experimental heart

A NOVEL

BY

JENNIFER L. ROHN

COLD SPRING HARBOR LABORATORY PRESS
Cold Spring Harbor, New York • www.cshlpress.com

Cover Design: Kris Franks
Cover Photograph: ©LabLit.com

All Cold Spring Harbor Laboratory Press publications may be ordered directly from Cold Spring Harbor Laboratory Press, 500 Sunnyside Blvd., Woodbury, New York 11797-2924. Phone: 1-800-843-4388 in Continental U.S. and Canada. All other locations: (516) 422-4100. FAX: (516) 422-4097. E-mail: cshpress@cshl.edu. For a complete catalog of all Cold Spring Harbor Laboratory Press publications, visit our World Wide Web Site at http://www.cshlpress.com/.

Library of Congress Cataloging-in-Publication Data

Rohn, Jennifer L.
  Experimental heart / by Jennifer L. Rohn.
    p. cm.
  ISBN 978-0-87969-876-8 (pbk. : alk. paper)
  1. Scientists--Fiction. 2. Women scientists--Fiction. 3. Medicine--Research--Fiction. 4. Pharmaceutical industry--Fiction. 5. Missing persons--Fiction. 6. Vaccines--Fiction. I. Title.
  PS3618.O486E97 2009
  813'.6--dc22

                                          2008042654

10 9 8 7 6 5 4 3 2

For David,
who was there from the very beginning

Contents

He is weary of analysis, the small predictable truths.
Rita Dove, "The Fish in the Stone"

Let me tell you something you don't know...

1 *Scrounge Culture*

*I*f you forced me to pinpoint the moment my tidy life began to tilt into the unknown, I'd have to say it started with a distraction.

Normally I performed experiments with the focus of a fanatic, but on this particular evening I had paused to notice what was happening outside my lab window. At first there was nothing extraordinary about the single square of bluish-white light across the courtyard. In fact, my gaze was drawn more to the darkened windows around it—but isn't that always the way? Maybe their power lay in their secrets, the sort that only take shape when you start to concentrate. Deep within the gloom, I translated these suggestions—the glow of ultraviolet, the silhouettes of machinery, a constellation of digital displays—into everyday items.

Everyday for me, that is.

Then time blurred, and I became hypnotized by the flickering red thermostat of an incubator in one of the dark labs. Soon I was day-dreaming about what lurked inside: stacks of plastic dishes nurturing millions of cells. And deeper still: microscopic ropes of genetic material replicating within, the chromosomes pairing and separating, the nuclei dividing. Two new daughters forming once a day in an orchestrated biochemical programme, halfway in spirit between a prim ballet and a drunken rugby scrum —

I blinked, dislodging the images from my mind, and the symptoms of my marathon workday returned: gritty eyes, dry mouth, the long-post-poned need to urinate. A vague headache. Shaky hands from too many vending machine Cokes, chocolate bars, cups of the bitter coffee that trickled out of an encrusted metal teat in the departmental common room.

It was easy to get existential at this time of night.

Resting my forehead against the cool glass, I surveyed again the windows visible across the courtyard, and then my own distorted, unshaven reflection.

"Maybe you're not the only one left after all, Andy."

I hadn't meant to speak out loud. Not that anyone was around to hear—just that one lit lab opposite and a few floors below my own.

As if in reply, a flash of white sliced past the corner of the window, so quickly that it was gone before I had really registered it.

I rubbed my eyes and tried to place the occupied room into context. It probably fell within Geniaxis, the start-up biotech company that had sprouted among the university labs of the Centre a few years ago. But Geniaxis had only moved into its present position the previous week, relocated from humble origins in the basement after a transfusion of venture capital, and rumours were already wafting through the corridors like a smelly experiment gone awry.

The new Geniaxis was said to be refurbished to gleaming modernity, conspicuous among the poorer academic departments huddled around. Somehow, the one room in the cellar had been tolerable, even appropriate, but this flagrant ascent crossed some unspoken boundary. The ivory tower was officially affronted: certain people were even hoping that its spending spree would lead to the company's downfall.

Nobody at that point—the critics, the company, and certainly not me—had the slightest idea that Geniaxis would be in danger so soon, and that its misstep would have nothing to do with overspending.

A series of creaks and groans drifted up behind me, and I turned away from the window. Old Bessy, our ancient centrifuge, had begun to shudder. This was my cue that its ten-minute spin was about to end, only in a laborious fashion, because the brake had perished in a spectacular incident long before my time. Soon afterward, lab myth had it, the dial had broken off in solidarity. Now the exposed screw had to be coaxed with pliers to one of several rough marks determined by trial and error to correspond to the approximate times by generations of students and post-docs. Still perfectly serviceable, according to Magritte.

The centrifuge convulsed to a stop and the lid-lock disengaged with a *clank*. Magritte was right, of course, as she always was. I wrestled open the centrifuge lid and removed my plastic tubes. As I held one up to see whether any DNA had settled to the bottom, another streak of movement caught my eye. This time, I was alert enough to identify it: the tail of a white lab coat rushing past the lit window across the courtyard.

This sighting bolstered my hypothesis that the lab now belonged to Geniaxis. Investors wanted their corporate scientists to look the part: serious, white-clad warriors with safety goggles, squinting into colourful test tubes bubbling over with steam. But it was becoming increasingly difficult to force the current generation of scientists to conform to this cherished view. The academic researchers in our building shunned the old-fashioned uniform like a viral infection. And as for the smoking test tubes, they were largely extinct.

The person reappeared in the window—a woman, probably about my age, late twenties or early thirties. She looked rushed but unruffled, and her lab coat was undone to reveal a trendy blue dress. At first I thought she was talking to herself, like I had been, but then I realized she was singing. Her accompanying movements afforded glimpses of sleek curvature and flashes of bare leg as the coat shifted about.

This is more like it, I thought, recalling the room's previous occupant: an ageing male post-doc sporting the slouch of irreversible disappointment.

Picking up a pipettor, the woman added a few droplets into a row of tubes in a rack. My mother had observed the last time she'd visited the lab that about ninety percent of the work going on involved the transfer of tiny amounts of clear liquid from one tube to another. It was an act of faith in the microscopic world, I had retorted.

The woman reached over with her free hand and fiddled with the antenna of a portable radio. After a few more beats, she executed a smooth dance turn, pipettor waving in the air, before going back to her task, and I burst out laughing. Even from this distance I could tell she was beautiful, but that wasn't what I found so fascinating. I think it was the way she moved, the way her careless grace betrayed an absolute mastery over her domain.

I doused the frenetic tune on my own ancient music player and switched to the radio, trawling the frequencies until I located the song corresponding to her movements. It was an old number, one of my favourites:

Here I am, baby
Come and take me,
take me by the hand...

I turned up the volume, letting the dreamy brass and vocals swell into the room. As the bass pulsed around me in slow heartbeats, I felt that the woman and I were somehow connected by these radio waves as they passed by, slicing through our laboratories on their long journey across the wastes of the universe.

Unaware of our shared cosmic convergence, the woman capped all her tubes and placed the rack inside a freezer. Then she switched off the radio and shoved it into a drawer. A few seconds later, the window became as dark as all of its neighbours.

Her departure jolted me back to my own solitary world, reminding me that it was Friday, nearly midnight, that I still had an hour's work before I could track down my friends on their mobiles. By then, I knew I'd be too tired to bother.

✦ ✦ ✦

Last one out, first one in.

I signed my name in the Centre register at ten-thirty the next morning, a bright summer Saturday. It seemed gloomier than ever in the lobby as the air-conditioning clamped down on my skin. I was about to dash for the lift when I had a thought. Turning back, I inspected the column of names in the register to find out who had signed out around 23:45 the previous evening. And there she was, nearly the first person to have arrived at work, but the second-to-last to depart—a performance that beat my thirteen-hour day easily. *Gina Kraymer*, proclaimed the script in a bold hand. Under the "department" column, which people usually ignored, she had written *Geniaxis, Vir & GT.*

Looking around furtively, even though the lobby remained empty, I flipped back a few pages to see what sort of hours Gina Kraymer, corporate lackey, normally endured. I discovered that yesterday's sixteen-hour stint was by no means unusual. The industrial lifestyle was famous for its nine-to-five mentality, so it didn't make sense for a company post-doc to be working so hard when she didn't have to.

Unenlightened, I restored the register page to its proper place and went up to the lab. I could hear Magritte before I'd taken two steps

4

out of the lift. Or, more precisely, I could hear her music. As usual, she hadn't signed in, but the genre was a giveaway: the Sex Pistols at maximum volume.

I turned the corner and poked my head into the lab. Old Bessy was competing with Johnny Rotten for airtime, howling and bucking ominously. Magritte never bothered to balance her tubes properly, either. I found her sitting at her bench in dye-stained jeans, a pale green T-shirt and old trainers. Her wavy hair was knotted into a bun with a pencil stabbed through the middle, and her brow was furrowed as she scribbled in her lab notebook and poked at a calculator. From this angle, she looked young enough to be an undergraduate, not a famous scientist.

I didn't worry about startling her; it was nearly impossible to sneak up on Magritte. Sure enough, she glanced over and smiled at my approach, setting off a reaction of fine lines that restored her appearance to the appropriate decade. When she got a better look at me, she reached for the remote control and subdued the music.

"Hangover, O'Hara?" There was an edge of amusement to her heavily accented voice.

"If only." I slung my rucksack down and hopped onto my stool, checking its forward roll with one hand on the bench. "Another late night here, I'm afraid."

"You look like shit, Andrew." She only ever called me by my first name, with its exotically trilled *r*, when she was feeling maternal. From her mouth, it came out like *Andryu*. "Working too hard. Should be going out, *getting* hangovers like normal person on Friday night."

"I had to finish those mutants so I could transfect my cells today in time for the next experiment on Monday."

"What big hurry? Your cells will never know difference." Her stare penetrated further. "You're young, should be out chasing girls, handsome devil like yourself."

"Don't worry...it was a one-off."

She snorted in disbelief.

"And anyway," I parried, "why are you here so early on a Saturday?"

"Boss allowed to work in mysterious ways." She started to turn away, then paused to inspect my shirt. "Where's your ID badge, O'Hara? You know rule."

"Same place as your *regulation* white coat." I looked at her with

5

surprise, only then noticing the laminated card clipped onto one of her belt-loops. "Since when have you worried about that?"

Magritte grimaced. "Had Kendall"—the head of our department—"in my office yesterday evening. He's paranoid about anti-vivisectionist break-ins. You hear what happened at Hammersmith last week?"

I nodded solemnly. Thirty cages of mice had been "liberated"—and a few PhD theses wrecked in the process.

"Thinks we're next," she went on. "Security staff is out for blood, so ID cards on person at all time, evenings and weekends, until Kendall gets distracted by something else. Understood?"

"Yes, ma'am!" I executed a flippant salute.

"And take it easy, yes?"

With one last thoughtful glance at me, Magritte nudged up the volume and went back to her calculations. Thankfully, Old Bessy compensated by clicking into the deceleration cycle, its bellowing diminishing with every revolution. I opened up my own notebook and started to organize my thoughts for the day. I knew Magritte was right about overdoing it, but I didn't have time to think about how to stop.

It was only when the solar calculator failed to register my jab of numbers that I realized dusk had fallen in a swathe across the lab bench, and that I had never turned on the lights. I was momentarily confused, thinking only a short while had elapsed since I'd finally given in to Magritte's nagging and ventured out into the blazing afternoon. After grabbing a sandwich from a deli in Covent Garden, I'd returned to find that she'd vanished back to her enigmatic world outside the lab.

Magritte obviously cared about our development, both in science and out, but she never talked about her personal life, and we sensed it wasn't appropriate to ask. I'd endured enough disgruntled reports from my colleagues about their own bosses to appreciate her. Not only was she brilliant, but she still found time to work at the bench instead of hiding in an office all day. And her stance about not working too hard was unusual among lab heads, especially in our particular field, where the competition was frenzied. We studied signal transduction, the biochemical processes cells use to communicate. As an animal is made up of billions of cells, it takes a fair amount of communication to keep the whole show running, and ours was just one lab of thousands around the world racing to unravel the nature of these complex signalling networks.

I suppose I was too preoccupied to see the real reasons why I worked too hard. Instead, I'd perfected the art of convenient justification, and one of my favourites was the fear that somebody else would beat me to the finish line. My most recent paper was still in shadowy limbo, under consideration for publication, and every day I opened up the major journals fearful that similar experiments would be displayed with fanfare under someone else's name. In fact, I'd recently received an e-mail from an old colleague warning me that another lab was close behind, but when I informed Magritte, she'd just shrugged.

"Not your business to worry, Andrew. Your business to do best, concentrate on living life too. The results come better when not so forced."

I switched on my bench lamp and the calculator's tiny screen woke up, offering me a belated series of zeros: nil to three excessive decimal places. The way I remember it now, this was the first time I really stopped to wonder about the rut that my life had become; why I let it exist, why I even embraced it.

What had catalyzed this dissatisfaction? Normally I liked being in an empty lab on the weekends or in the evenings, enjoying peaceful silence or the music of my choice. I liked the familiar grumbles of the machinery, and I even found the smells—agar, acetone, alcohol—subtly reassuring. I liked the concept of being a scientist, of doing what I had wanted to do ever since I was a child. And then when my interest in cancer research had become abruptly personal, the impetus had only increased. Still, coming back to the deserted building after my lunch break, I'd felt an uncharacteristic sense of loneliness.

Dusk had become dark around the pool of lamplight, another unremarked transition, until the fluorescent lights sputtered on and shattered my concentration.

"You'll go blind, Andy." Christine plopped down on a nearby stool, her entrance stirring up the pungent aroma of my *E. coli* cultures, still warm in their glass tubes.

"That's just a myth."

She grinned. "I was hoping it was you transmitting those depressing soul standards down the corridor. Wallowing, are we?"

"Who else would it be this time of night?" I turned back to my stack of Petri plates, noting with my peripheral vision that she was wearing something unusual over her standard uniform of T-shirt, jeans and Doc Martens.

"Well," she said, "there's always that remote chance you'd get a life in my absence. I live in hope, my friend."

"What's with the white coat?"

Soaking my glass spreader in alcohol, I wiggled it in the gas flame until it caught fire and burned itself clean.

"I'm up to my elbows in radioactivity," she said. I could sense her studying my technique as I flipped open another Petri dish and rotated the sterilized spreader around a puddle of bacteria until it was distributed on the surface of the agar plate. "But I'm nearly finished for the night. You?"

"I haven't even started my cell culture work."

"Sure I can't entice you down the Henry?" When I just shook my head, she hopped off the stool, emanating disapproval, and headed for the door. "Back to Chernobyl. Give me a ring if you change your mind about being a sad loser."

It was approaching midnight when I began my final task of the day, setting up a row of tubes to amplify some DNA overnight in the PCR machine. I had added all but one of the components before going into the freezer for the final ingredient, a dash of Taq polymerase enzyme. If all went well, the Taq would spend the night running off millions of duplicates of the DNA like a microscopic photocopier, so many that the invisible would eventually become detectable.

I stood with the freezer door half-open like a hungry, indecisive teenager and scowled at the empty tube of Taq. Maybe the fluid was just stuck on the sides of the tube. Optimistically, I spun it down in my mini bench-top centrifuge, but not a single drop collected at the bottom.

Swearing, I hurled the empty tube towards the yellow biohazard bin. It missed by at least a foot, bounced off the wall and ricocheted under a refrigerator. Where was I going to find some Taq at this time of night?

It wasn't time to panic yet. I did a quick window survey, but by now, the only lit square remaining was the one in Geniaxis.

It was a tricky question. Normally I would never hesitate to scrounge, even from a stranger. Scrounging is a universal cultural phenomenon in research institutes, more of an art than a science. You can't ask the same person twice in a row, and you try to borrow from people who have borrowed from you in the past. So if you've been working for a while in a building, you will ideally have built up a sizeable circle of people from whom you can obtain things, and who come to you in turn. While borrowing from someone you don't know can be awkward, it does help to expand your circle.

But the scrounge culture doesn't extend to companies, with their aura of prosperity. Asking a poor lab for an expensive enzyme or chemical would be like a rich man bumming a cigarette off a homeless guy, so corporate scientists avoided becoming part of the network.

I peeled off my latex gloves and stepped out of the lab. The shadowy corridors were a bit spooky, but I was an old hand at after-hours negotiation. I paused outside Christine's lab a few doors down and considered helping myself to her freezer, but taking reagents without asking just wasn't right. I pulled out my mobile phone, hesitated, then decided not to disturb her well-earned time off. Instead, I prowled through the rest of the department before expanding my search to other floors, pacing past lab after empty lab. After wavering in front of the stairwell leading to Geniaxis, I returned to my own room to find that Gina's window had darkened in my absence.

The unfinished reactions would have kept perfectly well in the refrigerator, but I upended the metal rack and slammed the tubes into the bin.

So there you have it: another day, going through the movements and manipulations of my chosen craft. You'd be surprised how many of them ended with similar disappointment, discarded moments rattling in the bottom of the biohazard disposal container. Bright spots were infrequent in a steady stream of nondescript grey.

I had no way of knowing then, but my life was about to become a lot more colourful.

2 *The Art of Public Speaking*

*K*athy swept into the lab, disrupting the collective Monday morning stupor with a cheerful greeting. Everyone else offered a limp response, but I couldn't quite surface from the depths of my lab notebook.

"Good *morning*, Andy," she repeated, her face glowing with health and a full night's sleep.

"It's just a bit early, Kath," I relented. Her work area abutted mine, so it paid to keep on good terms. Anyway, she was used to the surly post-doctoral phenotype after two months in my vicinity.

"I've been up for hours: first the gym, then the library." She struggled out of her rucksack, which was misshapen as usual with articles and textbooks relating to her undergraduate lab project. Even more amazing, I suspected that she had actually read them. I couldn't remember ever having been as enthusiastic myself, although the amnesia of embarrassment probably had something to do with it. I knew that she still harboured aspirations for a Nobel, but failing that, a cure for cancer would suffice.

"Just the thought makes me feel faint," I said.

"Why do you have to be so miserable all the time?" She dropped her rucksack onto the bench, and my glass tubes rattled in their rack.

I placed hand to heart. "It's my civic duty, as elder post-doc, to indoctrinate you into the inner sanctum of research academia. By demonstrating the proper behavioural response to financial hardship, vending-machine-induced malnutrition and, most importantly, sleep deprivation, I am preparing you for a lifetime of self-sacrifice, frustration, and —"

"O'Hara," Magritte called over. "You disillusion my student, I kill you." She was busy pouring molten agarose into a plastic mould. I wondered again why she was making more of an appearance at the bench recently.

"Not a chance, Dr V.," Kathy said. "According to feminist theory, male superiors can't function effectively as role models for women."

"*Superior*" is *not* the word I'd use to describe Andy." Paul, our chief technician, pelted me with a wad of aluminium foil, which bounced off my forehead and landed with a splash in the water bath. A Styrofoam raft containing a cargo of Eppendorf tubes nearly capsized, then attempted to tack to starboard.

"Now, children," Magritte said, gaze never leaving her handiwork. "All is fun and games until someone loses eye."

Paul raised his brows at me, no doubt remembering the time he nearly had done just that with one of his relentless practical jokes: a rocket fashioned out of plastic tubes and pressurized dry ice. I grinned back in acknowledgement.

"Who goes to the seminar?" asked Helmut, our German post-doc.

"Who's speaking?" I kept my tone noncommittal.

"I am not having a clue."

"Kathy?" Magritte and I asked simultaneously.

Kathy pressed a hand to her temples as if accessing a psychic seminar bulletin. "Dr Richard Rouyle, from Pfeiffer-deVries."

"Richard Rouyle?" Helmut brightened. "He's a celebrity in Germany, always appearing on the television, scientific panels and whatsoever, being quoted in the newspapers."

"Really, talking about what?" Paul sounded intrigued, but Magritte just sniffed.

"His big thing is that science should be more focused to clinical application and less abstract," Helmut explained.

"What's the topic of the seminar, Kath?" I asked.

She gazed into the distance. "Something about...boosting the immune system...applications for gene therapy?"

I woke up—this sounded like a subject Geniaxis would be interested in. Maybe Gina Kraymer would attend.

"Gene therapy?" Marcy, one of the PhD students, made a face. "*Bor*-ring. Besides, Pfeiffer-deVries is a pharmaceutical company, so the research will be crap."

"What about *Stan Fortuna*?" Magritte said. Fortuna, our biggest competitor, had recently moved with his entire lab from a Californian university to become a big-shot division chief at Metzger Pharmaceuticals in Frankfurt.

"Hmmm...okay," Marcy said. "But this Rouyle guy doesn't have a background in academia, does he?"

"Still," Magritte said.

"Whatever. I'm not going." She flounced off into the tissue culture suite. Marcy was in the late stages of her thesis work, when PhD students finally start to rebel; it was definitely time for her to be writing up.

Helmut extracted a seminar flyer from the clutter on his desk and waved it at us. "Rouyle speaks today about a new protein regulated by growth signals in the FRIP pathway."

"Isn't FRIP very similar to the SLIP protein that Helmut's studying?" Kathy asked, just as I recalled where I'd heard the speaker's name before.

"That's right," Magritte said approvingly. "Highly related cousins."

"Sounds like something right through both our alleys, Andy." Helmut didn't like attending seminars without an entourage.

"Anyone for the talk?" Christine popped her head around the door, with Cameron, her boyfriend, right behind.

"A thousand temptations await," Cameron proclaimed, gesturing theatrically.

"I'm coming," I said. I wasn't too keen, but the seminar topic was related to my work, and my mental block was showing no signs of clearing up. The prospect of seeing Gina was one reason that I wouldn't let myself put at the top of this list.

On the way down to the auditorium, a discussion about cell growth signals ensued, far too scientific for the early hour. I fell in with Christine a few paces behind.

"How was the concert last night?" I asked.

"Brilliant." She smiled at the memory, then shot me a particular look. "It's a pity you couldn't make it. What time did you escape from the lab?"

"About midnight," I said, then hastened on when her lips tightened into a shape I had learned to dread. "You can spare me the speech, because I'm already getting it from Magritte."

"She's an intelligent woman—why don't you listen to her? There's an entire world outside the lab."

"For some of us."

She glared at me. "Don't give me that pathetic tone. It's self-perpetuating: you don't have a life outside the lab, so you spend a lot of time *in* the lab, which means you avoid making the connections that would get you out."

"Meaning, a girlfriend."

"Not necessarily! Anything, really: hobbies, sport...self-reflection."

I smirked, even though I knew it was a bad idea.

"I don't know why I bother with you sometimes!" She focused her gaze ahead in eloquent indignation.

After a few more silent steps, I put a hand on her forearm and said, "I'm sorry. But you know how it is. The work's heated up recently, and I can't seem to stop piling on more experiments."

She sighed, finally nodded: all scientists went through such phases.

"It's been more than just recently, though," she said. "We used to go to gigs all the time—when's the last time you came out with me?"

A shake of the head seemed the best response.

"Look, Andy," she said. "I keep trying to open windows for you, but you're not even in the room."

We stepped out of the lift into the swarm of people streaming through the lobby towards the main auditorium. As usual, nobody had shown up until the last possible second, so a crush for seats was in progress. I scanned the crowd for someone who looked like Gina, only then realizing that the impression she'd made on me had been more visceral than visual.

Kathy and Helmut headed for the front: very uncool.

"Shall we skulk in back with the bad kids?" Cameron suggested— an observational vantage that suited me fine.

"I always like to be seated in the exit row, in the event of an emergency." I beckoned Cameron to file in after Christine so that I could have the aisle seat.

"If the speaker becomes excessively dull, floor illumination will direct you to the nearest exit," he said as I swept my gaze across the sea of heads in front of me, trying to decide if Gina's hair had been auburn or just dark brown.

A professor stood up and introduced Richard Rouyle's history at Pfeiffer-deVries, emphasizing his prominent public role in advocating

13

more clinically-based research before inviting him to the podium. Rouyle was powerfully built, well-dressed in a decidedly non-academic way and sported the craggy, middle-aged looks I associate with golf pros.

"Sexy." Christine was leaning forward in frank appraisal.

Cameron grinned at me. "If I said that about a female speaker, she'd impale me with my own pipettor."

Christine opened her mouth, no doubt to expound on one of her favourite feminist maxims, but then the lights dimmed.

"Thank you for the kind introduction, Professor Fujiwara," Rouyle said in an upper-class English accent, nodding towards the front row as he gestured with the remote control. Meanwhile, the first slide came up: a movie of live cells shot with timelapse microscopy. As many times as I'd seen such classroom-style videos—pretty, but imparting little information—I still watched with as much fascination as everyone else.

"The cells in our bodies have an immeasurable amount of information to worry about," Rouyle declared in a well-modulated tone, as the cells behind him seethed, crawled and occasionally divided into two in a spasm of activity. "An almost infinite amount of stimuli—both signals and noise—filter in from the environment. These must be processed correctly for us to survive. At the same time, there are only a finite number of cellular proteins at hand to do the job. In my talk today, I shall tell you the story of one such messenger protein—FRIP—and how it copes with this Herculean task."

As he called up a colourful schematic, I thought that, despite being known for promoting practical science, Rouyle had the poetic patter of a true academic.

"FRIP, like many proteins in the cell, leads a double life." He waved the laser pointer at the screen. "FRIP stands sentinel at a crucial point in the complex signalling network of cells. Its major function is to receive growth signals from outside and then pass them to the nucleus, where cell division is initiated."

Rouyle paused, his eyes sweeping the audience with an intense focus. "But under bombardment from certain viruses, FRIP can also join forces with the immune system, transmitting signals that vanquish the offending intruders. Like a routine postal worker who moonlights as a volunteer firefighter at weekends, FRIP is always ready to do what needs to be done."

14

"Very articulate," I heard Christine whisper to Cameron. "Brains as well as beauty."

I didn't know about brains, but Rouyle did appear to be one of those media-savvy scientists who enjoyed using humour and analogy to convince laypeople, not to mention funding bodies, that their research was a crucial pixel in the Big Picture. I felt a tingle of anticipation: maybe this seminar was actually going to be interesting.

But preliminary evidence is often misleading, and even well-grounded theories can turn out to be flawed. Just as I was removing the cap from my pen, it all went horribly wrong.

"As most of you probably already know," Rouyle went on, his lubricated voice picking up speed, "the growth factor-responsive protein family PT35 has several isoforms, including PT32 and PT40, which, when stimulated by mitogens,"—I lost focus for a deadly second—"... differentially phosphorylated on serine residues 91, 68, and 103, respectively, whereas in the unstimulated state..."

His words started to blend together as the red blob of his laser danced over the screen. In contrast to the previous slide, this one was densely populated with graphs and diagrams, all of which were difficult to make out.

"Oh, my God," Christine muttered under her breath.

I silently agreed. Rouyle, while skilful at generalities, seemed to lack even the basic skills necessary for communicating details to his peers—a far from uncommon trait in this business. As each slide would rely on information presented in the previous, a lost thread could seldom be regained. Despite my bluster about procuring the aisle seat, I was too intimidated to walk out of a major seminar. Like many aspects of my life at that time, I was comforted knowing that the option existed, even though I would never have the guts to follow through.

Defeated, I slumped deeper into my seat and allowed Rouyle's voice to slide into meaningless noise. Fortunately, I was practised in the art of seminar distractions. First, I made a leisurely list of all the tasks I had to complete for the week—a key strategy in my arsenal, because it gave the impression of enthusiastic note-taking. I lingered thoughtfully over certain experiments on my list, but eventually ran out of things to write.

Next, I observed my fellow audience. Cameron was well into REM sleep, his head swaying just inches from his chest. I admired his technique for a few moments, then peeked sidewise at Christine. She was still paying attention, but I noticed that her notepad was blank: not a good sign. In contrast, the woman directly in front of me was brazenly punching in a text message on her mobile phone. Far up the aisle, I made out Helmut hunched over his pad, scribbling furiously, and Kathy, blinking at the screen like a lost lamb. The hall was full of indications that others were growing restless: shiftings in seats, rustling of paper, throat-clearings and longing glances at the clock.

Motes of dust swirled in the shaft of light from the projector, and sleep began to steal over me. The initial symptom—that fatal heaviness of the eyelids—was always horrifying. I started to succumb, the screen swimming between weighty blinks, my head listing forward with utter inevitability. But unlike Cameron, I find it too disgraceful to sleep through a talk, no matter how deservedly, so I pinched my arm until the pain was unbearable.

A woman several rows in front of me stood up, crouched over and started struggling towards the aisle. We all watched as she made a show of looking at a lab timer clipped to her blouse, as if there was nothing she'd hate more than missing this talk, but a crucial experiment needed her attention. I had to admit it was a brilliant tactic.

"I take back what I said about him being sexy," Christine whispered to me over Cameron's slumped form. "And isn't it about time for the oxygen masks to drop from the panel above our seats?"

I was about to respond when I noticed someone near the front in the gap created by the escaped student: Gina, her face unmistakable in profile.

Adrenaline boxed me around the ears, dissolving my lethargy in one neat burst. She murmured something into the ear of the guy next to her, and he smiled in response. As I watched their banter, I felt a familiar sensation in my stomach, followed by a reflexive counterattack of disgust. I didn't even know her, so how could I possibly be jealous?

I forced myself to look at the screen. Rouyle had moved into the final segment of his talk, and was droning through a summary of the major conclusions of his research. Pens began scratching all over the hall as people took the opportunity to write down something comprehensible. The final slide was the obligatory cartoon attempting to tie together all the findings into one monstrous unifying model. It looked rather like a Miró, I thought critically. In his protein period.

"And with that, I will entertain questions," Rouyle said.

The house lights blazed on. Christine dug her elbow into Cameron's ribs and his eyes popped open, alert and innocent as applause sustained itself to the minimum that etiquette demanded and then haemorrhaged away.

A few moments of silence stretched out, and you could almost feel the concentrated weight of the crowd, yearning to be free. But then a hand shot towards the ceiling.

"Here we go," Christine said under her breath.

It was Mike Rexton, a new lab head in our department. Despite lots of practice, he still hadn't perfected the technique of the show-off question, designed to highlight his own genius at the expense of the speaker's. And sure enough, Rouyle deflected Rexton's effort with ease, like a man reprimanding an errant puppy.

Rexton flushed as he realized that his attempt had backfired, but when he opened his mouth to parry, Gina raised her hand.

"The young lady in the centre there," Rouyle said with a patronizing smile, pointing.

Young lady? What century was this?

Christine jolted up from her slouch. She was always observing that women were less likely than men to ask questions at high-profile seminars. Cameron's pet explanation was that women weren't assertive enough, whereas Christine insisted that they were just too sensible to put on a display. I kept well out of that particular running argument.

"Dr Rouyle." Gina's voice rang out with an unexpected American accent. "It's all very well to hypothesize that the FRIP kinase is coordinately regulated by"—and here she put together a string of jargon that I wasn't able to follow—"but your own data appear to contradict this theory, if I recall correctly the control lane on that last Western blot you showed. If FRIP were responsible, you'd see the phosphorylation there, and you clearly don't."

The auditorium went completely silent: not a single rustle or throat-clearing disturbed the hushed expectancy.

"I, ah..." Rouyle looked around the room, then gathered himself to make a rejoinder.

"Although," Gina continued calmly, "an alternative theory that would fit all the data would be..." She delivered a crisp description of her idea, then added, "At any rate, that model could easily be tested with the elegant series of mutants you described earlier."

Rouyle hung motionless as a murmur spread around the room. It was one thing to be clever enough to spot an inconsistency, but to have the courage to confront a speaker in public about it, come up with a solution, and then—the most impressive aspect, as far as I was concerned—bestow a face-saving compliment, was masterful.

"Well, then." It was Professor Fujiwara, belatedly recalling that it was his job to rescue Rouyle from further embarrassment. "We are running short of time, so I will have to ask that any further questions be addressed to Dr Rouyle up at the podium."

There was an eruption of noise as the audience stood up and began massing towards the exits. Gina and her friend joined the knot of people already nucleating around Rouyle. He had obviously recovered, his lips smiling and verbose. When he saw Gina, I was surprised when he stuck out his hand, shook hers firmly. Perhaps her performance had marked her out as one of the boys. She was smiling too as she rescued her hand and began to speak, gesticulating in enthusiasm. Possibly she was clarifying her theory further, and he would be a fool not to pay attention. At the same time, he seemed to be inspecting her breasts—so not exactly one of the boys, after all.

At that moment, a white flash illuminated the podium. Startled, I noticed a cluster of people off to the side with cameras and notepads. Rouyle, still talking to Gina, adjusted his stance to put himself to better advantage, charismatic smile widening further.

"They are from *Der Spiegel*!" Helmut announced, a dazed Kathy in his wake. He narrowed his eyes speculatively. "I wonder if they need any German quotes from the audience?"

"That was amazing," Christine said, still awed. I knew she wasn't referring to the press, but was still hung up on Gina's performance. "I've never seen anything like it."

"One exception for your feminist anthropological observations, anyway." I tried not to show my annoyance that Rouyle was being so smooth with Gina. They were even deeper in conversation now, almost rudely excluding everyone around them in their intensity.

"American, though," she went on. "They're meant to be more extroverted, aren't they? So it's not disproving my theory outright. Still, it opened a few male ears, no doubt."

"It must have been some talk," Cameron said as the flashbulb went off again.

"Don't worry, mate," I said. "You didn't miss a thing."

"Who *is* she?" Christine said.

"I know the guy she was sitting with," Cameron said. "Miles Nerek, a post-doc on my floor. Nice bloke, bit of a ladies' man, works on yeast too. But she's not from our department."

"I think she works at Geniaxis," I offered. If Christine found out that I might be even remotely interested, I would deeply regret it.

"What a waste of a brilliant mind," Cameron remarked.

I managed to acquire some Taq polymerase from a reluctant colleague in Medical Genetics who owed me a favour, and after a flurry of pipetting and a couple of short-cuts, my aborted experiment was back on schedule. At some point in the middle of the afternoon, the sounds and movements of my labmates faded into a haze as sleep tried to claim me again. I rested my chin in my hand, watching fluid drip off the bottom of the purification column perched on my bench. I was mesmerized as each droplet oozed out and grew to an agonizingly heavy maximum before eventually succumbing to gravity. The sun dazzled each distorted globule as it pinched off and fell into the collection tube below.

When I leaned over to adjust the blind, my gaze passed over the windows opposite, reminding me again of the mysterious Gina and the company where she worked. Unlike Cameron and many other colleagues, I had nothing against Geniaxis or its ilk. It seemed obvious that the commercialization of science was becoming increasingly acceptable, and that its ascendancy could well be inevitable.

Cameron's dismissive comment encapsulated the main complaint: that academia was healthy and pure, whereas corporate science was a capitalistic cancer in the system. And start-ups like Geniaxis were the hardest to swallow because they'd been spawned from academic origins. It was bad enough that they'd arisen at all, but the universities were actually incubating them.

Still, the idea that academic research was more rigorous because it wasn't tainted by financial interest seemed like mythology to me, fostered by those members of the previous generation who had been too cautious to establish a niche in the lucrative new food chain. While academic scientists didn't earn profits, they urgently needed funding, so it was naïve to assume that the imperative to obtain grants never inspired unbiased research.

Anyway, the whole idea of two separate camps was rather out-moded. As academia and industry ended their long period of nervous flirtation, the lines had begun to blur. Prominent university scientists acted as paid consultants for biotech companies or were head-hunted to become scientific directors, while their less famous counterparts tried to convince the university to support their start-ups. Meanwhile, industry kept soaking up fresh PhDs too jaded to continue in the tra-ditionally dreary fashion of post-doctoral research, yet too cowardly to leave science altogether. After having endured so many years of over-education, it could be terrifying to contemplate a completely new career.

Most scientists my age no longer avoided the obvious questions about the advantages of corporate science: what was so bad about earning decent compensation for one's hard work? About going home at a civilized hour in one's BMW to a normal existence of regular hot meals with a proper family in a proper house?

But Gina obviously wasn't conforming to that orthodoxy. Maybe the nine-to-five lifestyle was just spin propagated by companies to entice people away from the universities.

Night had fallen hours before, initiating its usual cycle: the ringing of mobile phones as spouses and friends reported in, the gradual scatter-ing of colleagues, and one by one, the lit squares across the courtyard going black. All but one, doggedly persisting as the hours eroded towards midnight. I eventually put down my pipettor with a sigh. I couldn't concentrate, so I decided to do something completely unscientific.

I slipped into the dark corridor and edged past the freezers clut-tering the passageway in blatant disregard for fire codes. I was just putting a hand out to push open the stairwell door when a throat rasped behind me.

"Your friend is looking for you." I inclined my head.

She turned around, startled, and Miles raised a hand, strode over. Gina's expression contained an edge that quickly smoothed over.

"I thought you were working late," she said.

Miles stuck out his hand to me pointedly, introduced himself with a smile. The grip was firm. *Nice bloke*, I remembered Cameron saying.

"Are you joining us?" she asked.

"Actually, something's come up," he said. "I managed to get a pair of last-minute tickets for The Chemical Brothers tonight. But you're obviously having a drink, so it seems rude to snatch you away."

"Go ahead," I found myself saying. "It sounds great."

Gina looked indecisively from me to him.

"I'm supposed to meet up with my friends anyway." I gestured towards Christine's table.

Miles was giving Gina a strange look now, but she kept her eyes on me. "You're absolutely sure?"

"Of course."

"We're going to be late as it is," Miles said.

"Okay," Gina said, drawing out the last syllable. "But you'll take a rain-check?"

I nodded, and Miles put a proprietary hand on the small of her back as he guided her out the door.

I became aware of the heavy bass of the jukebox rippling through smoky blue. Across the room, there was an uproar of merry laughter accompanied by a spattering of applause.

Gina and the entire vanished conversation now felt like a dream.

"Start talking, O'Hara."

I looked up to find Christine in Gina's abandoned chair. She slapped her elbows on the table and settled chin on fists, hazel eyes filled with a pity that couldn't remotely mask the curiosity underneath.

I hesitated, not sure I was in the mood to handle her incessant probing. Christine was a lovely person—tall and lanky, with the sturdiness and unconventional spirit of a wildflower blown into a formal garden. And I admired the single-minded focus and quirky theories she came up with in her field of study: metastasis, the deadly migration of cancer cells to other parts of the body. But she had a similar approach towards my personal problems; in essence, I had become one of her side-projects.

At first, this attention had baffled me, but when I finally asked why she was so obsessed with the topic, she had just smiled and confessed that she liked a challenge. And she was unusually adept at extracting meaning from my halting speech, at coaxing dark things out into the light, so I eventually learned to appreciate her efforts—although usually only in retrospect.

I shrugged. "It was hopeless from the start anyway...I already suspected those two were an item."

"Why didn't you tell me?"

"I didn't want you to get worked up over nothing."

She eyed me shrewdly. "Or maybe you didn't want to get yourself worked up."

"What's that supposed to mean?"

"I mean," she said, making each word crisp, "that working yourself up, even when it might facilitate your desires, is not one of your fortes."

"There's facilitation, and then there's futility." The comment stung, but I didn't want her to know.

"It's often a fine line, O'Hara, not distinguishable until you step over and see what happens."

"Nice sentiment, but too abstract to be useful." Where had I heard that analogy before?

"Then let's get more concrete, shall we?" Christine's voice sharpened to a deadly point. "You may think I didn't notice that you were interested in me when we first met, but you'd be wrong. And furthermore, I'm certain I made it clear that your attentions would be welcome."

I opened my mouth in dismay, but the look in her eye forced me to close it. It was one of those moments when your underpinnings shift, swatting you with your own shortcomings.

"I eventually convinced myself that you just couldn't be bothered," she said, "even that I'd imagined the initial interest. But I hadn't, had I?"

I shook my head, mute with embarrassment.

Christine reached over and took a sip of my beer. "I was disappointed, but finally concluded it was for the best, that I needed a man who was assertive enough to go for what he wanted." A shrug. "That turned out to be Cameron. And you've become a very dear friend, so everything worked out."

"For you," I muttered.

"Is that all our friendship means to you?"

Christine was difficult to hurt, but I could see I'd achieved it.

"That came out wrong." I covered her hand with mine. "I'm sorry—I didn't mean to be such a pillock."

"Don't be," she said, relenting. The corner of her mouth inched upwards. "And you're not."

There was something in her gaze that made me have to look away, and that's when I saw Gina, threading her way towards us with a frown.

"I think I left my purse here." She looked from me to Christine and back again, face impassive, and my hope slunk away.

Christine rummaged around her chair and produced a stylish handbag. "*Et voila*. Great seminar question, by the way."

"Thanks," Gina said. Took the handbag. "And thanks."

As she hustled away, I dragged my gaze back to find Christine studying me, eyes narrowed, a finger restless along her chin. Then she tapped the finger against her lower lip a few times. "How sure are you that those two are actually seeing one another?"

"Well..." I gestured towards the door of the Henry. "They spend a lot of time together. Besides, he seemed interesting—and he rides a motorcycle."

"Please, O'Hara." She looked disgusted. "First off, men only *think* women like motorcycles. Second, you're interesting too—amusing, intelligent, good-looking. Third, proximity is no indication. Just look at you and me—we spend a lot of time together as well."

You had to admire Christine when she flexed her neurons.

"We're scientists," she went on. "Let's review the evidence for the opposite situation—the null hypothesis, if you will."

"Be my guest." Despite my tone, I was secretly very keen.

"She hardly knows you, right?" She looked at me for confirmation. "Yet she asked you for a drink. Not conclusive, I'll admit, but suspicious. And did you see the look on her face when you two were saying hello earlier?"

"What look?"

"More intriguingly, she didn't seem at all pleased to see us head-to-head just now."

"I didn't notice anything."

"Of course not—you're a man." She sniffed. "These sorts of signals are transmitted strictly on a female wavelength. Did your male vibes pick up anything on him? How did he react when he saw Gina all cosy in the corner with you?"

I described his open demeanour, only then realizing that I might have mistaken confidence for amiability.

"Also a good sign," she said, not noticing my uncertainty. "And what were you two talking about before you were so rudely interrupted by the Road Warrior? Please don't tell me it was about science."

"Well..." I saw her disgust, added hastily, "though not in the nerdy sense. She was giving me the low-down on industry."

Christine smiled. "Trying to seduce you over to the Dark Side?"

"Not exactly."

"More importantly, O'Hara, not that it would've been like you, but did you react as if you weren't happy at them going off together?"

"I didn't want to put her in a spot," I said lamely.

"Bet you ten quid she wanted you to."

I just stared at her, and she sighed. "Listen, Andy—it's not a crime to assert yourself."

When I didn't respond, she reached over and helped herself to more of my beer. "But all may not be lost," she declared. "It's time to implement some covert ops. Cameron's in the same department as Miles, and someone's bound to know his current status. After that, we've got several options."

She paused, faraway eyes perusing a mental checklist. I wasn't thrilled by the prospect of her intervention. But then I thought about Christine's imaginary line between facilitation and futility, of hurdles that I usually didn't risk going over, of all the things I might have lost as a result. And I decided to leave her to it.

"By the way," she said, standing up, "the others are restless, want to move on to the Wall Flower. You coming?"

"Yeah, why not."

I felt under the table for my rucksack and connected unexpectedly with something soft and delicate. I bent down and saw Gina's blue silk scarf draped, forgotten, over my bag. I picked it up and tucked it into my pocket. It felt like an omen.

4 *Peer Review*

*I*t was a relief when Monday arrived, like a brash alarm after a night of uneasy dreams. Another spell of glorious weather had stranded me alone in the lab that weekend. Still smarting from Christine's lecture, I'd gathered up the courage to return Gina's scarf as a pretext for asking her out, but had been foiled by circumstance: her window remained stubbornly unoccupied. So I had buried myself in work, not soothed as usual by the peace of an empty lab, but tormented by a relentless internal dialogue that even loud music couldn't atomize.

I stopped by the departmental common room on my way in to check for post. The slot was stuffed full of colourful envelopes from biotech supply companies trying to sell me the latest enzyme or high-tech pipetting device. Automatically, I flipped them into the recycle box, where they landed on top of dozens of other identical, unopened envelopes. Then I milked a cup of acidic coffee from the machine and took an idle look at The Board.

The Board was a large square of cork, surface ravaged by the application of thousands of drawing pins over the years. It had been used originally for posting departmental memos, but in recent years the official channels of communication had gone over to e-mail, and the Board had enjoyed a cultural renaissance, now sporting news clippings, amusing quotes, droll scientific cartoons and compromising photographs from various drunken leaving parties. Most of the offerings were anonymous, but I had been in the department long enough to have a fair idea who had posted what.

A new item caught my eye, labelled in Christine's distinctive hand: "Hey, girls: I know it's a classic, but stumbled across it again and was just as enraged. Enjoy!"

It was a faded copy of the notorious *Nature* report proving that, all else being equal, female scientists had to be more than twice as productive as males for the purposes of getting a grant. Christine had circled the key paragraph: in the case of their publication record, women needed three more papers in a prestigious journal like *Nature* or *Science*, or alternatively, twenty more articles in lesser journals, to be considered as competitive as their male counterparts.

"*Twenty* more articles, ladies!" Christine had written in the margin. "Better stop reading and get back to work!"

I took a final gulp of coffee and was just turning to leave when I noticed another new offering in one corner of the Board.

Rouyle Overwhelms London Listener Public

The running title on top indicated that the article had been crudely computer-translated from the German by an internet search engine.

Dr Richard Rouyle, English scientist of Pfeiffer-deVries in Frankfurt and recent recipient of Georg and Anna Ulbert Award for Applied Biomedical Research, was the guest loudspeaker of the honour at prestigious RCC laboratories in London Monday before. Rouyle spoke to jammed chamber of commodious scientist employees, stopping those public in thrall while he spoke about his new researches.

I saw that some wag had scratched out *commodious* and scribbled in *comatose*.

Rouyle operates on a soil-breaking new gene therapy strategy, which is based on FRIP Kinase, one of the proteins in our bodies, acting out two roles: steering cell division and exhilarating the immune system during virus infection.

Rouyle is much known for his public speaking-out against wasting funds on researches being not likely to help patients or quickly translate to cures, even hugged by some as honorary German citizen for his genuine desires for improvement of society.

"The FRIP kinase is an exciting new agent who could make a real difference concerning the hospital," Rouyle said full of suaveness during an interview after his seminar.

The last two sentences were highlighted in lurid green.

Helmut Meier, a German post-doctoral employee at the RCC, which was into the audience, agreed with zest. "Dr Rouyle is paving the road towards excitement in novel new therapies."
   - Science NewsBytes, The Mirror Online

My grin faded as I noticed something in the accompanying grainy image of Rouyle, gritting his teeth with scholarly intrepidity on the Centre's podium. Putting my nose right up to the Board, I confirmed the identity of a slender arm and graceful hand not quite cropped off the left side.

✦ ✦ ✦

"Tea," Christine announced, appearing at my side in the middle of the afternoon. I was staring uselessly at a piece of film spotted with dark marks, the cryptic whispers and gossip of communicating cells. In my present distracted state, I had apparently forgotten the lingo. She poked me insistently on the arm. "Come on, then."

"Cheer him up, Christine," Paul begged. "He's been an especially miserable bastard all day."

I didn't have the energy to fend Christine off, and soon she had strong-armed me downstairs and into one of the tea room's sagging chairs. The silence stretched out as I blew on the surface of my steaming brew.

"You look wretched, O'Hara—what's wrong?"

"Nothing tangible. Just that I had decided to take your advice and be more proactive, but Gina wasn't in all weekend."

I'd been hoping for a dose of her previous bravado, but she just studied my face soberly before speaking. "Cameron had morning coffee with Susan—Miles's flatmate, a post-doc in the same department. Apparently, up until recently, Miles preferred to keep himself unentangled."

"So that spare helmet has seen some action."

"Hmmm. In fact, she says there's a not terribly exclusive club of women in the Centre who are rather disenchanted with his style."

Nice bloke. "Can you just cut to the *coup de grâce*, please?"

She sighed. "Miles and Gina have been together for a couple of months."

"I see." I didn't bother suppressing the spasm of disappointment—it was a waste of time trying to fool Christine. "Maybe there's such a thing as too much information."

"Nonsense: knowledge is power, and don't you forget it." She managed to make even the act of swallowing tea look disparaging. "For example, let me enlighten you further. Susan thinks it's not going well—they've been fighting, and last week, she's fairly certain he had another woman in his room."

41

"Maybe she was mistaken," I said.

"God. You don't know anything about human nature, do you? Rule number one, O'Hara, is that people don't change. Bounders remain bounders, cads remain cads, suckers remain suckers. Trust me, I'm a Doctor of Philosophy."

I couldn't help smiling. "So, Dr Edmonds, what's your philosophical recommendation?"

She swirled the dregs of her tea. "I reckon she's also attracted to you, based on the evidence at hand. She's bound to be distracted for a while, but Miles will probably move on eventually."

"Why can't she see what's wrong with him?" I scowled into my cup.

"Who can say what Gina sees in him? And remember, we didn't know about his reputation until today, either."

"True," I conceded.

"But the point is, O'Hara"—a touch of impatience, now—"when Miles leaves her, she'll be wanting a shoulder to cry on...and maybe you'll be alert enough not to squander the opportunity."

"Thanks!"

As usual, she ignored my sarcasm as it suited her. Then the timer clipped onto one of the loops of her jeans started to go off, which she silenced with practiced ease.

"My experiment is about to explode," she said.

I snagged her arm as she was getting up. "One more thing? If it's true people never change, then why do you even bother with me?" I was only half-joking.

She looked at me fondly, shook her head. "That's different," she said. "I happen to believe that you already have some spark...it's just hidden away."

Or, I thought to myself as I finished my tea in silence, temporarily misplaced.

❦ ❦ ❦

Back upstairs, there was a flurry in the air and people looked at me significantly.

"Will you join me in office, please, O'Hara?" Magritte approached, a sheaf of papers in her hand and a peculiar smile on her face.

Mystified, I followed her a few doors down the corridor. Magritte seldom observed formal niceties like meeting with us in private. She was much more apt to perch on a stool and chat about whatever was on her mind, whether the latest big paper in *Nature* or the lab's recent results.

Magritte's office was windowless, the size of a walk-in wardrobe and claustrophobic with a desk, two chairs, and wall-to-wall shelves crammed with books and scientific journals. Although it was probably just an optical illusion, the high shelves appeared to be leaning in as if the entire room was on the verge of collapse. There was also a scale-encrusted electric kettle, a stained cafetière and a couple of chipped mugs crowded on top of a refrigerator. Every other available surface was covered by dusty stacks of photocopied articles, one of which she dumped onto the floor so that I could sit.

"I'm dying of suspense here, boss. If it's bad news, can we just get it over with?"

"You are a pessimist," Magritte observed, "which is very British, yes?"

"We prefer to think of it as realism."

"Tea?" she commanded more than offered, reaching over to switch on the kettle. I fretted in silence, destined to spend the day drinking hot beverages and listening to the often inscrutable wisdom of women.

"I will cut to chase."

The sheaf of papers landed heavily onto my lap. The top sheet was an e-mail printout from *Cells & Cancer*, the very prominent journal to which I had submitted my most recent paper without much hope that it would actually get accepted.

"Don't tell me it's in!" I was too flustered to focus on the cover letter.

"Yes, but it's even better than that."

"Let me guess: they want to put one of my ugly films on the cover."

"Very funny. This is serious, yes? They are going to make deal." She watched me blink. "Seems that very similar manuscript arrived on desk just one day after yours."

My innards shifted. "They want to publish us back-to-back."

"Editor thinks ours is superior. Reviewers wanted to see one small experiment; if we have favourable result e-mailed by Monday, they will put us in alone, next available issue—that's September—and re-

ject other paper outright. No experiment, they run us back-to-back."
She shrugged. "And you have to share glory."

"What kind of an experiment? That's less than a week!"

She silenced my consternation with an upraised palm. "I want you to read all this stuff—three peer reviews, editor's synopsis and conclusions. Nature of missing experiment. You think you can't do it, I completely understand. Not worth killing yourself—either way gets published. I leave decision entirely up to you."

The kettle burbled over and clicked off.

"You stay here, Andrew." Her grasp on my shoulder was painful. "Drink tea. Use desk. Shut door if necessary. Madhouse in lab today— Helmut won toss for CD control this hour: Falco's *Greatest Hits*."

"But —"

"You decide to go for it, I arrange extra technical assistance for you. I can help, too, yes? Still know thing or two at bench."

With a wink, she whisked out the door.

In our lab, we focused on the growth signals leading to cell division. When—and only when—it's time for a cell to divide, signals from outside the cell alert messengers within, and the command is relayed step by step until the task is finally executed.

So much for how it's supposed to work. The sad truth is that these carefully regimented messages can go awry. All it takes is a few chance mutations in a person's DNA, and zap—a normal cell is transformed into a cancer cell, becoming deaf to restraining commands and multiplying out of control.

The experiments described in my paper implicated a protein I'd discovered as a major regulator in cells, responsible for integrating a variety of growth signals. In fact, it functioned as a cellular switchboard, like an efficient secretary who takes a dozen phone calls at once and then decides which message should be put through to the boss's office first. If this secretary became ill, the office would dive into chaos, and in a similar way, my protein often went missing in cancer cells.

I turned to the stack of paper. It was sobering to know that my article had slipped in just ahead of my mystery competitor's, and not a week later, when it would have been rejected altogether. Only novel papers fly, even if the news is just days old, and the scientific world resounds with tales of "scoops" inflicted and suffered.

I read each of the three anonymous critiques of my work. Two of them recommended publication if a few minor editorial changes were made. I felt a glow of happiness at phrases like *significant findings, answers a question long open in the field*, and, my favourite, *addresses the problem in an elegant and straight-forward manner*. At moments like these, all the hard work was worth it.

But the third reviewer was caustic, using adjectives such as *senseless, inconclusive*, and *inane*. Some of the accusations were flawed, betraying that the reviewer had not read my article very carefully. And the one valid criticism—that I hadn't ruled out an unlikely trivial explanation for the main result—had been inflated to an all-or-nothing condition, instead of an optional extra like the other two referees had viewed it.

I felt a searing sense of injustice. Maybe the referee had something personal against Magritte's steady success over the years. But from the safe vantage of anonymity, he or she could spin out misleading criticisms, despite the sportsmanlike objectivity that was supposed to rule the peer-review process. Just last spring, Magritte had reviewed one of Stan Fortuna's papers and had recommended it for publication in *Cell*, despite the fact that he was her closest competitor and bitterest rival. That was how the system was supposed to work.

Stan Fortuna. An intuition hit me: the paper jostling with my own on the editorial desk at *Cells & Cancer* must have originated from his lab—no one else could have been on such a similar track. The prospect of beating him was definitely inspiring, but how was I going to manage it?

I put the stack of papers onto Magritte's desk. True, the control experiment was important, and I'd been planning to do it for months. But there was no way it could be completed in less than a week, because I'd have to construct a new DNA plasmid first. Although the procedures of recombinant DNA technology had been streamlined in recent years, there were still basic bottlenecks that technology had not yet eliminated. The bacteria that produce your plasmid DNA during its construction have to grow overnight, and there are several overnight growth steps in the entire procedure. And once I'd finished the plasmid, the main experiment itself would take a few days. I could work non-stop with assistance from others, but it would still be impossible to beat the deadline—surely Magritte must have realized this.

I stormed back to the lab to find Paul and Magritte huddled together at her bench. She was pointing at something on a photo as Paul grinned and nodded his head. When they noticed me come in, they stepped apart and Magritte put the photo face down on her bench.

"It can't be done," I said, crossing my arms. Why did everyone look so amused? "Paul, you didn't fake this letter from *Cells & Cancer* as a practical joke, did you?"

Paul's grin stretched even wider. "No, but an excellent idea for the future."

"This is no joke," Magritte said, though it was clear she was trying not to smile. "*What* can't be done, exactly?"

I became aware that the entire lab had settled into rapt silence.

"You know perfectly well. For starters," I ticked off one finger, "I'll have to swap the mutation into the modified kinase plasmid. That's three days minimum."

Paul, obviously unable to stand it any longer, reached across Magritte, grabbed the photo and waved it in my face.

"She's already made it, mate! Right under your nose!"

As the photo vacillated in front of my eyes, I could see a few glowing bands of DNA cut into several pieces to confirm the correct pattern.

I snatched the image from Paul and stared at it for a few moments before looking up wordlessly at Magritte.

"Know it's been on your list to make mutant plasmid—but list is long. Still, had little feeling," she tapped a finger to her chest, "that reviewers demand this experiment before they let you publish." She shrugged. "So I made it myself. Just finished this morning, sent off to sequencing department for verification. But already know it's good." She pointed at one of the bands on the photo. "See here, this extra bit...S-to-E mutation must therefore be in."

Magritte's recent secretive behaviour fell into place. "Okay," I said in wonderment, "but there's still the H38 cells. How am I going to grow up enough in time?"

"Just so happens Jon thawed out a vial last week to test something completely different," she said. Jon was our first-year PhD student. I looked over to his bench, and he nodded affably.

"I've got stacks of plates going," he said, "and you're welcome to them."

"And to top it off, I've been assigned to be your personal slave for the week. Aren't I lucky?" Paul grimaced.

"So, O'Hara, what do you say?" Magritte said. "Know I told you decision entirely yours, but chance to scoop Fortuna maybe once-in-lifetime." She had an evil glint in her eye. It was, I would have sworn before that moment, a distinctly un-Magritte-like attitude.

I threw up my hands. "Okay, let's do it!"

The whole lab burst into applause. Even Marcy had a smile on her perpetually dour face. Kathy was looking on, enchanted by this melodramatic scene, which was probably cruelly reinforcing every misguided romantic notion she had about science.

Well, it did have its moments.

It was approaching ten o'clock that night. Paul was hidden away in the tissue culture suite, transfecting the first set of cell cultures for our big experiment, and I was sitting at my computer, hard at work revising the manuscript. Now that the euphoria of the afternoon had faded, I was starting to dread the coming week's efforts.

Something outside the window caught my eye. The entire side of the building opposite ours had been dark before, but now a window had filled with light—I had become so practiced that I no longer had to count along the matrix to tell it was Gina's. When nobody appeared in visual range, I forced my attention back to the screen. But after reading the same sentence several times with no comprehension, I removed the blue scarf from my rucksack, smelling for the last time that faint feminine something more subtle than any perfume, and went down to Geniaxis.

"Hello?" said the voice on the intercom.

"Gina? It's Andy. I —"

"Gina's not here." The accent was Irish, I realized belatedly. "But if you hang on a mo'..."

I felt the absurd urge to run. I didn't want to surrender the scarf to Gina's colleague because it was my only excuse to see her. But before I could move, the lobby lights came on and a woman came around the corner. She was slight, pale-skinned, and her long hair spilled like India ink around the shoulders of her white coat.

"Can I help at all?" Her eyes roamed over me with unabashed curiosity.

"I didn't mean to trouble you—a message would've been fine."

She slouched against the door frame and wrinkled her nose in a fetching manner.

"Truth be told, I was bored senseless with my tissue culture and desperate for any distraction." Her dark eyes laughed at me behind a composed expression. "So what's your story?"

"The abridged version or the full monty?"

"Oh, I quite like the sound of that second option." A dimple had appeared to one side of her mouth.

I gave her a second glance—this woman needed watching. "Gina left this in the Henry the other night."

She took the scarf from me, not even looking at it. "I'll make sure she gets it. Who will I say it's from?"

"I'm Andy." I hesitated. "I don't supposed you're expecting her back this evening?"

She shook her head. "Tickets to the theatre, alas."

"Well, if you could just give her the scarf." I received the uncomfortable sensation that the entire sorry situation was emblazoned across my forehead in red marker pen.

"Happy to help. And *I'm* called Maria, in case you were wondering," she added as I turned away.

5   Hot Lab

*T*he next few days passed in a blur of mounting stress. On Wednesday afternoon, Paul and I were fully entrenched in our big experiment, performing the radioactive assays that would tell us what messages Magritte's new mutant might be sounding off in cells.

Around noon, I paused to check my e-mail. It was the first chance I'd had all day, so lots of jetsam had washed up in my Inbox: tables of contents from online science journals, adverts from biotech supply firms, chain-letter jokes and memos from Admin about fire alarm testing and recent animal rights activities. I was deleting most of these without bothering to read them when I came across a message from one *glkraymer@geniaxis.com*. The date of receipt was yesterday evening, and the subject was, simply, "Thanks." I felt a tingle of excitement as I double-clicked and began to read.

Dear Andy,

I found your address in the online directory. Just a quick note to thank you for returning my scarf, which I'd feared was lost forever. Also was wondering if you'd care to meet in the Henry so we could finish having our drink? Even tonight, if you're free?

Gina

The words sank into my cortex, stimulating more pain than pleasure. Based on Christine's gossip, the invitation was probably a mere polite gesture to make up for abandoning me last Friday. In any case, going to the Henry, with her or anyone else, was out of the question until after the *Cells & Cancer* revision was sent off on Monday.

Taking a quick look at my lab timer, I realized I didn't even have ten seconds to phrase this delicately:

The alarm started to beep at me, so I sent the message into the void before dashing out of the lab.

Because of the large amount of radioactive isotope Paul and I needed for our experiment, regulations prohibited us from using the radioactive suite in the back of our lab. Instead, the entire Centre shared one high-level "B-complex," known colloquially as the Hot Lab. It was there that I found Paul working with his arms behind a thick Perspex shield, his Geiger counter clicking briskly.

"What kept you, mate?" Paul kept his gaze fixed on the set of four plastic cell culture dishes nestled on a tray of crushed ice, each of which contained an enormous dose of phosphorus-32. We'd labelled the cells with the radioactive isotope to catch Magritte's new messenger in the act of transferring its signal. "These beauties are ready to go! Precisely four hours."

"Sorry, I had to send a quick e-mail." I snapped on a pair of gloves and moved into the workstation on his right. We were operating relay-style: he would mash up the cells and put the resulting fluid into a tube, then I would further process the radioactively labelled proteins.

"So who's the lucky lady?" He flipped the lid off the first plate, pipetted in a glistening drop of detergent solution and started to scrape at the invisible carpet of cells with a small rubber paddle.

"What do you mean?"

"Come on, Andy." Paul carefully coaxed the viscous fluid onto one side of the tilted plate with the paddle. "Something's up, and it's got 'girl' written all over it." Deftly, he sucked up the gooey material with a pipette and squirted it into an Eppendorf tube before going back to the plate to collect the final dregs of the sample.

I pressed my lips together and began unwrapping a series of needles and syringes.

Paul risked a brief sideways glance. "This wouldn't have anything to do with the devastatingly gorgeous woman Helmut said was sniffing around you on Friday night, would it?"

I shook my head, disgusted. "The man practically subsists on gossip."

"And that's why we love him," Paul said. "So what happened exactly?"

"Exactly nothing."

"I'm surprised—Helmut said she was very keen." He snapped the lid of his tube shut and passed it over. Immediately, my own Geiger counter responded with a teeth-jarring shriek, its needle buried off the scale. I turned the nozzle away and the instrument settled down to a stream of rapid clicks.

"She's already got a boyfriend," I said, drawing up the radioactive cell mixture through the first needle and into the syringe barrel. As I passed the thick fluid back and forth through the needle, the consistency became less sticky as the DNA in the sample started to break apart. I could feel prickles of sweat on my forehead, and wished that Paul would drop the subject.

"Maybe not for long, from what Helmut was —"

He broke off as the heavy containment door swung open.

"*Hi*, Andy," somebody called out. "We meet again!"

Throwing a look over my shoulder, I saw Maria, Gina's colleague from the other night. She and her companion, a young man with a rugby physique gone to seed, were donning snazzy white coats with the Geniaxis logo emblazoned on the breast pocket.

I nodded a greeting before going back to my sample tube.

"Come here often?" She sauntered over to inspect my needlework, and I could feel her breath tickling my ear.

"Maria," the man said, the vowels dripping complaint. "We're already late."

"And whose fault is that?" she murmured so that only I could hear. I saw her wicked little smile reflected in my plastic shield before she retreated to the freezers. Paul raised his eyebrows, and I shook my head. Under the cover of their chatter, he murmured, "Your consolation prize, perhaps?"

"Listen, can we just focus on the work, please?"

"You want to get your priorities straight," he said, before lapsing into silence.

But the peace was temporary. Maria slipped into the workstation on my right, the stocky guy hovering anxiously next to her. He was taking notes, marking him as a newbie assigned to follow his more experienced colleagues around for a period of training. I remembered my own long-ago tour of duty in such a subordinate position and pitied him.

Maria proceeded to ignore her charge, manipulating her tubes with thoughtless expertise and firing comments at me instead. The guy just scribbled on his pad, casting resentful looks in my direction.

At first I answered her spirited queries with one-word responses. But as I settled into the routine of the work, I began to put more effort into my end of the conversation, especially as it became apparent that Maria was clever as well as attractive. Soon I had both her and Paul laughing—although the newbie just scowled.

The door opened again, admitting another group.

"Party in the Hot Lab," Christine remarked, emerging from the crowd and strolling over. "How's your magnum opus going, Andy?"

"No hitches so far," I said. "We're still on schedule to beat the deadline."

"Deadline?" Maria flipped hair out of her face, inspecting Christine under her lashes.

"Andy's finishing an experiment for *Cells & Cancer*," Paul said helpfully.

"Ooh, very impressive!"

Christine threw a questioning look at me, and I just shrugged.

"What brings you to my neighbourhood?" I asked Christine. "You're not normally this hot."

"That's not what I heard," Paul said. Christine threatened to whack him on the head, and he pretended to fend her off.

"I came to check up on you, but you're obviously in good hands." She exchanged glances with Paul then looked sidelong at Maria, who had turned her back and was suddenly explaining something expansively to the newbie.

"I'm absolutely fine." I wished people could mind their own business.

"Anyway, the B-complex is clearly *the* place to be," Christine observed.

The group who had come in ahead of Christine were setting up down at the other end of the row, and the room was now buzzing with chatter, laughter and a frantic choir of clicking, squawking Geiger counters. As I attempted to concentrate on the next sample, a rush of air blew against my face as the containment door opened yet again.

"Hi Gina," Maria said. "Sorry we're running behind."

"Christ," I murmured.

"This just gets better and better," Christine said under her breath to Paul.

Gina greeted me cautiously and came over.

"I got your e-mail just now," she said, a flatness to her eyes. "You must be busy."

With a quick look at the expression on my face, Paul's eyes widened as he made the connection.

"*Very* busy." Maria smiled at me in an alarmingly proprietary way. "Andy's been telling me all about the final experiment for his *Cells & Cancer* paper."

"We're all extremely proud of him," Christine said, gripping my shoulder in effortless counter-attack.

"How's Miles?" Maria asked Gina. "That was him on the phone when I left, wasn't it?"

"If you're just about done, I'm supposed to show Steve the virus labs now." Her voice sounded weary and resigned.

"He's all yours—I've finished here anyway."

Gina peeled Steve away from Maria and made a quick exit. Maria crossed herself carelessly with the Geiger's nozzle to check for hot spots on her clothing, betraying the rote movements of a Roman Catholic upbringing, and gave me a smile before following the others out the door.

There was a moment of silence, and then Paul whooshed out his breath.

I turned on Christine. "What were you trying to pull just then?"

Paul shook his head in wonder. "It's as if I woke up in a parallel universe where geeks rule the world, and Andy O'Hara is some species of super-stud."

"Don't tell me you've moved on so quickly," Christine said disapprovingly.

"Why shouldn't he go after Maria?" Paul was a man of simple calculus when it came to women. "He told me the other girl's taken."

"Would it be relevant to point out that I'm not actually interested in Maria?"

"It's not relevant at all, mate," Paul said. "Trust me."

"Forget Maria," Christine said. "The real information obviously went right over both your sorry heads."

When both Paul and I stared at her in confusion, she added, "Sometimes I can't believe men survive long enough to actually reproduce their genes. It was all there, in what *wasn't* said."

"Enlighten us poor unsophisticated males, then," Paul invited, grinning.

"Gina was a wreck. Puffy eyes—definitely been crying in the loo."

"All because I turned her down for a drink?" I was stricken with guilt, only then realizing how cold my e-mail must have seemed.

"You turned her down for a *drink*, mate?" Paul said.

"Don't be stupid." Christine sighed. "Although if you did, I'm forced to agree with Paul."

"Then why?" I considered Gina's despondency with this new insight and felt the sudden desire to abandon my experiment and find out if she was okay.

"Maria challenged Gina about Miles's phone call, no doubt to get her to admit in front of you that she's seeing someone else," Christine explained impatiently. "Instead, she looked as if she was about to dash to the ladies' for another round. Obviously, as we predicted, there's trouble with Miles. If that weren't enough, she comes up here to find her own colleague flirting with you —"

"And you're busy posing as my girlfriend on top of it," I said bitterly. "I don't get it."

"Me neither," Paul said. "Is this some sort of reverse psychology strategy?"

"I wouldn't put it quite so crudely." She brushed a speck of dust off her sleeve.

"So everything is going according to plan, then?" Paul studied her admiringly.

"Well, the Maria card was unexpected, but it should create useful tension."

"Don't I have any say in the matter?" I said.

Paul settled back on his stool and turned back to his samples. "If I were you, Andy, I'd leave it in Christine's capable hands."

The rest of the week blasted along at a similar pace like scenes whipping past a train window, until my conveyance finally deposited me at the end of the line: a quiet desk in the empty lab on Sunday night. As

I sat there, waiting the necessary hour before it was time to develop the final result, I should have been recording details in my neglected lab journal. But somehow, I hadn't quite caught my breath yet, and I needed to.

My labmates had been keen to find out how everything would turn out, but the few people who'd been around earlier had gone home one by one as it became clear that unforeseen delays would make the moment of truth much later than originally anticipated. Magritte had held out until about eight, whereas Paul, the last, had finally gathered up his things around nine.

"As much as I'd like to be there for the epic moment," he'd said, "Suzy'll kill me if I stay much longer."

I appreciated his support, but I'd been pleased to see him go.

So there I was, surrounded by calm. I could hear the whirring of the air conditioning fans, the humming of the refrigerators, the self-satisfied beep of the PCR machine every time it finished a cycle. I felt as if I were in a state of suspended time, with a clear sense that this was *before*, and soon it would be *after*—a temporal awareness that often coloured the moment before a pivotal result.

Although I was tired, my perceptions felt as lucid as the glittering rows of glassware in the cabinet across the room. It wasn't often that I allowed my scientific concerns to come to rest. And slowly, over the last few minutes, my thoughts had become full of Gina. I couldn't stop speculating about what had caused her to look so downhearted. As little as I knew of her, I was filled with an irrational desire to catch her fall—a curious immediacy I couldn't remember feeling for anyone before.

I was still irritated by Christine's outrageous behaviour in the Hot Lab. Even if she was right, that jealousy was a more powerful catalyst than simple attraction, her strategy felt wrong. I didn't like the idea of doing something backward to engineer the opposite result: it was terribly unscientific.

At the time, I wrote off Christine's interference as mere meddling. In hindsight, it's now obvious that she'd only been stepping into a vacuum of my own creation. But the thing she didn't realize was that I hadn't always been so unassertive about women. And even then I was aware that I had gradually lost some crucial edge. Yet when I bothered to think about it at all, I usually ascribed my flagging initiative to the ageing process, to something inevitable that I couldn't avoid. But recent events, and Christine's subsequent lectures, were starting to make me wonder.

✦ ✦ ✦

The notebook was still waiting, a restful blank page begging to be filled with my careful scrawl. I pulled open my desk drawer to search for a pen and was busy frisking the clutter when my attention snagged on the photograph stuck to the left inside wall of the drawer. Like the rest of my labmates, I had a number of snaps pinned up around my desk, but this one was kept purposefully out of sight. It was probably the most cherished item I possessed, but the truth was that I didn't want to have to see it all the time. As befits an old memory, I felt it should lie undisturbed in the dark except for the occasional discreet airing.

The photo was important because it encapsulated not just any memory, but my earliest. Sometimes I wonder if I just think I remember the actual scene. After all, I have been staring at the photo for most of my life. My brain might have adopted a changeling image as its own, this moment embedded in light-reacted chemicals on paper, defending it just as fiercely as if the neuronal connections really had been forged at the time of the shutter's click. But I have always been blessed—or cursed—by exceptionally vivid memories, and as far as I could ever truly know, I believed that this one was real.

So what was this memory? First, the setting: the molecular biology lab at Cambridge where my father had been a post-doc in the early Seventies—a splendid, high-ceilinged room with dusky glass windows, crammed with dark-brown wooden workbenches, quaint but still beautiful compared to the synthetic surfaces and accoutrements of the Centre's labs.

The supporting actors: Dad's colleagues, fifteen strong, all of them sporting the goofy hairstyles and naïve optimism of the dawn of the recombinant DNA era, when all human diseases were going to be swiftly eradicated in a puff of molecular logic. Arms about one another's shoulders, they emanated a rolling-up-the-sleeves vigour that wasn't at all apparent in the present day. Another outmoded feature of this lab was that the only woman in the room had been a wife: my mother, snapping the picture in her pink miniskirt and probably single-handedly responsible for several of the distracted looks.

The extras: Liz, my elder sister, hair lit up in a wispy halo and sitting off to one side on a lab stool, colouring with crayons and not deigning to acknowledge the camera. And me, perched nearby with two glass measuring cylinders, looking upward at Dad for approval before pouring water from one to the other, light blazing off the glass clutched in my three-year-old fist. I had never been as certain as Liz when we were growing up, but here in my father's kingdom, I'd felt the most secure. And he'd spent most of his time in the lab, so being with him was a rare treat. It was difficult to make out my expression because the photo was old and crumpled, and one of the spidery crease marks had replaced my features with a whitish fault line. But I could clearly remember feeling happy.

And the lead: Dad, lounging against the bench between my sister and me, one big hand on Liz's shoulder, the other on my head. Our trio was set apart at the end of the phalanx, distanced from the camaraderie. He was grinning carelessly at Mum with a look in his eye that I could have never interpreted as a child but whose meaning had gradually unravelled, years later. Like the other men, he wore a white coat—not an honorary coat but an honest one, stained with the chemistry of cruder methods.

And around us, everywhere, was light: dazzling the camera, all of us a bit too backlit, oval blobs of fiery white artefact dancing in one corner of the print.

After my father died of cancer at the age of forty-seven, my feelings about the photograph had changed. It wasn't too surprising that new emotions would override my earlier childhood nostalgia about the scene: sadness of course, but also, when I was in a certain mood, anger that he'd been taken away so unfairly, and the desire for revenge, to battle against cancer with every intellectual tool at my disposal. But more subtly, the celestial lighting began to impart an aura of strangeness, of downright unreality. Not only was my father gone, but it was almost as if he had never existed.

This evening, though, the photo was infused with a sense of authenticity that had been lacking for some time. Studying my father's face, I finally realized what it was. He looked uncannily like me, with his blond hair and easy good humour, more than he ever had done before. Doing the sums, I worked out that I had finally caught up: this stopped-in-time father was exactly the same age that I was now. It gave me an odd feeling that he had already produced two children— and I was about as far from that state as a man could be.

I was startled out of my contemplation by an unexpected voice pronouncing my name. Swivelling around, I saw Gina hesitating in the doorway of the lab. Just like that, the calm of the previous moments shattered, and my blood chemistry responded in kind.

I slammed the desk drawer shut and returned her greeting.

"I...don't have any excuse to visit," she confessed.

This time I noticed that she had recently been crying. At least Christine had been able to teach me something.

"You don't need one." I stood up and held out my hand, and she came over to me, took it. Then more tears were spilling over and I pulled her to me, held her while she shook with almost soundless sobs. She felt even more slender than she looked, and this seemed to increase her vulnerability.

Then something peculiar happened. Although her physical proximity was exciting, the quiet mood that had surrounded me all evening gradually returned and wove itself around us: tension and calmness effortlessly combined. I'm not sure how long we stayed like that after her crying finally ceased, but then my lab timer started to beep an insistent triplicate intrusion.

I swore, and Gina pulled away, face still streaked with tears.

"I should leave you alone," she said, disentangling herself. "Maria was going on about your deadline."

"Was she? I didn't even notice." I recaptured her hand in mine, reaching over to silence the timer with the other, and the abrupt cessation of sound was explosive. "I've got all the time you need."

"Your alarm must've gone off for a reason."

"It can wait. Tell me what's wrong."

She seemed torn by some internal conflict. After a few moments, she shook her head almost imperceptibly. I gave her hand an understanding squeeze before releasing it, and she seemed relieved that I wasn't going to push her.

"Fancy a distraction?" I tapped the timer with a finger. "It just so happens I've got some entertainment lined up."

She gave me a wan smile, nodded. When she started wiping her face with the back of her sleeve, I passed her a laboratory tissue, which would be coarse but effective, and she blew her nose while I grabbed an insulated glove from a drawer and led her towards the door.

"Where are we going?"

"Patience, Dr Kraymer." I took her arm and led her down the corridor to a bank of freezers. When I opened one of the doors, a supercooled fog massed out and sank around our shoulders. I donned the insulated glove, reached into the cloudy depths and pulled out two frost-encrusted metal film cassettes.

"Is this it?" she said. "The final experiment for your paper?" Curiosity had begun to restore her colour and animation.

"Yes—and it's so much better with someone to share the historic moment." I caught her eye, and this time her smile was convincing.

She followed me a bit further down the corridor to the departmental darkroom. The entrance was a rotating barrel door designed to allow people to gain access without permitting any outside light that would ruin unprotected film within. Not that there was likely to be anyone this late on a Sunday.

I gestured for her to precede me into the semicircular outer chamber, very conscious again of her closeness. As I pushed the heavy barrel around us, the movement stirred up a faint trace of her perfume—almost immediately, my heart rate sped up. When we were expelled into the darkness within, the delicate aroma was decimated by the strong chemical odour of the place, by the warm air being vented from the humming machine. Its single yellow eye winked at me conspiratorially.

"Hang on," I said, feeling along the wall until I'd located the switch. The room became bathed in the red glow of the safelight. In a few seconds my eyes had adjusted, and I made my way over to the workbench. Gina followed behind me, one hand on my arm for orientation. While I busied myself unclipping the safety catches on the cassettes, the frozen metal burning my fingertips, she hoisted herself up on the workbench to one side.

"What's your paper about, anyway?" she asked, swinging her feet back and forth. I couldn't make out her features, but I could picture the way her eyes became bright when she asked a question.

So while I extricated the first film and fed it to the machine, I gave her the abridged version of my major findings.

"That's quite good, isn't it?" she said, after digesting my explanation for a few moments. "I'm impressed. But how do you know that your protein is *directly* responsible? Maybe —" and here she unleashed a pointed, intricate salvo along the same uncompromising lines as her seminar question. Although I had done a large number of experiments, it was still formally possible that my hypothesis could be explained by a much less intriguing possibility. The only way to answer this criticism was with the experimental result that was about to come out of the developing machine—and I was amazed by her insightfulness all over again.

"Are you sure you weren't one of the reviewers?" I said. "That's exactly what we're about to find out."

"So you made and tested an activated mutant? How on earth did you manage that in one week?"

I grinned, even though I knew she couldn't see it. "Magritte was sneaking about the lab, cloning behind my back. The post-doc is always the last to know."

"Lucky you! I don't think my boss has touched a pipettor in a decade or so."

The developer beeped encouragingly, and I fed it the second film.

"So are you excited?" she asked. For most scientists, waiting for the film to emerge was one of those ritual activities that never seemed to lose its frisson.

"To be honest, I just want the damned experiment to be over, one way or the other, so I can get back to normal life again." I paused, wondering exactly what I meant by *normal*. "Here it comes now," I added, looking over at the delivery slot of the machine. The rollers extruded an indistinct rectangle, which flopped into the tray. I held the transparent film up to the safelight, scanning it anxiously.

"And...?" Gina leaned forward.

And...it was one of those rare moments when a film tells you exactly what you had been hoping for, to counter-balance the crushing disappointment of the dozens of other times when the news was bad, or, almost worse, ambiguous. I was flooded with triumph.

"Here's the regular kinase," I said, pointing at a crisp black band, the footprint of the radioactive tracer that Paul and I had dosed the cells with. "And here's the dead mutant..." I indicated the next lane, where no band appeared. "And this lovely thing"—I put a finger under the next band—"is Magritte's new activated mutant in the absence of upstream signals. Look at that whopping signal!"

"Congratulations!" I felt her hand squeeze my shoulder, sending a wave of impulses down my back. I was glad she couldn't see my face.

There was another clatter in the tray.

"What's on the second film?"

"A replicate experiment." I whipped it up to the light, and we could immediately see that the pattern was the same as the first.

"Result!" I said, waving the films in the air, and she laughed, treated me to a whimsical round of applause. When she slipped off the bench, I lifted her right off the floor and spun her around a few times before setting her, still laughing, unsteadily on her feet. She rested her head against my shoulder, and I put my hand on her head, stroked her silky hair. She seemed to melt into me.

"What would you say to a celebratory drink?" I asked eventually. "I know a certain place that will still be serving this late on a Sunday."

She didn't exactly stiffen, but I could feel the sudden discrepancy in her musculature. She angled her head up to look at me, though I was unable to see more than the moisture in her eyes and lips shimmering in the safelight.

"I'm sorry, but I'm supposed to see Miles tonight," she said. "It can't be put off any longer, I'm afraid."

My insides executed a roller-coaster lurch. "But I thought that you and he —"

"We are, I think. Through, I mean. But I want to hear it from *him*, in a situation where he has to look me in the eye."

"Is that all? Or do you still hope to salvage something?"

"Maybe I do," she said, but her arms slid back around me in con-tradiction, and I drew her in. "This isn't easy for me to talk about."

Her words dropped against the interface of my hearing and subse-quent comprehension like distinct pebbles hitting a surface of water. Somehow, I understood that it was only the darkness that was making this conversation possible.

"I feel pulled in two different directions," she finally said. "I wouldn't be with him in the first place if I didn't care—I can't just shut that off, even if he did do what he did." Her words trailed off bitterly.

"There are limits to what you're expected to endure."

She sighed. "I know, but in the past, I've given up when things got turbulent. I promised myself then that I'd try harder the next time. I promised..." She shifted her face against my throat, breathing me in, and my skin ignited into microscopic sparks. "I can't deny I'm strongly attracted to you, Andy. Even though I hardly know you."

"But."

"But I have to give him a chance first."

I dropped my arms, stepped away. If possible, my heart felt as if it were both swelling with joy and contracting in disappointment.

"Do you understand?" she said urgently, not moving from where I had released her.

"I think so." Other sentences crowded into my head. That I wanted far more than just a drink or a friendly conversation. That I was not only attracted to her as well, but completely entranced. That I wasn't the impatient sort, that I would be willing to wait for her to try one last time with Miles. That I'd still be there when they were finished. But I remembered in time how such confessions had only ever backfired, and suppressed the flood of inappropriate words. I still wonder how things might have played out if I hadn't.

"So can we just be friends, and...see?" she said, when I didn't fill up the silence.

"Friends," I agreed, busying myself gathering up the film cassettes, now puddled with melted frost, and the two crucial films. In the aftermath of our cutting closeness, the mere scientific data seemed anticlimactic.

6   *Acceptance and Rejection*

*M*onday morning brought a letter from my mother. In addition to the cheerful maternal missive, there was the inevitable newspaper clipping, which I pinned up dutifully on the Board as I enjoyed my morning coffee in the common room.

Gene Therapy: Scourge or Saviour?

Watson and Crick, the intrepid scientists who solved the structure of DNA in the Fifties, probably never dreamed that pieces of their humble double-helix would someday be ingeniously packaged into a fleet of viruses, charged with the noble task of ferrying life-saving genetic information into a critically ill patient. It is a satisfying irony that our ancient enemy, the common cold, could be dispatched on a dangerous mission into the human body, forced to dodge formidable immune defences and home in on cancerous growths, genetically-deficient tissues or fatally-infected cells...

The words went on from there, doggedly tedious.

"The mad clipper strikes again?" Christine had appeared soundlessly at my side.

"It's a never-ending supply." I folded the accompanying letter back into its envelope. "At the moment she's fixated on gene therapy."

"My father's the same way. I tend to receive these rambling e-mails sent off in the middle of the night, asking about the latest scientific finding that the media had managed to inflate beyond all recognition."

"I thought my mum's interest was unusual."

"Cameron gets enthusiastic interrogation from his family as well."

She frowned critically at a cartoon featuring horn-rimmed spectacled, white-coated geeks at play. "Gary Larson's behind the times—those glasses are actually in fashion now." She paused. "And I see our mysterious departmental poet's posted another instalment. One for you, eh?"

She pointed to a grubby piece of paper towel, scribbled over with the marker pen most people favoured for labelling Eppendorf tubes. The ink had bled from its original position like a chromatography experiment left unattended, so I had to squint to make out the words:

Post-Doctoral Haiku No. 14
by: Dr Anonymous

To work or to sleep?
Yet the dictum rules my life:
Publish or perish.

"Amen," I said, but I was still stuck on the previous topic. "Chris, do you think our families are interested in science because we're scientists, or do you think we became scientists after being subconsciously influenced by their interest?"

"I suspect it could be a bit of both," she said. "But your mother's case complicates the hypothesis a bit—your father was a scientist, wasn't he?"

Christine and I were close, but there were some conversational topics I avoided. Looking at my watch, I mentioned a sudden pressing need to return to my experiments.

There was simultaneous cacophony: a resounding pop and a chorus of cheers (and a squeal from Kathy) as Magritte expertly sent the champagne cork to the ceiling. The foam swarmed over the lip of the bottle and dribbled onto the floor, and everyone gathered round, thrusting out their Pyrex measuring beakers and good-naturedly elbowing one another as they manoeuvred for a favourable position.

"Andy first," Paul said, pushing me forward. Several people slapped me on the back as Magritte filled up my beaker with the fizzing golden liquid. Only minutes before, after an unbearably tense day of waiting, Magritte had received an e-mail from the American offices of *Cells & Cancer* informing us that my revised manuscript was officially accepted, and that the "aforementioned similar manuscript" had been summarily rejected.

I was feeling euphoric even without the champagne. Whereas Magritte had had many opportunities to stage the traditional lab celebration over the years, this was my first truly prestigious article. Getting published in a high-impact journal was as much a matter of luck as expertise, but still, we all craved this recognition that our work, aside from being merely solid, was worthy of fame. And, just like that, my future job prospects had increased significantly. It didn't seem particularly fair, but I wasn't about to complain when the apples had fallen on my side of the fence for a change.

And after what had occurred the previous evening, the distraction was welcome.

"The man of the hour!" Christine said, whisking into the lab with Cameron close behind.

"Typical you'd just happen to show up when the cork popped, Edmonds." Paul grinned as he fished out a few more beakers from the glassware cabinet.

"Coincidence?" Cameron intoned in an *X-files* voice. "*I don't think so.*"

"Call it feminine intuition." She gave me a hug. "Those better be clean, Paul, or you're paying the undertaker."

"I'll drag her body away later," Cameron said, shaking my hand.

Magritte proposed a toast, and after the scattering of applause, someone armed the CD player with a subversive groove. Under the cover of music and chatter, Christine homed in on me and asked if something was up—with that telltale suspicious look in her eye.

Since yesterday, I had been dreading telling her about my encounter with Gina, imagining all the disastrous counter-stratagems that might result. But the moment she asked, I wanted nothing more than to unburden myself, so I told her I had something to reveal later, when we could speak in private.

The party in the lab eventually migrated to the Henry, where we'd picked up a fresh crowd of well-wishers, including Maria, and lost the sort of people who had families to go home to. I had watched the door, full of ill-formed plans of action, but Gina never stepped through. After last orders, we tried out a few new after-hours places, the group whittled down to a hard core by the lengthening hours, before washing up at our standard haunt, the Wall Flower.

We pushed through the crowd standing outside the entrance, drinking from plastic glasses, sitting on kerbs, smoking and sending animated laughter into the dull orange sky. The summer darkness felt warm and dreamy, so removed from all temporal context that I had to check my watch—close to one in the morning.

Upstairs, people were crushed into every available space, both standing and interspersed underfoot on vintage sofas and cushions. We settled in, continuing a friendly argument that had been running since the Henry. As usual, it was everyone else versus Cameron, still gamely defending his latest outlandish theory *du jour*. The banter went a couple more confusing rounds (the *sequitur* having got increasingly *non* as the evening progressed), and then Christine turned, looking almost surprised to see me sitting on her other side.

"Andy—what news?" She slid down into a horizontal position and rummaged in her bag for a pack of cigarettes—this was a few years before the smoking ban. After lighting up, she pushed away her pint and slipped a flask out of her jacket pocket.

"Gina paid me a visit last night. Give me some of that, will you?" She passed me the flask, and I took an aggressive sip.

"She started crying," I said, "and I...comforted her."

"You devil! Right there in the lab?"

"Chris, please." I lay back against my cushion. "I mean, I gave her a Kimwipe, that sort of thing."

"I know, silly. Then what?"

"She accompanied me to the darkroom."

Christine dissolved into giggles, prodding my arm with her finger. "I can't decide if this is terribly romantic or hopelessly nerdy, O'Hara."

"It was atmospheric, at least." I couldn't help laughing myself, but my humour dwindled away as I told her the rest, ending with my terminal diagnosis: that nothing had really changed.

Chris chewed on this for awhile. I watched blue-grey threads of smoke creep along the plasterwork of the ceiling until she propped herself up at an angle that forced me to look at her.

"I'm not so sure," she finally said. "It sounds more as if she's got some idealized sense of what's right and is just going though the motions."

"I don't get it." In a rush, I remembered the sensation of Gina's lips whispering against my neck.

"Forgiving someone can often take more courage than running away—although it's obvious she doesn't know the full extent of his reputation."

"Exactly! She didn't specify what he'd done, but it's got to be another woman, hasn't it?"

She shrugged, unperturbed. "More likely than not."

"Doesn't she realize...?"

"That Miles is a hopeless case?"

"Whereas, I'm..."

"You're there, arms outstretched?" Christine had always possessed an uncanny ability to decipher even my worst specimens of inarticulateness. It was a short-circuiting phenomenon that amazed Cameron and, I suspected, bothered him with its implied intimacy.

"We girls can't read minds, you know," Christine added, unaware of her own contradiction. She blew a stream of smoke out the side of her mouth and tapped my forehead with a chastising fingertip.

"I'm sure she can tell exactly how I feel."

Christine shook her head dubiously, but let it pass. "Let me mull this over."

"Chris...I don't actually want to *do* anything at this point." I tried to put it nicely. "No more plans, okay?"

She reached over and stroked the stubble on the side of my face once with the back of her hand. "I'm not sure it's in my nature to mind my own business on something as juicy as this, but I'll do my best."

"Is there room on that cushion for me?"

I looked up to find Maria staring down at me.

"Take mine, I want to dance anyway." Christine scrambled up and disappeared.

I tried to sit up as well, but my limbs felt pickled in concrete. How much of that whisky had I actually drunk?

Maria sat down, expression gripped with uncertainty. Then I thought I might have imagined it because after I blinked, a smile had taken its place, and the room was tending towards an anti-clockwise spin.

"There's something I have to tell you," she said. The red colour of her top seemed to vibrate faintly against her milky skin, and as she leaned closer, I was treated to a tantalizing view of the world enshrouded behind her lacy bra.

"Andy, are you with me?" she asked insistently. "This is *important*."

"I'm listening." I could smell her perfume, which was about as brash as Gina's was understated. *There's an analogy in there somewhere*, my mind was trying to hypothesize, but such an advanced concept proved too much.

"The thing is..." She hesitated, hurried on. "I wanted to apologize for my behaviour in the Hot Lab—I'm not usually like that. It's just that it didn't seem fair, Gina playing you along when she already has Miles. She's always getting more than her fair share of male attention, you see."

"I can imagine."

She bit her lip. "And I felt bad for you...you looked so wistful the other night, clutching that scarf like a lucky charm. I guess I was trying to force her to admit it about Miles. But you already knew, didn't you? And I just made things worse."

My mind pushed through the alcohol, trying to process all the different elements of her candid speech. Then, one thing sprung out at me. "You mean, you *don't* like me?"

"I didn't say that." Her dimple appeared, an ironic punctuation mark. "Look, I —"

"Spare me the chivalrous let-down: it's perfectly clear what's going on. I'd rather stay out of it."

She tucked a strand of hair behind a delicate ear, a simple movement that struck me as forlorn.

"Thanks for being honest," I said. "I have no idea what's going to happen, but I'm glad we've met."

A smile crept in. "Yeah, well, I suppose if Gina and Miles —" Her eyes widened, and she smacked her hand to her forehead. "Jesus, I forgot the main point—when I was coming back from the loos, I saw Gina and Miles downstairs. There's still a hefty queue, but they'll be walking through the door at any moment."

"I've got to talk to her—she's making a big mistake!" I attempted to leap to a sitting position, but she held me down with unexpected strength.

"Don't be a bloody idiot!" she said. "You'll only make a fool of yourself, especially in your present condition. Better to lay low on the dance floor, make sure she doesn't know you're here until you cool off."

Maria hauled me to my feet and I felt a wave of dizziness. I grabbed her arm to steady myself, and then she was pulling me deep into the throng of dancers, slipping her arms around my shoulders. The Asian-influenced trance music had slowed to something throbbingly hypnotic, sitars and drums in a queasy mixture.

"What's up?" It was Christine, draped on Cameron and peering at us with suspicion.

"Gina and Miles are in the queue," Maria said. "I'm trying to keep lover-boy here out of trouble."

"Interesting strategy, but doomed in the long term," Christine said, nevertheless looking moderately impressed that someone else was doing some thinking on my behalf.

"The problem is that I'm not familiar with the layout of this place," Maria said apologetically. "There isn't another exit, is there?"

"I'm afraid not," Christine said. "That's one of its main disadvantages: no escape route."

The girls talked military tactics for a few moments, until Cameron cleared his throat.

"Miles and Gina at twelve o'clock," he remarked. "Battle stations."

In the brief second before Maria muscled me deeper into the crowd, an image dazzled my brain and set up shop in my long-term memory: Gina on Miles's arm in a clingy dress, hair piled up on her head and prisms of light glinting at her ears. I wanted to stride over, punch the self-satisfied leer off Miles's face, sweep Gina into my arms and—*God, was I drunk.*

"She didn't see him," Christine exhaled. "*Oi*—keep your head down, O'Hara."

"Could someone please tell me what's happening?" I begged.

"Gina seems a bit subdued, a bit insecure," Maria said.

"Miles is definitely upset," Cameron said. "He's scanning the room, as if he's looking for someone."

"Now he's gesturing at the bar." Christine sounded worried. "But she's shaking her head, pulling at his hand."

"She wants to dance," Maria said in alarm.

"They're headed this way," Christine confirmed.

"Wait a mo'," Maria said, standing on her toes. "Now Miles is pointing towards the other end of the room...I think he's spotted someone he wants to have a word with. Christine, can you see who it might be? I don't have the angle."

"Gorgeous blonde, over by the fake fireplace," she replied.

"I know that woman," Cameron said thoughtfully. "She's in our department. I've seen Miles and her together a few times in the coffee room last week, head to head."

"Looks as if the master juggler might be having a few problems keeping all of his balls in the air at once," Christine said.

"They've split up." Maria said. "Miles is hacking his way over to the blonde. Gina's at loose ends. A bit flustered. Oh—oops!"

"What? *What?*" I demanded.

"We've made eye contact," Maria said. "I think she's..."

"Yes, she's coming over," Cameron said.

"I recommend you just pass out, Andy, and we'll stash you in the corner," Christine said.

"That won't be necessary." I looked down at Maria, drenched with alcoholic calm. I was touched by her obvious concern, and it occurred to me that kissing her could solve many of my problems. I wove around the idea, measuring up the possible consequences.

"Hey, Maria, I didn't know you were..." Gina's smile froze when she saw me, saw us.

I dropped my arms from Maria's shoulders with a start. Over Gina's shoulder, I could see Miles entreating the blonde. She stabbed her finger a few times in Gina's direction.

"My paper was accepted today," I told her.

With no real detectable motion, everyone else had somehow faded back.

"That's great," Gina said, expression at odds with the sentiment. Behind her, the blonde leaned over to grab her jacket and handbag with furious movements. Miles took her arm, but she pulled away and stamped towards the door, her friend throwing him a murderous look before following suit. He stared after them for a few moments before whirling around and storming off to the bar.

"I think I'm going to make a move," I said. "I haven't got much sleep all week and it's starting to tell."

Before anyone could protest, I turned my back on the whole sorry affair. Halfway down the stairs I realized I'd left my jacket behind, and lurched to a stop. But I knew Christine would retrieve it, and there was no way I could go back now.

Outside, the alley was still crowded, the air thrumming with voices and shot with cigarette smoke. The blonde was leaning against the graffiti-splattered wall, weeping onto her friend's shoulder. I wondered how Gina could have been so deceived. But then I remembered that one of the things I found so attractive about her in the first place was that rare mixture of naïvety and deadly intelligence.

Thoughts woozy with self-pity, I stumbled a few steps in the direction of the night buses on Tottenham Court Road, but was forced to stop when a wave of vertigo clobbered me. I crossed the road and sank down on the pavement to wait for it to pass, and then things went murky. The next thing I knew, my body heat had been completely sucked away by the bricks and cement in a stealthy act of entropy.

I blinked the entrance of the Wall Flower back into focus and saw Gina standing there, holding my jacket and looking around until she spotted me. I nodded in acknowledgement when she started walking over, but I wasn't too keen to speak to her any more.

Gina peered down at me. "Are you upset? Can we talk?"

I took the proffered jacket and spread it out on the pavement next to me, and she settled onto it in a graceful orchestration of long legs, of slippery fabrics repositioning around the unconscious curves of her body.

"I'm not upset." And somehow, I wasn't, anymore. "Where's Miles?"

"I told him to wait upstairs. There was...an incident."

"I know, we all saw it."

"He slept with her last week, apparently." Her voice was serene. "I found out the evening before I ran into you in the Hot Lab."

The evening she'd sent me the e-mail.

"Why aren't you more angry?" I had to make an effort not to slur my words.

"It was an accident—an old flame that got out of hand."

I stared at her. "Is that what he told you?"

She flushed. "He promised it wouldn't happen again. I've given him one more chance." When I just shook my head, she hastened on.

"Listen, I'm not completely stupid: I know how he's been in the past. But he says he wants to change, and I owe it to him to at least..."

As clear as if Christine was whispering in my ear, I heard her often-repeated mantra in my head: *Bounders remain bounders, cads remain cads, suckers remain suckers.*

"Why do you owe him, exactly?" I demanded.

She just looked down, the epicentres of colour deepening on her fine skin.

"He's treating you terribly, and you're the only one who can't see it," I pressed on. "You deserve far better."

"Someone like you, you mean?" Her head jerked back up, suddenly angry.

"*Anyone* but him!"

"And I suppose you're Mr Objective at the moment—give me a break!" Her voice rose in volume as well as pitch, and I realized she wasn't entirely sober either.

"That's Dr Objective to you."

"Is that supposed to be funny?"

"I'm not just trashing Miles to promote myself—I care about you. God knows why, if this is how I'm thanked."

I felt furious at the perceived injustice, and then when Gina reacted, looked taken aback, a few key neurons misfired in my brain: I mistook hesitation for regret, and in the dim light, her confused eyes seemed cloudy with desire. But when I tried to kiss her, she shoved me away.

"Back off, Andy! I've told you where things stand."

"Fine." Full of bitterness, I found myself scrambling to my feet. The streetlights throbbed like pulsars and the pavement lurched towards me. Patches of black obscured my vision, dissolving the lights, the other people, Gina's angry face into one smear of colour. I wasn't sure what happened next, or how long it took, but then Gina was standing before me, and the aftermath of harsh words seemed to be echoing in my ears.

"Do you really mean that?" she asked, eyes wide.

"What do you care?" I had no idea what she was referring to, but I felt clever keeping up my end of the argument. "If you'll excuse me, I have a bus to catch."

"Andy, wait!" She began to cry as I whisked my jacket from the ground. When she grabbed my arm, I pushed her away, but the force was much more than I'd intended and she crashed against the corrugated wall. After a second of stunned silence, she turned and fled back towards the bar, cradling her shoulder, and I wove off down the alley, self-righteous anger not quite sufficient to cover up a growing sense of shame. Eventually, I noticed that the sky was lightening, a few birds were beginning to chirp experimentally and I had walked past my bus stop long ago.

7   At the Bench

A cancer eventually infiltrates the patient so thoroughly that the lines start to blur, the diseased and healthy tissues so intertwined that the surgeon cannot remove one without harming the other. The events of your life can be like this too, so interconnected that, in retrospect, it can be difficult to extract the mundane from the crucial—the benign from the malignant. So it was after my fight with Gina. Before I knew it, three months had slipped by with the ease of forgettable routine: I had literally lost the plot. Then one day I realized that the raw feeling of our falling out was suddenly months behind and, if not pain-less, then at least scabbing over, no longer at the top of the emotional agenda.

What triggered this thought at this particular moment was the sight of Gina emerging from the Centre's main entrance. As she stepped out of the shadow of the building, the glass doors swung closed behind in a blaze of reflected light and the wind and sun caught her hair in a shifting, reddish-bronze halo. Her wool sweater reminded me that the seasons had changed without my awareness either.

I didn't want her to see me, but I needn't have worried—I was hardly obvious, sitting on a bench in the small quadrangle park with more than a dozen yards between us. It was only my particular angle that provided an unobscured view of the entrance through the lilac bushes clogging the iron fencing. She was moving briskly, completely focused on the steps below, and after turning left at the bottom, she disappeared behind the foliage.

I realized with interest that the sight of her had not triggered the usual responses. Of course I was still aware of my continuing disappointment, but the immediacy of the emotions had deserted me. The shell of the memories was intact, but no small creature was lurking inside. If I held it to my ear, there'd be only an empty reverberation.

I looked back down at the laptop's screen, its cursor blinking patiently at the end of an abandoned sentence. I was supposed to be writing a paper about one of my side projects, and as the lab had proved too noisy, I'd come outside to enjoy the fine weather. But seeing Gina had derailed my focus, stirring up the mud of our fight and its unsatisfying aftermath.

Of course I knew I'd been to blame, in an abstract way, but I hadn't made it into a grand lesson as Christine would have, complete with a handy moral and advice for improvement. Not that she hadn't tried. I'd been harassed incessantly to disclose what had happened that night outside the Wall Flower, but I was too embarrassed by my brutish behaviour to tell her. Eventually, she'd given up in disgust, and after a few more weeks I managed to put the entire incident to one side. I still find self-analysis difficult, but back then, without someone like Christine to bully me into seeing the less attractive sides of my personality, it tended not to happen at all.

I gazed again at the primordial article on the screen, considering the paragraph I'd been struggling with. It dealt with an experimental result that failed to fit with my central hypothesis. In this portion of the paper, I was attempting to face the flaw directly instead of downplaying it as some of my colleagues were apt to do. It occurred to me that I didn't avoid critical examination when it came to scientific results, so why didn't I ever apply such discipline to my own life?

Only half seriously, I swatted a few keys, opened a fresh document and typed a title in bold-face:

Andrew O'Hara Blows It: A Case Study

KEY WORDS: Stupidity; Lout; Inebriation
ABSTRACT: Andrew O'Hara, a sensible and polite post-doctoral fellow, became enamoured of a colleague, a beautiful and intelligent woman who appeared to return his interest. Although it was clear the woman's relationship with her boyfriend was nearly over, and that the woman had feelings for O'Hara, he still managed to ruin his chances forever. In this study, we examine the causes and consequences of his folly.

Feeling a surge of embarrassment, I reached across the keyboard to snuff out the file. But something made me stop. I stared at the screen for a few seconds, then began another sentence.

> Hypothesis: the mess with Gina was caused by his actions
> in the alley. Therefore, alcohol was largely to blame.

This had been the explanation I had favoured all along. But did it actually fit all the data?

> 1. He failed to capitalize on Gina's invitation for drinks
> before the fight.

If I hadn't been so concerned about my wounded pride, our falling out might never have happened. In that critical period when Gina had just found out about Miles's affair but hadn't yet decided to give him another chance, things could easily have turned out differently. After Christine had alerted me to her state that afternoon in the Hot Lab, I could have sent her another e-mail. I could have *made* time.

> 2: He lost his temper in the alley.

Gina had clearly come down to apologize, and I should have just accepted it graciously and kept my low opinion of Miles to myself. After all, I knew from experience that people couldn't control who they were attracted to, but at least she'd had the integrity to be completely honest. Instead of returning the courtesy, I'd behaved like a thug and made her cry.

But I'd been drunk, and so had she.

> 3. He didn't apologize the next day.

Although I'd been angry during my long walk, stomping around Soho and eventually watching the sunrise from the upper deck of the N29 bus, I'd woken up the following lunchtime in a panic. If I didn't contact her and try to set things straight, I was convinced I'd regret it for the rest of my life. I spent a few madly inspired minutes at the kitchen table, navigating through the Yellow Pages online—I could send her an avalanche of flowers, parachute in with a box of chocolates, subject her to an American-style singing telegram.

But melodrama doesn't suit me, and after pondering the matter over several cups of coffee and sobering up a bit more, I resolved not to approach her. After all, she was involved with another man, and I had no right to interfere.

But only now did it seem obvious: an apology isn't interference. It's just decent human behaviour.

> 4. He didn't go downstairs when he saw her through the window.

My first glimmer that the relationship between Gina and Miles was finally over had come a few days after the Wall Flower celebration. Her lab light was on late for the first time that week, but instead of bustling around or singing to the radio, she was slumped at her bench, head in her arms and shoulders shaking in the unmistakable motions of grief.

I'd been paralyzed by indecision. I wanted to comfort her, but at the same time her window seemed miles away across the courtyard, a gap I couldn't bring myself to close. She knew full well that she was in my line of sight—was this some cryptic plea for help I was supposed to decode, or had she been confused into forgetfulness by her state of mind? Only one thing stood out as a certainty: if she truly didn't want me to intrude, I'd come across as the selfish opportunist yet again. So in the end, I turned my back and fled into the tissue culture suite, a difficult act that felt, at the time, like strength. When I emerged an hour later, her light was extinguished, and the dead black square hit me like the handing down of a sentence.

5. He didn't seek her out to make peace after things had settled down.

Of course at first, when seeing Gina was the last thing I wanted, I'd started running into her everywhere. The first few times were excruciating. I couldn't meet her eye, let alone greet her, even after the rumours reached me that she'd left Miles for good. Then the sightings ceased, and that was when I figured out she was on holiday. Her absence was an unbelievable relief, and when she returned, tanned and subdued, our silent encounters resumed, but the stretch of time had dampened their potency. And that would have been a good moment to approach her at last. But it's strange: the longer you let things go, the more permanently fixed they tend to become.

I scrutinized the list, and the pattern emerged with abrupt clarity. Item 2—my brutish, drunken actions—was an aberrant data point, a so-called *outlier* that didn't fit with the rest of the curve. Any sensible statistician would eliminate it from the analysis. And the other four items all pointed to the same underlying phenomenon: failure to take action at the appropriate time. Or, in layman's terms: simple cowardice.

My hypothesis had been wrong. And Christine, with her frequent lectures about missed opportunities, had been right. As usual.

At that moment, all the emotions I had so recently claimed to be free of came back to mock me, as if the fight with Gina had happened only the night before. Shutting the laptop, I edged my body away from the dappled shadow of the great old plane tree and into the weak September sunshine, feeling small all over again.

The first time Gina and I had spoken again had been only a few weeks before. The setting had been suitably dramatic: the hushed darkness of the fifth floor communal microscope room. It was the type of place where people tended to speak in low tones for no good reason, which always made me feel as if something crucial was about to happen.

I'd been teaching Jon how to use the confocal microscope. His slides were stained with three fluorescent probes: red, green, and blue, and as the machine scanned an individual cell, dividing it into visual slices that could eventually be reconstructed into a 3D image, I twiddled various knobs to equalize the colours. On one of the computer screens, the cell—blown up to the size of a fist—was taking shape as the computer continuously refreshed the image. Around the cell, tiny pixelated stars of background noise twinkled against a black universe.

"What a beauty." I tweaked up the red channel a notch. The cell featured a nucleus stained moonlight blue, ringed by discrete red globules, like droplets of blood. In the surrounding cytoplasm, a spidery emerald network of fibres radiated outwards. Where the red and green intersected, the computer coloured it amber, indicating that a subset of the globules were contacting the green fibres. This association, as well as being quite pretty, also happened to be Jon's first significant discovery in Magritte's lab.

"Think I can get the cover of *EMBO Journal?*" he joked.

"I'd say you could get that on *Cell,*" a familiar voice remarked behind us, "if aesthetics were anything to go by."

I looked over my shoulder, unable to conceal my astonishment when I saw Gina standing there with Steve at her side. When she recognized me, her cheerfulness mutated into confusion.

"What are we looking at?" Gina turned from me to Jon, while Steve glared at me with his baleful rodent eyes.

Oblivious to the awkward atmosphere, Jon started to rhapsodize about his experiment, pointing at the screen for punctuation.

"I think it's as good as it's going to get, Jon," I cut in. "You'd better capture the image before it starts to bleach."

He nodded, tapping away at the keyboard.

"I didn't expect to run into you up here." Gina's eyes flitted towards mine before performing an evasive manoeuvre. "I thought you were strictly biochemistry."

And that's precisely when the wall shattered.

"Despite my hard-core reputation, I'm actually somewhat of a Renaissance post-doc," I said. Then, more quietly, "It's good to see you."

She nodded, emotions tidied away again, before saying goodbye.

The next time we encountered each other, a few days later in the top floor library, we'd managed relatively normal greetings. I was cutting through the stacks on my way to the photocopier while Gina was leaning against one of the shelves, flipping through a fat blue issue of the latest *Virology*. We didn't stop to talk, but there was a quiet pleasure in the mundane feel of the interaction.

I remember learning how low-angled sunshine, under particular conditions, could strike tiny particles in the air just so, diffracting reality into an endorphin rush of colours, like a touched-up picture postcard where the green is too green, the blue too blue. That's how the afternoon had become when a scrap of distant motion caught my eye: Gina, striding back towards the Centre with a takeaway coffee cup. She hesitated by the steps, then backtracked and entered the park, seeming only half-real in the rose-coloured light. I just watched, not quite believing it in my Zen moment of serenity, until she was there, standing in front of me.

"I told myself that if you were still sitting here when I got back, I'd come over and drink my coffee with you," she said. She paused, then added, "That is, if I'm welcome."

"Of course you are." I made an effort to brush raindrops from the bench to cover up my amazement. And there I had been, feeling smug in my powers of invisibility.

"Are you sure I'm not interrupting your work?" Gina eyed the computer as she sat down—not too close.

"I was about as far away from work as it gets."

She looked intrigued. "You always struck me as more of a pragmatist than a dreamer. Where were you, then?"

"It will sound stupid."

"No...go on." She took a sip of coffee.

"My friend Christine says I'm not thoughtful enough. So I was trying it out." Now that I'd said the words aloud, I was no longer worried she'd find this explanation weird. For no good reason, I felt comfortable with her again, as if the three silent months had never happened.

"Were you thinking about science?"

"No...more about my life, about choices and options, the future, the past..." I dwindled off, afraid she would guess that the thinking had been largely about her, then hastened on with the first thing that entered my head. "I always liked that bit in the Roman Catholic confession about promising to amend your life. It sounds so convenient—just a quick amendment, and away you go."

"You're...?" She lifted an eyebrow.

"No, I'm a certified atheist."

"Good," she said, with perhaps socially unsuitable relief. Paused. "And while we're on the topic of confessions, you probably heard what happened with Miles."

I glanced over in surprise, but her gaze was lost somewhere in the rhododendrons.

"Thanks for not saying you told me so," she went on, "although you were probably quite happy to be vindicated at the time."

"I guess I can't blame you for thinking I'd be that heartless." I was about to add that I had been worried about her, but the evidence hardly looked convincing in my favour.

"I'm sorry, that sounded terrible," she said. I risked a look again, and found her grey eyes examining me. "If anyone was heartless, then it was me, calling your motives into question. I wouldn't blame you for not forgiving me."

I opened my mouth to protest, but she quickly changed the subject.

"I read your paper, Andy. It was totally impressive."

"Um—thanks."

"It actually inspired me to work harder."

"Now I feel guilty," I said, smiling. "That's the last thing you need."

She smiled back, and then I paused, seeing an opening. "You know, I have absolutely no idea what you're working on. Or maybe you're not allowed to say."

She put one boot up on the bench and wrapped her arms around her knee. "Up to a certain point, it's considered good PR to talk about our research with the academic community." Her mouth bent in private amusement—maybe it was an in-joke at Geniaxis.

"So what's your speciality?" This, at least, I had already guessed from snooping on the Centre register that long-ago June morning.

"I'm a virologist in the Gene Therapy group."

"What disease are you trying to cure?"

"I have some side projects in cancer," she said. "But my main focus is Vera Fever."

"I've not heard of it," I said, recalling the scanty reference on her company's web site.

"I'm not surprised," she said. "It's an African neurological disease caused by an emergent virus. It's only been around for a few years."

"Why would a start-up company be interested in such a minor disease?"

There was something wary about her gaze. "We're getting money from a Swiss pharmaceutical company to research various gene therapy strategies against this particular illness."

I reconsidered the matter. "I guess then my question becomes, why would a giant pharma be interested, either? It doesn't sound very marketable."

She flashed me another look, this time an unexpectedly sharp one. "Is that all you think is important?"

I blinked. "Of course not—I was just considering the business practicalities, that's all. Even in academia we have to consider what diseases will pull in the grant money. I just assumed the industrial mindset was even less sentimental."

"So you're only working on cancer because it looks good to the funding agencies, is that it?"

Her snide challenge felt like a kick in the stomach.

"No, I'm working on cancer because it killed my father."

A heavy silence filled the gap after my outburst, magnifying its resonance. Maybe the words had sounded too loud because this topic was normally restricted exclusively to my thoughts. Meanwhile, the usual mismatched feelings of grief and anger were massing out of their hiding place, but when I saw the distress on Gina's face, I forced myself to gain composure.

"I know it won't change anything," I said, in a reasonably normal tone of voice. I met her gaze briefly, which was deep and questioning. "My work, I mean. It won't bring him back, but it's very important to do *something*. Otherwise, what's the point? Life starts to look too random for comfort."

It was my turn to inspect the bushes.

"Tell me about him," she said at last.

"I can't."

"Why not?"

I shook my head, watching the wet leaves shudder in the wind. Of course she had no way of knowing how complicated that straightforward question actually was. I just didn't talk about him, even with my family—I guess I thought my anger was inappropriate. Half the time I didn't understand it myself.

"Andy, I'm truly sorry," she finally said. A fly hummed somewhere nearby, an ordinary sound blundered onto the wrong stage. "You were asking legitimate questions—and the upper management do think strictly in terms of money. Of course I know they have to, to survive." When I finally looked over, her expression pleaded for my understanding. I nodded tiredly, but couldn't bring myself to reply.

"I've been in a number of labs over the years." Her fingers were crushing the empty cup. "It seems like most scientists work in a vacuum, not thinking about real people suffering and dying. It's all just a clever puzzle to work out. I shouldn't have assumed you'd be the same."

She placed her hand briefly on my arm, a compassionate gesture that eased the pressure in my throat. Even after she removed it, I could still feel the warmth of her skin. And something else—a flare of desire, sweeping over my melancholy with unexpected intensity.

"Anyway, do continue about your work," I said hastily.

She seemed flustered too. "Okay...so you were asking why a large pharmaceutical company would be interested in Vera Fever. And you were right—for all the suffering it causes, it's nothing compared to epidemics like AIDS or malaria. But it's the type of disease and the therapy method involved that interest the Swiss."

"What's your delivery method? Adenovirus?" Most labs were using modified viruses for treating patients with foreign genes, because in the wild, viruses excelled at infecting human cells and delivering their viral DNA payloads. Adenovirus, one of the agents that causes the common cold, was a popular choice.

"Adeno's a bit passé now. Also, it doesn't naturally infect the specific type of brain cell this disease hits, and no one's been able to modify it so it will. That's the whole point. The Swiss feel there's an entire class of neurological diseases that currently can't be targeted by conventional gene therapy methods, and it might be worth their while to be the first company to develop such a brain-specific delivery system."

"How are you going to deliver the DNA, then?"

Gina's eyes brightened with enthusiasm. "I'm modifying a herpes virus."

"Herpes...as in cold sores, that sort of thing?" It didn't sound very glamorous to me.

"Yup. But the thing about certain herpes viruses is that they specialize in infecting cells of the nervous system. Not only that, but they can lie around dormant for your entire life, as opposed to something like a cold, where you're only actively infected for a few weeks."

"But surely if the virus spends most of the time being dormant, it wouldn't be that useful."

"Precisely—that's where my tricks come in." She leaned towards me eagerly. "I'm playing around with the virus, trying to modify it so that it remains constantly active, making sure at the same time that it won't damage the infected neuronal cells."

"That's quite cool," I said. "Not to mention a lot more practical than my stuff."

"Don't be silly," she said. "I read that review of your paper in *TIBS*. The author pointed out the implications for cancer therapy."

"Maybe in twenty years' time!"

"Well, some of the genes we want to put into my herpes vectors started being characterized in the 1980s. It's all part of the big picture, isn't it?"

"I suppose." We both were quiet then, a relaxed pause that had something to do with the sunshine and the ease of the moment.

"Anyway...I'd better get back to work," she said. "Are you coming too?"

"Not quite yet." I patted the computer. "I should try to make some progress on this article."

She executed a feline stretch before standing up. "I've been working like crazy, trying to finish up a key experiment before the Cambridge Symposium."

"You're going to the Symposium, too? I didn't know that Geniaxis was..." I almost said *invited*, but then quickly changed it to *involved*.

"They've added a gene therapy session this year...after Geniaxis agreed to sponsor part of the meeting, mysteriously enough." She smiled down at me. "I take it you'll be there?"

"Yes...won't everyone?" It was only a few days away, and many windows had been lit up at night lately.

"Well...I'll see you around, then. I..." She paused.

"Maybe..." I hesitated too, fighting back the sudden urge to ask her what she was doing later. It was just too soon, and felt wrong. Behind her clear eyes was an element that I hadn't noticed last summer: a wariness, a distancing, a subtle caveat. Her open personality had evolved, but I didn't know whether it was directed against the world in general, or me in particular.

"I'll see you," I said instead, and watched her walk away through the strange dappled light.

Later that evening, sitting at my laptop in the lab, I logged onto Google and slowly typed in the words 'Vera Fever'. There were dozens of hits. I read about the symptoms, about the panic its rapid spread was causing in a country whose name sounded only vaguely familiar. Hadn't it been called something else last year? Hadn't there been a civil war, or a famine? I couldn't remember. Clicking further, somewhat randomly, through the branching links of information, I studied images: crowded hospitals resorting to makeshift beds. A mother holding a sick baby. A CT scan of an infected brain, swollen grotesquely with encephalitis. An electron micrograph of geometrical virus particles, budding off in a sinister cloud from a ravaged neuron. I read statistics: percentages dead broken down by country, by gender, by age group.

Children seemed the most susceptible. I found a graph charting the annual incidence of the disease since its discovery in 1997: my scientific eye interpolated the rising curve of an epidemic. Diffident, carefully couched quotes from the World Health Organization about priorities, about limited budgets. I remembered my own choice of words, *minor disease*, and cringed with shame.

When I'd seen enough, I opened up the e-mail Gina had sent so long ago and hit "reply." What I really wanted to say was *Dear Gina, I think I'm falling in love with you.* Instead, I typed:

You're forgiven, by the way. What about me?

About an hour later, there was a message from her waiting in my Inbox.

What, for being drunk and telling me the truth? Hardly forgiveness material.

See you in Cambridge.

It was, if possible, both everything I wanted to hear and, at the same time, not even remotely enough.

8   *Scientific Stalker*

I stood next to my scientific poster presentation at the Cambridge Symposium, watching people flow past like a runaway experiment in fluid dynamics. The sound waves produced by several hundred people bounced off the walls and ceilings of the vast hall, constructing and deconstructing before finally fragmenting into an oceanic roar.

I took a sip of my bottled lager, which had succumbed to the inevitable laws of physics and grown warm. I had been nursing this drink for the last half-hour, thinking it would be prudent to stay sharp. I didn't want to babble away secrets to any winsome female post-docs that might venture by with ulterior motives. But for the first time in about an hour, the crowds around my poster had dissipated, and I realized that my throat had become parched from constant talking.

The guy stationed next to me looked over and caught my eye.

"All right?" I said.

"You've been mobbed with people," he said wistfully. His poster heading indicated a small university in the north of England. I had never heard of the lab head, whose name, by convention, was placed last in the author list. Certainly a PhD student, possibly his first scientific meeting.

I shrugged, trying to hide the fact that I felt sorry for the guy, who reminded me of myself at that age. My PhD work had been solid but unsung and my supervisor, similarly obscure. I had never quite acclimated to waiting alone by a poster like a loser, watching passing browsers read the title before looking away with disinterest. The cultivated nonchalance, while inside you suspect that everyone was secretly pitying you.

"It happens sometimes," I told him. "One minute there're droves, and the next minute you're all alone."

My neighbour wasn't convinced. "I haven't had a single visitor except for a post-doc from my lab who was trying to be nice. Whereas this is the first break you've had the entire session."

"Listen..." I glanced at his badge, "Robert. I just had a paper out, so people are curious about my follow-up stuff. And my boss is quite a name—so it's nothing personal."

He smiled. "You're Andrew O'Hara, aren't you? Do you think you could answer a few questions about your poster while there's a lull?"

"Sure." I had been planning to take advantage of the quiet spell to visit a few posters myself, but I felt strongly about showing solidarity with PhD students. "And then you can show me *your* work."

"Great!" He lit up like a Bunsen burner.

I was in the middle of showing him one of my films when I heard a male voice behind me that I thought I recognized.

"Ah, and this is the latest effort from the Valorius lab," the voice said to someone else, clearly meaning for me to hear. "It's such a shame to witness the decline of a formerly sterling example of scientific excellence." His female companion tittered obligingly.

Robert's eyes widened in outrage, mouth opening. With a wink, I shook my head.

"Shall we proceed to something more worthwhile?"

The unctuous voice moved away. I took a peek: it was Richard Rouyle, the man who'd given the incomprehensible seminar at the Centre a few months earlier, taking the arm of a glamorous middle-aged woman. In the brief moment before he hustled her off, I was struck by the luminous expression on her face, like a schoolgirl with a powerful crush.

"Charming!" Christine appeared at my side. "Did he actually say what I thought he just said?"

Maria came up behind, dark eyes radiant with suppressed amusement.

"He did," Robert confirmed, fuming. "He obviously doesn't know much."

Christine's smirk transmitted a clear question: *Who's the groupie?*

I introduced everyone, then stared significantly at Christine. "Robert's got a *very* interesting poster. I think you should both take a look."

She caught my request effortlessly. "Of course! I've recently developed quite an interest in..." and here, her eyes expertly scanned his poster title, "hormone-mediated growth signalling!"

"Yes, please do walk us through it," Maria said, smiling at me. Robert flushed and beckoned the girls closer. I watched idly as he summarized the various figures and graphs pinned to his board, noting that the work really was rather good.

"Andy O'Hara?" Another voice rose up behind me.

I turned to see a woman struggling out of the stream of conference participants milling around in the aisle between the long facing rows of posters. I was sure I'd seen her someplace before. She had tortoise-shell glasses, sun-bleached hair and was attired in what might charitably be called surfer-chic.

"That's me," I said, checking out her badge. "Sandra, is it?" Her lab affiliation denoted a German pharmaceutical company, but she'd sounded American.

"We met last year at a Keystone Symposium," she explained.

I shook my head at her, perplexed.

"We shared a semi-drunken moment on a chairlift to the top of a run that neither of us was in any condition to ski down...remember?"

The association clicked into place: she was from Stan Fortuna's lab. And I'd recently found out that she was the person I'd scooped at *Cells & Cancer.*

"I'm sorry about your paper," I said meekly. No matter how triumphant one might feel about defeating the evil competition, the sad truth was that behind every rival stood an actual post-doc, more than likely a perfectly decent one. Life was harsh in the scientific food chain.

She shrugged. "Yours was better, and it got there first." Then she flashed me a coy smile. "In fact, the scoop forced me to do some further characterization, so I got side-tracked and ended up with something even more interesting!"

"Really? What, exactly?"

"Never you mind!" She laughed. "You can read about it in next month's issue of *Current Biology.*" Seeing the look on my face, she added, "Don't worry, it's not gonna affect you directly, if this is what you're up to next." She glanced at the title of my poster. "But it might be invading the space of that German guy in your lab." She put a hand to her mouth, then added, "Oops, you won't tell him, will you?"

"Of course I will!" I grinned.

"It doesn't matter anyway...he won't guess in a gazillion years."

"Anyway, congratulations on your *Current Biology* paper." I wondered if I could get anything more out of her at the bar later.

"No hard feelings?" We shook hands, and then she dived into my poster, her nose so close to the printouts that it made me nervous.

After a few minutes, a middle-aged man approached, face pinched with unpleasantness. *Now where had I...*

"Shall I talk you through my work?" I asked him, gathering myself up for the usual spiel.

"Sandra, I've been looking for you everywhere!" he snapped in broad New York vowels, not even acknowledging my presence, and I realized with a start that it was Stan Fortuna himself. His hatred of Magritte—and everything associated with her—was legendary.

"Relax, boss, I'm just finishing up." Her attention was fixed on my most crucial experiment: it looked as if she was reproducing the entire graph, complete with labelled axes, legend, and error bars, onto her notepad.

"I don't know why you're wasting your time here when there're actually some *important* people I want you to meet." He cast me a disdainful look, but I remained impassive.

Sandra allowed Fortuna to drag her off, but not before she had made an apologetic face and mouthed "drink, later?" with illustrative hand gestures. Deciding that she would come out the wiser in any alcohol-inspired informational exchange, I resolved to avoid her.

"Is something in the air?" Christine had managed to extricate herself from Robert. "You're being insulted by some of the finest minds in the field."

"Thanks, by the way." I inclined my head in Robert's direction, where Maria's gaze begged for rescue over Robert's head.

"It's nothing," Christine said. "He's a nice kid."

The moment the girls had departed to spy on their competitors' posters, Robert turned to me, looking dazed.

"I think they really liked me!" he said.

I had soon discovered that being at the same symposium with Gina didn't guarantee that I would see her with any frequency. The organizers had arranged simultaneous sessions, dividing the therapeutic-based research, like Gina's work, from fundamental molecular biology where my topic was classified. I'd spotted her a few times in the bar, but she'd been flanked by labmates on every occasion and it hadn't seemed right to intrude. The only reason Maria had been so much in evidence was because she was skiving off most of the clinical talks. Gina was obviously more dedicated.

After I'd finished going through Robert's poster, I decided to do a bit of skiving myself and exploit a key opportunity to find out more about Gina. Unlike the rest of us lowly post-docs, she'd been awarded a very prestigious seminar slot, and I was keen to find out why. So I snagged Magritte in passing, told her I had an important poster to visit and asked her to stand by mine in lieu. Not even waiting for her reply, I'd rushed off, buzzing with anticipation and the charge of straying outside the lines of predictable behaviour.

I slunk out of the poster-filled hall, turned the corner and pushed open the back auditorium door, where the talk was already in progress. Immediately, I was enveloped in womb-like darkness, a heavy contrast to the bustle I'd left behind. Gina's amplified voice lapped against me as I scanned the room for a seat. In a moment I could make out that the hall below was packed, with people standing against the back wall and spilling into the steps between the aisles.

And there was Gina herself, standing in a relaxed posture by the podium and pointing at the screen with a laser. She was wearing a simple smoke-coloured dress and her hair was clipped back, accentuating the elegant lines of her neck and infusing her with an aura of authority.

I felt like a scientific stalker: I didn't, strictly speaking, belong there. And I knew I'd probably be lost after missing the introductory slides, but I planned to collect and dissect every scrap I could salvage, to learn more about what she was doing and how her thought processes worked. Even if I didn't manage to piece together anything useful, I was still filled with an ardent curiosity to find out how she would speak, and to examine her reflection in the reactions of her peers.

I sank down onto a free bit of floor and began to listen.

"Now that I've given you the background to Vera Fever Virus, I'll explain the strategy we're using to fight it," Gina said, clicking to the next slide. "A unique feature of the viral replication cycle offers excellent prospects for intervention by gene therapy."

Despite the missed preliminaries, I soon realized that Gina's speaking style made the story perfectly understandable.

"Vera Fever Virus has a linear, single-stranded negative-sense RNA genome..."

Gina launched into an easy-going explanation of the virus' replication cycle. Although viruses tend to hijack the proteins of the cells they infect, Gina described how Vera Fever was completely dependent on one of its own polymerase enzymes to replicate its genetic blueprint. This polymerase was packaged into the virus particle and delivered into the newly infected cell along with the RNA genome, helping to produce thousands of copies.

"The infected cell, thinking the RNA is its own, is duped into manufacturing the viral proteins," she said. "And the rest, as they say, is cell history."

The audience rippled with laughter.

"But blocking the Vera Fever Virus polymerase would result in a complete shut-down of viral synthesis. Fortunately, we have discovered a weakness that can be exploited...and we've devised a weapon, called Verase."

Gina described a feature of the polymerase that was vulnerable to attack by a modified protease protein, dubbed Verase, which would chop it to bits. I lost the story at that point, mostly because the virology got heavy, and I allowed myself to become distracted by the grace of her hands gesturing in empty space. I was pulled back in when she showed a few experiments proving that Verase had no harmful side-effects in normal cells, but could completely block virus infection and the associated cellular damage.

Gina surveyed the room. "It's all very well to have a powerful weapon like Verase, but how are we going to deliver it into the brain?" She paused, and I could feel the expectation of the listeners. "As most of you probably know, traditional vectors like adenoviruses or lentiviruses are not capable of infecting this particular cell type. So we needed a better virus to deliver our Verase weapon—and herpes fits the bill."

On the next slide, Gina introduced the subject of herpes viruses. "If any of you has suffered from a bout of inconveniently-timed cold sores, you already have first-hand experience with one key element that we need to modify in order to use Herpes Simplex I virus as a gene therapy vector against Vera Fever."

She explained how cold sores erupt because a resident herpes virus has been awakened by an outside stimulus—stress, sunlight, hormones—and abandoned its latent state, where it may have resided peacefully for years. Once activated, the herpes crawls down out of nearby facial neurons and begins an active infection in the tissues around the mouth. Later, for unknown reasons, the virus retreats into the nerves and goes back to sleep.

"Of course, there have been past attempts to use Herpes Simplex viruses as gene therapy vectors, but no one has totally solved the reactivation question," she said. "To make a safe and effective vector, we modified the natural virus so that it could not spontaneously reactivate. Deleting these two viral genes," she circled each in turn with a swift oval of red laser light, "is sufficient to keep the virus from hearing the wake-up call."

Two people sitting near to me started to murmur to each other heatedly, scribbling something on one of their notepads.

"Okay—so now we've got a perpetually sleeping virus," Gina said. "What good is that if we want to express a gene to combat Vera Fever? Time to tinker a bit more with the natural herpes genome."

She went on to the next slide. "As you can see, this particular herpes virus preserves its own latency with a series of selective viral transcripts..." Clearly and expertly, Gina described how the herpes virus maintained its dormant state, and how, with a few modifications, the Verase weapon could be inserted under the same controls so that its powerful antiviral effect could be constantly produced in a patient's brain. "The net result is a modified herpes virus that can infect a patient and undergo a permanent pseudo-latent state, during which Verase is constantly on duty, ready to destroy the Vera Fever Virus the moment it appears."

Tricking one virus into defeating another: it was a satisfying concept. I was thoroughly drawn in to her story. In fact, the entire audience seemed enthralled. It was funny, and sad, too, but watching her gave me a pang of what I suspected was jealousy. And I don't mean because her performance might be better than anything I could muster. No, it was far more personal: her delivery had a strange intimacy about it, as if she were having a one-on-one chat with each audience member. Selfishly, I didn't want to share her with everyone else. I wanted, with the deep cravings of an addict, for her to direct that smile only at me.

At that moment, my adoration was irrevocably fixed.

Gina finished to sustained applause and a forest of raised hands. I noted with approval the minimal amount of posturing in the questions and the easy competence with which she fielded them.

"Dr Kraymer." That familiar unctuous voice again, issuing from the front row. It was Richard Rouyle, with the roles reversed this time. Would he try to humiliate her out of revenge?

"It strikes me," he continued, his tone bristling with genuine excitement, "that the modular nature of your vectors makes delivering *multiple* genes possible. Would it be feasible to supplement Verase with a second gene, perhaps one such as FRIP kinase, whose secondary ability to boost the cell's own natural defences against viral infection is already well documented by my own laboratory?" He paused, added eagerly, "That way, you'd get a double attack, increasing the probability of success."

The audience murmured, clearly intrigued. "That's an interesting suggestion," Gina said.

Personally, I was sceptical—I dimly recalled something about FRIP in the context of Gina's viruses that wasn't compatible with Rouyle's idea, but I couldn't think what this was.

"Yes...you could easily put in another gene," she went on, sounding increasingly enthusiastic. "The virus packaging process could accommodate a longer RNA strand, and the second gene could be spliced separately. Perhaps we should talk about it afterwards, but it's a very good idea." She looked reluctant to move on to the next person.

After a half dozen more questions, the chairperson called an end to the afternoon session and people began streaming out of the auditorium. A subset of the audience surged up to the podium to speak with Gina, and Rouyle was at the head of the pack.

The lights came up, making me feel exposed. I didn't think she'd notice me in the back, but I moved behind a column just to be sure. Rouyle and Gina had another intense discussion, raptly followed by the crowd gathered around the podium. Soon, he had her by the elbow and was leading her out the side exit.

I loathed his air of familiarity.

❖ ❖ ❖

By the time I stepped out of the auditorium, the poster session had already finished and the conference bar was crammed with people, winding down after an intellectually intense afternoon. As I pushed my way into the main press, I was bombarded by random snippets and bytes of information.

"Wasn't she the woman who got two *Cell* papers during her PhD work?"

"And then he didn't even acknowledge my work at the end of his seminar! Yes, I'm *sure* it was deliberate!"

"— and I was looking at this graph, thinking, this has *got* to be faked. I mean, you just don't get such perfect error bars..."

"— this really foxy post-doc with a great set of...reference letters! Mate, I could have offered *her* a job!"

"— think *you're* having proteomics problems—I know a guy up in Edinburgh who..."

"So he says, if you give me some of your antibody, I might be able to send you the mutant plasmid before it's published. I said, listen, don't e-mail us, we'll e-mail you."

"Everyone knows about them! He may be this close to a Nobel, but when it comes to pretty secretaries, he just can't..."

Wading through the crush, I finally located Christine, Cameron and a few others standing near the back, clinking lager bottles together. I adjusted my angle and started tunnelling towards them.

"— not as if *he's* ever discovered anything interesting. He just skulks about the lab, sponging off everyone else's projects and passing them off as his own ideas!"

"— heard that more than two hundred people applied for that lectureship position in..."

"— know she's *meant* to have a boyfriend back in Paris, but I'm telling you, I saw them coming out of the same room this morning!"

"Andy! Yo! Andy O'Hara!" A strident American voice managed to cut through the chaos: Sandra, waving at me from the other side of the room. I swerved onward, pretending I hadn't seen her.

"Where've you been?" Christine gave me a bright, only marginally suspicious smile.

Cameron passed me two bottles. "You've got some catching up to do, O'Hara."

I glanced over my shoulder, but Sandra had vanished.

"Good poster sesh?" Jon asked me. "I tried to visit you but I couldn't get within a two metre radius."

"What's wrong with you?" Christine asked as I threw another glimpse behind me.

"Sandra, Fortuna's post-doc, is determined to extract information from me." I took a heroic gulp from the first lager. "After a couple of beers, I'm useless in the hands of the enemy."

"Doesn't sound so unpleasant to me." Cameron winked at Christine.

She stuck her tongue out at him. "If that's the way you feel, I had about six decent-looking men practically drooling over my poster. Shall I invite them back to my room later?"

He kissed her on the cheek. "The sacrifices I make in the name of science."

"Having good time, kids?" It was Magritte, smiling over her usual double vodka, no ice. "You enjoy herpes seminar, Andrew?"

"*Herpes* seminar?" Christine looked at me sharply.

"I thought you were manning my poster," I stammered.

"Relieved by Jon...good practice for him. Was very stimulating talk, yes?"

"Why did *you* go?" I was deeply embarrassed to have been caught out.

"Little-known fact, but I did initial PhD work with Epstein-Barr virus before getting side-tracked. That woman is something else, yes? Very bright." She had a knowing glimmer about her.

"Which woman?" Christine narrowed her eyes at me.

"Andy, you promised me a drink!" It was Sandra, holding out an immense glass inscribed with a notorious logo: one of the highest alcohol content beers ever created by Belgian monks. For herself, she had a modest half of lager.

"I've got to go to the loo!" I blurted out, bolting away.

"Ooh, Dr Valorius," I heard Sandra coo. "Just the person! Care for a beer? Can I call you Margaret?"

Gina's mouth moved in animated conversation at the corner table she was sharing with Rouyle.

I froze at the sight, still with a bottle in each hand. Rouyle nodded, and she leaned over and sketched something on a cocktail napkin, no doubt elaborating on his double gene idea from the seminar. Again I got that odd feeling in my brain, that not-quite-remembering as I tried to connect up to that elusive memory. And an odd feeling in my gut, seeing them with their heads together. No problem interpreting that emotion: it was jealousy again, swift and absolute. I remembered Rouyle's careless denouncement of my poster and glowered with anger.

When I passed through on the way back from the gents, I couldn't resist another glance. They'd stopped taking notes. Rouyle spoke and Gina shook her head with a laugh, eyes echoing the sentiment. He put a hand on her forearm and murmured something else that made her smile. The scientific portion of their discussion was obviously over.

I turned my back on the pair, cursing myself. What had prevented me from asking her out after we'd made up in the park? Why hadn't I even attempted to speak to her here at the symposium? Caution was clearly useless when forces like timing were against me. Gina was a stunner and not likely to stay single for long; at a conference like this, she could have any man she wanted. Doing nothing was, as usual, going to get me exactly nowhere, but now it seemed as if this less than earth-shattering realization had come too late.

Listlessly, I returned to my group. With this latest development, I didn't care about avoiding Sandra. But both Magritte and Sandra had disappeared.

"All clear," Christine informed me.

"Look over there." Cameron angled his head.

Magritte and Sandra were lounging against the bar, conversing. Or rather, Magritte was lounging, whereas Sandra looked rather unsteady, as if she was actually relying on the support. Magritte tossed back her vodka, started on a fresh glass. She waved a hand at Sandra, who reluctantly finished the last of the lethal Belgian beer. Magritte pushed a second glass towards her, and Sandra began to talk.

"Confucius say, never try to out-drink someone from former Soviet socialist republic," Christine said with satisfaction.

9   *Scoring Tips from Shakespeare*

*I*t was the final night of the symposium, and the farewell party was overheating to a drunken frenzy. Feeling claustrophobic, I stepped out onto the rear terrace to cool down. A wedge of moon glowed down on the Backs, highlighting the Cam in twists of mercury, and the way the scraps of clouds scuttled across the sky seemed to reinforce my own restlessness.

Despite my preoccupation, I couldn't help enjoying myself. The banquet had been spectacular, with decent wine and conversation, and now a talented DJ was in firm command of the dance floor. I had met many people during the past week, and it was intriguing to see how they performed. The final party was always the big equalizer. It didn't matter how many *Cell*, *Science* or *Nature* papers you had published: if you were too dignified to at least try to execute a decent boogie, then nobody wanted to know you.

The only blemish on the evening was Rouyle's monopolization of Gina. Even I had to admit that he was a practised dancer, twirling Gina around the floor with old-fashioned finesse. She had said a few words to me by the drinks table, which I'd answered amiably enough, but as she was so obviously enjoying Rouyle's company, I hadn't made an effort at a proper conversation, let alone at trying to dance with her myself.

It suited my mood to stand on the interface: the peaceful night in front of me, the lights and music from the party pulsating out of the terrace doors behind. That's how I was when Maria found me.

"You're positively Byronic out here," she teased.

"And you're looking smart." I admired her dress, a red gauzy affair that hid more than it revealed, while at the same time managing to convey the opposite effect.

"I'm not intruding at all?"

"Of course not." I motioned her towards a nearby bench.

"It's just that I was worried about you. You've seemed down these past few days." The shifting tree branches splintered moonlight and shade across her face, preventing any interpretation of expression.

"And you came out to check that I hadn't flung myself into the water feature?"

"Can't you ever be serious?" A warning edged her tone. "I was only concerned."

I apologized, not wanting to be disagreeable on such a lovely night, then added, "I'm touched you even noticed."

"So something is the matter?"

"The same old refrain," I finally confessed. "Gina."

"What about her?"

"I think something's going on between her and Richard Rouyle." Maybe I'd been paranoid, seeing things that weren't there. Maybe, to the rest of the well-balanced population, they came off merely as colleagues bent on scientific collaboration. After all, he was nearly twice her age.

"It certainly seems so, the way they've been carrying on tonight." She took note of my reaction, making me realize that I was clenching my teeth. I forced my jaw to relax.

"The dancing, you mean."

"Not just that," she said. "He sat with our group at dinner, ostensibly to speak with the boss about Geniaxis's lines of research, but he spent most of the time flirting with Gina—and she was lapping it up."

"How come nobody else notices how slimy he is?"

"It's all in your head," she said with a shrug. "He's a charming man, no question. There is a seductive quality beneath that I find a bit unsettling, but no one else but you seems to find him disagreeable. Definitely not our boss, who shamelessly courts all the big pharma connections he can get. And especially not Gina."

"I can't believe this."

"But Andy, why would this be bothering you now?"

I stared at her. "Just because a few months have passed doesn't mean I can forget about her just like that."

"So you actually have changed your mind!" She frowned. "When did this happen?"

"Now you've lost me," I said. "I've been mad about her since the moment I first saw her."

"That's not what you told her. In fact, you said pretty much the opposite."

"I did? No, I didn't." I blinked at her in complete disorientation. "And how would you know, anyway?"

Now Maria was confused. "Because she told me. I admit we aren't the closest of friends, but she was so upset that night, I think she was reduced to —"

"What did I say?" I grabbed her by both shoulders, dimly aware of a lost memory struggling to get my attention. "When did I say it?"

She made no move to free herself, eyes solemn. "I found her in the lab a few nights after your celebration party at the Wall Flower—in a right state. She described your fight, your parting confession—that you weren't interested in her, that you never had been."

I wanted to protest, but her words were exerting a paralytic effect.

"I pointed out that you might have reacted from wounded pride, but she said you'd made it plain." She tilted her head at me. "And anyway, you hadn't come round to see her after the fight, so you must've meant it. She was inconsolable."

I let go of Maria, slumped back on the bench.

"She was so unhappy she took unpaid leave back to the States," she went on. "The boss was furious—and I had to look after Steve the entire time!" When I just shook my head, she studied me with pity. "You daft idiot—I was right, wasn't I? You hadn't meant it—it was just drunken spite."

I didn't have to say anything, just kept shaking my head, even though we both knew the answer was yes.

"Then why didn't you go to her after she left Miles?"

"She was angry," I said, in a very small voice. "I didn't want her to think I was trying to make a move in her weakest moment."

Maria flung up her hands. "But that's exactly what she wanted you to do! What in hell is wrong with you, Andy? Do you need an instruction manual?"

I started to laugh: I couldn't help it. "I've had more than *three months* to make it up with her, but now she's dancing the bloody tango with that —"

I stood up, strode away a few steps, whirled back. She stood up, too, and put a tentative hand out.

"Listen, Andy —"

"Byronic? You've got it all wrong! I'm like some Shakespearean character who worries about consequences and never just acts. Like Hamlet—he should've stabbed the uncle outright, but he was too busy cross-examining himself on the battlements. Or Romeo—he could've just run off with the girl.., instead he overanalyzes everything and ends up topping himself!"

There was a moment of shocked silence. Then Maria started to giggle. Wide-eyed, she put her hand to her mouth, but it was no use. Despite everything, I began chuckling too. Soon, we were gasping for breath, wiping tears from our eyes.

Behind us, a truly appalling ballad swelled out from the party, indicating that the DJ had a sense of humour.

"May I have this dance?" I held out my arms with a flourish.

She made a face. "You're joking, right?"

"Hey...he *is* your fellow countryman, if I'm not mistaken."

"Don't remind me."

She moved into my arms, pressing close. Her pout slipped into a smile, very alluring in the tricky moonlight, and then the smile became something else altogether. When I leaned down to kiss her, her arms went around my neck—and there's no denying that I sank into the moment for more than a few seconds before finally managing to wrench myself away.

"This isn't a good idea," I said. "I'm sorry."

She gave me another smile. "You don't have to apologize for *that*."

"I must be an idiot."

"Don't look so tragic, man," she said, sounding her usual brisk self. "It was just a snog, not a proposal of marriage."

I studied her with concern. "I thought I sensed some feeling behind it."

"Let's just say I've got a thing for blue-eyed Shakespearean types who know one end of a pipettor from the other."

"I'm trying to be serious here."

She crossed her arms. "Sorry, but I'm not giving anything away till you've sorted out this unfinished business with Gina."

"I'd say it was finished."

"Don't be such a defeatist!" she said. "Go in there, cut in, drag her off, do whatever you have to do to get her away. Knee Rouyle in the testicles or something. Then spell it *out* to her, Andy: explain the whole misunderstanding, proclaim your undying love or whatever it is you feel for the girl, get down on one knee if you have to, but don't just give up!"

She started to move away. "Do *something*." Transmitting a final look like an ultimatum, she vanished.

I collapsed down on the bench, almost feeling as if the correct "something" was to go after Maria, pull her into the shrubbery and carry on where we'd left off. But that was just an after-effect of the kiss. Meanwhile, the panic that had been mounting inside had dissipated. Maria was right: if it wasn't too late, I should be able to explain. Anyway, I had nothing to lose.

I went back inside and stood on the fringe of the dance floor, taking the whole scene in. I didn't see Gina anywhere, but there were now hundreds of people seething about in the flickering light show. A dramatic piano glissando swooped down, then the first strains of Gloria Gaynor's girl-power standard. I dodged the stampede of men leaving the floor as the women clustered together, yelling along with the lyrics, but Gina was not revealed by this exodus.

But I did see Christine, shoving away the hands of a very drunk, very middle-aged, very famous American scientist. She said something angrily, but he continued to paw at her. I was just about to dash to her rescue when she threw her drink in his face. The man sputtered, wiping his eyes, and stumbled against a line-up of Italian PhD students writhing in synchrony, who recoiled in contempt. Christine looked pleased with herself, and, spotting me, headed over.

"I've always wanted to do that," she said. "Just like in the movies."

"Chris," I said, in awe. "Do you realize who that was?"

"Oh, yes. I've never been groped by a Nobel laureate before; do you suppose I could put it in my CV?" She got a closer look at me. "What's up, Andy?"

"Have you seen Gina?"

"She's over there getting cosy with that long-winded man from Pfeiffer-deVries." Christine pointed. "Why?"

I turned around, absorbing the shadowy corner scene in painful detail.

"Great." I sank down into a nearby chair. In that one motion, my previous momentum evaporated. It was all very well to talk about kicking someone's testicles, but when faced with the actual opportunity, it wasn't all that straightforward. You could see where Hamlet was coming from, actually. Then too, there was the growing suspicion that both parties, not just the male rival, might construe the approach as an intrusion.

Christine glared down at me, hands on hips. "What do you care, anyway? I thought you'd gone off her ages ago. Not that you'd ever had the courtesy to tell me, your own best mate, what happened."

"I still don't want to talk about it."

"Come on, O'Hara, don't be cross." She put a hand on my shoulder. "I promise I'll say no more about it for the moment. Meanwhile, shall I get us some drinks?" She smiled wickedly. "I seem to have misplaced my own beverage."

She slipped away, leaving me to lapse back into turmoil. For a few minutes I vacillated between warm and cold, savouring the memory of Maria's kiss, then rebounding into appalled disgust at the image of Rouyle doing the same with Gina.

"Andy O'Hara? I don't believe it!"

I glanced up, startled by the familiar voice.

"It is you, mate! I thought I caught a glimpse of you yesterday," a guy was saying. "It's Dan Lamont. From Leeds."

My confusion cleared. "Dan! What are you doing here?" I leapt up, clapped him on the shoulders. "I thought you were a chemist! I haven't seen you in, what...?"

"Seven, eight years," he supplied, looking me up and down. "The post-doctoral existence is obviously treating you well. You haven't changed at all."

"Well, you're completely different," I said. "I think you've lost about two stone, all of it in hair." His former Iron Maiden-inspired mane was shaved to stark, laddish minimalism.

"And I'm a neurobiologist now—there just weren't any jobs in chemistry."

After we'd caught up for a few minutes, he shook his head admiringly. "So do I have it straight so far: you own a flat, you're in a hot-shot lab and you have a famous paper just off the presses—I suppose you've got a gorgeous girlfriend as well?"

Christine appeared right on cue, laden with an armful of Newcastle Brown. Dan flashed me an expression of undisguised approval as he helped her unload the bottles.

"They were out of lager, so I took it as a warning to stock up on whatever was going," she explained, pulling yet more bottles out of the pockets of her denim jacket and looking inquiringly at Dan, then me.

I introduced the two, adding, "Dan and I were at University together."

"Are you Andy's girlfriend?" Dan looked even more enchanted when Christine produced a bottle opener from her handbag.

"Someone else beat him to it, I'm afraid," Christine said. "And he's in his bachelor phase."

Dan blinked. "That's a bit of a departure, mate."

"Are we talking about the same man here?" Christine sat, scooted her chair closer. "Do elaborate." You could practically see her gossip antennae unfurling—and there was no doubt she possessed the skills to extract more than a few compromising details.

"You wouldn't want to let the side down, would you, Dan?" I said.

"You owe me one, then," he said. "But seriously, you must be interested in someone at least." When I turned my head involuntarily towards the corner where Gina and Rouyle were entwined, he contemplated the pair, then remarked, "If that's the one, it looks as if you'd better hurry."

Christine just smiled and settled back in her chair, waiting to see what I'd say.

"She was the one, but I blew it." I shifted my gaze from Dan and met Christine's surprised eyes.

"Blew it?" Dan said.

"Yes, Andy...how exactly? I can't quite remember," Christine added sweetly.

I sighed. "Let's just say I missed my opportunity—multiple opportunities, acted like an unfeeling idiot on top of it, and now she's given up on me."

Dan took another glance at the corner, then turned back, brow furrowed.

"I'm sure I've seen that guy someplace before. Do you know who he is?"

I gave him the highlights on Rouyle.

"Mediocre science, big ego," Christine summed up, only half focusing. I could see thoughts drifting over her face like those sped-up films of clouds moving across the sky—an uneasy forecast of the interrogative storm that was going to break out later when she caught me alone.

"Maybe you saw him on television?" I offered.

Dan shook his head. "I'm sure it was in person, but I don't have any connection to his field. The memory feels...older."

"Perhaps from your earlier incarnation as a chemistry student? But he definitely wasn't at Leeds."

"*Maybe* chemistry," Dan said. He scrunched up his forehead with the palm of his hand and rubbed and wrinkled the skin a few times.

"It doesn't matter," I said. "Maybe he just looks like someone else."

"No," he insisted, taking one last quick glimpse in Rouyle's direction. "I'm sure I know him. And there's something associated with the memory...something not quite right."

"Not right?" Christine prompted, intrigued.

"I mean...the memory's associated with something negative. I can't quite explain." He stared into space, then shook his head. "Never mind. It doesn't matter who he is...I'm just sorry he's got your girl."

I slipped outside and walked back to my room, the moon bathing the universe in an aloof blue.

There is nothing quite like the feeling of watching the woman you desperately want leave a party with another man—especially when you have made absolutely no effort to prevent it.

10 Close Collaboration

I unfolded my mother's latest newspaper clipping and pressed it into the Board with a drawing pin. Her accompanying letter mentioned that I might like to know what my neighbours "were up to." Unlike many of her offerings, I actually read the article to the end once I realized that it was probably describing one of Gina's projects:

British biotech firm to begin US cancer gene therapy trial

The London company Geniaxis unveiled plans yesterday to initiate its first Phase I clinical trial for a gene therapeutic anti-cancer agent called GeniVir-MetaStat (GVMS). GVMS will be tested next month on thirty patients in Bethesda, Maryland, in conjunction with the US National Institutes of Health.

GVMS is a herpes simplex virus—the micro-organism that causes cold sores—which bears a modified coat protein designed to home in on metastatic cancer cells. Metastatic cells are cells from a primary tumour that acquire mobility and spread to secondary sites in the afflicted patient. While primary tumours can often be successfully removed, it is the metastases that tend to foil surgical intervention.

Once the GVMS virus reaches the metastatic cell, it initiates infection and delivers a bacterial toxin gene that kills the cell. Because only metastatic cells, not healthy tissues, are recognized by the GVMS agent, it is hoped that the treatment will have few side effects. An assessment of toxicity is the main goal of a Phase I trial.

Thomas Boyd, PhD, the Scientific Director of Geniaxis, said: "We are confident that GeniVir-MetaStat will prove its merit, and look forward to introducing several more gene therapeutic viruses into similar trials within the next year."

The trial is expected to give a modest boost to Geniaxis, which has experienced a steady decline in its valuation since it floated on the stock market earlier this year.

As I read the article, something very peculiar happened. Of course I knew intellectually what gene therapy was all about: putting foreign DNA into a human. At first, all that occurred to me about GVMS was that the strategy of attack was very ingenious. But then I found myself imagining what it would feel like to be one of those test patients. I could picture the microscopic viruses scattering, seed-like, into the warm currents of my bloodstream, burrowing into my cells like blind insects under a rotten log, and that was when I began to wonder if everything that could possibly go wrong had been predicted and circumvented.

A very unscientific shiver passed over my skin, but then the moment passed.

✦ ✦ ✦

In the week following the symposium, Magritte began working late in the lab. At first I tried to guess why, but her trail of routine protein gels didn't give me any clues. Then, when I found myself alone with her for the third evening straight, I finally just asked.

To my surprise, instead of telling me to mind my own business, she put down her pipettor and confided in me.

"Heard rumours in Cambridge that Kennedy's lab may have stumbled onto Jon's most recent stuff."

"They've co-IP'd fil-A with ERG-3?" I asked. "Or seen a co-localization by IFA?" The most important thing you learn in your PhD, after adapting to chronic sleep deprivation and low glucose levels, is how to speak in sentences composed almost entirely of impenetrable acronyms.

"Something like that. Don't know how much else they've managed to work out—or how close behind."

"Have you told Jon about this?"

She shook her head. "Not sure that's wise—already panicked enough."

Jon had only started in the lab six months before, and was still suffering the novice's inability to handle more than one task at a time.

"It's part of the game, though." I kept my tone neutral; the last thing I wanted to do was criticize someone as experienced as Magritte.

"Thought best to check out a few angles myself first, but..." She sniffed and went back to her samples, but I could see I'd made her think.

Fortunately, Magritte's interloping didn't extend to taking over the CD player's remote control—the night was still my acknowledged domain. We were working along to a bit of Motown in otherwise companionable silence when Gina entered the lab.

"Knock knock."

"Who's there?" Magritte asked obligingly. She delivered a droplet into the last tube on her rack and looked up.

I nearly dropped my own pipettor. I always find it startling when someone you're thinking about shows up in person. Of course, she'd been on my mind so often since the symposium that this coincidence wasn't really surprising.

Gina gave us a tentative smile, and I noticed that she was holding a glass measuring cylinder discreetly at her side.

"You must be Dr Valorius," she said, when I failed to regain my powers of speech in time.

"Must be and am," Magritte acknowledged, looking Gina up and down. "Know who *you* are. Very much enjoyed seminar—clever work, clear presentation. Look forward to seeing in print. And maybe in clinic."

Gina thanked her, rather flustered from the matter-of-fact praise.

"Andrew liked your talk, too." Magritte nodded in my direction, but before I could pin down her expression, she'd shifted her eyes away.

Gina stared at me in pleased amazement. "You went to my seminar? Why didn't you come round afterwards? I would've appreciated your input."

I cleared my throat, not wanting to say that Rouyle had been supplying enough input for the both of us.

"Must excuse me, kids." Magritte leapt up from her stool. "Forgot I left cells trypsinizing in tissue culture suite."

She delivered an inscrutable smile and promptly disappeared around the corner.

"I sense I'm about to lend you something," I said to Gina.

"I know it's two in a row, very bad etiquette, but you're the only one still around and I've run out of methanol." Now that we were alone, she seemed softer, shyer.

The scrounge made me feel as if we were starting again. I was pouring the methanol from a plastic bottle when the words just popped out.

"Have a drink with me," I said, topping the fluid up to the 250 ml line and looking her in the eye. "I'd love to hear more about your research."

A slow smile spread over her face. "Okay, but I prefer ethanol."

"If you insist." There were suddenly several maybes crowding my head: maybe she felt like starting again too. Maybe she really hadn't gone back to Rouyle's room after the party. Maybe I was actually going to be handed another chance, even though I didn't deserve it.

She checked her watch. "After I finish up this experiment, I've booked a couple of hours in the Timelapse Room. Are you free after that?"

"Actually, I'm due in the Hot Lab at ten o'clock." I kicked myself mentally, but it was too late to retract.

Gina thought a moment. "Why don't you join me down in Time-lapse? I'm just babysitting an experiment that needs occasional read-justment, and there should be a few beers left in the communal fridge."

"You keep leading me astray: first the covert radioactivity opera-tion, and now drinking in the lab."

"It'll be our secret." The corners of her eyes crinkled with mischief.

After she left, I poked my head around the corner into the tissue culture suite. Magritte was sitting at the microscope, her face in reposed profile, peering down the oculars at a dish of cells.

"What was that all about?" I demanded. "Trypsinizing cells, my arse."

She didn't even look up. "She's a one-of-kind girl. Try not to blow it, yes?"

"We're just friends." I felt the heat creeping up my face. She raised a sceptical eyebrow at me before returning her gaze to the micro-scope's binocular eyepiece.

"By the way, I'm off home now," I mumbled.

"Don't stay down there too late, O'Hara."

❦ ❦ ❦

"Take a look."

Gina put a hand on my shoulder as she leaned away from the microscope. We were sitting in near darkness, the sole occupants of the Centre's cramped basement timelapse microscopy facility.

I took her place at the eyepiece, peering at the elongated neuronal cell that glowed red against the blackness. The round cell body was bristling with hundreds of branched extensions, the dendrites responsible for passing along the brain's electrochemical signals: impulses, commands, feelings, memories. At the same time, I was hyperaware of the weight and warmth of her hand lingering on my shoulder.

"It's beautiful, Gina. I've never seen a live primary neuron before. What's the red colour?"

"That's just a membrane stain, so you can see the outline and integrity of the cell. But if you wait a moment..." Her hand left my shoulder and flowed over the computer keyboard. There was a mechanical click and the view through the oculars went black for a second. Then a new filter slipped into place, and a swarm of green speckles had appeared inside the cell.

"What am I seeing now?" I spun the fine objective knob up and down. The spots were floating in three dimensions, so as I made adjustments, various points of green light prickled in and out of focus.

"That's the antiviral Verase agent, tagged in green, being produced by my herpes vaccine."

"What are you trying to find out?" I looked over my shoulder, struck by her animated expression.

"I've treated this brain cell culture first with the vaccine, and then with Vera Fever Virus. It proves that the vaccine has worked—that it's stopped the Vera Fever cold."

I backed off reflexively. "It's not contagious, is it?"

"Of course not." Her hand returned to my shoulder for a moment, a teasing acknowledgement of my nervousness. "These are crippled lab strains."

"How do you know the Vera Fever's really destroyed?" I returned my attention to the eyepiece.

"Because..." Gina leaned over me again, so close that a strand of hair whispered against the side of my face. The filter mechanism clicked once more, and then the view went black. "There!"

"I don't see anything now."

"Exactly." The excitement in Gina's voice increased. "There's nothing to see because the virus has been shut down. You remember that my vaccine destroys one of Vera Fever's replication proteins?"

"The RNA polymerase you mentioned in your seminar."

"That's right. I've tagged that polymerase in blue so it can be tracked. But you're looking through the blue filter now—and there's none left. My vaccine has completely trashed it!"

"Yeah, but how do you know the Vera Fever infection was even there in the first place?" It was always hard for me to control scientific scepticism, even among friends.

"Negative controls, Dr O'Hara," she said, laughing and not offended in the least. "Let me convince you."

She removed the tiny tissue culture dish from the microscope, opened a nearby incubator and swapped it for a second dish. I rolled my chair away as she leaned over and adjusted the microscope again. It was strange how a simple thing like the fall of her hair around her face could hit me so powerfully.

"Okay...take another look," she said. "This culture didn't receive the protective dose of vaccine before I hit it with Vera Fever; it was completely vulnerable to attack."

A new cell floated in space, packed with lurid, lapis-blue clusters.

"Christ. What's going on here?"

"This is a few hours after Vera Fever infection, and its early genes are peaking in expression," she explained. "The blue-tagged polymerase protein you're looking at is in the process of running off thousands of copies of the viral RNA genome. The host cell looks fine now, but in a few hours, it will literally explode."

I pushed my chair back. "But pre-treatment with your vaccine completely kills the Vera Fever—I know you said as much in your seminar, but I had no idea it was so all-or-nothing."

"It's far better than I'd dreamed," Gina admitted. "This is the first time I'm filming a live infection with both coloured proteins. I want to pinpoint the exact timing of the various events, see if there's anything I can improve in the next version."

I looked down the oculars once more at the sinister masses of blue virus proteins, poised to hijack the neuron in a microscopic terrorist act. "How can you improve on one hundred-percent destruction?"

"I'm afraid it's not so straightforward in the wild." Her enthusiasm deflated somewhat. "What I'm going to film this evening is our standard Vera Fever lab strain compared to a new mutant, called B1, that's recently emerged in Mbomba, my African village. I want to see if the vaccine does as well against B1."

"Why wouldn't it?"

"B1 first showed up in the village this past February," Gina said, playing with a cluster of silver bangles on her wrist. "It's a highly virulent strain—it spreads faster, kills faster. My preliminary experiments suggest that the polymerase doesn't get destroyed as efficiently by my vaccine. These colour videos ought to give me a clue how B1 manages to win the race."

"So your vaccine might be out-of-date before it's even approved?"

She sighed. "It's always the same with micro-organisms. They evolve so fast that we can never be more than a few steps ahead. Just look at flu—resistance crops up eventually, then sweeps through the population. The problem with gene therapy is that it takes even longer than simple drugs to pass through the bureaucracy of animal testing and human trials."

"Don't take this the wrong way," I said, "but why even bother with gene therapy for Vera Fever if it's always going to be obsolete?"

"You have to be cleverer than the enemy." She dealt me a small smile. "The key to fighting resistant micro-organisms has always been with combination therapies."

"Hitting the disease with multiple weapons, so it's more difficult to evolve evasive mutations?"

"Exactly. It's working with AIDS, and HIV is a master of mutation. I've designed my vaccine to be modular, and I've been thinking about giving it a second genetic weapon for ages. But it wasn't until Cambridge that my boss was finally convinced."

"Rouyle," I said, closing the link, "and his idea about putting the antiviral FRIP gene into your vaccine vector." *No wonder she'd been captivated.* "So Pfeiffer-deVries has agreed to collaborate?"

Gina nodded. "FRIP seems to be a suitable candidate, and Dr Rouyle convinced his superiors."

"But surely if you've been thinking about this for a long time, you've come up with even better ideas, something more tailored for Vera Fever?"

She held my gaze for a second or two. "Very perceptive, Andy. Frankly, there are dozens of genes that are more appropriate and better understood than FRIP. But Geniaxis is a very small company. So far, we have no products on the market. To date, we have only one even scheduled for human trials, after which five or six more years will elapse before we can recoup our costs—that is, if it succeeds at all."

"Are you saying Geniaxis is in trouble?" I sat up straighter. "I saw something in the papers..."

"I shouldn't be telling you this." She shifted in her seat, glanced back at the open doorway. "But basically, the entire strategy of using herpes vectors to treat brain diseases—my main project—has run out of funding. Geniaxis needs venture capital, but the investors are reluctant to commit without evidence that a major pharmaceutical company has the confidence to invest in our clinical trials."

"But you were telling me before about your Swiss pharma collaborators. I thought they were paying for neuronal-specific delivery systems."

"They were...until there was a reshuffling of their upper management. Now they won't buy into developing more advanced delivery systems until we prove the principle with my prototype—using someone else's capital."

"Can't Geniaxis just reallocate funds internally?"

"I'm afraid our cancer programme has a far bigger market, and therefore more priority...I'm lucky they even initiated the project." She said this calmly, but I could detect an undercurrent of frustration.

"So you have to settle for something suboptimal out of desperation."

"It's not that bad." Her expression became guarded. "Pfeiffer-deVries is loaded with cash, has a strong gene therapy programme, dozens of candidates in clinical trials...and Dr Rouyle is particularly enthusiastic."

"Is he?" I suppressed a surge of anger.

"He's remarkably passionate about the plight of the Vera Fever patients we've been studying. He's very outspoken about the need for more applied research in developing world diseases, and demanded to know all the details. I can tell he cares."

"How?"

"Pfeiffer-deVries doesn't need us." Gina flushed. "It was only his eloquence that persuaded them."

I cleared my throat. "Didn't you say something about beer earlier?"

"Right." She jumped up and headed out the door. Blood seething, I looked down the microscope again and forced myself to breathe deeply. Maybe it was my imagination, but in the past few minutes, the neuron seemed to have become more swollen, more pregnant with viral proteins—one step closer to annihilation.

By the time Gina returned with a laboratory ice bucket stuffed with a few bottles, I had myself largely under control. I observed her while she was distracted, setting up her virus "race" under two adjacent microscopes.

"That's it." She broke into my brooding contemplation. "I've programmed the filming to start. All I have to do now is keep an eye out for the first few passes, make sure the cells don't slip out of focus or crawl away from the cameras." She sat down opposite me, opened up two lagers and passed one over.

"This is probably the weirdest place I've ever had a beer," I said, trying to slip back into my earlier relaxed mood. A flash of purple lit up the room, and Gina's face, as the microscopes illuminated the cells for one of their periodic exposures.

"It's nice having company; I spend quite a few late hours alone in this building." She looked thoughtful, and then smiled at me in a way that made my head feel light. "And I haven't come across many at the Centre who are interested in talking science."

"The whole place is infested with scientists, you know."

"Yes," she said. "But haven't you found that most people think it's antisocial to even mention their projects outside of work? There's a bit of peer pressure not to be so..."

"So nerdy?" I grinned at her. "I'm hopeless on that account, too."

"I really enjoy telling you about my research—you aren't afraid to be critical."

"And I like hearing about it."

"Then why didn't you come up after my seminar?"

Her manner was curious, not challenging, and I chose my words carefully. "I felt a bit out of my element," I admitted. "And...you were already being monopolized. Both on the podium, and afterwards, in the bar." And at the party, I didn't need to add.

She blushed again, took a quick sip of her beer. "Maybe I did spend a lot of time talking to Richard, but honestly, it felt like you were avoiding me the entire symposium."

Richard. I wished I knew exactly what had happened between them, whether she was ever going to see him again. At least he lived in another country.

"The last thing I wanted was to avoid you," I said. "But after what happened a few months ago, I haven't known how to act."

Gina was, I saw, suddenly on full alert.

"I behaved like a real brute," I said. She tried to protest, but I

113

silenced her with an upraised hand. "Although the stuff against Miles was out of line, it was certainly understandable. But I definitely shouldn't have got physical with you like that—and being drunk was no excuse."

She shook her head impatiently. "It was no big deal, Andy—I'd already forgiven you, remember?"

"Yes, but I never apologized properly. And there's something else you don't know."

"Hold on. What are you talking about?"

"What I said at the end about not liking you any more. It was all lies. I was completely off my head, Gina—I can barely remember any of it."

She gaped at me. "You mean —"

"And later, I wanted to say I was sorry, see if we could make a go of it, but I was afraid you were still angry. So I let it ...slide."

Gina just stared at me as the microscopes flashed hot red.

"I didn't even realize what had happened until Maria clued me in," I said. "But it was all a misunderstanding. Maybe..."

I trailed off when she started shaking her head.

"I can't believe this." Her words were barely audible. "I can't *believe* you didn't come around when I needed you! Do you have any idea how..." She kept moving her head back and forth in wonder.

"Look at it from my perspective: you were furious. I thought you didn't want to see me."

"The whole time, you *cared* for me? And you never said?" She paused, eyes gone bleak. "I was suffering, Andy. And I really liked you."

I was smitten into silence by the past tense.

"I'm not sure what I feel now," she said, more quietly. "I spent months trying to get over things...you, the break-up with Miles, and how that reminded me of —" She looked away. "Everything at once. I've only just regained my equilibrium—I'm a different person now."

"Different how?" I demanded, as the microscopes glowed green, dwindled back to darkness.

"Besides," she said, chin set. "This collaboration with Pfeiffer-deVries has the highest priority, so I won't have time to even think about anything else."

"Listen," I said, "despite how it may have looked, I never stopped caring for you."

There was a long pause.

"Things have become a bit more complicated since summer," she finally said.

And just like that, she seemed lost. I put a tentative hand on her arm and she turned her head away, clearly forcing back tears. I felt like that neuron under the microscope, packed with alien words but not yet ripe enough to let them fly out of my head, my heart, my mouth. Now it's obvious I should have shaken her by the shoulders, clarified the depth of my feelings and insisted that she give me a chance. Or I didn't even have to speak—I could have put my arms around her and let nature take its course. Instead, I just removed my hand from her arm, and eventually she turned back to me.

"I think what I need right now is a friend," she said softly. "Do you think you could be one?"

We gazed at each other for a second or two more, and I felt a distinct tug of gravitation like a tingling under my skin.

"I know I could," I finally replied, my voice sounding too hearty.

Gina passed a hand over her eyes. "I'd better check the focus on those cells."

I moved out of her way, watched her fuss too attentively with the machinery. My thoughts raced, unable to find a purchase. I had the feeling that something very important had just occurred, and that I had somehow misplaced it.

"Actually, I'm glad we can be friends, because I could use your help," Gina said, as if continuing her own mental monologue. She sat back down, took a gulp of beer.

"How?" I was disarmed by her abrupt shift in mood.

"It's about this Pfeiffer-deVries collaboration. I'm a virologist, so my knowledge of signal transduction is somewhat unspecialized."

"Stunning seminar questions notwithstanding."

She waved a dismissive hand. "That was just close observation and common sense. Of course I know the basics, but not the finer details of FRIP kinase. I can read the literature, but I'd be lacking the insider perspective."

"So what do you want from me?" I was secretly pleased by the praise. It was so pathetically easy back then for science to divert me from more pressing issues.

"I just need someone to listen to my plan and point out any inconsistencies. But it all has to be confidential."

"Does your boss know you'll be talking to me?"

She shook her head. "It's too complicated—I don't want to bother with confidentiality agreements or other paperwork. I'd have to rely on your discretion."

"Well, I'm happy to help." I hoped that her confidence in me wasn't going to be misplaced.

"So if we're in agreement, this calls for a toast." She raised her bottle, not noticing my hesitation.

"To the collaboration, then."

I had meant between us, but I realized that she thought I was toasting her and Rouyle. I could sense the cosy twosome ambience becoming more crowded.

11 Fag Break

*I*t was one of those rare autumn weeks when summer makes a brief reappearance. People start leaving their jackets at home again, and the women put on an encore performance of bare shoulders, arms, feet, and—if you're lucky—legs while lounging on the grass in the quadrangle park over lunch. It was teatime, and I was heading outside to savour some of the sunshine myself.

The Smoker's Wall—the portion of the park's squat stone perimeter that faced the main entrance of the Centre—was jammed with people. A few years ago, the PR department of the Centre realized that it looked hypocritical for a high profile cancer research institute to have a main entrance cluttered with scientists enjoying cigarettes. Smoking was consequently banned from the Centre grounds. However, the Centre were powerless to prevent smokers from migrating philosophically across the street to the public park, and had to be content with issuing stern, unenforceable memos.

I scanned the Wall until I found Christine sitting with her usual group.

"I'm telling you, it's a great project," Cameron was rhapsodizing as I approached.

I settled in next to Christine and popped the lid off my polystyrene cup. "What is?"

One of Christine's labmates, on my other side, snorted in amusement. "Cameron's getting a new student to look after, a boy who's interested in pharmacology, and Cameron's come up with a rather controversial thesis."

"I'm telling you, it's got all the elements," Cameron insisted. "Universal appeal, one of those questions that has plagued mankind for millennia, now totally within our grasp by harnessing the power of yeast genetics." He stared off into the distance, eyes taking on the half-mad gleam that usually accompanied his scientific rants.

"What are you on about?" I asked, not sure I really wanted to know.

"The question has been posed throughout the ages, with most cultures even coming up with instructive poetry to guide their youth." The wind pushed a generous section of sandy-brown hair into his eyes, but he seemed oblivious to the obstruction. "But the data are conflicting! The English say, *beer before wine: always fine*. The Yanks, *beer before liquor, never sicker*. Why this disparity, assuming that wine and liquor are loosely equivalent substances, and can we use science to finally learn the proper way to mix alcoholic beverages whilst on a bender?"

Christine's colleague nodded thoughtfully. "In my country, we say something that can be loosely translated as, *wine before beer is the surest course towards a sudden trip to the toilet*. That would support the English hypothesis, no?"

"Hang on a minute, isn't it actually *beer before wine, never fine*?" I asked.

"That's the whole point!" He waved his arms in the air. "We all know mixing is bad, but no one can ever agree on which order is less toxic."

"And here we come to Cam's brilliant idea." Christine nudged me in the ribs.

"It's dead easy to grow yeast on medium spiked with all manner of substances," he said. "Yeast cells are related to ours, after all, much more so than those of bacteria. Why not dose their food with trace amounts of beer or wine, in various permutations and orders? Once you found a phenotype, maybe you could discover a resistance gene. You know, the key to those annoying people who can drink all night and still remain *compos mentis*."

"What's your toxicity read-out?" someone asked. "I mean, how do you know whether they do better with beer or wine first?"

"Yeah, can yeast get hangovers, and how could you recognize it?" Christine added, winking at me.

"Simple viability tests should tell you something," Cameron insisted.

"But alcohol is actually a by-product of yeast," I pointed out. "That's how you make beer and wine in the first place. So yeast aren't going to mind floating around in alcohol, are they?"

He looked crestfallen. "I hadn't thought of that."

Christine grinned. "Looks as if you'll have to come up with another project, Cam. I don't think your boss would've been too keen, anyway."

The others laughed, and Cameron collided a palm against the side of his head. "I'm supposed to be meeting that new student at half three. Hopefully I can think of something clever while I'm waiting for the lift!"

This inspired a general exodus, leaving Christine and me alone in the extraordinary sunshine.

"How's it going?" she eventually asked, rummaging around for another cigarette. There was nothing suspicious in her question, and when I thought about it, I realized she had entirely stopped prying into my affairs recently.

"Okay," I said. "In fact, it's been quite interesting these past few days."

"Oh?" Her tone remained casual, unobtrusive.

"Chris—I miss you."

"How do you mean?" She glanced over at me curiously.

"I mean, I can't believe I'm actually saying this, but I miss you hounding me all the time."

She put cigarette to lips, looked forward again at the sporadic flow of people entering and leaving the building.

"Spit it out, O'Hara—you've obviously got news."

"You haven't been angry with me, have you?" I examined her familiar profile, the distinctive bump on the bridge of her nose.

"Nah...don't be silly." She finally met my eye. "It's just that Cam thought I was being too nosy and overbearing, and that's why you didn't tell me about Gina and your little misunderstanding. It made me realize that I'm always trying to manipulate your affairs—I've been meaning to apologize for weeks, but the right moment never came up."

"My misunderstanding...hang on, how do you know about that?"

"Maria." She shrugged. "We recently had a lovely chat—and the topic came up."

I shifted uncomfortably, wondering whether Maria had also mentioned our aborted kiss.

"And...what do you think?"

"You don't really want to know, mate."

"No, really. I do."

She regarded me for a moment. "I think you behaved like an utter idiot, and if you'd had the intelligence to confide in me, I'd have forced you over to Gina's the next day on an emergency, damage-control mission, made you clear things up and plead for absolution. Then none of this unpleasantness would ever have happened!" Seeing my wince, she added, "Well, you did ask."

"I know, you're absolutely right—you're always right." I paused. "That's why I was hoping I could brief you about more recent developments."

She gave me a luminous smile. "If that's the way you feel, you know I can't resist a good bit of gossip."

So I sketched out what had happened the previous Friday night in the Timelapse room, omitting only the existence of the confidential Vera Fever collaboration. When I'd finished, she smoked in Buddha-like equanimity, leaving me in suspense for an entire minute.

"I'd give that six out of ten."

I blinked. "Give what?"

"Your *performance*, O'Hara." She tapped a column of ash off her cigarette. "I'm impressed you had the courage to bring up the subject of your falling out. For you, that's progress."

"Why only the six, then?"

"Unless you've left something out, I don't recall you emphasizing how much you still like her."

"I should think that's painfully obvious."

"I have no doubt it's painfully obvious to *you*."

"I'm almost positive she's still interested in Rouyle." Especially, I didn't add, now that he was single-handedly responsible for saving her beloved project.

"All the more reason to spell out your feelings, Andy."

I knew she was right, but it wasn't always easy, in the moment, to commit to such powerful things as words. Words, once uttered, could never be retrieved—or so I used to believe.

"It sounds as if Rouyle is being quite articulate," she pressed on, ruthlessly.

"I wish I knew what she saw in him."

Chris eyed me sympathetically. "It's not always that simple. I suspect she's a bit star-struck at the moment—literally—by Rouyle's celebrity, by his unexpected attentions. But this sort of glamour tends to wear off if there's not a lot underneath. Meanwhile, you should be happy that you've talked things over, repaired the damage somewhat."

"Yeah, but I've lost so much ground with her—and I never had much to begin with."

"I'm not sure I agree. I suspect that the attachment between you two is even stronger now. Shared emotional history, even if it's not all pleasant, can be potent." She studied me fondly. "Be patient, though...it could take time. She's definitely worth it."

I took her hand, squeezed it one time. She squeezed back before releasing it.

I was just thinking about heading back inside when Christine broke nearly five minutes of contemplative silence.

"Andy, now that I've been officially reinstated, could I ask you about something your friend Dan mentioned back in Cambridge?"

"Hmmm...go on." I was lulled into complacency by the sun on my skin, practically melting into the hot stones of the Wall in reptilian bliss.

"What did he mean, that you being single was a departure?"

I woke up, fighting back another animal instinct, this one the urge to scuttle away into the safety of the shadows. "I was hoping you'd have forgotten about that."

"Please," she scoffed. "You couldn't possibly have expected me to pass up a comment that suggestive."

"No, I suppose not." After lobbying to return to our former intimacy, I couldn't very well refuse to answer now. It was a dazzlingly shrewd manoeuvre, I had to admit.

"And first, you have to explain why you haven't told me this story before."

I sighed. "The entire topic's a bit...laddish."

"Afraid of offending my delicate feminine sensibilities?"

I backed away hastily from this dangerous ground. "Nothing to do with you, Chris. I just don't feel comfortable talking about certain things."

"How scandalous could it be? Don't tell me you were a sex god at University." She couldn't help snickering.

"Do you want to hear this or not?"

Christine patted me on the knee, and I continued. "What happened was, I'd been a slow starter. Being intelligent in my school was hardly a route to romantic success."

"It isn't anywhere, my friend."

"Many of my mates learned to mask it, but I never got the hang of it. Frankly, I never wanted to."

Christine smiled. "Now why doesn't that surprise me? You always struck me as the know-it-all at the top of the class. So let me guess—you got to Leeds and..."

"Precisely. I was surprised to find that women were suddenly interested in me, and I got charmed into sleeping with quite a few of them. Dan was my flatmate for two years; he probably deserves a medal for patience and discretion."

"That doesn't sound terribly traumatic, O'Hara."

I watched a few leaves rasp across the pavement in the breeze. "I was very serious back then, and —"

"Back *then*?" She slapped a hand over her mouth at my warning glare.

"— and not experienced enough to realize it was just a game to them. Each time, stupidly enough, I thought these relationships were the real thing. It was very...educational."

Silence crept in, and I took a sip of cold coffee.

"Something odd happens to women at University," Christine remarked at last. "All that abrupt liberation makes them want to explore their own sexuality—I'm sure it was nothing personal. You shouldn't demonize them...us, I should say. Things are never that black-and-white."

I examined her kind face, trying unsuccessfully to put her in the same picture. It was strange how close one could be and still know so little.

"So what happened between then and now?" she asked. "Girls eventually grow up, start wanting commitment. But I can't remember you going out on a single date since I met you." She was using the carefully neutral tone she adopted when trying not to offend me.

"I kept trying during my PhD years, but never ended up with any-thing lasting." I shrugged. "Then after a few unsuccessful forays at the Centre, I changed strategies. Time was limited, so I decided to restrict myself to suitable contenders. In true scientific fashion, I drew up a list."

"A list?" Christine's lips twitched.

"You know, the ideal woman. She had to be sympathetic, easy-going and attractive, but above all she had to be intelligent. Really intelligent."

She snorted. "No wonder you've been celibate for so long."

"It's not an impossible combination, though." I tried to catch her eye, but she looked down.

"Anyway,"—brisk, businesslike—"I can understand now why Gina's captured your imagination. But a *list*, for Christ's sake…it's not healthy."

"Come on—everyone has an idealized partner in their heads. I just decided to be pragmatic about it."

"But, Andy." She looked off into the distance with a faint smile. "It's often dangerous to consider only one set of options. Sometimes things creep up on you, qualities not necessarily on your shortlist."

Uninvited, the thought of Maria entered my mind: her cutting commentary, the outrageous way she could flirt—and the feeling I'd experienced when we'd kissed.

❖ ❖ ❖

Back upstairs, the lab was a study in orchestrated chaos. It was Paul's hour for the CD player, and, predictably enough, we were being assaulted with Van Morrison at maximum volume. Everyone was rushing around, almost but not quite colliding with one another as tubes were loaded in and out of centrifuges and refrigerator doors were opened and slammed shut. Kathy walked across the room, balancing an unsteady column of several dozen Petri plates under her chin, while Marcy, bearing a tank of buffer solution, swerved casually to avoid hitting her, the liquid mere millimetres from slopping over the rim. It reminded me of a paper I had seen once in *Science* about hidden mathematical patterns in the seemingly random dynamics of crowd movement.

I was approaching my workbench when I caught a glimpse of Paul, leaning back in his chair, feet on desk, a thick sheaf of printouts in his hands. When I stopped to stare at him, he looked over the top of his glasses at me.

"All right, mate?"

"Those wouldn't happen to be your latest sequencing results, would they?"

He looked down at the papers, shrugged. "They might be—who wants to know?"

"I submitted my DNA samples *two days* before you did!" I had stopped by the sequencing department on the way up from tea, and my results still weren't ready.

Paul shrugged again, resumed his scrutiny of the colourful DNA sequence traces. "Must've been a mix-up," he offered.

"It's not fair!" I raised my voice a notch. "Just because the sequencing guy is a personal mate of yours doesn't make it right that he keeps bumping your samples ahead of mine in the queue!"

A few people had stopped what they were doing to listen.

"Hey, O'Hara, easy there." Paul held up a restraining hand. "It's got nothing to do with me. Why don't you ask Xavier what happened?"

"Fine." I marched over to the nearest phone, dialling with angry jabs.

"Yes, hello, is this Xavier?...Yes, it's Andrew speaking, from Cell and Molecular. Yes, hi, I'm fine. No actually, I'm not fine. You see, I'm a bit impatient for my DNA results, and it seems that, yet again, you've processed Paul Gray's samples ahead of my own...I just don't think it's very professional behaviour..." I listened, then said, "I beg your pardon? No, he's got them just now, he's holding them in his hand...of course I'm sure, Xavier, I..."

Paul, unable to control himself any longer, was bowed over his lap, laughing helplessly. The rest of the lab were starting to chuckle, too, as they realized what was going on.

"Actually Xavier...I...I'm sorry, I was mistaken about Paul's results. No, he hasn't got them after all...yes, I realize you've got a lot on, and I...yes, I *am* sorry...hello? Hello?"

I slammed down the receiver. "Damn it, Paul!"

He was laughing so hard that scarcely any sound was coming out.

"A good scientist doesn't jump to conclusions!" he finally managed, wagging a finger at me.

"It's not funny—Xavier was seriously pissed off. Now he'll probably take even longer with my sequences out of revenge!"

"Should have thought of that before you were so nasty to him on the phone," Kathy said. "Serves you right, you miserable old sod."

124

"That's *Doctor* miserable old sod to you!" I couldn't keep the smile from breaking over my anger, and then I started laughing too. He'd scored a fair hit. But he was going to pay...eventually.

"Nice one, Paul," Marcy said.

"But seriously, mate." Paul got his voice under control, wiped his eyes with his sleeve. "That foxy girl was up here looking for you during tea."

"Which foxy girl?" I whirled back.

"Which foxy girl, he asks me." Paul peered around at an imaginary crowd. "There are so *many*."

"You know, Andy," Helmut chimed in. "The one with the splendid attributes."

"The super fashionable woman with the great seminar question," Kathy added eagerly. "I wanted to talk to her, but I was too shy. Anyway, she was very rushed."

"You missed her by ten minutes." Paul stuck the old sequencing printouts back into his file drawer.

"Did she leave a note?" I was already scanning the surface of my bench and desk.

"She said to check your e-mail," Kathy said.

Feeling Paul's knowing eyes on me, I strolled over to my desk, slung myself into the chair and roused the mail programme.

```
This is a bit short notice, but something urgent's come up
and I need to talk to you about the stuff we said we'd talk
about earlier. Are you free after work, say around seven?
```

I sat back, did a mental inventory: minimal tissue culture, a brief bit of Hot Lab work, a couple of PCRs...I could probably get it all done in time.

I replied that I'd drop by Geniaxis to fetch her, then stared vacantly into the screen.

A Mars bar dropped onto my desk: truce.

Paul peered over the divider between our respective desks. "Good news or bad, O'Hara?"

I shrugged. "Absolutely no idea, mate."

12   PubMed Revisited

I stepped out of the lift on the top floor, but instead of taking my automatic left turn towards the library, I headed right, down the corridor towards the Mouse House—a route I had managed to avoid for my entire stint at the Centre.

I'd rung the Geniaxis after-hours bell at the appointed time, but one of Gina's colleagues speculated that she must be running late in the animal facility. The closer I got to its entrance, the more the telltale odour increased, propelling me into the past. I had worked with mice throughout my PhD years, but what the smell reminded me of most was the very beginning, when the grief at losing my Dad had been a raw sore, and the mouse facility, a sanctuary where I didn't have to speak or keep up appearances.

I swiped my pass and pushed into the foyer, where the musky fug was almost unbearable. Squinting into the gloom, I made out rows of white coats lining the walls, open boxes heaped with masks, gloves, paper boots and hats. Several heavy doors, skirted with sticky mats and guarded by red-blinking keypass units, formed the other wall, and at the far end by an untidy desk, light was issuing from a single inner window.

I walked over to the observation area and peered inside. Gina sat alone at a workbench within, not one metre away, completely enveloped in white protective garments. Her eyes appeared more emphatic framed between the paper cap and the horizontal slash of mask folded over her nose, and she didn't notice me in her absolute concentration.

There was a cage of white mice swarming next to her right elbow, and on her left, I recognized the nondescript black box where they could be placed for lethal doses of carbon dioxide gas: a humane but irreversible visit.

I stepped back further into the shadows to watch. Her movements were suffused with the confidence that had first attracted me across the courtyard as she consulted a clipboard, reached inside the cage and captured a creature by the tail. After inspecting the identification marks on its ears one last time, she turned towards the black box. The mouse was oblivious, but I was feeling trepidation enough for the both of us—a familiar heaviness in the gut.

She reached for the lid, and then something went wrong. She froze, lashes fluttering as if she had something in her eyes. The mouse tried to squeeze through her gloved fingers, and she looked at it blankly, as if she had never seen one before. I stepped forward without thinking, and her face jolted up, pale and panicked, her stare colliding with mine through the glass.

Suddenly off-balance, I steadied myself with a spread hand against the window; simultaneously, Gina seemed to restart, pushing the mouse back into its cage and running for the door. I came over to meet her as she burst through, pulling off her mask and hat in two swift movements, her freed hair tumbling around her shoulders like a wild thing.

"Are you ill?" My voice came out rough with urgency as I reached over to steady her. She sagged against the containment door, moulted the gloves into a crumpled pile at her feet and rubbed her hands harshly against the sides of her white coat.

"I'm sorry...I..." She passed a fluttering hand over her face.

"You *are* ill—sit down." I rolled a chair over, but she didn't move.

"I couldn't do it." A single tear bled down her cheek, wiped away absently with the back of her hand.

My bafflement transmuted into comprehension then, but I kept still.

"I've probably sacrificed hundreds of mice throughout my career." She looked up at me appealingly. "I've never liked doing it, but I was never unable, either. I...you probably don't want to hear this."

"No, please go on." I took her by the shoulders and made her sit down, then pulled up a chair of my own.

"I'd been having a bad day anyway."

"Why, what happened?"

Her eyes seemed shadowy. "I didn't have time to eat lunch, so I was already feeling shaky. Then I had a fight with the boss. I wanted to postpone this experiment, but they've reached a crucial stage: we need to know the answer for the next step." She took a deep breath. "There was just something about that mouse. I felt faint, and sick, and...I couldn't do it."

There was a small pause, and then I said, "These things happen sometimes, Gina."

"You must think I'm pretty stupid, an animal experimenter crying over her subjects." She almost couldn't look at me.

"Don't be ridiculous. I hate killing mice too. In fact, I'll tell you a secret no one else knows, not even my labmates." I leaned closer, resisting the urge to take her hand in mine. "I used to work with mice. And I firmly support the need for animal research. But one of the reasons I chose Magritte's lab was because she doesn't use animals— and I wouldn't have to kill them anymore. Now who's stupid?"

"I respect that." Her eyes were filled with earnest intensity. "Anyone would."

"I think it's hypocritical," I said. "If I don't feel comfortable killing animals personally, how can I support a system that does? It's like enjoying a steak but not wanting to know how it magically got off the cow and into the shrink-wrapped packaging."

Gina shook her head. "No, I don't buy that. We contribute in our own ways, to the best of our abilities." Unexpectedly, her mouth curved into a half-smile. "The clinicians would probably feel queasy doing your biochemistry."

Despite myself, I smiled too, and we found ourselves gazing at one another. I wanted to touch her hair, her face.

"You probably just need fresh air and some dinner," I finally said. "Can't you save that lot for tomorrow?"

Gina pressed splayed fingers over closed eyes. "They've got to be put down before they start suffering. But I don't know how I can face it right now."

"Then let me do it for you."

Her eyes widened. "But Andy, you just said —"

"I know what I said. But I've killed dozens of mice in my day—a couple more won't make a difference." My words sounded harsh, mostly because they were true.

"You're not authorized! If Theresa finds out —"

"Everyone's gone home," I said firmly. "Let me just get some gear on."

We walked past the alley leading to the Henry and headed towards the main road. It was a foul night, the wind gusting up leaves and stray pieces of litter, the streetlights bleeding into the puddles. We'd fallen silent after a short spate of chatter, and in the absence of words, a strange sense of closeness had stolen into the space around us. For me, at least, our recently shared bloodshed had seemed almost more intimate than sex.

"Where are we going, anyway?" I inhaled cold air to erase the lingering uneasiness of rodent from my nostrils.

"A pub too obscure for anyone from Geniaxis to show up," she said.

"Which one?" At the moment, she was leading me through Covent Garden towards Soho. The most logical venue, with guaranteed privacy, would have been one of our flats, but as she didn't suggest it, I decided that our growing friendship was still too precarious.

"It's a bit geeky," she confessed, giving me a self-conscious glance.

"That's about the last word I'd use to describe someone like you."

"Ah, but you don't know about my secret hobby yet."

I studied her, intrigued. "This ought to be good. I can see the headline in the *Centre Monthly* newsletter: *Geniaxis's most fashionable post-doc caught jotting down train numbers at Paddington Station.*"

She giggled and pressed the button at a traffic light, jumping up and down to keep warm. "I've got this thing about historic sites of microbiological significance."

"Really?" I asked, when it became clear she was serious.

"It was one of the many reasons I came to London—the entire city is dripping with ancient plagues." She met my eye. "It's a bit twisted, don't you think?"

"No, it sounds fascinating," I said. She looked unbelievably sweet with tiny droplets of rain clinging to the fine hairs curling around her forehead.

"The funny thing is, you go to these places now and you'd never know," she said. "People walk by and have no idea what used to be there. But if I stand still, and close my eyes..."

The light changed and Gina bounded across, forcing me to lengthen my stride.

"Give me an example," I said. "I'm interested in the history of science, but I don't know much about microbiology."

"How about Blackheath? It's an ordinary green—but there may be thousands of plague victims underneath the turf. Even though most people say it's a myth, I had to go—and true or not, it was totally creepy to walk across."

We'd hit another red light, and Gina paused. "When I first moved here, I didn't have any friends and I was really homesick. I spent my weekends tromping around London to keep my mind off things, and those historic places gave me the illusion of familiarity because I'd read about them in class."

She poked the kerb with her toe, balanced on the other foot with thoughtless grace.

"You have no idea what London is like for an American," she said. "This mixture of the alien and the recognizable."

"Like coming home to find someone has moved into your house and changed all the furniture?"

She looked at me intensely, nodded. "That's it exactly. And not only that, but I saw where a hundred different things I thought were typically American came from—and it turns out they're actually British. It throws you."

"The light's green." I put a gentle hand on her back, but she didn't move.

"I was living in this dismal room off the Bayswater Road, and I used to escape to Hyde Park to sit next to a statue in the Italian Gardens." She was gazing fixedly at nothing in our current coordinates of space-time.

"Edward Jenner," I said, dredging up the memory. "The Father of Vaccination."

"That's right!" Gina came back to me, momentarily delighted again. "You've been there?"

"My mum has a thing for Jenner; apparently there's some distant hereditary connection. She took my sister and me to see him when we were kids."

"I think I'd like your mother," she said. "Jenner's ethical practices were loose by modern standards—he performed the equivalent of a Phase II clinical trial with smallpox virus on an eight-year-old boy. But the statue became like a friend. I would lean against his pedestal and read, and he was always there."

Her mood pressed in around us. The light went green again, and when we were halfway across the road, Gina slipped a tentative arm though mine. I tucked it in more firmly and had to remind myself to breathe. After about ten more minutes of walking in silence, she steered us down a deserted tributary off the bustle of Wardour Street.

"This is it—The John Snow." Gina pointed out a pub up ahead. "Do you know it?"

"I'm afraid my mother failed to brief me on this one."

"Then let me show you something first." She dropped her arm from mine and crossed the street to an old-fashioned water pump protruding incongruously from an octagonal platform on the pavement.

"People have no respect." She ran a finger across its undignified layer of peeling old flyers and stickers. "Notice anything funny about this pump?"

"Er..." I stepped back, shook my head.

"No handle," she said. "This is a replica of the original. A doctor named John Snow realized that a pattern of cholera outbreaks in this neighbourhood correlated with the source of drinking water. It was a brilliant feat of epidemiological insight; no one knew anything about the bacterium—*Vibrio cholera*—at the time. He removed the pump handle, and sure enough, the disease petered out."

She turned, and I followed her across the intersection to the entrance of the pub. "Look, here's where the contaminated water pipe used to be." She rubbed a metal plate on the pavement wistfully with her booted toe. "The first time I came here, I was expecting some sort of shrine. But it's just an ordinary pub." She shrugged. "They do great fries here. Shall we go in?"

The pub was warm, murmuring with people, the chrome of the taps glowing in the dark woodwork. The two people behind the bar greeted Gina by name when we entered, and one of them, a young woman, threw me a curious second look.

"This is nice. Did you used to come here with Miles?"

"Miles wouldn't be caught dead in a bar this un-trendy," she said shortly. "Can I get you something to drink?"

"Let me."

"Don't be silly—I'm the one who's inconveniencing you, after all."

I paused, remembering my recent scolding from Christine. "You already know how much I enjoy your company, so this is about as far from inconvenient as it gets."

My confession evoked a confused reaction from Gina. The overriding emotion seemed to be sadness, which caught me off guard and neatly prevented me from following through. After a few flustered seconds, she turned away to fetch our pints, leaving me to find a place to sit in bewilderment.

Both of us had recovered by the time she slipped into the booth across from me and pulled her rucksack onto her lap. As I took a sip of beer, she extracted a thick stack of papers and pushed the top document towards me.

"What's this?" I asked in surprise, examining the official Geniaxis logo.

"Confidentiality agreement."

"But I thought this was off the record?"

She looked sheepish. "It is. And it's not that I don't trust you, Andy—I'm actually not going to log this back at the office. I just thought...well, if I get caught, this way I probably won't get fired. You don't mind, do you?"

"Nah." I took the proffered pen. "Who would I tell, anyway?"

I scrawled my signature and date on the bottom, not even bothering to read it. Now that scientists were realizing that intellectual property could translate into money, such documents were increasingly commonplace.

"On to the interesting stuff." She began to dismantle the stack: diagrams, charts, articles. I recognized the cartoon representations of her herpes virus vectors reoccurring on several pages.

"It's unfortunate I haven't had a chance to do my homework." If she'd given me more notice, I would have downloaded a few of Rouyle's recent FRIP kinase papers. If he wrote anything like he spoke, it would have taken more than a few hours to wade through them.

She glanced up. "It's okay—I've done all the reading already. I even brought copies of the most relevant articles." She patted a separate pile of reprints. "I just want you to listen and let me know if something doesn't seem right."

"Let me get one thing straight first," I ventured. "Rouyle's supposed to be a FRIP kinase signalling expert. Don't you think he's got his portion under control?"

"Well...let's just say that I trust him, but I'm suspicious about Pfeiffer-deVries. I know I keep saying how great industry is, but..."

"There's a big difference between a small biotech firm like Geniaxis and a monolithic pharmaceutical company like Pfeiffer-deVries?"

"Exactly. Also, the whole collaboration has been rushed, so I don't want to make mistakes. I'm sure his people are checking my virology as well."

"What was the urgency you mentioned in your e-mail?"

Her eyes dipped down to the diagram in her hand. "They're sending me to Germany to supervise production of the first batch of virus."

"You're joking—that *is* rushed." From cocktail napkin to reality in less than two weeks: it seemed unbelievable.

She just nodded, continuing to worry the piece of paper.

"So how long will you be gone?" I said.

A pause. "A month or so."

A month!

"Oh," I said.

"I leave tomorrow morning."

Tomorrow morning!

She seemed to be appraising me carefully, so I kept my disappointment hidden as I gestured at the mess of papers fanned out between us. "Are you truly ready for this step yet? It looks as if you're still at the thinking stage."

"The thing is," she said, "inserting the FRIP gene into my vaccine turns out to be straightforward. So it's not the actual mechanics that aren't ready...just the feasibility."

"In other words, you still haven't decided that it's actually going to work."

"In a way, yes," Gina said. I could sense her underlying tension. "But Pfeiffer-deVries is convinced. You see, they've already tested the FRIP gene alone in Phase I clinical trials using adenovirus delivery. And we've recently completed our pre-clinical animal trials on my Verase herpes vaccine."

"And both were successful?"

"Yes. So as each component works separately, Pfeiffer-deVries is ready to streamline the process towards animal trials on a new combination vaccine."

She leaned back in her chair, gauging my reaction. "Our skittish Swiss collaborators are more than happy to let Pfeiffer-deVries pick up the tab. Not surprisingly, my boss has decided to run with this. It's a great opportunity for my own career, as well—another clinical trial on my industrial CV would be worth three *Cell* papers. It's just not my style to be so..."

"Sloppy?"

"Hasty," she corrected, making a face.

"No wonder you're nervous." I thought for a moment. "Even if your Verase vaccine and Rouyle's FRIP strategy work perfectly by themselves, it's a formal possibility that having the two proteins present at the same time could cancel out their beneficial effects. Worse, the combination could add up to an unexpected—even harmful—outcome. It wouldn't be the first time something like that has happened. Cell signalling networks are notoriously complex."

"That's exactly what I was afraid of."

"I haven't seen any of the details yet, but I would insist on extensive tissue culture experiments before this new combination vaccine goes anywhere near a live animal."

"Then I'll make that a non-negotiable point." She nodded at me. "Shall we get to work? I'm particularly interested in your opinion about Dr Rouyle's unpublished research. For example, this new alternative PT35-like isoform..."

At my blank look, she added, "You were paying attention at his seminar, weren't you?"

"Er, actually..."

I swiped my keycard and let myself back into the Centre. It was nearly midnight and I was exhausted, but I'd told Gina I had suddenly remembered something I'd forgotten to do in the lab. This wasn't strictly true. In reality, our brainstorming session had sparked off a few suspicions and privately, I was starting to wonder about Rouyle's credentials. As I didn't want to let on to Gina that I was critical of yet another man she might be involved with, a discreet PubMed search seemed the best place to start—but I'd left my laptop at work and knew the anticipation would prevent me from sleeping if I put it off until the morning.

Superficially, there wasn't a great deal to criticize. I had caught two mistakes in his part of the plan, so obvious that I had picked up on them immediately, and then was able to show Gina why they were errors using Rouyle's own articles. Neither was serious enough to invalidate the entire plan, and Gina hadn't seemed too concerned. It was just carelessness. But as Magritte was fond of saying, she was always suspicious of manuscripts with lots of typos and minor mistakes. If people weren't careful enough on the things that didn't matter, how could one be sure that they'd taken care over those that did? It just seemed as if he hadn't put much thought or effort into his end of the project, which was remarkable considering that the final product would be injected into actual people.

The building, of course, was dark and deserted.

"You are an idiot," I whispered to myself in the lift. Not only was I tired, but I'd also missed the chance to take the Tube with Gina as far as Finsbury Park. It hadn't seemed like such a big deal at the time, but now I realized that even fifteen more minutes with her were precious considering how long she'd be away. I couldn't stop thinking about how we'd parted ways at Oxford Circus, the brief kiss on the cheek, the way she had pressed herself against me before slipping into the Underground. Now that it was too late, it became clear that I should have capitalized more on the opportunity, grabbed her hand to prevent her flight, said or done *something* to cement our fragile new bond into a more substantial state. I shouldn't have allowed her anywhere near Rouyle until I'd infiltrated her defences further.

I walked into the dark lab, which was powered down but still very much in stand-by mode. Lights flashed and various pieces of machinery hummed their familiar tuneless songs. A purplish glow leached around the corner leading to the tissue culture suite: the ultraviolet sterilization lamps, busy zapping away any traces of microorganisms. I put my hand on the light switch, then decided not to break the peaceful midnight spell, flipping on my desk lamp instead.

While waiting for the computer to warm up, I noticed Paul's peace offering still sitting on my desk. I peeled off the wrapper and demolished the Mars bar. We'd had a few rounds of chips in the pub, but dinner had been forgotten in our preoccupation. Gina had listened to my opinions with intelligence and respect, always seeming to grasp instantly what I was trying to say. I couldn't help noticing how well our thoughts worked together, how we could build on one another's concepts in a complementary fashion—in short, what a good team we made. There was no doubt that our intellectual synergy had a strange intensity to it. I tried to convince myself that I could be satisfied with such a friendship if that were all that was possible.

Still hungry, I searched through my desk drawer for the emergency stash of peanuts, only to be distracted by Dad's stare from the old photo within.

"Rouyle's up to something," I told him. "I can just tell."

Munching on the nuts, I clicked open the web browser, went into PubMed and typed in 'Rouyle R'. After a few moments, PubMed gave me forty-one abstracts—not a great number of papers for a senior lab head. I scrolled down the list. Some of the abstracts were obviously not even relevant, by someone else with the same name, because the titles had nothing to do with molecular biology, such as:

13. Rouyle, R, Jefferson, AD, Venkatu, L.-D. and Yakimoto, Y. Mass spectrometric elucidation of reductase domains that control chirality mediated by the modular polyketide synthases. Chem Biol. 1998 Aug 25 (3): 32-38.

Or,

40. Rouyle, R, Viknar, PM, and Maaros, E. Dominant passivity factors and pliancy criteria in rhesus macaques exposed to the PAX fraction. Arch Lat Psychiatry, 1993 Apr 5, 2:134-143. (No abstract available).

The first example was obviously written by a chemist—I could barely understand the title. As for the second, I had never even heard of the journal. Archives of...Lateral Psychiatry? Latent? Latex? The fact that PubMed could not provide an abstract of the paper might mean that the journal itself was too obscure, which sometimes happened with the smaller foreign-language publications. Basically, if a scientific paper wasn't in English, unfair as this might seem, it practically didn't exist. English was the lingua franca of science, and science was now a global enterprise. PubMed was littered with such forlorn, forgotten specimens.

So among my forty-odd Rouyle hits, a good handful were almost certainly written by someone else. The rest, however, were clearly my man. For example,

17. Rouyle, RF, Ullrich, A, Rudolph, HE, and Bohr, T. FRIP

kinase is differentially phosphorylated in response to distinct upstream stimuli: mapping the viral response determinants. J Biol Chem, 1996 Jan 11: 410: 11456-11461.

About halfway through the list, Rouyle's name migrated from first to last, indicating that he was now in charge of his own group. None of the papers was in the best journals, and there were not a few in very obscure journals, all of which betrayed a below-average track record.

I double-clicked on his oldest title, number 39, to call up the associated abstract. A text box bloomed onto the screen, displaying the title and authors, the location of the laboratory and a long paragraph summarizing the research reported in the paper. This information told me that Rouyle was already at Pfeiffer-deVries when he wrote his first paper. I found it a bit odd that he had published nothing from his PhD and indeed, had no other post-doctoral publications prior to this abstract. How had he managed to secure a job at a major pharmaceutical company with no publications in his CV? I supposed that back then it was more difficult to entice people into the taboo-enshrouded halls of industry, and the standards for hiring must have been lower.

I sat back, rolling my neck around to diffuse the accumulated tension. The search hadn't told me anything. I didn't know what I had expected to find, but it was clear that, while not sterling, his publication record didn't condemn him either. Of course Gina would have checked up on him as well. Meanwhile, she was packing for Frankfurt—and there was a night bus with my name on it in Trafalgar Square.

I was just about to shut down the computer when I remembered that I hadn't checked my e-mail. I had one new message, sent only a few minutes before.

Dear Andy,

I hope you didn't have to work too late. Just a quick note to let you know I got home safely, and to thank you for all your help this evening. I know it was work, but I really enjoyed myself. Forgot to tell you that I'll have access to my e-mail account in Germany, so please write to me.

I'll miss you.

Gina

Her final words hung there on the screen in irrefutable black on white. I appreciated their solidity, but wished she'd been able to say them in person.

13 *Opposing Parties*

"*A*ny guesses on the genus and species?" Cameron speared the glistening cube of meat with his fork and examined it gingerly.

Christine sampled hers and did not look encouraged. "It almost tastes like chicken, but chicken gone horribly wrong."

"Wasn't that meant to be the Lamb Provençale?" I looked down at my own plate, which contained a shrivelled fish filet nestled on a bed of flaccid broccoli. It was called Haddock Primavera, and it tasted terrible.

"I can't eat this," Paul said, shoving his tray to one side. "I'm going back for a salad. Not much they can do to raw vegetables, is there?" He got up and squeezed through the space between the long tables.

"Now that's what I call an optimist," Maria said, tucking into some fantastic-looking, and fantastic-smelling, lasagne she'd brought from home.

"How did you know it was going to be this bad today?" Cameron peered longingly into her Tupperware.

"It's not exactly rocket science, is it?"

Cameron resumed his inspection of the meat. "Okay, I'll concede that it could've been derived from a lamb...but which organ or gland?"

"Can we talk about something else, please?" I pleaded. "It's easier to get it down if we're not dwelling on it."

"What about this animal rights protest tomorrow?" Kathy looked up from the edge of our group, where she and Helmut had been discussing science as usual, oblivious to mere mortal considerations like the taste and texture of food.

Christine shrugged. "It's going to be a major demonstration, according to the *Guardian*."

"What if we can't get inside the building?" Kathy sounded nervous. "I've got a big experiment on tomorrow."

"Don't worry, kiddo, they're usually all talk," Christine said. "Just don't let yourself get handcuffed to one of the protesters." She winked at me.

"Handcuffed?" Kathy looked horrified. "Then they'd have to come to lab with me, and if it was my right hand, I wouldn't be able to pipette very easily."

"She's just winding you up," I said. "There're usually police about to make sure no one gets martyred."

"But seriously," Helmut said, "does anyone know why we are targeted in the particular? The Centre is having only a small-scale animal experimentation programme. Who actually does much —"

"Define *animal*," Cameron said. "People here work on fruit flies, frogs, zebrafish, nematode worms...even my yeast are complicated organisms, and I can decimate several million of them in one go."

Christine snorted disparagingly. "Everyone knows the 'animal' in animal rights means 'warm, furry, and cute'. They don't get worked up about unappealing species."

"Then who does much work on mammals?" Helmut persisted.

"It's you lot, isn't it?" Christine said to Maria.

She looked up from her lasagne meekly. "I'm afraid so. We had a memo about it last week. There was an internal leak to the press, and a witch-hunt atmosphere ever since."

"What sort of leak?" Christine asked.

"It's all very mysterious," Maria said. "Somebody inside must have gone to one of the tabloids and helpfully revealed the details of our rodent experiments. We've been performing a number of gene therapy trials in recent months. Not everyone, of course—just a few key people. But they've involved quite a few animals."

When she met my eye, I could read her perfectly: *Gina*.

"Did the mole actually name and shame?" I asked.

"Well, it's not clear." Her eyes were troubled. "The article implied that the activists know exactly who's been performing the experiments, and they made a few veiled threats, but so far no actual scientists have been mentioned."

Just as well that Gina was still safely in Frankfurt, although her last e-mail had implied she'd be back any day now.

"Well, the protest should be exciting at any rate," Maria said, spearing another forkful of pasta.

"I don't know," Cameron said. "If Julie's party is as good as promised, perhaps we'll sleep through the whole thing."

"*You* lot are going to Julie's party?" Marcy was roused from her sullen contemplation. "It's just going to be a bunch of PhD students."

"Precisely," he replied. "Students indisputably throw the best parties. And even more promising, it's rumoured that Julie lives with three non-scientists, and they're inviting all of their friends as well!"

"Why do they have to have it on a Wednesday?" I said. "I'm getting too old to keep up the pace."

The turn of Marcy's mouth was scathing. "No wonder post-docs are so boring. Everyone knows that Wednesdays and Thursdays are the coolest nights to go out. The weekend is too *obvious*."

"And talking of boring post-docs," Paul said, appearing back at his chair with a bowl of wilted salad, "are you all invited to Mark's birthday party as well?"

We all nodded, except Maria, who asked, "Who's Mark?"

"He's a post-doc in Chris's lab," I said. "You're welcome to come along with us." I looked at Chris for confirmation.

"Definitely," Christine said. "We plan to go early to Mark's, put in a polite appearance, load up on free food and then escape over to Julie's as soon as decently possible."

"Sounds like fun." Maria gave me an agreeable smile.

Paul smirked at me, and I shot him back a look telling him, essentially, to get lost.

The evening's adventures got off to a slow start. First, there'd been a chain reaction of signal failures on the Underground. We'd had to suffer through a sweaty scrum on the platform at Camden Town waiting for that most elusive of all beasts, the Edgware-bound train. Then we'd inexplicably stalled halfway to Chalk Farm for nearly half an hour, crushed in the airless carriage with tempers rising on every side. After the slog to Mark's, the scene awaiting us was dour—only a handful of guests sitting in a loose circle who looked up expectantly as we entered the room. When Christine and Cameron were ensnared in lab gossip, I seized the opportunity to steer Maria over to the side table laden with an optimistic excess of enticing dishes. It was the first promising indication I'd seen all night.

"Sorry about this," I said softly as we heaped our plates high. I hadn't managed to eat much of my sorry lunch, and it was already past nine. "It was bound to be a bit boring, but this feels positively funereal. And of course you don't know anyone."

"Don't worry, it's exactly what I was expecting," she said placidly. "Post-doc parties are always the same."

We made our way over to a sofa in the corner.

"There's no *a priori* reason why these affairs have to be so dull," I said, appraising the room. "With the right tools, I could get this place going."

Maria just looked at me. "Andy, *nothing* is going to get this place going."

I felt myself responding to her challenge. Maybe it was some vestigial piece of genetic information, urging me to dazzle this impressive female of the species with my prowess, but as there was no elk at hand to bludgeon, I was forced to improvise. Also, it beat joining the group conversation, which had degenerated to the usual nihilistic diatribe about the academic post-doctoral experience. I had enough of that in my own head without indulging in it during social gatherings.

"We'd have to contrive to get the lights lowered without anyone noticing," I said. "It's like a police examination room in here."

"There's a dimmer switch over there."

"Well, that's one for the arsenal—we can nudge it down later. Let's inspect the CD collection, shall we?"

Currently the stereo was whispering Eric Clapton *Unplugged*, the graphic equalizer twitching almost imperceptibly like a patient about to flatline.

Amused, Maria knelt down in front of the chrome rack and joined me in skimming the titles. "I'm afraid it's fairly bleak," she remarked. "*Billy Joel's Greatest Hits*...Dire Straits...Hey, Sting, *The Dream of the Blue Turtles*—I think I lost my virginity to this album!"

"I never thought I'd say this, but I wish they had some ABBA at least—there's absolutely nothing useful here." I made myself more comfortable on the floor and started to demolish my dinner. "It's times like these I worry that all the stereotypes are true."

"About scientists being boring, you mean?"

I nodded, mouth too full to reply.

"Don't despair, Andy. There're only a few rogue boffins giving the rest of us a bad name."

"Then why are these parties always so grim?" I said.

She leaned against the bookcase and thought about it. "It's age, not profession. My brother has the same complaints about his work gatherings—and he's a lawyer." She started twirling her hair around one finger. "Believe me, if his stories are anything to go by, scientists are far more interesting."

"Hmmm."

She reached over and squeezed my knee. "Even you, on second glance."

"Are you saying I'm a nerd on first glance?"

"Possibly." Her eyes laughed amid an otherwise neutral face. "But I haven't got you entirely figured out yet."

"Do let me know when you've finalized your analysis." I grinned at her.

"Haven't you found any livelier music to put on?" Christine collapsed beside us on the carpet, feigning cardiac arrest.

"Sorry, but it's out of my hands," I said. "Have you worked out our escape plan yet?"

"Pierre's offered us a lift to Julie's." She righted herself and snagged a piece of bread from my plate. "But to be courteous, we should stay long enough to offset the way we've decimated their food supply. You'll cope okay until then?"

Maria smiled at my expression. "I'll keep him entertained, don't worry."

After Christine moved on, Maria pulled out a CD case and studied the song list before looking over at me. "She's due back any day now, you know," she remarked.

I sat up straighter. "You don't know exactly when?"

She shook her head, prised the liner notes out of the CD case and flipped through the glossy pages.

"Have you not heard from her?" She held the booklet sideways to examine a centrefold photograph of the pouting boy band.

"The occasional e-mail here and there...I gather she's been busy."

"Has she mentioned anything about Rouyle?"

"His name has come up a few times when she was writing about the lab, of course."

Maria turned a page, still avoiding my eye. "I meant more...on the romantic side of things."

"No, she hasn't." When she didn't comment, I took a breath through tensed airways. "Why, has she said anything to you?"

She finally looked at me, her dark eyes reflecting a jumble of emotions. "We're not that close, as I've mentioned before. I've had a few e-mails, strictly work-related. But I have heard some rumours."

"Such as?" I wanted her both to continue and, urgently, to stop.

"You know how small the scientific world is." Then she leaned towards me, put a hand on my shoulder. "Hey...it might not be as serious as people are saying."

I shook my head, not wanting to believe this latest development, but now that Maria had broached the topic, I had to admit that Gina's e-mail messages had gradually tailed off over the weeks, and the few I'd received recently had been brief and detached.

"I was hoping Rouyle was married," I said, slumping.

"Like that's any impediment!" She laughed outright. "You are so hopelessly old-fashioned, Andy. But anyway, he's not."

"How do you know?" In the background, I was aware of the doorbell.

"That was the first intelligence the Geniaxis rumour network sniffed out when it became clear something was up between the pair of them." She shrugged. "Everyone was disappointed that it wasn't more scandalous."

"Marvellous," I muttered.

"We haven't had a chance to really talk since Cambridge," she said. "There's been something I've been meaning to ask you...do you still —"

Paul called out a cheery greeting as he entered the lounge in a swirl of cold air. In the space of several seconds he'd insulted Mark, bantered gallantly with Mark's wife and registered marked dismay at the morose grouping in the centre of the room. When he noticed me, he perked up and strode over, kicking me on the leg and winking at Maria. She closed her mouth, clearly miffed at the interruption.

"Where's Suzy?" I was grateful for the reprieve.

"Hen night! Which means I'm free to be one of the unencumbered tonight and can join you all for..." he lowered his voice out of respect for the hosts, "Julie's piss-up." He rubbed his hands together in antic-ipation. Or was it emancipation?

"But first you'll have to serve your time," I said.

"Hmmm." He surveyed the scene thoughtfully. "You know, what this party needs is a spot of decent music."

"And what do you do?"

The woman waited expectantly. Mary, I reminded myself, in her second year at the London School of Economics. She was attractive, conservatively dressed and was sampling her wine with birdlike sips.

"I'm a scientist," I said. It was always best to start off generally.

The brightness of her expression clouded over, and I sensed that my appeal was starting to wane. This often happened at the outset, but it was worth persisting: when you hit someone who was truly inter-ested, it made you feel like a star.

"What sort of scientist?"

"Cancer research," I said, giving her my most charming, heroic smile. At times like these, I was thankful I didn't work on something embarrassing, like the sexual organs of intestinal parasites.

"Cancer?" Her eyes widened, and she leaned closer. "You know, my aunt died of cancer."

"Um...I'm sorry." Foiled at the crucial moment by the unsolicited medical anecdote! I knew from experience that my chances of im-pressing her with molecular details were now slim, and that I might very well be in for a protracted siege.

"Lung cancer," she said, "which seemed really unfair, as she'd never smoked a cigarette in her life. The doctors said..."

I lost the next part of her story as the stereo's volume was boosted yet again. Julie's flat was so full that even movement was problem-atic, let alone an easy escape. I'd heard rumours of an impressive sup-ply of alcohol in the kitchen, but so far I hadn't been able to get anywhere near it. And I'd managed to lose the others within minutes of entering the fray.

The woman seemed to be waiting for a reply. "Listen...Mary, it's been nice talking with you, but I've just spotted someone over there I have to..." I produced a few more pleasantries before diving into the crowd.

Orientating myself, I located the entrance to the kitchen. After a few hard-won steps, someone collided into me, and I felt a cold splash soak into my leg.

"God, I am *really* sorry." A deep-voiced bohemian-looking woman steadied herself with a strong grip on my upper arm, pulled back her dripping bottle of beer. She was pretty, with blond dreadlocks and cornflower blue eyes.

"It would be a disappointing party if I didn't get covered in booze," I replied diplomatically, starting to move off, but she'd settled into chat mode.

"So how do you know Sylvia?"

"Sylvia? Is that one of the flatmates? I'm a friend of Julie's."

"Julie...the biochemist? So are you a scientist too?" Her friendly smile faded somewhat. "What's your position on GM foods?"

"My position? I think it's a big fuss over nothing."

"That is just so typical!" she said. "How can you condone the release of such potentially harmful organisms into the environment?"

"Well, it's a bit difficult to prove they're actually harmful if eco-terrorists keep uprooting all the test crops," I said.

"You don't *need* proof—you can't deny it's completely unnatural to modify plants like that!"

The right thing to do was to excuse myself, but there was something patronizing in her last statement that I found impossible to ignore.

"Are you aware that crops have been genetically modified for thousands of years?"

"What do you mean?" She was caught off guard, and then her eyes grew larger. "Do you mean by aliens?"

I sighed. "No, I mean by farmers. They've been tinkering with the DNA of fruits and vegetables since the dawn of agriculture."

"Bollocks!"

"What do you think cross-breeding does?" I produced the smile that tended to drive Christine mad. "None of the stuff in your fridge bears any resemblance to the natural ancestor plants, most of which are long extinct."

"That's —"

"Ever wonder why strawberries are suddenly so large? Because they're polyploid, that's why—they've been forced to carry multiple copies of their chromosomes by traditional breeding methods. If that's not genetic modification, I don't know what is."

"Typical scientific propaganda." She systematically upended the last of her beer on me before flouncing off.

"Hey, is everything all right?"

A chic woman now stood before me, dressed entirely in black and holding a plate of party snacks.

"Well..."

She passed me her paper serviette. "Relationship problems?"

"Philosophical differences," I corrected, starting to blot at the spreading beer stains.

"Oh? On what topic?"

"GM foods," I mumbled.

She flashed me a sympathetic smile. "Was she one of the many scientists floating around tonight? They can be quite frustrating."

"Yeah, I know what you mean." I looked over her shoulder in the hope of discovering some handy excuse for terminating the discussion.

"Just a few minutes ago I was speaking with this guy, some sort of researcher, who seemed perturbed about the animal rights protest tomorrow. We're preparing quite a —"

"We?"

"Yes, we, as in FUR-IE." At my vacant expression, she added, *Fighting Unethical Research, Investigation and Exploitation.* I'm the Central London branch secretary."

"Ah —"

"Like I was saying, we've arranged quite a show. Serves them right, the animal-murdering bastards...don't you agree?" Her eyes were cool-green and expectant.

"Absolutely," I gasped, spotting Paul waving at me from across the room. "Listen, I've got to go now. It's been quite..."

I bolted past her, negotiated a thrashing patch of dancers and emerged relatively unscathed on the other side.

"Where've you been?" Paul said. "Mate, there's a truly amazing spectacle out on the terrace. It's too late for me, as I'm already spoken for, but you should go and check it out."

"What are you on about, Paul?"

"Persian physicist." His eyes went distant with appreciation. "She's holding court out there, surrounded by a flock of lads and expounding on various enlightened topics. I reckon you could make some progress—many of the contenders are quite young and inexperienced."

Cameron appeared. "Have you by chance met the Persian physicist yet, gentlemen?" He seemed rather dazed. "Spectacular. A prime example of what I was saying earlier, my theory about beauty and intelligence being synergistic rather than merely additive. If you could somehow quantify her qualities and plot them on —"

"I think Andy was doing fine chatting up the talent inside," Paul said. "That's what it looked like from this vantage."

"Let's just say that our occupation is a distinct liability when it comes to scoring," I said.

"And that's precisely where you've been going wrong." Cameron wagged a finger at me. "Never even *admit* you're a scientist until the second date."

"A-ha, so you were trying to score?" Paul nudged me painfully in the ribs.

I sighed. "No, it was just an observation."

"If you ask me, you've already got it sorted." He nodded his head towards where Maria stood in lively conversation with Christine. Christine leaned over, mouth moving in sardonic commentary, and Maria laughed, sending her curtain of dark hair shimmering down her back.

I noticed that Cameron had been studying me curiously. For the hundredth time, I wondered how much Christine talked about me, whether he knew all about my dealings with Gina.

"We're just mates," I said firmly, wishing I had a drink in my hand.

"I'm not so sure that's what she thinks." Paul's expression was serious for a change.

"She's a very nice woman," Cameron agreed, similarly earnest.

Christ, this was the last thing I needed—a heart-to-heart with the lads.

"You're not leading her on intentionally, I hope?" Paul persisted.

"Of course not! She knows exactly how I feel."

"Maybe she doesn't entirely believe you," Cameron ventured.

"Listen, this has all been very thought-provoking, and I'm touched by your concern, but I'm going to get some drinks in—anyone else coming?"

I strained against the press of bodies bottlenecked firmly in the kitchen's entrance. Momentarily defeated, I pondered the almost universal magnetism of the kitchen at parties. They are usually cramped spaces, brightly lit and uncomfortable, but even when the alcohol is stored elsewhere, the kitchen retains its mystical pull. It was a problem that modern science had failed to explain.

"Can someone pass me three lagers, please?" I yelled optimistically into the crowd. "Preferably cold ones?"

There was a stirring within, the smack of a refrigerator door, and then a small fleet of bottles was dispatched hand to hand overhead. Halfway across the sea of heads, a disembodied pair of hands reached up and popped the caps off, and then the beers resumed their journey until they had safely reached me.

I took a bracing sip of lager and tried to locate Paul and Cameron, who had vanished from their previous coordinates. Now that I was applying no counter-resistance, the throng's seething Brownian motion gradually nudged my body into the thick of the lounge. I came aground at an island, a man and woman in heated discussion at the edge of a larger group. A few key words alerted me that, instead of the normal party topics of football, work complaints or the solo careers of various lip-syncing pop stars, another scientific debate was in progress. The woman looked familiar; I was fairly certain she was a PhD student in Julie's lab. The man was a clean-cut City type, the sort who comes across as formally dressed even in casual clothing.

"Okay, forget pre-implantation embryos, then," the PhD student was saying. "How about abortions? If it's legal to have one, why not allow the foetuses to be used for research? They're just going to get chucked away."

"Hey, Anja," the man said, touching the arm of a stylish, etiolated woman with spiky henna-coloured hair on his other side. "Your government has the right attitude about stem cell research. Why don't you try explaining it to her?" He gestured with a thumb at Julie's colleague.

"Sorry to disappoint, but I am actually in disagreement over the extreme position of the *Bundestag*," she replied mildly.

The PhD student smiled in triumph at the City type.

"Don't tell me," the man said in disgust. "You're a scientist as well."

"No, I am in advertising," she replied, one plucked eyebrow arching. "Can I not still hold such an opinion? There are all sorts of horrible diseases that this type of research may be able to cure—do you really wish to prevent such a thing?"

"Of course not," the man admitted. "The point is that relaxing the laws might create a legal loophole for human cloning."

"Ridiculous," she retorted. "Surely they can just pass further laws to permit the one without the other."

"Lawyers can worm their way out of anything." The man looked genuinely worried. "It's just not worth the risk: human clones are crimes against nature."

"My *brothers* are clones," the German woman said, flushing. "Identical twins. Of course I am not in favour of laboratory cloning, but I would ask you to watch what you say!"

It had to be the particular composition of flatmates that had led to this uneasy cocktail of so many scientists and modern-day Luddites in one room, rubbing shoulders with people of every shade in between. Wondering at the sheer width of the ideological chasm, I moved on.

149

14 *On the Sofa*

We were standing outside later, shivering in the dark. The murmur of voices and the thumping of music encased the back garden in a bubble of activity. Every few minutes someone would trip the motion detector over the terrace door, spotlighting the partygoers in fleeting tableau.

"It's exhausting," Christine was saying.

"Like trying to reason with a Jehovah's Witness," Cameron added. He manipulated two beer bottles, attempting to pry off the cap of one with the other. It was a trick that tended to work only early in the evening, when motor control skills were still intact.

"I don't quite see the parallel," Maria said. Unlike the rest of us, she'd had the sense to bring out her jacket, and looked snug in the thick leather.

"Religious fervour," I said. "Facts being irrelevant in the face of faith."

"Exactly—*damn*!" Cameron's bottles skittered apart yet again. Christine passed her cigarette to me, took the beers from Cameron and popped off a cap with one proficient movement.

"I don't think they've necessarily got their facts wrong," Maria said.

"We can't do medical studies without animal research." I passed back Christine's fag. "Drugs can't be tested in humans without animal trials. It wouldn't be ethical."

"But that doesn't make it right, necessarily. And anyway, ethical to *whom*?" The set of her chin was cantankerous, but her eyes were wisely amused.

Christine looked at Maria, intrigued more than alarmed by this sudden renegade opinion. "Are you saying you're against animal research? I see you up in the Mouse House all the time."

"It's not a question of me being for or against," —a gust of impatient exhalation— "it's what other people believe, and whether that opinion is necessarily as crazy as you lot have been making out."

"Maria, they're nutters," I said incredulously. "They put bombs in laboratories. They handcuff themselves to stationary objects. They set HIV-infected chimpanzees free in populated areas."

"I'm not saying I agree with their methods." Maria was unruffled. "I'm only saying that the personal belief that an animal's life is just as important as a human's is not necessarily something we should be laughing at."

"It's hard to separate the extremist methods from the beliefs," Cameron remarked.

"Crazy behaviour invalidates reasonable discussion," I agreed. "You can't *talk* to these people."

"It doesn't sound as if you try very hard." There was a dangerous constriction to Maria's eyes. "What about that woman you just told us about, the one advocating caution over GM foods? Aside from a self-righteous—and not completely accurate—lecture about the history of agriculture, can you honestly call what you had a *reasonable discussion*?"

"She dumped beer all over me!"

"I can't say I blame her—it sounds as if you showed no sign you were willing to listen to her, let alone have a balanced conversation."

"What do you mean, not completely accurate?" Christine was obviously enjoying Maria's performance at my expense.

"Direct genetic modification changes plants more drastically than old-fashioned breeding methods," she responded smoothly, obviously more up on this particular topic than I. "Thousands of years of husbandry are never going to produce antibiotic resistance markers, for example, and some of the changes could cause allergic reactions. Test crops may very well spread to the wild, causing problems with the food chain and biodiversity. Not that most scientists will give these issues much credit."

I didn't have a clever answer for this.

"No wonder lay-people think we're arrogant," she said. "For all our famous objectivity, we can be bloody pig-headed about the inviolate nature of science—and anyone who disagrees with our sacred opinions must be too uninitiated to understand." Maria had been speaking to everyone, but she was staring at me.

There was an awkward pause.

"No pigs were harmed in the uttering of that last sentence," Cameron quipped.

Everyone laughed, dissipating the tension. I joined in, but I couldn't help feeling that I'd been put in my place, along with the uncomfortable impression that I'd deserved it.

Later on, I was negotiating the house in search of food and got obstructed by a traffic jam in the narrow corridor.

"From what I've read, you don't actually need to test drugs on animals," I heard a woman say.

Was there no escaping these people? But I was still smarting from Maria's outburst in the garden, and I found myself pausing.

"New drugs are risky," her companion replied. I could tell he was a scientist by his jeans and promotional T-shirt from a biotech supply company, and looked forward to hearing how he'd set her straight. "Half the time we have no idea how people will respond."

"I've read that animals make poor predictors, and that there are loads of human volunteers who would be willing to take that chance."

"The liability issues alone would bring the system to a standstill," he replied.

"Still, if it's wrong to risk humans, why isn't it wrong to risk animals? Just because we're more intelligent doesn't necessarily give us the right."

The woman opens the scoring: one-nil.

"If that's truly the issue, why isn't there more fuss about killing animals for meat? Why aren't they bombing supermarkets?" A trace of frustration had bled into his tone. "There are a thousand times more animals affected by that industry."

He pulls one back.

She hesitated. "That's different. Most people believe that eating animals is natural: we've always done it. But testing medicines on them is a modern conceit. We shouldn't be stooping to torture."

"Ever been to an abattoir?" The man gave her a faint smile. "I understand it's not a very pleasant experience."

Two-one—our lad creeps into the lead!

"Whereas we have to restrict our experiments severely if there's even the slightest whiff of pain. I agree with that policy, but it sometimes means we have to stop before we've completely answered our questions."

This might be true for his own project, I thought, but the guy surely knew that some procedures, like giving mice heart attacks or strokes, were unavoidably painful and distressing.

The woman rubbed her nose reflectively. "What about that other option people always talk about, tissue culture? Doing it all in plastic dishes?"

The T-shirted guy shook his head. "Not good enough. I once had a brilliant idea, but it turned out to be a spectacular flop in mice. You can't get an immune response in a dish, I'm afraid." He paused dramatically. "Mice and humans are basically indistinguishable at the molecular level, and every single mouse I sacrifice brings us closer to desperately awaited and important cures."

"Do you really believe that?" I butted in, so amazed that I forgot where I was.

He stared at me coldly. "If you were a scientist, you'd know what I mean."

One of Christine's most often-quoted laws went: if you want to last at a party, *never sit down*. And sure enough, the minute I sank into the loose-sprung expanse of sofa, the first fatal stirrings of weariness came over me. It was only around midnight, so I had no excuse. Marcy's disdain for the geriatric nature of the post-doctoral state was probably justified.

A few minutes passed while I observed my fellow species, as an anthropologist might, engaging in routine human behaviour. Just as in my own field of study, communication networks seemed to be crucial: signals transmitted, signals received, signals ignored. There were layers of body language behind the crude verbal utterances, and still further beneath, fantastically subtle feats of pheromones: chemicals engaged in their own acts of molecular seduction.

A man shifted position among the dancers, bringing Maria into view. Her streamlined and unpretentious movements were appealing to watch, transmitting the idea that she wasn't dancing to please any-one except herself. Of course such heedless behaviour only made her more attractive, and several males were posturing around her, trying to capture her attention. But she remained stubbornly oblivious.

Just as I was formulating this thought, she turned her head my way, and when she caught me staring, she came over and joined me on the sofa. Gravity and the worn springs conspired to bounce her body into the same valley that my own occupied. I didn't correct the slight impropriety of her thigh resting against my leg, and neither did she.

"You're not fading out on us, are you?"

"Merely a temporary lull," I promised, breathing in her usual insistent perfume. Not to say that it was unpleasant, mind. I thought again about chemistry.

"Still friends?" she asked, after a slight hesitation.

"I can admit when I've been out-debated." In fact, I found her con-troversial stance compelling, but I wasn't about to admit it.

"You must think *I'm* a bit of a nutter." Her smile indicated that it wouldn't bother her in the slightest if I did.

"Absolutely." I paused. "No, seriously. Your points were valid and made me think."

She looked almost disappointed—maybe she'd been spoiling for a second round. Just then, the stereo fell silent. Someone put on a num-ber with a familiar saccharine introduction, inspiring good-natured groans and a few squeals of feminine approval.

"They're playing our song." Maria looked sidewise at me, and I belatedly recognized the soundtrack of our Cambridge kiss. "I insist on a rematch!"

She wrestled herself out of the sofa, took my hand in both of hers and started tugging. Laughing, I allowed her to lead me into the throng of couples swaying half ironically, half drunkenly. The fabric of her blouse felt smooth against the palms of my hands as she pressed against me in a distinctly less-than-oblivious manner. Over her shoul-der, I noticed a few of those aforementioned males glaring at me: no mistaking *those* signals.

"There's no easy way to ask this," Maria admitted, "but since I've had more than a few drinks, I'll just spit it out. Considering that Gina is seeing another man, have you given up on her yet?"

"Why are you so keen on this particular topic?"

"I should've thought that was obvious."

I sighed. "No, not officially."

"You're a bloody idiot." She stared at me, all traces of playfulness blown apart. "They're obviously *shagging*, man—shagging!" She pretended not to notice when I flinched. "Why don't you give up while you still have some dignity, like?"

My feet lapsed to a standstill. "I can't."

"Can't?" She stepped out of my inert arms and faced me squarely, an immobile obstacle in the flow of dancers. "It's simple: you just accept the truth and move on."

"Before she left, there was something." I was speaking more to myself than to her. "It may not be completely decided—I've got to wait and be sure."

"Wait and be sure? Maybe you can just *wait* until you're *sure* she's tried out every other available man on earth, and then she might just consider giving you a go!"

"That's enough." Stung, I backed away from her scorn and her flashing eyes. And then I saw Gina herself, scanning the crowd from the far end of the room—a hallucination that stubbornly persisted.

Maria turned to see what had distracted me.

"Oh, this is grand—I'll just leave you to it, lover-boy." Almost trembling with outrage, she stranded me on the floor.

Gina had turned her head towards me in the meantime. When our eyes met, a slow smile—conveying uncertainty more than any sense of happiness—took over her face, causing my breath to catch in my throat. We stared at each other for a few seconds, and then I approached, the noise and people on either side fading away as if she was standing at the end of a tunnel.

"Welcome back." I stopped a respectable distance away.

She acknowledged my greeting, studying me with those lunar-pale eyes, and made no move to come closer for a kiss. In the back of my head I could hear Maria's voice repeating the word *shagging!* like a playground taunt, and finally, I could internalize its truth.

"Are you just back?" I asked.

"I flew in late this afternoon. When I heard about the party, I thought I might as well check it out. I was hoping you'd be here, actually."

She sounded far from enthusiastic, and the air in my ears buzzed faintly as if the room were compressing.

"Are you here with Maria?" she asked.

"Among others."

"It looked like you were together just now." She could have been reading aloud from a cereal box.

"Well, we weren't—she's not the one I'm interested in."

For the first time, a trace of feeling passed over her face. "I've been meaning to talk to you about that. That's why I came, actually. I —"

"Don't," I said. "Please, not yet. Shall we sit down and catch up first?"

I led her over to the couch. She sat down next to me, bemused but unprotesting, and the springs didn't do their let's-get-cosy trick this time.

"Tell me how the virus production went," I said.

She looked at me in surprise, shrugged. "It was a success. The FRIP gene integrated on our first attempt, and when we tested the new combination vaccine in cell culture, we could see both proteins, my Verase and his FRIP."

The contrast between the banality of our conversation and the unacknowledged emotions running just underneath made everything feel unreal.

"Any toxicity?"

"Nothing," she said. "The cells were fine."

"But did you test whether the new vaccine actually worked?"

She paused. "We did a few pilot tissue culture infections, and the combination vaccine still shut down Vera Fever Virus. But of course in the absence of an intact immune system, FRIP isn't switched on, so we couldn't evaluate its contribution."

That wasn't strictly true—surely Rouyle had access to the appropriate peptide analogues. Before I could mention this, she added, "And then there's the species problem: even live mice wouldn't produce immune factors similar enough to the human FRIP activator."

"So you'll have to use a more appropriate animal model to get the full answer."

She looked away, fingers fiddling with the zip of her jacket.

"What?" I prompted.

"There aren't going to be any animal trials," she said at last. "We're going straight to Phase I clinical trials."

"You're *what?*" I stared at her. "You're going to infect *humans* with this combination virus after—what—a couple of tests in cell culture?

Aside from being ethically questionable, that wouldn't be legal in Europe or the States, would it?"

"We're not doing the trial in Europe or America. We're doing it in Africa."

I gaped, speechless for several seconds. "Where there are no pesky laws to stop you?"

"No, where people are dying in droves from Vera Fever!" She met my eye again, forced her voice to soften. "Listen, Andy, I know exactly how you're feeling because I've been through it all myself, but you've got to take certain things into account: Richard's solo FRIP virus has already passed its Phase I, and my original vaccine succeeded in mice."

"But —"

"The new combination vaccine was fine in cultured *human* cells, and was still able to shut down Vera Fever. Therefore, they concluded that the combination is ready for a limited Phase I."

"And do you agree...honestly, Gina?"

"It doesn't matter what I believe," she admitted bitterly. "It's going to happen whether I like it or not."

"So you did try to stop it!"

She nodded, failing to hide her mounting agitation. "I've lodged a formal complaint with Geniaxis. But I'm sure it will never leave the Director's office. If I make too much fuss, they might take me off the project altogether. As it stands now, at least I've got some power to express my opinions."

For all the good that seems to have done so far. "And what about Rouyle?"

"He knows how I feel, but I've been asked to trust him on this, and considering his experience in such matters, I have acquiesced." She looked down, but not before her expression betrayed that their discussion hadn't been quite as civilized as she was making out.

"Anyway, it's happening, so I've just got to believe in my work," she said, head still bowed.

"It's not your work I'm worried about."

She raised her head, but instead of the angry retort I was expecting, I saw the shine of tears.

"Hey, what's this?" I said, surprised.

She just pressed her lips together, and before I knew what I was doing, I had gathered her up in my arms and she'd started crying.

"I'm scared, Andy." I could hardly hear her words. "He's so driven, and he won't *listen* to me. I'm afraid it's gone completely out of control, and once it starts rolling, no one will be able to call it back."

I didn't know what to say: she was right to be scared, so I wasn't going to utter meaningless platitudes. Instead, I just stroked her hair as her tears stilled, as her reserve thawed with every ragged breath, inhaling the warmth and the scent of her. Somewhere in the process, our comfort began to evolve into desire—and it was definitely mutual.

She clung to me, conflicting signals coming off her like radiation, before making a strangled sound and pulling away. Her face was streaked with tears and her eyes looked darker now, almost wild.

"This isn't...I have to go!" She struggled from the sofa and pushed violently through the crowd.

I collapsed back, stunned to immobility. A few moments later, Christine appeared, perched on the arm of the sofa and shoved a plastic tumbler full of clear liquid under my nose.

"It's gin—the only strong stuff left," she said. "I just happened to be walking by, and I couldn't help noticing."

I took a few gulps, the fiery trail imparting an after-image of numbness to the room. She put a hand on my shoulder, not saying anything, but the question hung between us and gathered momentum.

"She's chosen Rouyle over me," I said eventually.

"It didn't look like that from my angle."

I glanced up and was struck by the intense look waiting there.

"It's hopeless, Chris." I tried to shrug off her hand.

"Is it?" Her fingers squeezed my shoulder, resisting dislodgement. "Rouyle had her to himself for a whole month. She's only been around you five minutes, and look how far back she's slipped already."

I just shook my head, not wanting to hear.

"Why don't you go after her?" she said. "You might still catch her."

I just kept on shaking my head, and then she said, "Can I tell you something your friend Dan mentioned in Cambridge while you were in the gents?"

"I can't believe you two actually discussed me behind my back!"

Christine continued as if I hadn't spoken. "He said the old Andy O'Hara wouldn't have let another man steal his woman without a fight."

I fumed, refusing to comment.

"What's changed?" she persisted softly.

After a minute of silence, she sighed and turned her attention forward. We both watched the dancers for awhile, not saying anything more. I could vaguely make out Maria getting heavily physical with some guy, neither of them bothering with the formality of dancing at all. I didn't feel bad noticing this, but, then again, I wasn't feeling much of anything.

15 Under Protest

I knew how bad I looked by the expression on Christine's face.

"Sorry, there isn't any milk," she said, passing me a mug of tea. "Well, at least none still in liquid form. I'll find the others."

When I finished blinking, she'd already vanished. Sipping the harsh brew, I slumped down further at Julie's dining room table and rubbed the skin on the side of my face, still imbedded with grit and embossed with carpet-like indentations. I couldn't believe we were still here: how had that happened? When had night become day, and vertical, horizontal? The post-party carnage was spread out before me: unconscious bodies, empties stacked on every available surface, the stench of stale alcohol and a fresh snowfall of fag ends caught in the smudged daylight oozing through the French doors.

Eventually, Christine mustered up Cameron and Paul, dazed but intact and nursing their mugs protectively.

"Where's Maria?" I fished out my shoes from under a nearby chair.

"She left around three with that bloke," Christine said. "I imagine their cabbie probably got an eyeful, the way they were at it."

I avoided everyone's eye and concentrated on fumbling with my laces.

It wasn't until we'd ventured outside that someone asked, "Does anyone actually know where we are?" We all stared at each other, shaking our heads and blinking in the sunlight.

"Don't panic, gentlemen." Christine whipped out a battered copy of *The A–Z* from her handbag. "We'll walk to the nearest corner and take a reading."

I fell in a few paces behind the others, mind filling with the previous night's occurrences. Everything pivoted around Gina, the crushing rejection I hadn't let her deliver, the accidental moment of passion we'd shared on the sofa. Despite Christine's assurance, I didn't take the evidence of Gina's desire for me seriously—she'd just been confused by her unhappiness. And I knew very well that it was possible to be attracted to someone without loving them: my mixed feelings towards Maria were a good example. Walking down the pavement and breathing in the crisp melancholy odour of geraniums and dried leaves, I felt the relief that endings bring, even unhappy ones.

"Right, lads." Christine stopped at the corner, flipping pages into an unrumpled section of the booklet. "This is Stanmore."

When Cameron groaned, she said, "For Christ's sake, it's Zone Five, not Siberia."

"We're practically in Hertfordshire!"

"I hate waking up outside my own post-code," Paul muttered.

The noise of amplified shouting and the subsequent surge of crowd response reached our ears long before we'd even turned off the high street towards the Centre.

"Oh, joy," Cameron said. "I'd forgotten about the animal rights protest."

Paul rubbed his head. "If that megaphone gets near my hangover, I'm going to shove it somewhere interesting."

The street outside the main entrance was seething with people. The area had been cordoned off from traffic, and though there were a few empty police vans parked discreetly in the Centre car park, their actual owners were not in evidence. Placards bobbed above the chanting crowd depicting gruesome photographs of cats, monkeys and dogs (none of which were actually studied in the Centre) being subjected to various torturous practices that weren't ever performed in our building. Some were clearly old photos recycled onto shiny card, because the activities they displayed had been outlawed in Britain years ago. On the fringes, men were loading up an ITN News van with dismantled equipment. Next to it, a local newsreader sat on the Smoker's Wall, touching up her make-up and sharing a furtive cigarette with one of the crewmen.

"Give the scientists a taste of their own medicine!" a woman shouted into the megaphone. She was standing at the top of the steps, peppy cheerleader's smile clashing badly with the bloodstained lab coat.

Her disciples roared in fevered response.

"Maybe we can slip in through the back loading dock?" I was put off by the sheer venom of the demonstration.

"Please," Christine said. "This is our place of employment and we have the legal right to gain access to it. Besides, these sorts are all absolute invertebrates."

"Invertebrates?" Paul could occasionally play the role of straight man, especially towards attractive females.

"Spineless," she explained dismissively, moving out.

I exchanged looks with Cameron and Paul—they didn't appear to share her opinion either, but we followed her determined back closely. Knowing Christine, she could easily get herself into trouble here.

We kept our eyes down and sauntered into the throng. Maria's scathing remarks from the previous night came back to me then. Probably I had been self-righteous and condescending to the bohemian woman about GM foods, indulging in a knee-jerk response, even showing off. Frankly, I didn't have a strong opinion either for or against that issue.

But animal research was another matter altogether. I was vehemently against the use of animals in the cosmetics industry, and had recently decided that doing studies on higher primates was wrong— any species that could communicate with humans in complicated sign language didn't even belong in a zoo. Yet while I was fond of animals, and absolutely hated killing them, I would never hesitate to prioritize human life over that of a mouse when it came to developing medicines for serious diseases. Testing the finished product was only one application that animals were useful for. More importantly, the initial idea for a drug had to be grounded on intricate information about how intact bodies actually work. And there was no question that basic animal research provided fundamental knowledge culminating in important cures—especially in my field, where the study of animal tumour viruses had sparked the field of modern cancer genetics.

In the abstract, my position probably was immoral, but I could never forget the one key life I had lost. My father's malignant melanoma had been particularly vicious and sadly resistant to all known forms of therapy. The day he died, there were probably hundreds of new therapies that could not be attempted because they had been delayed by the glacial bureaucracy of obtaining test animals, a bureaucracy aggravated in part by fear of these sorts of protestors. It was hard to stay *abstract* in the face of that.

As we reached the Centre steps and began pushing our way up in a tight phalanx, it soon became apparent to the hive mentality of the crowd that we didn't belong. The almost tangible sensation of coming into focus—predator spotting prey—was unsettling.

"Heads up, everyone," Cameron breathed. There was a pause as the hoard seemed to inhale expectantly, then a mighty roar broke out and hands started grabbing us from all sides.

"Murderers!" A woman bore down on us, face blanched with hatred, but the rest of her accusations broke up in another surge of crowd noise. I attempted to mount the next step, but a man held me back, flapping a pamphlet in front of my eyes. I could vaguely make out a rabbit covered with electrodes.

"I've never experimented on a rabbit in my life," I said. "I don't even *work* with animals here—I'm just trying to do my bit for cancer."

"But you *use* antibodies made in rabbits and other animals, don't you?" he asked.

I was thrown off by his knowledge. "Yes, but I didn't personally —"

"Hey — it's you! I knew there was something suspicious about you!" It was Madame Branch Secretary herself, bulldozing through the crowd behind and trying to follow me up the steps. "You misled me!"

I whirled away and crashed into Cameron, who had paused to address a sandwich-munching protester.

"Do you realize how many yeast organisms were murdered to make that bread?" he was asking conversationally.

My grin froze half-formed when I noticed a suspicious huddle of people off to one side. Despite the chaos, my ears homed in on a familiar voice issuing from within, scared but defensive.

Gina.

Breaking away from the others, I shoved aside a few clinging activists and strode up to the pack. It was indeed Gina, backed against the wall, face pale but otherwise defiant. One of the men had her by the arm, emphasizing his words with an occasional rough shake. A man bearing the unmistakable aura of leadership was waving a piece of paper at her: an enlarged photocopy of her company ID card.

"This is definitely you, Dr Kraymer," this man said, towering over her, "and we know all about the mice. All *one hundred of them*, to be precise. And we know where you live."

"Leave her alone!" I called out authoritatively.

The knot of protestors turned around. When Gina saw me, her eyes widened with relief. I became aware of the steadying presence of Cameron on one side and of Christine and Paul on the other. However, after the leader had measured us up, he didn't seem to be impressed.

"Chris, go and get Security," I said out of the corner of my mouth, "while everyone else is distracted."

She nodded, promptly melting into the quiet and expectant crowd.

"This woman has murdered hundreds of mice in the past year alone," the leader declared with a sneer. He was scrawny, but there was a virulent look in his eye that I didn't underestimate. "That's sacred, innocent life, taken in vain."

"I'm sure the thousands of children in Africa who will someday receive her vaccine, and be spared a painful death as a result, would disagree with you," I informed him in a clear, carrying voice.

The crowd stirred uneasily in response.

"That's irrelevant!" the leader said.

"Have you had all your inoculations?" I kept my tone respectful: if they wanted reasonable discourse, I'd give it to them. "Smallpox was a bit before your time, and the millions of lives saved by that vaccine, but what about rubella, pertussis, polio, mumps, tetanus, measles? Do you have any idea what the quality—or length—of your life would have been without medical research? Ever had an antibiotic? Or popped a Neurofen Plus? They're all the fruits of animal research, too, whether you like to admit it or not."

The leader drew himself up to reply, features sharpening in fury. Behind him, Gina looked directly into my eyes and began to smile, a slow, dazzling smile that made everything else go momentarily out of focus.

"We'll take it from here, lad."

I felt a hand on my shoulder and turned to find Eddie, the Centre's head of security, his habitual cheery grin tinged with feral anticipation. While certainly an imposing figure, the three Metropolitan policemen he'd brought with him didn't look like they were going to tolerate any resistance either.

"If you'll just take your hands off the lady and step aside," one of the cops ordered.

I tried to move in to speak to Gina, but Eddie held me back.

"You lot have to go inside now. We'll look after Dr Kraymer for you, don't you worry."

I caught one last glimpse of Gina before I was tugged away into the safety of the building.

When Paul and I entered the lab, everyone burst into applause.

"Thought you were both dead, vivisected by protestors," Magritte said, looking theatrically at her watch. It was about quarter to twelve.

"She's just joking." Kathy's eyes were glowing. "We've already heard how you knocked those terrorists unconscious, Andy! Like a knight in shining armour!"

Paul and I exchanged knowing glances: as usual, the rumours had spread throughout the Centre and had seriously mutated in the process, all in the brief time it took to get questioned by the police in the lobby.

"Nice shirts, you two," Marcy said. "They look strangely familiar, somehow."

"At least you get here in time for my presentation," Helmut said matter-of-factly.

"Presentation?" My residual high plummeted when I remembered what day it was. After two hours of sleep, a persistent hangover, no breakfast and braving a pack of hostile activists, the last thing I needed was one of Helmut's tortuous research-in-progress talks.

"Lab meeting, twelve o'clock Thursday, same as usual," Magritte said. "Late night or no late night. Shining armour or no shining armour."

I was sitting at my desk later, going over the notes I'd taken during Helmut's presentation. As I stared at the page of scribbles, an undeniable fact was starting to solidify. It was one of those quirky coincidences that often happens in science: an important clue issuing from an unexpected avenue. In this case, the insight had come from my own labmate's experiments, which pointed towards another flaw in

Rouyle's science. Only this time, it wasn't just a minor error—it might render the FRIP protein useless altogether as a cofactor in Gina's gene therapy strategy against Vera Fever. Gina, I was suddenly convinced, had a serious problem on her hands.

On any other occasion, such a realization would have propelled me to gather together Helmut and Magritte, along with whoever else might be standing around. We'd thrash through the evidence, throw a mix of facts, intuition and wild speculation into the pot and stir it into a manageable theory. Helmut would be his usual cautious self, reluctant to believe in his own data, while I would push forward my opinions more boldly, and Magritte would act as low-key mediator, occasional contributing the key idea that would help the entire soup hang together—or blast it into vapour.

But this wasn't academic science, mere abstract musings into the secrets of signal transduction. This was the real world: an international collaboration to develop a vaccine that would soon be tested in human patients, a world where microscopic details could have serious consequences. There was big money associated with the entire endeavour as well as reputations. I could certainly discuss the result in the abstract, but I didn't dare betray the nature or depth of my interest.

"What's the matter, Andy? Are you going to lose your lunch too, like Paul?"

I glanced up at Kathy's round, face anxious.

"Some of us actually know how to handle their alcohol," I retorted. "I'm still bothered by that odd result in Helmut's presentation, that's all." Kathy, I reasoned, was hardly a threat.

She looked down at the drawings in my notebook. "I'm afraid that part of the discussion went over my head."

"Take a seat." In the fluid apprenticeship of modern science, looking after the development of students was a group effort. "Do you remember Richard Rouyle's seminar, when he explained that FRIP was like a postal worker moonlighting as a volunteer firefighter at weekends?" As much as I hated the man, I couldn't deny that the analogy was illustrative.

"Of course," she said. "It wasn't *that* over my head. I just don't get why Helmut's peptides didn't —"

"That's what I'm trying to explain, Kath. So FRIP acts like a growth factor most of the time, passing along signals that instruct the cell to divide. But when certain sorts of viruses attack, it can double as an *ad hoc* firefighter, transmitting a warning message to a protein called TRAP, which in turn destroys the virus's genetic material."

"I already knew that too."

"Today's youth are too clever by half," I said, and she stuck her tongue out at me. "And of course Rouyle's FRIP protein is just one member of a small family of related proteins."

"Including Helmut's SLIP," she said loyally.

"And not to forget CLIP, which the evil Stan Fortuna is more interested in. But here's the key thing: we always thought that, because these family members were so similar, they must behave in roughly the same way."

"Why have three versions, then?"

"Well, imagine that FRIP works for the Royal Mail, SLIP for DHL, and CLIP, for Federal Express. The basic function is the same, but they've got different speeds and modes of transport. More importantly for clearing up your confusion, they might behave differently in different types of cells."

"Mmmm. So that's why you were going on about the fibroblasts versus the neuronal cells."

"Exactly. We focus on the postal stuff in this lab, but as a routine control, Helmut tested the antiviral signalling function of SLIP in two of our standard cell lines—fibroblasts, originally isolated from skin, and neuronal cells, derived from brain tissue. He fully expected to see evidence that FRIP was turning on TRAP in both."

"I see the problem now," she said excitedly. "It went wrong: SLIP switched on the TRAP protein in the fibroblast cells, but not in the neuronal cells." She paused, thinking furiously. "Then you asked him, how did he know that SLIP was actually active at all in the neuronal cells, and he said...he knew the experiment had worked because SLIP was still passing on the growth signal."

I smiled at her. "Well done. SLIP could deliver the mail in neuronal cells but not put out any blazes."

"I'm going to go write this down in my book," Kathy said. "Thanks a lot, Andy."

My good humour faded as I looked back down at my own notes. Helmut had dismissed the anomaly as some uninteresting technical error—maybe a database search could tell me more.

I turned to the computer and accessed PubMed, but the results were disturbing: whereas the growth-regulating "postal" properties of the FRIP family were well-established in many cell types, including neurons, there was not a single report that their antiviral "firefighting" effects had ever been tested in cells derived from the brain. And such neuronal cells were often the exception to the rule, biochemically speaking. This was of more than just academic importance, because Gina's vaccine would have to be functional in the neuronal cells of the patient's brain in order to be effective.

I sauntered over to Helmut's desk, where he was busy filing away his notes from the talk.

"I'm still hung up on that weird result," I told him. "Could I see the original film?"

"Certainly." He flipped back a few pages in his notebook and detached a piece of blue transparent film from the page. I held it up to the light, inspecting the lanes of the gel, labelled in his precise script, and the various black horizontal bands underneath.

I pointed. "And this one here, lane three...that's PC12s after peptide treatment, right? Where there's no TRAP phosphorylation? You're sure about this?"

"Absolutely. Of course I have done it only once, and I could possibly have switched the tubes or something, but that is not like me."

"No, you're right," I said. Helmut was careful to a degree that struck me as obsessive-compulsive. "You realize this goes against the dogma."

Helmut nodded. "In fact, it is a pity I did not have this result when Richard Rouyle was here. I would have enjoyed bantering with him about it. You know, gnawing on the fat."

"Indeed." I returned the film and walked back to my desk.

There was someone else who might know more. I started up my e-mail, and while the ancient laptop considered the pros and cons of my request, I rummaged in my file drawer, pulled out the Cambridge Symposium programme and flipped through the participants list until I had located Sandra's e-mail address.

I sent her a light-hearted message, telling her I had a bet with Helmut about the behaviour of FRIP-like proteins in neuronal cells and asking if she'd ever explored that particular issue with CLIP. I was afraid she would be too worried about helping the enemy to answer, but there was no way I could reveal the true reason for my interest.

It was nearly midnight before I had capped the last tube and stowed my samples in the freezer. I hadn't found a moment to check my e-mail since I'd sent the message to Sandra.

My Inbox was full of tantalizing mail.

From:	Date:	Subject:
msoconnor@geniaxis.com	Today 14:45	apologies
e.mitchell@rcc.sec.ac.uk	Today 15:02	commendation
glkraymer@geniaxis.com	Today 18:50	my hero
breckenridge@metzger.de	Today 20:17	you lose, dude
dan.lamont@neuronet.ac.uk	Today 23:09	Memories...

I couldn't decide which to read first, so I just took them in order.

Dear Andy,

Well what can I say??? I was a tad drunk & stepped way out of line. I hope you'll forgive me. On more sober reflection I'm afraid my original impression that you're acting like a bloody idiot still stands, but it's your life & I'd no right to interfere. I suppose your loyalty is even admirable, if misguided. Anyway, I ended up going home with a right plonker & had a miserable time. He had nothing on you.

Still friends (again!!)???

xxx,

Maria

p.s. Heard you wrestled a few activists to the ground at the protest this morning. Did G. swoon into your arms???

dr o'hara,

just writing to thank you for your help today in standing up for dr kraymer. it was a brave thing to do. anyway, thought you might want to know that i nominated you for an official commendation with Admin. don't know if anything will come of it, but...

cheers,

eddie mitchell, rcc security

Hi Andy,

You have no idea how relieved I was to see you this morning. They hadn't actually hurt me, but the atmosphere was
definitely getting tense. Who knows what might've happened
if you hadn't shown up - so a million thanks. Also your
speech was very touching. I wanted to go in and find you,
but I was hustled away to the police station! By the time
they got through with me, I decided just to go home (I'm
writing this from my study).

Also...I wanted to apologize for acting so crazy last night.
We should talk about this sometime, but not by e-mail. I
value our friendship, and don't want this to get in the way.

Gina

✦ ✦ ✦

Andy,

You owe Helmut ten pounds, however much that is! There IS
a difference in the antiviral response of FRIP-like kinases in neuronal cells, even though the growth signalling
part of the pathway is still intact. At least, I can say
the same about CLIP kinase in a primary sympathetic neuronal cell situation. But given the similarities in function among the FRIP family, SLIP probably wouldn't
phosphorylate TRAP in neuronal cells either. I've never
looked at FRIP myself, and I don't remember reading if
Rouyle's lab has either, but if two out of the three...

Please keep this info to yourself - I'm already telling
you against my better judgement.

By the way, you now owe me a SECOND drink.

catch ya later,

Sandra

✦ ✦ ✦

Andy, mate!

I *finally* remembered where I'd seen that bloke before,
the one who was putting the moves on your woman at Cambridge. He was a member of the academic department where I
did a summer stint, back when I was trying to decide whether
to bail out of chem and move into the molecular neuro field.

It was in Estonia, believe it or not. I don't know if I mentioned my time in Tartu, but to cut a long story short, I
was going out with this Estonian woman at the time and I
thought I could combine a summer of romance and research.
It turned out to be a good project, despite the exotic lo-
cale and the political/infrastructural instability! (the
project lasted longer than the girlfriend, actually.) This
was a long time ago, back in 1992. Anyway, he was working
down the corridor but was forced to leave under dubious
circumstances. It seemed like there was a cover-up. Anyway,
I always thought it was a stupid reason, like he slept with
the professor's wife, but I remember there were other theories, rumours of scientific misconduct and so forth. I was
just a student volunteer at the time and I didn't speak the
language, so I didn't know what was going on. But I've got
the e-mail address of the man I was working under at the
time. We're still in touch, he's a cool bloke, and if anyone would know what happened, it'd be him. I don't know if
you still care, but I just thought I'd let you know.

Stay in touch this time, yeah?

Dan

p.s. oh, nearly forgot the address, it's raidula@ut.pui.ee.
The name's Raim Aidula.

I stared at the screen, thoughts whirling. Then I dashed off a barrage of messages, only lingering carefully over two of them:

Dear Gina,

Any time you need rescuing, I'm happy to be of service. It
was no big deal, and I'm glad nothing serious happened.
About last night...please don't worry about that either.
I want you to know that I understood what you were trying
to tell me at the party, and, disappointed as I am, I accept it. There: now there's no need for a discussion,
which would be painful for both of us.

Look out for yourself...those activists are a nasty piece
of work.

Your friend

Andy

❖ ❖ ❖

From: a.ohara@rcc.cmb.ac.uk
To: raidula@ut.pui.ee
Subject: a mutual acquaintance

171

Dear Dr Aidula,

You don't know me, but I'm a post-doc in Magritte Valorius's lab in London and an old friend of Dan Lamont, who once worked with you in Tartu. This is a bit of a strange request — and also I'd ask that you keep it confidential — but I'm interested in Dr Richard Rouyle. He has become involved scientifically and personally with a friend of mine, and I have a few questions about him. Anything you might be able to tell me — in particular, the details surrounding his departure from your department — would be greatly appreciated.

Yours sincerely,

Dr Andrew O'Hara

16   *Several Visits*
(One of Them from My Subconscious)

I was sitting in my favourite place in the Centre—the top-floor library—at my favourite time—after hours. There were rarely people around this time of the evening, but on Fridays especially, everyone had fled to the pub and I was almost assured of privacy. The main lights were dimmed and I was installed on one of the sofas in the periodicals room, in a cone of halogen light from one of the reading lamps, flipping through the latest issues of the scientific journals. Heavy rain pelted against the windows, shrinking the room into a cosy universe.

Even though most of the key journals were available online, I often had the urge to flip through articles the old-fashioned way. Sometimes I scribbled a few token notes on my pad, but usually I just read for the sheer pleasure of it. There was something satisfying about the feel of the glossy pages beneath my fingers, the distinctive smell of the binding, even the incongruous adverts, with their bizarre mixture of 21st century marketing and sheer nerdiness:

> *Don't let your DNA fragments play hard-to-get! Purification is a breeze with our UltraEez-500 column—because your samples deserve the very best!*

But on this evening, I was preoccupied by several of the e-mail messages I'd received yesterday evening, primarily the one from Dan. But I agreed that it wasn't safe to assume anything sinister behind Rouyle's dismissal. People can get fired from academic departments for a variety of reasons—lack of political support or funding, imprudent romantic alliances and so forth. And no matter what the actual cause had been, there were bound to be a wide range of rumours, ranging from the staid to the ridiculous, propagated at the time. So without further details, I shouldn't presume that scientific misconduct had occurred, let alone run to Gina with the story. In the event of a simple explanation, she would be furious with me.

I had a similar feeling about Sandra's information. While it did suggest that Rouyle's FRIP gene was never going to work in Gina's vaccine, definitive proof was still lacking. Both Helmut's and Sandra's results, although complementary, were preliminary and unpublished. More importantly, neither Helmut nor Sandra had studied FRIP itself, but only its related cousins, SLIP and CLIP. It was still quite conceivable that FRIP was an exception. Besides, even if FRIP was useless as an antiviral messenger in the brain, it was always possible that Rouyle was innocently ignorant—that he hadn't ever tested FRIP in cells derived from the nervous system. This might be a useful weapon for Gina to force an animal trial for the combination virus, but it didn't implicate the man in anything more serious than lack of adequate preparation.

I tossed aside one unarresting journal and picked up the next one on the stack—the latest *Nature*. After failing again to lose myself in any of the research reports, I flipped restlessly to the back section and skimmed the job advertisements: a traditional post-doctoral time-waster.

A colourful square finally managed to snag my attention:

Melanex

Transforming Theories into Cures

We are a small biotechnology company focused on discovering drug targets against malignant melanoma and related cancers. Our intellectual property portfolio is extensive, and we are currently seeking enthusiastic young scientists at all levels to expand our initial findings and join the quest to propel our knowledge of basic biological processes into rapid, intelligent cures for this serious disease...

Something about the slogan—probably the heartless creation of a highly-paid PR agency—nevertheless resonated. Maybe if it had been any other disease but melanoma, I might have turned the page. Instead, stumbling across this advertisement put months of abstract consideration about leaving academia to the test for the first time.

And almost the first thing that occurred to me was that I wished my father were around to consult. He'd always had strong opinions about my career path, even though he'd been too busy to advise me as much as I'd wished. The perspective that he could never give—the wisdom of a son working on the very disease that had killed his father—was the one I found the most crucial. I was aware of a muted feeling of emptiness that I would never know his opinion, on this question or any other.

When the prickly sensation didn't go away, I looked up from the page to find Gina poised in the shadowy entrance to the periodicals room. We both jumped involuntarily.

"You've got to stop sneaking up on me." I couldn't help smiling at her expression: as if she'd been caught raiding the biscuit jar. I wondered how long she'd been observing me—and what emotions had been evident on my own face.

"I'm sorry," she said, still hanging back. "I was trying to decide whether to disturb you."

"Don't be silly," I assured her, putting the journal down. "It's only science."

She smiled at this, and when she reached the perimeter of light, she transformed into vivid colour, flushed skin and burnished hair radiating vibrancy. Despite what I had written in that e-mail, the mere sight of her made my heart stall momentarily.

I shoved aside the pile of journals and she dropped easily beside me.

"I've been looking for you everywhere—I even poked my head into the Henry. Christine said you might be hiding up here."

"Christine has been studying my behavioural patterns for quite some time now."

"Has she made any progress yet?"

"Very funny."

She was quiet a moment, a smile still lingering on her lips.

"So what was it you wanted?" I prompted.

"Two things..." She looked sideways at me, picked up the journal I'd discarded, put it down straightaway. "About your e-mail—I didn't deserve to get let off so easily. But...it's not easy to talk about, so I appreciate that you already seem to..." Her words began to spill out. "I mean, you're being very understanding and kind, and the fact that you don't want me to explain makes it almost too..."

I cleared my throat. "You're talking an awful lot about something we've decided not to talk about."

She flashed me an intense look that I couldn't interpret. "Okay. But it doesn't seem fair to leave it without at least telling you that my decision didn't mean that I didn't...that I don't..."

"I have a pretty good idea where you're coming from. You don't have to explain anything—really. As far as I'm concerned, the case is closed."

She stared at her shoes, looking rather sad for someone who had presumably sorted out her love life to full advantage. As for me, despite my calm exterior, I felt a terrible sense of falling, so far downward that she seemed to be shrinking to a tiny point in the distance.

"The second thing?" I reminded her, keeping my voice even.

"Oh." A layer of recalled anxiety altered her features yet again. "I'm afraid I want to commandeer you for another brainstorming session...tonight, if at all possible?"

A dose of adrenaline, microscopically administered.

"I'm up here killing time while my gel is running." I glanced at my watch. "Then it just has to be set up to blot overnight. So...I could be finished by eight."

"That's great. I really need to talk to you about the project." She looked over her shoulder, relief dissolving into nervousness again.

"Back to the John Snow?" I asked.

"It's more...sensitive this time. I was thinking we could go back to my apartment. I can cook dinner."

It doesn't mean anything, I told myself sternly after she went away.

Gina was still laughing across the table in the aftermath of my absurd story about Leeds. I liked the way she threw herself into a laugh with no apology or restraint, the way her mouth and eyes retained a glimmer a while after it had ended. We'd been having one of those free-ranging discussions involving frequent digressions, in turn sparking good-natured arguments about what the original point had been. It seemed to me that I was seeing the original version—the woman who had flirted with me in the radioactive annex, wept over the condemned mouse, taken my arm in the streets of Covent Garden and told me with childlike delight about the plague victims under Blackheath—and not the cool doppelgänger Rouyle had swapped in her place.

The remains of the impromptu dinner were spread out between us, and we had nearly finished an excellent bottle of wine.

"It sounds like you have such a different academic system over here, at least for the biomedical sciences," she said. "Don't take this the wrong way, but I think it's amazing how well you turned out after only a four-year PhD."

"And I have no idea how you could've survived six, even in an environment as pleasant as Berkeley. But it must've made the next step easier with that much preparation."

Gina looked down at her plate, pushed a bit of salad around with her fork.

"Have I said something wrong?" I asked.

"Actually, I had a hard time during my first post-doc."

"Dead-end project?" As soon as I said the words, I recalled the contrary evidence of her non-stop publication record.

She looked up, eyes searching mine. "Actually, I spent every moment I could working on it. I used to arrive at the lab at five in the morning, leave at ten at night. Sometimes I didn't go home at all."

"That's crazy."

Her face was devoid of all emotion. "It was a convenient escape from what was going on in my private life. I published five papers in two years."

I was caught mute, unable to exhale my last routine breath for a moment.

"I'm so sorry, Gina."

"Nothing running away to England didn't solve," she said shortly. "Listen, I'm going to get seconds—you want anything else?"

When Gina returned, there seemed to be an unspoken agreement to forget about the previous thread of conversation. Though our earlier good humour eventually returned, we focused more on concepts—politics, music, cultural differences between Americans and the British—than on personal details.

When we'd finished dessert and Gina disappeared into the kitchen to make coffee, I stood up to stretch my legs. Keen to capitalize on this rare glimpse into Gina's behind-the-scenes existence, I wandered around the large main space that served as both dining room and lounge, cataloguing details with a scientist's eye. It was clear that her salary was more comfortable than my own: she'd gone for real quality over the mainstay Swedish design that most post-docs opted for.

She had a massive digital music collection running off a state-of-the-art computer, which I approved of, and an even more massive assortment of fiction. But I was disappointed to see no photographs, no traces of family or friends or much solid evidence about the things she cherished in life. It was as if the environment she'd chosen to display to strangers was a reflection of her characteristic guardedness.

"Coffee's ready," she called from the kitchen, and I hastened back to my chair. When we had settled down to our steaming mugs, I watched her play with the lid of the sugar bowl for a few moments, the nervousness that had infected her in the library slowly returning.

"Why don't you just tell me what's wrong, Gina?"

Her candid eyes assessed me for a few moments, and then she began to nod.

"I didn't know where to begin," she confessed. "And there's no confidentiality agreement this time. What I'm proposing is essentially mutiny, so it doesn't matter how many forms get signed—I'm fired for sure if this gets out."

"Well." I paused as the implications registered. "You can trust me not to say anything."

"That's why I've asked you here. It's not just the pressure of having no one to talk to—although that's been considerable. I also think you can actively help me."

"Hopefully nothing illegal," I joked.

Her expression dared me to contradict her. "I'm going to perform my own animal trial on the combination virus."

I choked on my coffee, then finally spluttered, "That's *extremely* illegal!"

She clamped her lips together, but a flush appeared on her cheeks.

"How can you possibly get away with it?" I demanded. "It's difficult for me to do even a simple experiment on the sly without Magritte finding out. Believe me, I've tried. And that's just a couple of tubes, hidden away in the freezer—where are you going to hide all the mice?"

"We're not as closely supervised as you might imagine." Despite her agitation, she kept her voice serene. "I'm performing an authorized trial on a number of mice currently, so no one's going to notice a few extra cages. But I'm still left with the problem of the species requirement for FRIP activation...and that's where you come in."

"Me?"

"I did a PubMed search on you a while ago," —she hurried on before I could comment— "and I know you did your PhD work on immune system signalling in mice...in SCID/pbl mice, to be precise."

"That's right. But I —"

"Just listen." Her eyes were fierce, defensive. "We've already discussed that it's useless to test the combination virus in a normal mouse, because in our patients, the *human* immune system has to activate the FRIP in response to viral infection. It's not even clear that higher primate test animals would respond identically to humans— but human FRIP will be inert in a regular mouse for sure."

I nodded, finally seeing where she was leading. SCID mice are a mutant laboratory strain unable to muster a natural immune response to any infectious challenge. A while back, scientists had discovered that these deficient mice could be transplanted with human tissues, which would flourish inside the mice and, in many cases, react in a human way. And as Gina was well aware, you could gain insights from studying an animal's response that were impossible to glean—or even predict—from a thousand tissue culture experiments.

"So you want to use SCID/pbl mice for your trial," I said. "That's a great idea."

"And I want you to get me some from your old lab," she said.

I put down my mug. "You what?"

"I'm desperate," she said simply.

I broke away from her potent gaze and took another sip of my coffee, trying to keep myself sensible. The stupendously complex laws around animal experimentation, though grumbled over by my colleagues, were in place for a good reason: to ensure that the animals were treated as humanely as possible. And enforcement of these laws was notoriously strict.

"That's a fairly drastic request," I said at last. "The animal folks in my old university are totally by-the-book, and I could never persuade them to shift some cages without the proper authorizations. You know I think very highly of you, but hacking into an animal facility in the middle of the night and stealing some mice is out of the question. I mean, I could go to prison for that."

"Can't you request them for your own research, all above-board?" She had a pleading edge to her voice that I had never heard before.

"It's out of the question, Gina. For starters, Magritte would have to rubber-stamp everything, and I'm afraid I can't invent a compelling reason for such mice in my own line of research. And second—haven't you ordered animals from outside the Centre before?"

She shook her head. "We've got our own colonies."

"Otherwise you'd know that the Home Office takes ages to authorize new projects. Christine once waited five months for a shipment of transgenic mice, and those were only coming from down the road at the Chester-Beatty. I don't think you have that kind of time."

"These things are much quicker in America." She was struggling to control her disappointment.

I drummed my fingers on the table, staring absently at the steam curling out of my mug. As the tendrils of vapour twisted upwards and dissipated into the air, an idea formed in my mind. It must have been evident on my face, because she was leaning forward, demanding, "What? What is it, Andy?"

"We can make our own SCID/pbl mice," I said. "Rupert Flack's lab has the bog-standard SCID strain—Christine uses them occasionally for her metastasis studies. All we have to do is convince her to slip us a few cages. If we explain to her what a good cause it is, I'm sure she could arrange —"

"Absolutely not! We can't take the risk of too many people knowing."

"I'd trust Christine with my life. Besides, if you truly want to go through with this, I don't see any other way."

Gina still looked dubious. "Okay...but what about the human xenograft?"

"That's the easy part. I've got a mate in the department who gets a weekly shipment of human whole blood from Bart's Hospital for his research—I'm sure he can spare a bit. The procedure for reconstituting the limited immune system from adult peripheral blood lymphocytes is relatively straightforward—I can help you with that."

"How long does it take for the immune system to establish?"

"About a week, for the factors that your experiment needs," I said. "By the way, do you actually have some combination vaccine for this trial?"

"The main stock is in Germany, but I put up such a fuss about the lack of animal trials that they agreed to send me a small batch for more extensive tissue culture testing."

To shut her up and keep her happy. It obviously hadn't worked.

"I've got enough virus to infect two litters of about six mice each," she went on. "Then I just need another litter for the control injections...so three cages all together."

She seemed to be cheering up whereas, on further contemplation, my own earlier confidence was deteriorating.

"You think this is a really bad idea, don't you?" Her gaze travelled over my face.

"Not necessarily." I hesitated. "The African Phase I trial will involve more than a handful of subjects, won't it?"

"They're talking about forty individuals. I can't stop thinking about those people. I could never forgive myself if —"

"But say this mouse trial proves the virus is toxic or ineffective," I said. "You could be in serious trouble for having done unauthorized animal work, even if you *had* saved the day."

She thought about it. "I guess I'd have to appeal to Richard. He couldn't let things go further if I had that kind of evidence."

I wasn't so sure, and was just thinking of a polite way to voice this when the doorbell rang.

She rose, puzzled. "Who could that be?"

While she was away, I swirled my coffee mug and watched the residue circle at the bottom. I heard the deadbolt retract with a *thunk*, and almost immediately, cold air rushed into the room.

"Hello?" Her voice sounded uncertain.

I put down the mug and turned around curiously in my seat. The front door was ajar and Gina had disappeared. Feeling a tingle of apprehension, I was just standing up to investigate when there was a muffled scream, followed by the sound of shattering glass.

"Gina!" As I dashed over and flung the door wide, various images flashed into my mind, frozen like film stills: Gina, sprawled out on the step below me, face hidden in a bent arm; blood everywhere—sprayed over the step, splattered on her clothing, mixed in with sparkling shards of glass; a dark figure, racing down the pavement towards a car idling on the road a few doors down.

I was too stunned to move for a few seconds, and then the film restarted with a flickering jolt and I knelt down, reaching for Gina's slack body with immense fear pumping in my heart and sabotaging my shaking hands.

181

At that moment, she began struggling to a sitting position, and simultaneously, a car door slammed like a shot. Looking up, I saw someone leaning recklessly out the passenger side window.

"This is the last time we'll ask nicely, Dr Kraymer!" the figure yelled back at us. "If you keep experimenting on animals, you're *dead!*" Then tyres screeched, and the red tail lights dwindled into the night.

Gina exhaled audibly, and I turned to find her slumped against the brickwork of the building, watching the retreating car in a daze.

"Where are you hurt?" I tried in vain to determine the source of the blood: there was so much of it, it didn't seem possible that she could have sat up by herself.

"I'm absolutely fine, Andy," she insisted faintly, with a little smile.

Several nearby doors had opened up, porch lights switched on, heads poking out. From within one of them, a dog was barking furiously.

"Can I help at all?" It was one of the nearest neighbours, a young man with a pale, fearful face.

"If you wouldn't mind calling the police," Gina said, removing a shard of glass gingerly from her lap.

"Don't you need an ambulance as well?" He hesitated in the doorway, blanching at the carnage.

"Of course she does—and make it quick!" I shouted.

"No," Gina said calmly. The man blinked in confusion, looking back and forth between her and me. "It's not my blood," she explained in a louder voice, exploring her upper arm with careful fingers. "I've just got a bit of a bruise."

The man nodded and disappeared.

"Are you *sure* you're okay?" My voice sounded coarse with worry. Now that my mind was working again, I could see that the blood on her clothing had splattered from an impact; a glass jar had hit the concrete front step and exploded, expelling its contents.

"Positive." Gina peeled up the sleeve of her blouse to inspect a nasty contusion swelling up on her arm.

"What happened?"

She touched the tip of her finger to the bruise, winced. "I didn't see anyone at first. Next thing I knew, something heavy smacked into my arm, knocked me over—there was a big crash, and this guy was coming out of the bushes towards me. You must have frightened him off."

"You heard what he said, didn't you?"

"The police warned me that something like this could happen. But there's no way they're going to intimidate me into stopping my research." The set of her chin took on a stubborn resolution I was starting to recognize.

"The most important thing is that you're all right."

I sat back on my haunches, trying to smile, but my breath caught as I thought about the darkly clothed man coming after her. I put a hand on her forearm, and she placed her own reassuringly on top. We were both in the process of becoming drenched from the drizzle, but I don't think either of us noticed. Despite all I thought I knew about my feelings for her, I was still surprised by the intensity of my fear earlier, and now, by the magnitude of my relief. Her own smile faltered, and it seemed as if she might also be aware, and similarly surprised.

"Thanks for seeing them out," Gina said, closing her eyes. I sat down next to her on the sofa as the police car's engine roared into life outside. "I'm really tired all of a sudden. Must be the excitement on top of all the wine." A small curve appeared to one side of her mouth.

I took the half-empty mug from her slack hand and put it on the coffee table. Leaning back, I pulled her against me, and we sat like that for a few peaceful minutes, not saying anything.

"I think I should stay over tonight," I said.

She stirred, and I realized she'd been dozing. "I'd like that...though I'd hate to put you out."

"Nonsense—it's no trouble, and you shouldn't be alone after such a fright. Besides, what if they come back?"

At this, she half-opened troubled eyes, and I cursed myself for even introducing the possibility.

"Anyway," I continued hastily, "I won't get in your way. I'll just kip here on the sofa, keep a watch."

"You don't have to sleep on the sofa." I felt a surge of hope like an electric charge, which was promptly squelched when she added, "I've got a spare room."

I hurled myself into a sitting position, frightened awake by a sound. It was still ringing in my ears, but I could somehow tell that the fragment of noise had leached out of a forgotten dream and wasn't actually real. I was sweating in the twisted duvet. Forcing myself to lie back down, I waited for my heart to stop pounding, for the adrenaline that had shot to my extremities, and pooled there with painful pressure, to disperse back harmlessly into circulation. My eyes slowly accustomed to the dark with the help of streetlight dribbling in through a chink in the curtains. Eventually, I could make out the desk, the rectangular lines of a flat-screen computer monitor, the ergonomic chair heaped with my discarded clothing.

Gina's computer. Gina's spare room. That's where I was. The disturbing events of the evening came flooding back, and then something else, a memory from the dream, something insistent that I'd realized just before the illusory sound had kicked me into consciousness. Something about...Estonia...about Dan Lamont...about PubMed...about Rouyle. The various threads tickled at my brain, and I felt that familiar stretching feeling I often get just before a collection of diverse experimental results consolidates into a theory. I struggled to create the link, to pull out the last forgotten connection that would make the entire idea crash out of solution.

When it did, I was propelled upright again, mouth actually hanging open in shock. Dan Lamont, in Estonia—he said he was doing neurobiology there. But Rouyle was a molecular immunologist: I had failed to realize that it didn't make sense for him to be in a neurobiology department. And one of those old abstracts in PubMed, among those I'd ignored as irrelevant...hadn't it something to do with neurobiology? Or psychiatry? What if it wasn't irrelevant, after all? What if it was written by the correct Rouyle? Dan said all this had happened in 1992; what had been the date on that abstract? I couldn't remember. And if it was Rouyle, why hadn't he published more on the same topic later? Why had he switched fields completely after having been dismissed? I thought about the rumours of scientific misconduct and cover-up that Dan had mentioned, mind racing around all the details faster than I could keep up.

The luminous green clock hands hovering over the bedside table told me it had just gone 3 a.m. There was no way I could sleep now. I looked calculatingly at Gina's computer. It was definitely wrong to poke around someone's workstation behind their back. Then I remembered how Gina had fallen into an exhausted sleep almost as soon as her head had touched down. She would never find out.

I slipped out of bed, turned on the computer and performed the same PubMed search. Found the reference that had snagged at my subconscious. Gazed at the title, still baffled.

40. Rouyle, R, Viknar, PM, and Maaros, E. Dominant passivity factors and pliancy criteria in rhesus macaques exposed to the PAX fraction. Arch Lat Psychiatry, 1993 Apr 5, 2:134-143. (No abstract available)

The year of publication was consistent, just a year after Dan's internship. The other names could be Estonian, I reckoned. I had no idea what *passivity factors* and *pliancy criteria* referred to; they sounded like psychiatric mumbo-jumbo to me. And PAX; there was a very large gene family called *pax*, involved with animal development, but in this context it didn't sound like the same thing. Unfortunately, PubMed was unable to provide the brief summary that could shed light on my questions, as for some reason the abstract was unavailable. Probably because the journal in question was so obscure; maybe it was in some unusual language as well—Estonian, for example.

I continued to ponder the title. *PAX fraction*...the word *fraction*, in biochemical terms, often referred to a tissue extract that demonstrated a certain biological activity. In neurobiology, it was often an extract derived from the brain. In the old days of classical neural biochemistry, scientists had patiently ground up tonnes of cow brains from the slaughterhouse, separating their components in search of elusive hormones, neurotransmitters and other microscopic messenger molecules.

I did another search, this time on the keyword "PAX," but, as expected, I only managed to pull down thousands of articles about the more familiar developmental pax gene. More tellingly, this keyword did not come down with either of the other co-author names, and searches combining the words "PAX fraction," or PAX with "pliancy" or "passivity" came up with nothing.

My disquiet was far more piqued than appeased, but I had reached the limit of what I could do with the information at hand. There was no other way: I had to get a copy of that article. With a few clicks, I determined that the journal didn't have an online home, so I couldn't exercise a pay-per-view option. The old-fashioned way, interlibrary loan, could take weeks. On the other hand, there was a service available online that offered quick electronic copies of print-only papers for a fee, and I resolved to order the article using my credit card once I was safely back at the lab.

I closed the browser window, restoring the desktop to its original tidy appearance. As the column of icons reappeared along the right side of the screen, a familiar white envelope caught my attention. It was a shortcut to Gina's e-mail Inbox.

Looking over my shoulder, I pushed the mouse's cursor over to the envelope icon. It felt peculiar, as if my hand were not connected to my brain but had become sentient in a fit of muscular mutiny. A slow seeping of chemical tension entered my bloodstream as I clicked my way in.

The Inbox spread out before me, oblivious to this lapse in propriety. I cast a calculating glance over the chronological list of e-mails Gina had received at her Geniaxis account over the last few days. Not surprisingly, it was infested with correspondence from Rouyle.

I opened up his most recent message. It was brief:

Darling,

I am convinced that if you think a bit more about our discussion last night, you will come around to my way of thinking. It is clear that more people than I would be disappointed if you changed your mind — many more, if you take that argument to its logical conclusion. But as you are highly perceptive, I trust you have realized this already, and see the wisdom of preserving the status quo.

Love,

Richard

I puzzled over the odd tone, but was unable to understand its significance out of context. Perhaps he was referring to their disagreement over the animal trials. Meanwhile, the words *darling* and *love* had collided disagreeably with my stomach, despite the distinct lack of affection sandwiched between.

A noise creaked behind my back, just outside the door. Going dry-mouthed and motionless, I strained my ears, one index finger poised to snuff out the computer, the other hand reaching for the lamp switch. The house sighed again, shifting in its foundations. It was nothing, I realized: only the wind.

This had clearly been a stupid, masochistic idea. I was about to quit the programme when one of the newer subject headings caught my eye: *Watch your step*. The sender was called Lillian Marzan [*L.marzan@u.mass.edu*], and it had arrived yesterday morning. I couldn't resist having a quick look.

Dearest Gina,

I have to confess you've got me worried now. Why prolong things if you're not feeling comfortable? Or — you don't have to do anything drastic, but why not step back and con- sider what you're doing, and why? Contrary to what you say, I'm not concerned about the age difference or the distance. The issue is that he's not listening to your point of view on legitimate grievances — even if they're scientific as opposed to personal — and you shouldn't ignore the warning signs. You sound like you're being your usual protective self, hiding the full story, but I don't need to know the details to be fairly certain it's a bad idea.

And by the way, if you really are still feeling jealous, and torn, isn't that just another warning sign of a dif- ferent sort?

Don't be an idiot. I mean that in the nicest possible way.

love,

Lill

I had a suspicion what the jealousy might be about. Heart racing, I opened the Sent Mail folder and scrolled up the list, but I couldn't find a message to L.Marzan in the week before her reply. Maybe it had been in response to a phone call. Just to be sure, I sorted the sent items by recipient, trawling through her frequent e-mails to her friend, shame forgotten as I gathered momentum skimming through message after message.

I didn't find what I was looking for, but there was a lot about Rouyle. Going backward in time, during Gina's Frankfurt visit, the descriptions of him became more positive, less dissatisfied. I began to build up a random picture of my rival, the reverse flow giving the bizarre sense that I was uncovering his character as Gina knew him less and less well. He was good at giving compliments, I learned. She noted the way he exuded confidence and never hesitated about deci- sions or regretted them afterward. He possessed a strangely intense passion for his scientific research that sometimes bordered on the obsessive. His tireless defence of applied biomedical research fitted well with her own ardent views about Western science's neglect of developing world diseases. She was impressed that he was always the first to be approached by the German press and television for quotes about the latest scientific developments. He seemed to move in a more adult and cosmopolitan world, and she was trying to learn how to fit in there because it seemed new and exciting.

At last, I found an old e-mail containing what I assumed was a reference to me. It had been sent in September, probably just after we'd run into each other in the park.

> I saw HIM again, and we finally had a real conversation. It wasn't as bad as I'd been expecting. I managed to put my foot in my mouth, as usual, but it ended up okay. I was surprised at my own feelings. The anger and hurt are gone, just evaporated away. But there's still something beneath. I'm too jaded to call it by a name. Let's just say that I like the way he listens, and there's a quietness around him that lets me be myself. The chemistry was still there, too. I can't tell if he cares for me, that way. But anyway, I know in my heart I don't deserve such kindness, and I would probably only end up hurting him. It's so much easier, isn't it, when they're not so nice.

I suddenly felt repulsed by the idea of seeing anything else that I hadn't ever been meant to know, especially information that had been rendered irrelevant by the passage of time, that pointed out yet more lost opportunities. But it was only when I started erasing my footprints, deleting the history links and temporary files that might betray my transgression, that the uneasy lump of shame returned to lodge in the back of my throat.

17 The Morning After

A sound roused me from a dreamless sleep. Unlike my earlier jolt into reality, I was clear-minded, aware of exactly where I was. I could tell by the red-bathed glow behind my eyelids and the warmth on my skin that it was fully morning. The noise had been the creak of a floorboard, but for some reason, I didn't want to betray the fact that I was awake. I could sense that someone was still standing in the room watching me. Gina, it had to be, undecided about whether to disturb me. But the odd thing was, she was taking a long time at it. The seductive smell of fresh coffee drifted over the bed, so enticing that it was difficult to keep up the pretence. Finally, I heard her approach, and the click of ceramic on wood as a mug touched down on the bedside table. Then, soft footfalls out of the room, and the door being pulled gently shut behind.

My eyes flew open. The mug sat in my field of vision, glazed a cherry red. The clock indicated about half past eight, and sunlight streamed between the slightly parted curtains. I sat up in bed and reached for the coffee cup, only then realizing I hadn't been completely decent while Gina had been observing me. A tangle of duvet had obscured the pertinent area, but I'd been sprawled bare-chested and bare-legged, most of me freely available for inspection. I felt my lips curling into a smile.

As I was pulling on my clothes, I noticed an ensemble of framed photographs clustered at the back of the desk that hadn't been apparent during last night's furtive hacking session. Leaning in, I feasted on this unexpected lode of personal information. I could tell that most of the portraits were of Gina's family from the marked genetic resemblance, but the more I studied them, the more this small tribe of handsome, grey-eyed people seemed to close ranks protectively, excluding me from the sphere where I so much longed to be central.

Closer to the front of the assembly, two smaller photos pulled me in. The first depicted a younger Gina, probably in her late teens. She was sunburnt, dirt-smeared and squinting into the sun with her classmates and a group of African villagers, standing proudly next to a recently constructed well. The second photo seemed much more recent. She was obviously back in Africa, looking very American in a blue Geniaxis T-shirt, khaki shorts, white trainers and a deep tan. Her eyes burned with scientific focus as she watched a local medic draw blood from the child at the head of a queue. I remembered the way she had talked about the place where she obtained Vera Fever Virus samples: *my* village. This, I thought, was a person far more involved in her research than your average post-doc, dealing with abstract molecular riddles, playing the publication game and trying to score enough points to ace the next job application.

The photo was about the size of my palm. I had to suppress an acute urge to slip the thing into my pocket, to take her perfectly captured expression of curiosity home with me.

The front door was open to another spectacular autumn morning. Gina was on her hands and knees in paint-spattered jeans and a flannel shirt, sleeves rolled up, scrubbing at the concrete with a brush. When she saw me, she sat up, pushed a stray hair out of her eyes with a forearm and wished me good morning with a radiant smile.

"Hey, Cinderella." I stepped outside. "How's the arm?"

"Not too bad," she said. "And I slept amazingly well. Last night almost doesn't seem real, does it? Except for the evidence..." and here she gestured at the sudsy concrete, which was still coming up a faint pink.

"But it was real, you know—I hope you're going to be very much on guard."

"Don't worry, I'm taking it seriously."

"Good." I sat down on the threshold, angling my body to catch the warmth of the sun. I shut my eyes in pleasure, and when I opened them, I found her studying me.

"You're wearing that 'I've got something to say' look," I said fondly.

"I must be getting predictable." Her tone was teasing, but it was delivered with a self-conscious smile. I sensed a bit of tension in the air.

"No, that'd just be my sheer intelligence and finely-honed powers of observation."

She laughed, diffusing whatever it had been. "No, you're right: I do have something to say. I wanted to thank you for everything: tending to my arm, mopping up the worst of the glass and blood, helping me deal with the police, putting me to bed. And this morning, I came downstairs to find you'd done the dishes too."

I shrugged. "It was nothing, really."

"It wasn't nothing, it meant a lot to me. So please let me thank you properly for looking after me." Her eyes were full of something indefinably meaningful.

I looked down, not wanting to say that, given the slightest bit of encouragement, I'd be happy to volunteer for that job on a permanent basis.

"*And*," she continued, "before we were so rudely interrupted, you had also agreed to help me out of my scientific predicament, at no small personal risk. I've been thinking a lot about that this morning— it wasn't fair to ask. I could always try to take full responsibility, but I don't think that would be an option if we were caught. You and Christine would both be consenting parties."

"But I *want* to help you."

"Exactly. So it's not fair. I shouldn't have allowed myself to ask when I knew full well that...sentiment could influence your decision." She forced me to meet her eye, and I didn't look away, feeling stripped bare.

"Forget about it, Gina—I'm still in."

"You're absolutely sure?"

"I'm not afraid to take responsibility for my own actions," I said. "Besides, there's more than one category of sentiment flying around here: there are those innocent patients to consider as well. And besides..."

"What?"

"We're too clever to get caught."

She couldn't help smiling. "And what about Christine?"

"Christine's perfectly capable of making her own decisions. And you can rest assured that sentiment won't be clouding *her* judgement."

"Are you completely certain of that?" Her eyes were carefully wiped clean of any implication.

"Listen, Chris and I are close, but I can't see her doing something stupid purely in the name of friendship." As I said these words, I suddenly wasn't so sure.

❦ ❦ ❦

I sat at a window bar seat, watching the sporadic Saturday traffic, mostly black cabs, streaming past. The tiny sandwich shop wasn't very exciting, but it was the only place ever open on weekends in the office zone around the Centre. I was alone, except for two Spanish girls—the usual Saturday shift—bustling around quietly behind the counter.

I was thinking about how the rest of the morning had gone. After a pleasant but uneventful breakfast with Gina, I realized I'd forgotten to switch my mobile back on after dinner. When I did, I found two voicemail messages from Christine. The first had been left around midnight.

"Hi, Andy...I take it Gina found you in the end, as we missed you in the Henry. Hope you're not currently doing anything I wouldn't do! No, I take that back. Listen, I've got some interesting news...ring me the moment you get in, it doesn't matter how late."

The next message was left around nine this morning, her voice sounding distinctly more sly. "Looks like you got lucky, Andy my man. Give us a ring once you've slunk home. On second thought, lunch at the El Cid. Noon?"

The coffee was crude but effective, and I was indulging in a sneak preview to fortify myself for dealing with Christine. I was doubtless going to get harassed for not making it home, but I was suddenly dreading asking her to play a role in the mouse plot. Now that I'd had a chance to think, I wasn't convinced that she would go along with it. It was all very well for me to feel bravely vigilante helping Gina, but I couldn't get into too much trouble for diverting some human blood cells her way; it wasn't much riskier than the time I'd bent the rules and lent her some radioactive isotope. It was actually Christine who would suffer the bulk of any punitive measures if we were found out.

Just then, I saw Christine through the window, rounding the corner and turning towards the El Cid. There was a distinct jauntiness about her stride, and I recalled the news she'd mentioned in her first phone message. She looked terrific in her suede coat with the fringe on the bottom, worn jeans, heeled boots making her seem even more long-legged, cropped light-brown hair shining gold in the sun. When she reached the intersection, she dashed across against the light, sticking two fingers up at a honking cab, and a grin transformed her face when she noticed me in the window. I wondered how long that mood would last when she heard about Gina's plan.

The bells above the door jingled cheerily as she pushed inside.

"Andy, you dirty dog!" She bounded over and kissed me on the cheek. "Glad you managed to get here."

"You're looking great, Chris," I said with a smile. "Something to do with your news, I expect—what's up?"

"Nice diversionary tactic, O'Hara, but completely futile, I can assure you." She smirked and whirled away to the counter before I could comment.

"You want something besides that coffee?" she called over after a few minutes.

"No thanks." I wasn't looking forward to breaking the news that my evening with Gina had not gone remotely as suspected.

"I should think you'd need to refuel." Her eyes were wide in mock-innocence as she deposited her usual BLT and Coke onto the bar.

I shook my head, only mildly annoyed. "I had a big breakfast."

"A-ha! So it wasn't one of those sneak-out-while-they're-still-sleeping sorts of mornings? A nice cosy brekkie as well? I know Americans like them large...their breakfasts, I mean."

I rubbed the faint ache behind my forehead with a thumb and forefinger. "Chris, it's not what you think."

She pulled her stool closer to mine. "I sent Gina upstairs to the library last night—she was practically frantic to find you—you don't return my calls, you meet me here in yesterday's clothes and it's *not what I think?*"

Why is it that women can always keep track of precisely what you'd been wearing the day before? Maybe the talent was controlled by some gene on the X chromosome.

"I slept in her spare room."

"You what?" She put her sandwich back on the plate, untouched. "Andy, you're allowed to sleep together on the first date."

"It wasn't a *date*, you idiot. We were having dinner—a just-mates sort of dinner—when we were interrupted by —" and here I filled her in on the attack. "As you can imagine, she wasn't in any condition to be left on her own."

"A death threat!" She bit into her sandwich, mumbled, "Frankly, I'm surprised. Do you think they're really that serious?"

"They sounded like it, but Gina's not the least bit deterred."

She chewed thoughtfully for a moment, then poked my shoulder. "At any rate, those activists aren't doing you such a bad turn."

I looked at her, puzzled.

"Think about it," she said. "That's twice now their actions have put you in the best possible light with Gina. First the high-profile, dazzling speech on the steps of the Centre, and now this—the late-night crime scene, complete with a gallant bout of post-traumatic stress counselling. It's all very romantic."

"Being up to your elbows in fake blood is hardly romantic. And it's never been clearer that our current relationship is strictly platonic."

She studied me for a moment. "Are you sure there's no evidence she might be starting to change her mind?"

I hesitated, then shook my head.

"Because I think she'd be mad not to." Her smile contained equal parts affection and sympathy.

"On that very subject..." I paused. "Would you mind explaining something from the female perspective?"

The eyebrows went up. "Not at all."

"What is it about women that makes them go for older blokes?" I was unable to suppress my frustration. "Miles at least I could understand. But Rouyle must be in his late forties. Sure, I guess you could call him handsome, in a distinguished way, but..."

"But he's not exactly a virile stallion like yourself?" She pushed my shoulder again, making my stool wobble.

I filtered the impatience from my voice. "But it's not only Gina. Just look at all the leathery old men in the movies with leading ladies young enough to be their daughters."

"Or even their grand-daughters." She rummaged for her pack of cigarettes, a clear sign she was settling into analysis mode. "But that's Hollywood. Still, it's only exaggerating something real."

"So what's the attraction?"

The lighter snapped, its flame nearly invisible in the pool of sunlight dappling her shoulders. "Let me tell you something about women, Andy. Nine times out of ten, when they're choosing a man, they're reacting to something in their past."

"You mean, they're on the rebound?"

"Sort of. When Gina encountered Rouyle in Cambridge, she was reacting to both Miles and you—two careless young men who had messed her about." She held up a hand, forestalling my outraged response. "*Despite* the misunderstanding in your case."

I was silent while she pensively refuelled on nicotine, watching the sun lighten the freckles on either side of her nose. I had asked for this, so I might as well try to learn something.

"So along comes the older bloke," she continued, "handsome, articulate, obviously openly admiring of her work and her person, right when she was doubting her desirability. Did you actually see him on the dance floor?" I nodded reluctantly. "He probably charmed the pants off her, just when she was longing to be charmed. And, say what you want about him, he's not likely to display the flaws of youth. Moreover, he's powerful, self-confident—women are intensely attracted to self-confidence—and he's probably quite sexually experienced." She saw the expression on my face. "Shall I go on?"

I didn't have to shake my head. She just watched me think, a curtain of smoke wavering between us.

"It doesn't completely fit," I finally said. "Of course people can be deceived by appearances, but..."

"I know what you're getting at." She tapped a precarious inch of ash off her cigarette. "The way she overreacted to her problems this summer, and then falling into Rouyle's web—these are classic symptoms of low self-esteem. But then we've got this extroverted, hyper-confident persona asking killer questions at seminars."

"I sense a hypothesis coming on."

"Of the worst sort—one backed by insufficient data." She shrugged. "Still, it's all pointing towards a negative experience in the not-so-recent past...recent enough that she's still dealing with it, not so old that it happened before her fundamental confidence had developed."

I wrote five papers in two years, Gina had told me. And if I'd followed up on her clues like she'd probably wanted me to, I might not be fumbling around in ignorance now.

Anger flared up then at my own inadequacies, when I had always considered myself so eminently capable. I could strip down biological processes to their molecular essences, but I was too focused on this microscopic world to interpret real-life interactions as they unfolded in front of my eyes. I felt a stab of longing for my previous grey equilibrium, when distressing occurrences just rolled off me and my experiments gave me all the fulfilment I needed. Like a captive animal released into the unknown, I was yearning for the simplicity of the cage.

"Do you think I should just give up?" Even airing the possibility was depressing.

"I wouldn't classify it as hopeless yet," she said in surprise, putting a hand over mine. "I can't stop thinking about your little tussle on Julie's sofa. I reckon she's got mixed feelings about you, and circumstances are bringing you closer all the time. Rouyle's in Germany—who knows what might happen? Besides, she asked you over for supper, so she must enjoy your company at the very least."

"Actually, there's something I haven't told you about that."

She blinked at me, narrowed her eyes.

"It's a long story," I added. "And you have to promise not to say a word to anyone, not even Cameron."

"And I thought *I* was the one with the news!"

We changed venues to the quadrangle park to take advantage of the sunshine. In contrast to the weekday bustle of Centre scientists skiving off on lunch or tea breaks, the grounds were largely deserted at weekends. Now, only a few children played under the plane trees, watched indulgently by their mothers, and a dog zoomed around off his lead, looping between his owner and the great beyond in larger and larger hyperbolas.

I had just finished telling Christine about Gina's collaboration and my reservations about it, keeping strictly to my scientific suspicions of FRIP's untested efficacy in the human nervous system. My more personal concerns about Rouyle's past were too vague to air, so I skipped that aspect and told her directly about Gina's plan.

As I waited for Christine to break the silence, the dampness of the earth seeped into my jeans, a cold reminder that summer was officially over. I was just about to suggest we forget the whole stupid idea when she turned to me at last.

"I'll do it." The mild tone belied the fierceness of her gaze, which was currently penetrating me like twin pneumatic drills.

"You...will?"

"On *one* condition," she said, tossing her spent cigarette into the grass.

"Name it," I breathed.

"That I get to talk to Gina about it first, alone. And I have to be satisfied on that front as well, before I agree."

I looked at her, confused. "Yeah, but what could you possibly —"

"Do we have an agreement or not?"

I knew that tone well enough to know it was no use arguing.

"Sure, Chris. And...well, thanks."

"Don't thank me yet," she warned, gathering her things together. "It all depends on what Gina says." She grimaced at her watch. "I'm way overdue in the Mouse House."

"Wait, I'm coming too." I scrambled to my feet as well, aware of a funny awkwardness between us. We walked together wordlessly towards the Centre, and when we were going up the steps, I put my hand on her arm.

"I am such an idiot—your big news...in all the excitement, we never..."

At last, Christine gave me a tired smile and patted my face with her hand. "Ask me next time. There's no way my paltry bit of gossip can compete with the amazing array of sex, violence and intrigue you've treated me to this afternoon."

✦ ✦ ✦

From: raidula@ut.pui.ee
To: a.ohara@rcc.cmb.ac.uk
Subject: RE: a mutual acquaintance

Dear Dr O'Hara,

Many apologies for not answering sooner, but I have been out of town, and only again in Tartu this one day before departing again. First I must tell you that naturally I remember Dan, but more importantly you should know that any friend of Magritte Valorius should also be mine — she is rather a hero in this part of the world and I have only the highest esteem for her person and work.

It would give me great pleasure to relate the events you mention in your e-mail. Unfortunately, I cannot write further now, as my flight leaves in but two hours, and the history requires some telling indeed. On the rather lucky side, after brief stay in Helsinki I am off to London to give a seminar at the Institute of Child Health. This hap-

pens Wednesday next. I would be honoured to have coffee
with you that day.

with best regards

Raim

****

Dr Raimar Aidula
Institute of Brain Research
University of Tartu
Tartu, Estonia

✦ ✦ ✦

I carefully depressed the pipettor's plunger, releasing a heavy droplet
of purple liquid into the last lane of my DNA gel, and watched as the
glistening fluid settled into the small rectangular well. Helmut's voice
floated up the corridor, forecasting an end to my spell of Sunday solitude in the lab. Magritte was about, too, but she'd been concealed in
her office all afternoon.

"Andy! You are having a visitor!" Helmut cried out. He added
something else I couldn't hear, and a generous, familiar laugh rose
over the top.

I stood up in surprised consternation.

"Hello, love." My mother wafted into the lab, Helmut hovering so-
licitously nearby. I blinked, momentarily unnerved by the incongruity.

"How did you get up here?" Recovering myself, I strode over with
a smile and kissed her on the cheek.

"I was negotiating with that unpleasant man on the door when this
handsome fellow rescued me, smuggled me through Checkpoint Char-
lie." She patted Helmut on the arm and he made a face at me that she
couldn't see.

"Mum!" I passed a hand over my eyes. "You could've just rung
from the lobby extension."

"True. But this way, I managed to get all the lab gossip in the lift."
She winked at Helmut.

"And may I suggest also to take your coat, Mrs. O'Hara?" Helmut
held out his arms with ceremony.

"Such delightful Continental manners!" It was my turn to receive
the maternal wink as Helmut, oblivious, hung up her jacket on a peg
amidst all the unused white coats.

✤ ✤ ✤

Sunlight poured through the courtyard window of the departmental common room, highlighting the ink-blue veins beneath my mother's skin, the silvered blunt angles of her fashionable haircut. Maybe the same light didn't flatter me as much, because as she studied my face, her customary good humour degenerated into a frown.

If I'd known she was going to be in town, I would have shaved, made more of an effort with my appearance. As it was, I was rough and exhausted after another late Saturday night in the lab. It definitely wouldn't help if I told her I felt worse than I looked.

"Cup of tea?" I attempted to head off the inevitable interrogation.

"From this place?" She wrinkled her nose. "I don't fancy imbibing any escaped second-hand viruses or genetically modified whatsits."

I knew better than to take her seriously. She did more than just clip out articles for me; she was an avid reader, and I suspected she knew more about some branches of science than I did, bogged down as I was in my micro-specialized niche. On the other hand, despite her breezy bantering with Helmut, it was clear that the Centre made her nervous. Most parents, no matter how confident, found the environment intimidating, a feeling exacerbated by the careless proficiency of their offspring. And labs had become a lot more high-tech and alien since my father's day.

"So what brings you to London, Mum?"

"I reached critical mass." She leaned back in her chair, eyes still roaming over my sorry state. "The errands build up when you're mired in the suburbs. I'm the last of my friends to see that new Jasper Johns exhibition at the Tate Modern. And Jane and I are going to the theatre tonight."

"I don't know how you keep up the pace." Although I was happy to see her, I couldn't help doing a mental tally of several experiments I'd left running back in the lab, including a protein gel that would shortly need attention.

"*And* my local Waterstone's is woefully deficient—there's a particular biography of Rosalind Franklin I'm dying to get my hands on."

"You know, Mum, you can order books on the internet and they arrive on your doorstep twenty-four hours later."

She waved a hand, wedding ring sparkling. "And neutralize one of my excuses to visit London?" When I smiled, she went on, rather diffidently, "We were hoping we could entice you to come along tonight."

"Actually, I'm quite busy." I felt the usual defensive guilt arm my shoulder muscles. "If you'd given me more notice..."

She sighed and ruffled at the pages of a coffee-stained *Nature* lying between us on the table. "Is everything all right otherwise?"

"This isn't just a spontaneous visit, is it, Mum?"

"Not completely," she said. "I had a call from Liz last night."

"So that's it." My sister had caught me in a foul mood on the phone the previous week, and though I'd tried to keep the conversation cheerful, she had obviously picked up on something and duly reported back to the mother ship.

"She didn't say anything specific, Andy. But she was concerned."

I started shifting a paperclip between my fingers.

"Liz worries too much." *And so do you.*

"That may be true, but frankly, dear, you do look awful. And something *is* bothering you—I know that expression too well. Your father used to have the same one."

I mutilated the paperclip, stretching it out into an imperfect line and then forcing it into various unnatural shapes. It was a game we played: she would mention my father, trying to get me to acknowledge his existence, and I would side-step the reference like I always did. Both of us were old hands.

"I have had a lot on my mind recently," I admitted.

"Such as?"

"There's this woman." I exhaled in gusty resignation. "It's all very complicated."

Her surprised expression invited continuation, and I sketched in very general terms Gina's problems with the animal rights activists and the Pfeiffer-deVries collaboration.

"Just a friend?" she inquired lightly, obviously more interested in potential grandchildren than in corporate intrigue.

"Despite all my best attempts," I said.

"Have you actually tried?"

I paused. "What's that supposed to mean?"

She put her face in her hands and rubbed her eyes before looking back up at me, face still framed by her fingers. It hit me then that she was an old woman, and that, inevitably, she was going to die.

"I shouldn't..." She hesitated, shook her head. "It's just that sometimes it seems as if you surrender before you even begin."

I felt my shoulders stiffen again. "I do my best, Mum."

"You do no such thing!" The words scorched out of nowhere. "Don't think I haven't noticed. You used to be a fighter—what happened? Now all you do is *work*, work at the expense of everything else. Nothing else matters to you—why? Is it something to do with Charles? Is it...?"

She put a hand to her mouth, and there was a stung silence. Why did she always have to drag my father into everything? My face started to burn in an unexpected rage, but when I opened my mouth to defend myself, no words emerged. My next instinct was to storm back to the lab, a world where I had some semblance of control, but my body seemed pinned down by gravity. I bowed my head, struggling to control myself.

"Why are you so *angry?*" she said.

The last word was half entreaty, half bewilderment, and I knew exactly how her eyes would look, her mouth. I breathed in, out, concentrating on the way the sunlight reflected off the surface of the table. I can still recall it now in astonishing detail: the scratch marks, the crescent imprint left by someone's mug, the way it felt when the forgotten paperclip snapped between my fingers.

After a few more seconds of strained silence, a throat cleared at the open door.

"Sorry to interrupt." Magritte's face was composed. "Your samples about to run off gel, Andrew...shall I set up blot apparatus for you?"

I leapt up. "No, I'll do it. Back in ten minutes, Mum."

My mother laboured to her feet, and I felt a stab of shame. "Don't worry, dear...I'm due at the museum shortly. I'll be along in a moment to say goodbye."

She extended a hand to Magritte. "Always a pleasure to see you, Dr Valorius." How many times had I begged her not to be so formal? "I trust my son is working hard, fighting the good fight?"

I slipped into the corridor before either of them could see the expression on my face. As I swerved into the lab, I heard Magritte's response: "Am looking out for him, Mrs O'Hara, not to worry."

It didn't sound like the right answer to my mother's question. Or at least, to the one she had asked out loud.

The album had ended, but I was reluctant to dispel the accumulated silence. It was close to midnight as I sat in the tissue culture suite, arms resting inside the bio-safety cabinet. I was supposed to be seeding cells into dishes, but I found myself adrift in thought, still churning from the encounter with my mother. Was she right that work was the only thing that mattered to me? And if so, was my research really worth the sacrifice?

I'd been spared a close experience with death until the age of twenty-one. At first, losing my father had spurred me on, inspiring me to switch my focus to cancer biology. I'd galloped forth in a fierce crusade that didn't leave much time to dwell on things, but I had been unable to sustain it. I eventually realized how hypothetical my research was, how far it lagged behind the real world of patients and suffering. I was an insignificant bit-player in a vast production, churning out theories instead of cures. In the end, my noble career choice left a hypocritical aftertaste, especially when I was subjected to my mother's pride. She failed to distinguish between courage and just being swept along: it was as embarrassing as being praised for the act of breathing.

I leaned my forehead against the cool protective screen and allowed my stacks of dishes, with their gleaming ruby contents, to blur into the reflected light. After Dad died, cancer was no longer the abstraction it was for so many of my colleagues. His legacy was a dark understanding, the ability to see it, almost *feel* it, multiplying in black tendrils, overwriting good systems with rotten ones. It was unnerving to learn that cancer wasn't purposefully evil, but rather subject to the vagaries of natural selection, driven by a blind biochemical programme of survival much like any other organism—an insight that made the simple comfort of demonization impossible. It was also disheartening that the more my colleagues and I discovered about cancer, the more complicated and unconquerable it seemed to become. So as my idealistic hopes faded, all that was left was a vague sense of being out of control, of being mired in hesitation while the rest of the world marched purposefully by. Somewhere along the way I had retained the work ethic but lost the underlying meaning that would have made the sacrifices worthwhile.

18   *Girly Chat*

Post-Doctoral Haiku No. 22
by: Dr Anonymous

Tinkering with genes
I ponder consequences:
Will I go too far?

I repositioned the latest effort from our elusive departmental poet
to one side of the Board to make room for a clipping from my mother,
as if this dutiful act could somehow make up for the immature way I'd
behaved. It had been enclosed in a note whose light-hearted tone puzzled me until I realized it had been posted before our fight. Scanning
the article, I wondered what maternal instinct had led her to choose a
topic so dangerously relevant to her son's current exploits:

Stem cell research grows up

*As anti-abortionist opinions gain sway, biomedical scientists scramble
to find viable alternatives to foetal tissue. But these new compromises
may not be the answer, says Frederica Lawson.*

To my untrained eye, they were just white mice, but as they scurried
in their cages, ran on their exercise wheels or slept in a heap in the corner, these particular rodents were unaware of the momentous changes
going on inside them.

Born with a natural genetic deficiency in their immune systems, these
so-called SCID mice are unable to reject foreign tissue grafts as normal mice would, and they had just been injected with a strange brew
indeed: carefully harvested neuronal stem cells from adult human
donors. As I contemplated the oblivious rodents, their microscopic
invaders were even then spreading throughout their brains.

The method of creating such human/mouse hybrids has been known
for years, but the use of adult neuronal stem cells is new and controversial. These particular primitive progenitor cells, long considered the
Holy Grail for the treatment of devastating neurodegenerative diseases
such as Alzheimer's and Parkinson's, were not thought to exist in
adults until recently. Indeed, scientists still debate their authenticity.

But campaigners against the use of foetal tissue have latched onto this alternative method of repairing brain damage, muddying the waters around the unestablished new science even further...

I was experiencing my usual Monday caffeine low, but all that trickled out of the coffee machine in the common room was a sludge of scorched remains. Checking my watch, I saw I was due to meet Christine downstairs in about twenty minutes time, so I decided to grab a few articles and head down early for a proper cup. I was just rounding the corner to the tea room when I spotted Christine and Gina head-to-head in a private cluster of chairs near the back exit.

I slammed to a halt.

"Hey!" Someone collided into me from behind. "Are you coming or going?"

"Sorry, mate," I said, and the guy gave me a funny look as he shoved past.

I was clearly intruding. I hesitated, knowing I should just sneak back the way I had entered and return at the appointed time. On the other hand, I was consumed with curiosity. What could Christine possibly have to say to Gina, and in what way would her response dictate whether our plan could go forward? At the moment, Christine was doing all the talking, body poised in a tensed configuration, whereas Gina was just nodding her head in sobered capitulation.

I found myself backtracking through the canteen and negotiating the corridor between the serving area and the main kitchen. I walked behind the swinging door of the tea room's back exit and squatted down, prepared to do up my laces in case anyone happened by. The corridor was deserted, but I could hear the radio echoing in the kitchen and occasional scraps of laughter as a man tried to sing along and was ridiculed by a choir of flirtatious female jeers. When the canteen staff fell momentarily still, I could hear Christine's voice behind the door, muffled but somewhat intelligible.

"...clear-cut case of exploitation, Gina...hard for me to believe that you had the cheek to...him like that. Given the way he feels about you, how could he possibly have..."

Gina's reply was too soft to understand, and then Christine was saying, scornfully, "...sure he *thinks* he's being objective. But the man's completely gone on you...probably jump off the Waterloo bridge if you..."

At this point, one of the women in the kitchen started scolding someone and I lost the next thirty seconds or so.

Maybe Christine had shifted my way, because now her voice came at me with crisp clarity.

"Listen, Gina, I know it doesn't sound like it, but I approve of what you want to do and I'm more than willing to help. I don't give a toss about regulations, but I am worried about Andy. I care about him... a lot. And while I can't stop him from getting hurt because you won't come to your senses and give him a go, I *can* try to make sure that he doesn't get blasted by any unexpected fallout. It's completely unnecessary for all of us to go down if we get caught. If it's just the blood and the know-how he's providing, I can easily engineer that as well."

For the first time, Gina's voice was also audible. She sounded shaken, as you would be if you weren't accustomed to Christine in self-righteous mode. "I see your point. He said the blood was readily available from some guy in your department —"

"That'd be Antonio in the Dermont lab. I can ask him just as easily. In fact, my research is a lot more relevant than Andy's when it comes to inventing a pressing need for human blood components. I already have a protocol for the SCID/pbl reconstitution...it's a classic procedure." She sounded eager—it would be like her to relish any opportunity to get one over an evil capitalistic entity like Pfeiffer-deVries. "Anyway, you want to steer well clear of Magritte—she's scalpel-sharp, and definitely not the type who'd look the other way."

A classic George Michael song came on in the kitchen, inspiring ragged cheers and a significant boost in volume, so I had to strain to make out the next bits.

"...we're agreed, then?" Christine was asking.

"Absolutely."

"So who's going to break it to Andy that his manly services are no longer required?"

Gina giggled. "I think you should have that honour."

"I'm meeting with him in a few minutes' time anyway."

There was a pause, and then Gina started to speak in a very low voice.

"...what you said earlier, about coming to my senses..."

I leaned forward, trying not to breathe.

"I just think you should know that —"

A rumble of sound exploded into the corridor. A trolley loaded with milk cartons extruded itself from the kitchen, a haggard young man at its other end. Muttering under his breath, he wrestled the thing around and steered it towards the service entrance. I made a show of doing up my laces, burning with frustration. By the time the trolley had rattled into the canteen, whatever Gina had been about to reveal was over.

"Are you blind?" Christine's voice bristled with disbelief. "How could you possibly doubt that he..."

"...know what he's *said*." Gina sounded uncertain. "But before, I could always sense this underlying...hesitation. I assumed it reflected doubts about me...or that it wasn't a question of how much he cared about me, but how much he cared about anything. I've gone that route before, and it doesn't work."

"I do know what aspect of his you're referring to. But you said, *before*..."

Another pause. "... might be my imagination, but it just seemed, recently...that I was wrong."

"It's not too late, you know." Christine's manner was casual. "Nobody's forcing you to..." then, "Gina? Are you okay?"

The silence oscillated in my head, and I crouched frozen, trying to filter out the sound of my own heartbeats.

"I'm fine." Gina sounded very odd.

"Is there something you want to tell me?" I recognized Christine's tone immediately: compassionate suspicion, her trademark form of coercion.

"No, it's nothing. The problem is..." Her voice dipped below my radar momentarily, then I barely made out a couple of words: "...that simple...both of them."

"I know how that feels, too," Christine said, and another pause stretched out. My mind scrambled, trying to fill in the missing scraps to form a cohesive whole, but I didn't have enough information—expressions, body language, eye contact, the signals of the complex communication network that would make the messages make sense.

A timer went off behind the door, swiftly placated.

"Listen, I've got a meeting with some patent lawyers in a few minutes," Gina said, sounding briskly normal.

"Don't forget...not a word to Andy about what we've said here."

"You can count on me...and, Christine...thanks for everything. You'll never know how..." The rest of it was muffled in what I suspected was an embrace.

"I'm happy to help, Gina. With the trial...and if you ever need a listening ear. Just..."

"What?"

"Watch your back, yeah? I know you've got those animal rights goons on your mind, but I'd be a lot more concerned about what Pfeiffer-deVries would do if they found out about our scheme. And I'm not just talking governmental regulations here. I know that you and Rouyle are..." a bit lost, here, "but you've got to make damned sure you don't give anything away, I don't care *how* close you think..."

A chair screeched on lino. I realized that Gina might very well go out the back way, so I scrambled to my own feet, unsteady as the blood returned to my legs in a prickly wave.

"...sure he would never let anything..." Gina's voice was coming my way. "Thanks again, Christine...I'll be in touch."

I dashed into the nearby gents, managing to make it inside just before Gina emerged into the corridor. I could hear the clicking of her shoes as she walked past. Unthinkingly, I ran some cold water from the taps, splashed myself with cupped hands and watched my face in the mirror as it dripped. My emotions were all mixed up: anger, disbelief, confusion. I felt like a pawn in the hands of women. I was angry with Christine for having the gall to pressure Gina, not just about my role in the animal trial but also about our private affairs. I was irritated at Gina for going along with Christine's over-protective plan—the whole SCID/pbl thing had been my idea. And above all, I hungered to understand exactly what Gina had been saying about me, yet doubted that my friendship with Christine would overcome the sanctity of the girly chat confessional. And if she didn't confide in me of her own volition, I couldn't very well try to persuade her to tell me without betraying the fact that I'd been eavesdropping. And then, as my anger cooled, guilt at my shameless covert activities moved in smartly to take its place.

I dried my face and hands and checked my watch: not too early to make a real appearance. I poked my head out of the loo, looked both ways then sauntered past the kitchen. Coming around the corner, I blended in with the anonymous throng queuing up in the main entrance for their afternoon tea. After paying for my cup of coffee, I pretended to scan the seating area for Christine. She raised her hand to get my attention and I went over and sat down. Although it was probably my imagination, I fancied that the cushion was still warm, and that I could detect a residual trace of elusive perfume.

"Not like you to be so punctual," she said with a smile, although I noticed that she looked tired and tense.

"Don't tell me you've drunk yours already?"

Christine glanced down at her lap in bewilderment: the polystyrene cup was not only empty, but completely shredded as well. "Um, yeah...it's been quite a day."

"I'll get you another," I offered, retracing my steps. I'd been so preoccupied with my own clandestine problems, I'd forgotten that, thanks to me, Christine now had secrets of her own to deal with. True, it wasn't my fault they'd decided to hide things from me, but I was learning that secrets, once formed, tended to breed like bacteria. And Christine was one of the most open people I knew, so keeping things concealed was probably stressful for her.

"This'll sort you out," I said, settling back down and passing her the cup. "Now, tell me your big news at last—I promise not to upstage you again."

"News?" Her smile seized up, smoothed out again. "Oh, *that* news. Well...do you remember the guy I told you about who was chatting me up at my poster in Cambridge—career-wise, I mean?"

I nodded. "A vacancy in Newcastle, wasn't it?"

"That's the one. I received an e-mail from him on Friday evening on behalf of his department's search committee. They've specially requested that I interview for a lectureship position."

"That's great! Newcastle's a bit remote, though."

"Far from London, you mean." She sighed. "But jobs are scarce, and this one is quite promising. Generous funding, with the possibility of becoming a permanent position...in the event of good behaviour, of course." She winked at me. I thought about the illicit animal trial and felt a flicker of apprehension on her behalf.

"And it's flattering to be head-hunted like that."

She shrugged. "It would be quite a coup to secure this job so soon—the last thing I want is to become trapped in a post-doctoral holding pattern."

"Amen and hallelujah. You must be thrilled."

"They're very keen about my work here, want to give me the resources to develop it into a major line of research." Her cheeks had taken on a rare flush. "And the best part is that I'd be free to keep my projects as fundamental as I want. They showed a refreshing lack of this current fixation on translational research."

The last two words sounded like a curse in her mouth. I decided not to mention that this precise phrase—referring to the process of applying scientific results directly to the clinical treatment of diseases—was one I actually tended to scan for in my restless forays through the job adverts.

"Is Rupert fine with you taking your project out of his lab?"

"I haven't told him yet, but he'll definitely be relaxed about it," she said. "He's not one of these clingy bosses, neurotic with separation anxiety."

"And Cameron?"

She deflated. "He's...pleased for me, of course. But he had his heart set on a position in London, where all the buzz is."

"Have you two ever talked seriously about...well, things?"

"We've only been together two years, so it's premature to be making any life-changing decisions. At least, *hasty* ones." She looked away. "We're starting to talk about it, yeah, but...it's tricky."

The subject was obviously closed. I gave her a sideways glance, surprised that she had even the slightest doubt about Cameron.

"So the interview's next Friday," she said. "I'm going to spend the whole weekend there, of course, have a look around. I've never been there, actually. You?"

"Nope." I went silent, drinking my coffee and becoming aware of the sadness rumbling under my pleasure like the Tube trains that passed beneath my flat when I tried to sleep late on Saturday mornings. I thought back to the people I'd met and lost touch with throughout my career, and then imagined what it must be like for someone like Gina, who was so far from home. We were a migratory species, forced to respond to the winds of job availability. It was the nature of the business; I understood it, but that didn't mean I had to like it.

"You okay, Andy?" She flipped a penny playfully into my lap from her pile of coffee change.

"It's nothing. Just that I'd miss you." Feeling silly, I smiled at her and picked up the coin, rubbed it absently between my fingers.

"The feeling's mutual, mate." She paused, a bit emotional, then said, "I've got to go in a minute, but there's one more thing." Her voice transformed yet again. "About the plan, Andy..."

I was sitting at my computer, waiting for the mail programme to extricate itself from whatever sector it was currently skiving off in. Kathy had put on an album by one of those indistinguishable girl-boy bands where only the girls sing and the boys are reduced to prancing around in the background with air traffic control headgear and soulful expressions. I looked over, unable to suppress a smile: she was concentrating so hard with her pipetting that her lips were moving, counting as she deposited a droplet into each tube.

"All right, Kath?"

She nodded, eyes never leaving her tube rack. "Yes, thanks."

She was becoming more self-sufficient every day. This must be how parents feel: a peculiar mixture of pride and regret.

The computer beeped my attention back to the screen. There was a new message from Gina in my Inbox, asking whether I'd have a free moment later in the evening for a "chat" in the Henry.

Perfect timing. Though I'd accepted my official relegation from the mouse trial after a convincing display of outrage, I had secretly resolved to do a small *in vitro* trial of my own. But for this, I needed some tools, and I had reason to believe that Gina could supply them. I sent back a swift agreement and was just preparing to do something productive when the computer emitted another beep.

```
From: queries@litsearch.uk
To: a.ohara@rcc.cmb.ac.uk
Subject: your reprint request, ref. no. 389975602

Dear Dr Andrew O'Hara,

This is an automated response to notify you that your
local library [code WC2A569] has confirmed its agreement
with LitSearch Central, and that the requested document(s)

* PMID: 120188831   Rouyle et al. Arch Lat Psychiatry,
1993 2:134-143

if available, will be e-mailed to you as arranged with
your local library. In the event that the e-file is un-
```

"Duck, everyone!" Paul warned. "Pissed-off post-doc approaching, fully armed."

I glanced over as Helmut stalked in, laden with an armful of supplies from a trip to the darkroom. Ignoring Paul's needling, he dumped everything onto his bench and retreated to his desk, clutching a piece of film.

I strolled over, but Helmut was still frowning at the film and didn't see me.

"Bad news?"

He looked up, a pained expression on his chiselled face. "Andy, just who I want to talk to. I repeated that SLIP experiment I showed you earlier."

"The one where SLIP failed to activate the antiviral TRAP protein in the neuronal cells?"

"Ja, and it is reproducible." He tapped a pencil onto the relevant black marks. "Only this time I do even more controls and am super careful. As expected, SLIP has no problem whatsoever activating growth signals as usual in both neuronal cells and fibroblasts. But at the same time, you see here that TRAP lights up only in fibroblasts and not in the neuronal cells."

"So why do you look so disappointed?" I tried not to reveal my own uneasiness. "You could be onto something big here, mate."

"You think so?" He employed a fatalistic tone of gothic proportions. "Maybe SLIP is some funny exception, and FRIP and CLIP can still act as antivirals in the nervous system. Or perhaps it is a trivial cell-type difference, PC12s being strange in some way."

I longed to tell him about Sandra's data on CLIP in a completely independent neuronal cell type, but knew that wouldn't be honourable. Instead, I said, "Maybe the dogma is wrong. Why don't we follow it up?"

"*We?*"

I held up a hand. "Don't worry, I'm not trying to muscle in on your next paper. I'm just...intellectually curious. I wouldn't mind doing a few transfections on the side to save you the trouble. Also, I think I can get hold of some FRIP reagents—an antibody, a DNA construct—quite easily."

"I already have a FRIP DNA construct, but the antibody would be most useful." He had straightened in his seat.

"You've got FRIP already?" I demanded. "Where from?"

"I requested it from Rouyle's lab a long time ago, and to tell a long story short they *finally* send it to me last week. Think I must've worn down his technician with my weekly e-mail reminders." He grinned.

"So can you spare a few million cells and a dollop of Rouyle's FRIP DNA? I'm doing transfections tonight anyway," I said.

"Well, this is sounding quite stimulating, Andy, but shouldn't we talk to Magritte first?"

I sidled up closer. "Why don't we just keep it between us lads until we've got the result? Only she's been putting pressure on me lately, and I don't want her to think I'm being distracted by something else." I gave him a look of fellow-post-doctoral angst.

There was nothing Helmut liked more than being in on a secret. "The cat gets my tongue on this one. I can give you some cells right now, in fact."

It was a slow Monday evening in the Henry, so it was obvious that Gina had not yet arrived. But Maria was leaning against the bar, making what looked like flirtatious small talk with the young bartender as he topped up her pint of Murphy's.

"Hi, stranger," she said, with a big smile. "Can I get you a drink at all?"

"Are you here alone?" I sloughed off my jacket.

"No, just arrived, conveniently missed a round with those folks." She jerked a thumb towards the far corner where Geniaxis employees huddled in their usual clique. "But I could stay awhile if you're at loose ends?"

"Half a lager, then. Thanks." I watched her cajole another beer out of the barman. On closer inspection, her cheer seemed forced. "Is everything all right?"

She sighed, running a hand through her hair. "Stressful day, and a crucial experiment that failed spectacularly."

"What project are you working on, anyway?"

She made a face. "Please—I'm off-duty now. Not only that, but Steve is driving me mad."

"Isn't Gina his supervisor?"

"She *was*—until she scored the lucrative, high-priority Pfeiffer-deVries collaboration. Now she's got more important things to do than look after a high-maintenance technician." Maria took a downcast sip of her stout.

"If he's that incompetent, why did Geniaxis hire him?"

"Actually, he's got a way with the mice—he's always mooning over them, anyway. What I *meant* was, it's clear he's messed up in some way, and I don't have much patience with that sort of thing. Gina was much better at handling him." She peered over my shoulder, frowning. "And speaking of which..."

Gina was pushing through the door, her cheeks flushed from the cold. When she saw me, her complexion glowed even more around her smile.

"You must have the touch," Maria muttered in my ear. "That's the first time she's looked happy in days."

Gina approached, and Maria offered, with forced enthusiasm, to buy her a drink. Gina declined, leaving me to explain about our prior engagement.

"Well, I'm meant to be with the others anyway," Maria said. "I'll leave you to it, will I?"

Maria walked off, her posture spelling out hurt dignity, and I watched with a twinge of remorse. When I turned back, I found that Gina had been dissecting my reactions. Yet there was nothing informative in her composed features, and when she realized I'd caught her out, she signalled to the barman.

"Any word from the police?" I asked as she dug around in her handbag for coins.

She glanced up at me. "Apparently FUR-IE has denied all responsibility for the attack, although the police said the particulars conformed to their *modus operandi*. But nobody noticed the car's license plate number, so there's not much to work with." She came up with a few fluff-covered pennies and sighed.

"That's it?" I demanded. "They're not going to do anything?"

Gina shoved the change back into her bag and gave the barman a ten pound note. "They're still checking out a few leads, but it's been totally quiet since the attack. Besides, now that FUR-IE has lost interest, I'm feeling more secure."

"Hang on—lost interest?"

"Haven't you been reading the papers? They've officially moved on. The Centre's 'Mouse Mass-Murder' scandal is old news—they've got higher organisms to fry." At my blank look, she added, "Dogs: much more photogenic than rodents. Apparently some neuroscientists up in Leicester have attracted their wrath."

"That's a relief." The understatement of the week: I could almost kiss that fickle Madame Branch Secretary.

She took a sip of her G&T. "So, Andy...I take it Christine has spoken to you?"

"Yes—didn't I tell you she'd be happy to help?"

Gina nodded, obviously waiting for more.

"I understand," I said, "that she found a better source of blood and has the reconstitution protocols well in hand, so it sounds as if I won't have much to do after all. It's a bit of a shame."

"Maybe it's for the best," she said, flustered.

"Maybe," I agreed. "But there's something I would like to do, with your permission and help, of course. After all, it's not fair to let you girls have all the fun."

"What?"

"Don't look so alarmed," I said. "I just thought I could do an *in vitro* test of FRIP in our standard rat neuronal cell cultures. Helmut's got these handy peptides for his SLIP research."

"What sort of peptides?"

"They mimic the FRIP activating factor secreted by the immune system, the one that your SCID/pbl mice"—I lowered my voice, remembering where I was—"should be pumping out fairly soon."

She looked puzzled. "I'm surprised Richard hasn't...what did you have in mind?"

"First I'll just confirm that FRIP can activate the antiviral TRAP protein in cells derived from the nervous system," I said.

"But Richard says —"

I held up a hand. "Only a formality, Gina. I'm sure he's confirmed it himself, but it's not been reported in the literature so I think it's important to cross-check." I moved on briskly. "And if my pilot experiment shows that the FRIP response is fine, I'd like to mix your Verase DNA with some FRIP DNA and see if the two actually complement one another, as opposed to —"

"Doing something bizarrely unexpected." She began to nod, alight with that scientific radiance I liked so much. "That's a great idea. It will be a nice data set to compare with the animal tri—with my experiments," she amended hastily. "Are you sure it's not too much trouble?"

"It's dead easy, Gina. All I need from you is an antibody that would recognize human FRIP, so that I can detect the protein."

As she nodded, eyes intent on mine, I became aware of the extent of her trust and confidence in me. I felt a stirring of uneasiness: not telling her my doubts about FRIP in the nervous system, no matter how preliminary, was wrong. And now would be the perfect time to bring it up.

"Andy, are you okay?"

"I'm only tired." I took a sip of beer. "The antibody would be great, and some FRIP DNA, if you've got any."

If I was going to keep my suspicions to myself until I had stronger evidence, there was no point in letting on that Helmut already had some FRIP DNA from Rouyle's lab. Safer just to work with the same material Gina had used to clone her combination virus vectors.

"It wasn't strictly permitted for me to transfer any DNA or antibodies back from Germany, but as it happens, I accidentally borrowed a few tubes on my way home." She shrugged. "Of course, both DNA and antisera are notoriously stable at room temperature, so I'm confident they survived the flight."

"Gina, you're amazing," I said. "We make a fantastic team!"

Her smile slipped, and I sensed a familiar pull. With the certainty of a fool, I became convinced we were going to kiss, right there at the bar in front of all our colleagues.

"Listen, Andy. I..."

She stopped, eyes alive with shifting emotions, and I waited, not daring to say a word.

"I'm grateful for your help," she finally said as she lifted the glass to her lips.

19   The Ex-Colleague

*L*ate Wednesday morning, my first *in vitro* FRIP experiment was nearly completed.

On Monday night, after our illusory moment of intimacy in the Henry, Gina had taken me back to Geniaxis and given me the materials I required. I'd stayed late in the lab, zapping her FRIP DNA into cell cultures using a standard transfection procedure. Tuesday evening, after the cells had had a chance to manufacture a suitable amount of protein, Helmut had stepped in while I was busy with other tasks. He'd treated the cell cultures with a peptide that would mimic the action of the human immune system—in essence, the cells would be fooled into believing that a nasty viral attack was imminent. After enough time had elapsed to allow FRIP to be alerted by the warning call of this artificial signal, he'd mashed the cells up in a detergent solution to isolate their proteins.

I'd come back upstairs from the Hot Lab around midnight to find poor Helmut slumped at his bench, fast asleep and murmuring vague German phrases about being attacked by molecules. After gently sending him home, I'd taken up where he left off, running the proteins through a gel matrix under an electric current. This technique would separate the proteins by size in a neat ladder: largest at the top, smallest at the bottom. All that remained today was to reveal the key proteins we were interested in—the needles—amidst the haystack of thousands of other cellular proteins. The basis for this specific detection was the antibody, a specialized molecule designed to recognize only one unique protein, homing in on its target and grasping it with a lover's fervour.

Gina's unauthorized acquisitions had made it possible to answer once and for all whether FRIP could muster an antiviral attack in neuronal cells—and thereby, whether having FRIP in her vaccine would do any good.

And if the answer was no, Rouyle had some explaining to do.

I hadn't quite finished the experiment before my much-anticipated appointment with Raimar Aidula, Rouyle's ex-colleague from Estonia. I fretted impatiently in the reception of the Institute of Child Health. He was late, which wouldn't have been so bad except that, in my nervousness, I'd arrived fifteen minutes early and was unable to concentrate on the articles I'd brought with me.

I was just reading a sentence for the fourth time when a voice called my name. I jerked out of my slouch to find the porter staring at me over her steel-rimmed bifocals, gesturing at the man leaning against the counter.

Raimar Aidula was not the sort who would blend into a crowd. He was as towering as an ancient pine and startlingly fair. His eyes, when they met mine, were a weird milky aquamarine colour.

"Dr O'Hara, I presume?" He approached me with alarming momentum, beefy hand stuck out.

"Andrew, please." I stood up and prepared for the painful crush that never came. Instead, he just pumped my arm firmly and released.

"Call me Raim," he said, his smile dispelling the aloof polar bear aura. "Could we drink something? Been talking all day and my voice is going."

"Coffee?"

"God, no." There was an avuncular glint to his gaze that put me at ease. "Something stronger, yes? I need a double vodka."

The porter met my eye, the corners of her mouth twitching amidst otherwise professionally arranged features, and soon Raim and I were ensconced in the Irish bar around the corner. He held up his glass and produced a string of words in his throat like the sound of ripping cloth.

"Cheers," I said, lifting my Coke and deciding it wasn't worth trying to repeat the sentiment.

"Now, *Andryu*..." He downed half the drink in one leviathan gulp. "You have developed an interest in Richard Rouyle."

I detected a distinct change of atmosphere in the room.

"He's...collaborating with a female friend of mine."

"Both in lab and bedroom, I take it?" He raised a pale eyebrow.

I nodded, embarrassed.

"And you would prefer this girl in *your* bed, yes?" The eyebrow performed a suggestive wiggle.

I shifted uncomfortably this time, and didn't need to nod.

"He always *was*...how do you call it, a ladies' man." His voice trailed off, gaze distant with memory.

"Is that why he was dismissed?"

"Oh, no no *no*, not at all." He stabbed the table with each word for emphasis. "If only. But if *that* grounds for dismissal in our department, it would be a great empty building!" He grinned at me, now more wolf than polar bear. "There was this one time —"

"So," I interrupted hastily. "About Rouyle..."

"Sorry, yes. Well, I'd been there a few years, studying cognitive aspects of vision, when Rouyle was hired as a new PhD student."

I did some rapid maths. "But wasn't he a bit old?"

"Indeed not *truly* new," he said. "Understand he transferred from England a few years into his studentship—and even with that, you're right he was much older than usual students—maybe mid-thirties. Those ones always hard to control, yes? Especially as brought his own project with him, switched supervisors to my colleague Dr Laar. But Rouyle alienated Laar straightaway."

"How?"

"Laar runs a clinical neurology lab focused on Huntington's disease, and Rouyle made no secret he hated the work."

"Let me guess," I said, nodding. "Was it too abstract, not patient-oriented enough for his liking?"

"No," Raim said with surprise. "Quite opposite. Laar's focus was—still is—very applied, testing new cures directly on hospital patients. Rouyle didn't like Laar's neglect of fundamental research into disease mechanism."

"Oh." I blinked. "So what was this project Rouyle brought with him from England?"

"Don't know precisely, for he was very intense, focused...kept research close to chest. What I do know is he wanted to test something in monkeys."

"Monkeys?" I sat up, on full alert.

"Yes, monkeys...don't know English name, but Latin is *Macaca mulatta*." He pantomimed with hands around his face. "Funny nose, dark hooded eyes?"

"Macaques," I breathed, thinking about the title of the *Arch Lat Psychiatry* paper I'd ordered from LitSearch. "Rhesus macaques."

"That's it." He took another swallow of vodka. "Mind if I smoke?"

When I waved him on, he pulled out a bag of tobacco and some papers, mammoth fingers assembling a cigarette with surprising deftness. "Anyway, Rouyle tried to get approval for monkey...for macaque experiments, but was turned down."

"Do you know why?"

He shook his head. "Rumours that animal committee questioned ethics of project. On the other hand, monkeys very expensive, very rare in Estonia. Could be just didn't make cut."

"So what happened next?"

Raim looked down at me with those alien iceberg eyes, cigarette lighter poised. "We managed to keep worst rumours down, reputation of university more or less intact. Even *I* not in on full story. Was a long time ago, but old stinks have a way of hanging around...have I your word as gentleman that this stays between us? Except for the general idea, what you can use to warn off this lady friend?"

"I swear."

"Okay." The lighter flared in the gloom of the pub. "Well, our man Rouyle developed a sudden interest...an interest of *passion*, you understand...with female head of animal facility. She had keys to all areas...mice, rabbits, monkeys. And soon, he had all *her* keys."

"Christ." I felt a rush of recognition.

"But one day, got careless—got caught." Raim's voice was intensifying. "We all thought—okay, this stupid guy, he's finished. And sure enough, they tried to boot him out without degree."

He was staring down, simmering with anger.

"*Tried* to?" I prompted.

Raim raised his head, shook it. "And what do you know? Rouyle fights back. He threatens to go to presses, confess sins, get our university in the muck! Everything was very unstable with aftermath of whole Soviet mess—we were lucky to be in business at all."

He paused to inhale a hefty amount of nicotine. "Not only that, but animal caretaker, who stood to get in biggest muck, was daughter of very important university official, connections with Parliament et cetera. This VIP guy convinced university to keep the whole affair hush."

"So they bought Rouyle off?'"

"Yes," he said darkly. "Awarded big degree, packed off to cushy job at Pfeiffer-deVries—high-ranking favour pulled in there—all on condition he keep quiet. I can still remember when news hit department—nobody could finish work that day." His eyes were awash in bad memories. "This stupid guy, he does such a bad thing and now he's smelling roses!"

"Amazing." I shook my head, unable to quell a spasm of admiration for the younger Rouyle's resourcefulness. I still thought he was a bastard, mind you, but a clever one—one I ought not to underestimate.

"He eventually got some of the work published, didn't he?"

Raim scowled into his glass. "One of his demands, publishing results of tainted monkey trial. Compromise was that it couldn't be submitted to prestigious journals—not that any would have accepted it. Took him a long time to get it in anywhere. Laar refused co-authorship, you see, though it was his lab. Understandable—most editors could smell dead rat."

"Have you read it?" When he shook his head, I asked, "Who were those other co-authors, Viknar and Maaros?"

"Made-up names—Rouyle's work was a one-man show."

"And the journal? *Arch Lat Psychiatry*?"

Raim snorted. "*The Archives of Latvian Psychiatry*. Went bust after only two years. All its papers were as bad as Rouyle's."

"Latvia," I repeated, everything becoming clear. "And Raim...do you remember if this journal was in English?"

He banged his glass against the table. "Latvian. For certain."

I looked at him hopefully. "I don't suppose you...?"

"Not a word, boy." His brow creased. "But why you care about his research topic? Now you know enough to warn your lady friend and save the day, yes? Anyway, bet you a hundred *kroon* you never find a single issue of that god-awful journal left in entire world."

I thought back to the automated response I'd received from the biomedical reprint service. Come to think of it, its routine preliminaries had contained no indication that the article had actually been located. Part of me thought I already had enough information to go to Gina.

But then I sifted through the various scraps of evidence: visceral doubts, unpublished research results and a second-hand account only slightly more solid than gossip. Considering Gina's relationship with Rouyle, these items, even taken together, weren't much more than a flimsy construction. Besides, a lot could change in so many years: a man could reform. I happened to disbelieve this fervently, but without proper proof, Gina just wasn't going to be convinced.

Raim finished the last of his vodka and leaned back in his chair, heavy lids closed almost to slits.

"Now I've told you my story, boy, you can return favour." His wolf expression returned. "Your Magritte Valorius...what's she *really* like?"

I slipped into the lab, failing to achieve an inconspicuous entrance due to the water streaming from my coat, hair and face.

"Nice lunch, O'Hara?" Paul gave me a conspiratorial smile. "Which one of your harem, then?"

I removed my sodden jacket; the rain had come without warning and pummelled me into submission on my jog back from the pub. "*He* was a colleague, no one you know."

"Whatever you say, Andy my lad."

"You got a phone call," Marcy said, too busy with a Petri plate full of bacterial colonies to look up.

"Who was it?"

"Janice." Marcy impaled one of the tiny colonies with a wooden toothpick, as if neutralizing the undead, and shoved it into a flask full of lager-coloured nutrient broth.

"What did she want?" A little thrill ran through me: Janice was head librarian at the Centre, so this must be about Rouyle's article.

"I left a sticky note on your desk." Her tone indicated that the effort involved had been heroic. Privately, I thought that if I were one of those bacteria in her flask, I'd be too intimidated to multiply.

"Janice, eh?" Paul was giving me the eye. "Bit of a departure from your string of young super-scientist babes."

On the note was a request to come upstairs at my earliest convenience. I took the lift up to the library, charged with anticipation. I wasn't put off that the article would be in Latvian. I'd studied German extensively in school, so if Latvian was even remotely related to other European languages, I could improvise. And if not, most scientific words were based on English, and scientific graphs and figures should be universally understandable.

I stepped into the hush of the library, greeting Janice at her customary position on the front desk. I liked Janice, with her matronly solidity and that competence only certain reference librarians command. If Janice couldn't find something, no one could.

"Thanks for popping in, Andrew. I've got some news about that article you requested. And it's not all good, I'm afraid."

I leaned against the counter in anticipation. "There's no e-file available?"

Her lips took on a prim curvature. "E-files are the least of our worries. The article doesn't seem to have ever been copied—even on paper—by any reputable repository in Britain or America. And Helsinki and Stockholm, which normally carry material from the Baltic region, also couldn't help us."

I stared at her. "Are you telling me there's no way to obtain this article?"

"Not at all." She ruffled slightly at my lack of faith. "Just that it's turning out to be trickier—and more expensive—than you may have originally envisaged. They've managed to track down an actual bound journal, but there's an extra fee involved in the copying and faxing, so I need your signature for approval."

"How much?"

She rummaged around her desk and pushed a pink form and a Biro across the counter towards me. "Thirty-five pounds. Sign here, please."

"*Thirty-five pounds?* Where's it coming from, Venus?"

"Close," she said serenely. "Vilnius."

"Christ."

She paused, thought a moment. "If this article is for your research, surely you can just charge it to Dr Valorius's grant. I can process it for you with her budget number now, if you like."

"Um...actually..." I thought fast, not wanting Magritte to get wind of my little side-project. "That'll delay things, won't it, if the paperwork has to go through Admin?"

"To put it mildly."

I was already reaching for my wallet. "Don't worry about it, Janice—I'll deal with the reimbursement later." I scribbled my signature, slapped several notes onto the counter and watched them discreetly disappear.

"Shall I have it faxed to your departmental office?" she asked.

"No!" Several secretaries seated behind Janice looked up collectively in displeasure, and I lowered my voice. "No, actually, could you have it faxed here and then pop it into the interdepartmental mail?" I was stammering, aware of how idiotic I sounded. "Only they're notorious for losing faxes down there, and after investing thirty-five pounds..."

"As you wish," she replied, unperturbed and obviously not believing a word I'd said. I could see her storing up my odd response and filing it, fully indexed and cross-referenced, into her mental archives for some possible future use.

❦ ❦ ❦

Helmut homed in on me immediately when I returned from the library, holding a piece of film.

"Is that it?" I stared at him, excitement rising.

"I couldn't stand to wait," he confessed in a low voice. "I sneaked into your fridge and finished the experiment while you were at lunch."

"Is Magritte around?" I sensed the heaviness of Paul's curiosity, but didn't look over.

"No, she's gone across town for a seminar."

"Good—let's have a look."

He pulled up a chair and held up the film.

"It's a mixed result, Andy. SLIP acted the same as the last two times." He pointed a finger at one blank area of the film. "See, here. It's totally clean again, *ja*? TRAP is *not* activated in the neuronal cells after immune stimulation." He pointed out a few more places where, in contrast, very dark bands were evident. "But here, TRAP is nicely lit up after immune stimulation in fibroblast cells."

"But the results were mixed, you say. Did FRIP not act the same as SLIP?"

"Well, we cannot say for sure." Helmut frowned. "Here you see no TRAP activation in neuronal cells expressing FRIP, *ja*, but *con-*

trols have failed...I cannot see any evidence that FRIP protein is even there, and the growth signalling is also absent—even in the control fibroblasts." He tapped a finger on the film, which indeed showed no black bands in those lanes.

"That's odd," I said slowly.

"Are you sure Rouyle's FRIP DNA was okay? I didn't have time to test it."

"I didn't use his DNA in the end—his stingy technician hadn't sent you enough to transfect an amoeba," I said. "And as I didn't want to waste time growing up more, I borrowed some FRIP DNA from that friend I mentioned before, the same one who gave us the antibody."

His forehead pleated. "Maybe your friend's antibody wasn't any good."

"I doubt it—if it was just antibody failure, you'd still see the growth signal being passed on if FRIP were there, even if FRIP was invisible to us. More likely to be the DNA."

"There was something..." Helmut tapped pencil to chin. "I didn't think it was worth to mention at the time."

"Tell me."

"Before I harvested the proteins, I took a routine look at all the cell cultures under the microscope. They all seem healthy—*except* for the neuronal cells transfected with FRIP."

"What was wrong with them?"

He shrugged. "Hard to describe. They looked...funny. Neuronal processes shrivelled, withdrawn. Not so...shiny, you know? Maybe your friend's DNA was contaminated with mycoplasma or something."

"Were the fibroblasts that got FRIP DNA also sick?"

He regarded me thoughtfully. "No, they weren't. That is a good point; if it was mycoplasma or whatsoever, both cell types should be infected."

I was stumped. "Listen, Helmut, you've shown three times now that SLIP is violating the dogma in neuronal cells. If we can prove it's more universal by showing it with FRIP, I reckon you could knock up a quick, sexy paper for *Current Biology*. How soon can you prep more of the FRIP DNA you got from Rouyle's technician?"

"I already transformed it into bacteria—the Petri plates are in the refrigerator."

"I noticed that Marcy is growing up some bacteria today. Maybe if you're nice to her, she'll prep your DNA in parallel?"

He just looked at me. "You are joking, right?"

"Marcy," I called over, voice laced with sweetness.

"I don't like the sound of that," she grumbled. "If it's a favour you want, it'll cost you. And I mean actual cash."

"You tell her, Helmut," I said breezily, and he shot me a nasty look.

"What on *earth* are you two up to?" Paul said.

I winked at Helmut, who scowled back, and made a show of strolling back to my desk, but in fact, I was disturbed by this result. Both Helmut and I were quite experienced, not prone to making stupid errors. Gina wasn't likely to have stolen the wrong reagents by mistake, either. She had clearly stated that the DNA she'd taken from Rouyle's lab was the same batch used to clone the FRIP gene into the new combination vaccine, and that the antibody was the same lot she'd used to detect that FRIP.

Something strange was going on, and it was going to take time to repeat the experiment. But scientists are accustomed to delayed gratification, and I thought I had no choice but to be patient, to prove the point with my usual meticulousness before presenting the damning evidence to Gina with triumphant fanfare.

If only I had ignored all my training and trusted what was already in front of me.

20 *In Vivo*

$\mathcal{F}$ollowing my disturbing revelation that Rouyle's FRIP might be a random and potentially dangerous element in Gina's new vaccine, nearly a week slipped by without any significant communication with her. I hadn't seen her in person since the evening we'd met in the Henry. A few days later, there'd been a cryptic, impersonal e-mail from her about generating the SCID/pbl mice for the trial. She was spending most of her time in the Mouse House, according to Christine, so I hadn't caught so much as a glimpse of her. Until this evening.

It was late, and the lab had gone dark in my brief absence. My stomach was queasy from a fast food supper eaten faster than intended. I went over to my desk, hand outstretched towards the lamp, but then stopped when I spotted the sole lit square across the courtyard. Concealed in shadows, I stood by the glass and watched Gina ricochet about her workspace like a subatomic particle in a supercollider. Serious, purposeful and fluid, she seemed to be multitasking dozens of experiments with grim ease.

I must have observed for more than ten minutes, longing and desire eating away at me. She didn't appear at all happy or charged with her usual animation. She just looked tired, and about as far away as a person could be while still remaining in visual range.

The next morning, I stood at the Board, dazed over my cup of coffee. Paul, I was almost certain, must have pinned up the latest clipping:

Boffins get wiggy with it

We all saw the classic snaps of the mouse growing a human ear on its back and wondered what the world was coming to, but now things are getting really hairy.

Scientists in Italy say they've created a hybrid mouse that can grow a complete pelt of human hair. Pieces of human scalp were transplanted onto immune-deficient mutant mice and after a few months of hormone treatment, the Italians report three inches of luscious locks.

Head boffin, Dr Sergio Taratula, stressed that several colours and types of hair had been produced so far, including blond, brunette and Afro, and that someday soon they would be attempting to transplant the world's first mousy hair-do onto bald human volunteers.

No thanks, Serg: I think I prefer a rug.

And the departmental poet had struck again:

Post-Doctoral Haiku No. 25
by: Dr Anonymous

Lonely midnight gel
With cursèd old electrodes:
Tragic explosion

I went to lab, turned on the computer and was confronted with an e-mail from Gina:

Remember the things we discussed earlier? They'll be ready tonight around eight. I'm a bit swamped, so it would be great if you could swing by — sorry for the bother.

I couldn't stop the smile; she probably had no idea that she'd just made my day.

The "things we discussed earlier" were the first exploratory blood samples from the fledgling SCID/pbl mice, which I had offered to analyze. There were several antibodies in my fridge that could detect growth factors and proteins normally secreted by a healthy human's immune system. If I could identify the relevant factors in the blood samples, it would indicate that the human xenograft had "taken," and that the hybrid mice were ready to respond to the new combination vaccine. And if so, the unauthorized trial could finally begin.

Christine had been as scarce as Gina had recently, but I'd managed to pin her down for a more complete update earlier. Downstairs, I'd found her already queuing up for the tea machine. Cameron was with her too, laughing as she whispered in his ear.

"Joining us?" Cameron asked me amiably.

"Actually, Andy and I need to talk about something in private. He's having woman trouble, you know?" Christine rolled her eyes as if I were a lost cause. Which in many respects, I realized, was true.

"Sure." Cameron went a bit quiet. "I'll go catch up with Susan and those folks, then. Have a nice therapy session."

227

He took his cup of tea and pushed on ahead.

"He's been acting funny all week." Christine shoved her polystyrene cup under the metal teat.

"Maybe it's this Newcastle business."

She released her breath in frustration. "The interview isn't until tomorrow, and even if I decide I want the job—*if*, I stress—there are lots of other applicants. It's premature to be so worried, wouldn't you say?"

"From the male perspective..."

"There's a switch, eh?" Her voice sounded light, but I heard the expectancy underneath.

"We do worry, Chris. We get irrational. We sometimes take things personally even when they aren't intended that way."

"Going for this interview has nothing to do with how I feel for Cam." She kept her voice low as we negotiated the cashier and made our way through into the seating area. She seemed to be heading for that same cluster of chairs near the back exit, with their deceptive atmosphere of privacy, but considering what we were going to be talking about in a moment, I corralled her firmly towards the opposite side of the room. After hearing Raim's account of Rouyle's primate experiments and *in flagrante* discovery, I was feeling even more paranoid about the mouse escapade.

"Yeah, but Chris, it's never too soon to panic, especially if you're not talking to him about it. You're not, are you?" She scowled, shook her head. "He'll read even more into it if you avoid the issue."

She took a sip of tea, evading my attempts at frank eye contact. "I thought we were here because you wanted an update on the mice, not my love life."

I sighed. "Fine."

"The cage transfer went smoothly." Her voice dipped so low that I could barely make it out. "We had too many litters born last month anyway, so it was easy to move them into Geniaxis's area and fudge the records. Physically, you can't tell the SCIDs apart from some of the other strains Gina's got going, so it would be difficult to catch us out now. If the cages weren't numbered, even I couldn't tell which was which."

"And the human blood?"

"I collected it from Antonio last Tuesday evening, purified the correct cells and treated them with the appropriate factors to enrich for the right progenitor population. It went fine...good yields. We injected the mice on Wednesday, and now it's been a week, which should be sufficient for complete xenograft establishment."

"There's no way anyone could have seen Gina doing the injections?"

Christine shrugged. "Gina's injecting mice all the time. But we made sure no one was around, though sometimes it's difficult to lose that weird guy, the one with the beady eyes..."

"Steve?"

"He's creepy—and always underfoot."

"Gina's drawing blood from the mice tonight for me to test."

Christine nodded in confirmation. "It's all going swimmingly. With any luck, the actual *in vivo* trial can begin tomorrow, and if the combination herpes vaccine is toxic, we should know sometime next week."

"Then she's going to challenge the mice with Vera Fever Virus, right, to make sure the therapy has worked?" It was a secondary question to whether the vaccine was safe, but just as important in my view.

"Just try to stop her—she's got a brutal schedule lined up." Christine shook her head admiringly. "After the Vera Fever challenge next week, she's got this mad idea to monitor the mice's progress every three hours for four days straight. She'll have to sleep in the lab; I told her to count me out between midnight and nine in the morning. I've never seen anyone so fired up—I don't know where she gets the energy."

"So it sounds like things are under control," I said.

"Don't tax your delicate neurons, Andy: the ladies have it well in hand."

"As they always seem to when we hapless men are out of the picture?" I grinned at her, but she had paused, worrying her lower lip with an absent thumb.

"What is it, Chris?"

"Only...speaking of hapless men, I was wondering how things were going between Gina and Rouyle."

"We don't talk about that. Why?"

"It's just that she's been acting a bit...skittish."

"She's risking quite a bit on this enterprise you're cooking upstairs."

"No, that's not what I meant at all. She's..." Christine paused, strangely indecisive.

"Have you two talked about him? Or me?" I leaned forward—was I about to receive some privileged information at last?

"No, forget it," she said. "By the way, Gina mentioned you were doing some parallel *in vitro* trials of your own. How're those going?"

I waggled my hand back and forth. "The first go was a failure, but I think it was just for trivial technical reasons. I'll let you know what happens with the repeat experiment."

At that moment, it occurred to me that I still hadn't told Christine about Rouyle's past. The confession was long overdue—after all, unlike with Gina, I had no good reason not to tell her. I was just opening my mouth when Christine's timer started to go off.

"Hey, that's me, Andy, due back in the tissue culture suite." She paused mid-flight. "If you've got the time, could you take Cam down the pub on Friday or Saturday?" I got the message: *talk some sense into him, please.*

I stood in the corridor, peering through the glass into the twilight murk of Geniaxis. My skin was tingling with expectation as I pressed the buzzer.

"Dr Boyd speaking." A male voice, clipped and impatient. "Can I help you?"

Who the hell was Dr Boyd? I thought fast.

"Yes, it's Dr O'Hara from Cell and Molecular." I crafted a smoothly professional tone. "I'm here to see Dr Kraymer."

"One moment." The intercom emitted a burp of static and died. Boyd...the name was familiar for some reason.

I crossed my arms, uncrossed them, then finally dangled them at my sides. To my relief, it was Gina who appeared in the sudden flare of fluorescent lights, frowning as she opened the door.

"You're early!" she whispered, grey eyes flashing at me. She stood there flushed and emanating impatience, and I was struck by the furtive glimpse of low-cut silk blouse and clinging wool skirt beneath her undone white coat.

"I know I am." I tried to cover my discomfort. "I should've rung first. Who's the bloke?"

"My boss." Now I remembered the name. "He sometimes stays late and pesters us while we're trying to work."

"Should I go away?"

"No, he's curious now. Just follow my lead, okay?"

I had to hurry to keep up.

"It's absolutely no problem, Andy," she announced as she strode into the lab. "I can certainly spare ten microlitres of Taq."

I took in the scene over Gina's shoulder. The radio was absent from its accustomed late-night position, but the rest of the bench was a disaster: multiple ice buckets crammed with sample tubes, racks and racks of more tubes obviously waiting their turn, measuring cylinders full of various freshly-prepared solutions, spills and empty containers and crumpled packaging. An older man with dishevelled hair and loosened tie was leaning against the bench, eyeing me with interest.

Gina said, "Andrew's a post-doc in the Valorius lab," before crouching down to poke around in her freezer.

I smiled winningly and stuck out my hand, hoping it wasn't damp with nervous perspiration. He smiled back, gave me a firm shake. "Thomas Boyd, scientific director of Geniaxis."

"I've heard good things about you, Dr Boyd," I said.

"And I'm quite impressed by your Magritte—we approached her about a consultancy a few years back when we were struggling to get established."

"Really?"

Meanwhile, Gina was removing a polystyrene box full of ice from the bottom shelf of the freezer. I looked back up at Boyd, not wanting to draw attention to what she was doing.

"But she was having none of it," he continued ruefully.

"I wouldn't take it personally, Dr Boyd. She's about as academic as it gets." Out of the corner of my eye, I saw Gina manipulate something in the box.

He peered at me more carefully now, eyes inquisitive behind thick plastic spectacles. "Are you one of Gina's many admirers, then?"

"Thomas, please." She stood up, colour deepening, with familiar blue tube of Taq lodged inconspicuously in the centre of the crushed ice in the box. As she busied herself with her pipettor in an absurd parody of our first meeting, the sensation of lost time and wasted chances settled over me in an unexpected weight of sadness.

231

"I saw her seminar at Cambridge," I said, putting on the voice I used to use when addressing the parents of prospective girlfriends. "And I was very impressed by her herpes gene therapy strategy. So I guess you could call me an admirer of sorts."

I caught a glimpse of Gina's smile, quickly squelched, as she operated the pipettor.

Boyd nodded. "Yes, we're all very excited here about her work. I can't go into any details, of course, but let's just say that things are looking promising...*very* promising of late with regard to moving her viruses out of the lab and into the clinic."

Just then, a mobile phone went off somewhere on his person. He patted his blazer pockets until he'd located the offending item, then cringed at the number on the screen. "It's the wife—excuse me, please."

While he withdrew and started murmuring into the receiver, Gina finished with the Taq. She was just about to whisper something to me when Boyd stashed the phone back in his pocket, said, "Right, kids, I'm off home now, probably via the florist's. Shall I escort you out on my way, Andrew, so that Gina doesn't have to interrupt her assay?" His voice was solicitous, but I clearly received the message.

"You can keep the box, Andy." Gina's intent look was trying to transmit a message of her own. "It's just recycled packaging."

"Coming, Andrew?" Boyd grabbed his coat and briefcase from a nearby chair.

"Still up for that drink at the Henry later?" Gina asked me.

"Absolutely," I replied smoothly. "That is, if I manage to finish before last orders."

Boyd beamed at me, obviously an aficionado of hard work.

"I'll call you when I'm done," she said.

"She's one of the best—and most committed—scientists I've ever had the pleasure of working with," Boyd confided to me in the foyer.

I didn't know how to respond, so I just nodded at him, and we parted ways in the dark corridor outside.

The phone was already ringing as I walked into my own lab. There wasn't anyone else in the main room, but I could hear music issuing from the tissue culture suite. Probably Helmut, by the doleful choice of artist.

"I've got it!" I dashed for the phone.

"Andy?" It was Gina, breathless.

"That was close." I wedged the receiver between my shoulder and ear and dug my hand into the cold chips of ice.

"Closer than you think," she said, just as my fingers contacted the plastic tubes hidden underneath. "All the blood samples are on the bottom of that box."

"Elementary, my dear Kraymer. Why did you risk it?"

"I panicked," she said. "I thought he'd never leave, and I knew your tests would take time. I don't suppose you can come back down for a moment?"

"My pleasure," I replied. "Hey—do want your Taq back?"

"Just hurry up!"

✦ ✦ ✦

Gina was already waiting at the door.

"We've got to stop meeting like this," I quipped as she ushered me inside impatiently.

"You're telling me—I've got like a million things left to do tonight before I have to..." She paused, went on, "before I get to go home." She shot me a business-like smile, and I followed her obediently, awash in *déjà vu*.

"So the Henry thing was just a ruse," I said to her back. "That's good, because I wasn't joking about the last-orders bit."

"I just didn't want you to disappear before we could talk again."

"I reckoned." I was disappointed despite myself.

She pulled out a file folder from a pile on her desk and extricated a sheet of paper with a column of numbers and acronyms.

"It's easy," she said, passing the paper to me. "S stands for the basic SCID mice, and SP are the candidate SCID/pbls. The numbers are just the individual mouse codes. Not to pressure you, but do you think you'll have the results by tonight?"

I looked at my watch. "I've already set up the ELISA plates, and Chris gave me a quick blood prep kit, so it shouldn't be a problem. I'll e-mail you the results —" I held up a hand as she opened her mouth to protest. "Gina, I'm not stupid, you know. Just a 'yes' if the SCID/pbl mice are producing the relevant human immune proteins in sufficient amounts, and a 'no' if there's a problem. Agreed?"

She sighed, seeming to thaw for the first time that evening.

"Sorry, Andy. I didn't mean to be short with you," she said. "I'm really rushed tonight, and the boss's visit didn't help. I do appreciate what you're doing. If your test results are positive, we can start the mouse trial first thing in the morning."

"Don't worry about it," I said. "Hey, I know tonight is out, but how about getting together tomorrow for a meal? Chris was telling me about this fantastic —"

"I can't." She looked down. "Richard will be in town. I have to meet him in a few hours, actually."

My innards collapsed. "Business or pleasure?"

"Final preparations for the Phase I." She twisted the pearls around her neck with anxious fingers. "There's a lot to arrange with Geniaxis. For the next week or so, I'm likely to be...unavailable."

"I'll have dinner with you," someone said sweetly from the doorway.

Gina hissed a swift intake of breath, and I jerked my head around to find Maria slouched against the door frame, looking like a femme fatale in leather jacket, miniskirt, black stockings and boots. I wondered how long she'd been standing there, and I rummaged back through the conversation, trying to figure out how many sentences had elapsed since we'd said anything incriminating.

"How about it, Andy?" The shrewd shadow about Maria's eyes concealed just how informed she actually was.

"Fine." A numb impetus was pushing me forward. I saw the stricken look on Gina's face, but refused to care—I'd had about as much as I could take.

"Wonderful." Maria's attention flicked towards Gina before focusing back on me. "My cell cultures await...don't let me interrupt your cosy chat." And with that, she disappeared down the corridor.

Gina had gone pale. "Do you think she actually...?"

I shrugged. "Possibly. We weren't being terribly quiet."

"This is all I need right now." She slumped onto her stool, cradled her head in her arms on the workbench.

"I can try to find out...tomorrow."

"Just be discreet about it." Her voice sounded smothered.

I looked at the back of her head for a moment. "You know, I realize the two of you don't get along, but if she did overhear something, I think we can trust her not to say anything. She's a decent person."

She raised her head, eyes gone dark with emotions I couldn't read. I could almost sense her tension triggering the hairs on my arms, and at that moment, I wanted to hate her as much as I loved her.

"It's not Maria I'd rather have dinner with," I said.

"Then you're a fool," she said, with a sad little smile.

I walked away and didn't look back, though I somehow retained the sensation of her unhappy eyes following me long after I'd left the Geniaxis complex.

"I'm off—wish me luck!" Christine called out.

I glanced up from the rectangular ELISA plate in my hand, its ninety-six tiny wells glistening as the yellow colour started to develop. She was standing at the door, coat on and rucksack slung over one shoulder.

"You're leaving it a bit late, aren't you?" I was aware that my voice sounded flat.

"The interview's not till the afternoon." Then she got a closer look. "What's the matter?"

I shrugged, tapping at the plate to help the droplets of solution mix together. "I just found out that Rouyle's come to town for an entire week. And Gina and I quarrelled, sort of."

"Ouch. Anything else?"

"Well, I *do* have a date with Maria tomorrow evening," I said with false brightness.

Christine's eyebrows scrunched downward into perplexed new shapes. "Are you sure you know what you're doing?"

I clenched my jaw, refusing to answer on principle.

"Maria's a nice woman, but she's not right for you. She's too..." Christine searched for the word. "*Together.*"

"Thanks a lot!" I scowled down at the plastic plate as its chemical reactions went inexorably forward.

"I don't mean that the way it sounds." She moved behind me,

mussed my hair. "It's just...people who are that together can be a bit impatient. Can have unrealistic expectations."

"In other words, she'll eat me alive."

Christine sighed in exasperation, patted my hair back into place. "I've really got to run now. You'll be okay?"

"Of course." I swivelled around on my stool and pulled her down for a kiss. "And best of luck."

✦ ✦ ✦

From: a.ohara@rcc.cmb.ac.uk
To: glkraymer@geniaxis.com
Subject: YES

✦ ✦ ✦

I stood in the crimson dusk of the darkroom, waiting for my film to traverse the developer's chemical bowels. It was nearly midnight. The film was the repeat experiment about FRIP that I'd been itching to see all week. Not only that, but the SCID/pbl mice had established gloriously well—it was a vindication of my whole idea. I should have been energized. But at the moment, I just didn't care.

I gripped the edge of the counter, dizzy from the lack of visual cues, from the sting of the fixer and developer solutions, from the fact that I'd had nothing to eat since lunchtime. I had no idea I'd allowed so much optimism about Gina to accumulate until it had been shattered earlier in the evening. It was clear from her brittle impatience that she was anticipating far more than mere clinical trial negotiations from Rouyle.

A dozen thoughts and images, both real and imagined, flashed through my mind like a movie trailer: Gina and Rouyle on the dance floor in Cambridge, his hand sliding down the low-cut back of her dress. Rouyle and the Estonian animal caretaker, trysting illicitly among the cages. Rouyle, carelessly insulting my poster in Cambridge. Gina in the canteen, leaning over to murmur something to Christine about giving me a go. The undeniable sensation that she'd wanted me to kiss her in the Henry, and the feel of her hair when I'd embraced her in this very spot, so long ago.

"You're a fool." I repeated her parting words softly in the darkness, unable to deny their patent truth. I couldn't help chasing up the words with a bitter laugh. Here I was, trapped once again in late night lab purgatory performing tasks that had nothing to do with my own work, whereas Gina was long gone to meet her lover. My behaviour was utterly stupid, but since it was entirely self-inflicted, that left me with no one to blame but myself.

The top of the film appeared at the exit slot. I yanked it out savagely instead of letting the rollers do the work as you were supposed to. Held it up to the bordello brightness of the safelight. Looked, and then looked again, stunned. Was forced to brace myself on the counter once more as the chemical air pressed in on me.

I grabbed the film and propelled myself through the barrel door, bruising an arm in my haste to escape. An infestation of brown spots swarmed into my eyes and blotted out the corridor. I leaned against the wall until the dizzy spell passed, then returned to my desk and fell into the chair. Heedless of my physical discomfort, I held up the film to see if I had imagined what I thought I'd just seen in the darkroom.

I had performed a similar experiment as before, except this time I'd included both Gina's FRIP DNA and Helmut's FRIP DNA side-by-side, pitted against one another in a molecular marathon.

The first part of the experiment dealt with Helmut's FRIP DNA, the new stuff Marcy had grudgingly prepared fresh from the batch sent by Rouyle's technician. Just like last week, I could see no black band where FRIP ought to be: the lane was completely clear. But unlike last time, the "firefighter" TRAP signal as well as the "postal" growth signals were strongly activated in fibroblasts, suggesting that FRIP—though not recognized by Gina's antibody—had indeed passed on both messages.

But just as I'd feared, in the brain-derived neuronal cells, although Helmut's FRIP had stimulated a hefty growth signal, the antiviral TRAP protein had not been activated: the lane was empty. Here it was at last, proof that Rouyle's idea was never going to work in Gina's gene therapy strategy. FRIP would be defunct in the brains of any African villagers who received the vaccine, and would be unable to help fight off any Vera Fever infections.

I went on to the second half of the experiment, identical to the first except that I'd re-tested the FRIP DNA that Gina had stolen from Rouyle's lab. As in the previous week, the film showed no growth signal or TRAP activation in either cell type. But Helmut's FRIP DNA had turned on some signals, so it was obviously different from Gina's, even though they were both supposed to encode the same gene. Very strange.

But there was something even more bizarre going on. In contrast to what had occurred with Helmut's DNA, I now saw a thick black band in the lane where I'd transfected in Gina's DNA and used the antibody Gina had provided to detect the presence of the protein. The only problem was, the signal corresponded to a protein of completely the wrong size. It was almost forty kilodaltons too small, in fact, at the very bottom of the gel, instead of being nestled in the middle as it should have been if it were FRIP. I lined up the film to the ladder of coloured size markers I'd run down one side of the gel for reference, but it wasn't necessary: even a child could see that the protein being produced could not possibly be FRIP.

What was different from the previous week, when Helmut and I had tried out Gina's FRIP DNA and nothing at all had been visible? I dashed over to Helmut's desk, flipped back a few dozen pages in his notebook and studied the old film in bafflement.

Then it hit me: in my hurry to finish this evening, I had taken short cuts and run the gel for a much shorter time than I had for the previous experiment. I could see from the ladder of size standards on last week's attempt that the mysterious small protein had probably run right off the bottom of the gel. As it was, I was lucky the same thing hadn't happened this evening: the black band was only a centimetre from the edge of the membrane.

I went back to my desk, sat down again and examined the latest film once more. Why didn't the lanes with Helmut's FRIP DNA react with Gina's antibody, show that same small protein? And how had Gina failed to notice this drastic discrepancy in protein size during her tissue culture experiments back in Germany?

I rubbed my forehead, trying to remember what she'd told me at Julie's party. She said she'd infected cells in culture, and that she'd been able to detect both FRIP and Verase. But then I remembered that Gina wasn't a biochemist—she was a virologist with expertise in cell biology. She wouldn't have ground up the cells and fractionated the proteins by size like I had done. Instead, she would have fixed the intact cells, stained them with fluorescent antibodies and looked at them under the microscope. Visualizing proteins this way told you where they were located in the cell, but gave you no information about their molecular mass. For all she knew, the bright red or green speckles she was seeing corresponded to FRIP. Why would she have had cause to think anything else?

I drummed my fingers against the desk, forcing my tired mind to think. All the results together strongly suggested that Helmut's DNA encoded *bona fide* FRIP, but that Gina's DNA was not FRIP at all, but some other, smaller gene. Moreover, the antibody Gina had taken from Germany was not specific for FRIP, but for that smaller mystery protein.

What was going on?

The answer clicked into place with an almost physical impact. Gina had inadvertently inserted the wrong gene into her herpes virus vectors, having been led to believe that it was in fact FRIP. Clearly, Rouyle had never had any intention of using FRIP in combination with her gene therapy vectors at all.

I slammed my fist onto the opened notebook. The conclusion was inescapable. And there were now two key questions remaining. One, what was the mystery gene that had been swapped in FRIP's place? And, two, was this substitution a secret only of Rouyle's, or was Pfeiffer-deVries in on it as well? Or even Boyd? My mind reeled at the possible layers of conspiracy.

I had to tell Gina everything before it was too late. What more proof did I need? It was stupid that I didn't have her phone number, and a hasty enquiry soon determined that both her home and mobile lines were ex-directory.

I called up my Inbox. E-mail was probably the last thing on her mind at the moment, but tomorrow morning would be soon enough. It was too risky to spell anything out, but I asked her to contact me first thing, making the urgency clear.

After stashing the disturbing film in my drawer, I slipped out of the lab and headed towards Holborn station. I didn't know why, but I had to suppress the sudden urge to pelt down the pavement like a fugitive.

21   *Dirty Weekend*

*A*ffecting a casualness I didn't feel, I sauntered into the lab and murmured a subdued but civil greeting of the morning variety.

Kathy looked up at me in confusion, blinking. It had similarly disturbed her equilibrium the one or two other times I'd made it in before nine o'clock.

"To what do we owe honour, O'Hara?" Magritte asked. Then she got a closer look at my face. "How late were you here last night?" She actually clucked in maternal sympathy. Now that I thought about it, she'd been in an unusually good mood for the past week.

"You look like shit," Paul clarified helpfully.

"Good morning to you too." I slung down my rucksack and turned on the computer.

"Fresh coffee in my office," Magritte said. "Better than that battery acid from departmental machine. Surely can spare five minutes."

Tempting. It would probably take that long for the computer to get going, but meanwhile I had some pressing data-doctoring to perform.

"Or perhaps a whole pot intravenously," Paul suggested.

"Helmut in yet?" I asked, off-hand. He was one of the few lab members who could also be relied on to be late: a time-honoured post-doctoral prerogative.

"No sightings of any morose Germanic types yet," Paul said, narrowing his eyes at me.

I opened up my lab notebook, managing to appear so industrious that it inspired a collective, unspoken decision to leave me alone. When the epicentre of the morning buzz had moved away, I pulled out the previous night's film and a pair of scissors.

It was standard practice to crop a piece of film to save room in one's notebook. What wasn't standard was carefully trimming off incriminating bits of data. But that's exactly what I did, slowly and methodically, on the portion of film containing the lanes transfected with Gina's mystery DNA. I hid this strip of film with its puzzling, too-small black band in my file drawer; when the time came, I could line it up with the rest of the film and prove to Gina what her DNA actually was...or more pertinently, wasn't.

The computer chirped at me. I clicked open the mail programme to see how Gina had responded to my last e-mail, already tensed to rise from my seat and run down to meet her.

Unbelievably, my Inbox was empty.

A wave of disorientation swept over me. Gina had probably had a late night as well (I didn't want to dwell on the details), but she had been very clear: she needed my ELISA result so she could begin the animal trial straightaway. There had to be a logical reason why she had failed to get in touch.

I decided to ask Maria, since I had to contact her anyway. I didn't have the energy to be subtle, either. After a few pleasantries and logistics about getting together later, I typed:

    By the way, I don't suppose you've seen Gina today? Only
    I sent her an important e-mail late last night and I wanted
    to know if she'd read it yet.

"Well?"

Helmut stood behind me, fair complexion still bruised red from the cold. Then, in a lower voice, "I pass the boss just now, going towards her office, so the beach is clear. Oh, by the way, I check my post on the way in and I notice also this comes for you." He thrust a worn interdepartmental envelope at me, leaning in to get a glimpse of the tempting film stuck into my notebook.

I took the envelope, only having time to notice that it had come from Janice at the library before Helmut had pulled up a stool.

"Helmut, my man." I deployed a tone of collegial enthusiasm. "I think we're in business."

"Marcy's prep of DNA is better?" He scanned the first bit of the film, face falling. "But there is still no FRIP band."

"That's true," I said. "But look at that glorious growth signal activation, only in the lanes where I transfected in Marcy's FRIP DNA, and not in the controls! There's got to be FRIP there! And you can see the antiviral TRAP activation in the fibroblasts."

"But not in PC12s." Helmut was starting to nod. "So neither FRIP nor SLIP can phosphorylate TRAP in neuronal cells, just as you hypothesized. This is most interesting! I am starting to obtain your drift vis-à-vis a *Current Biology* paper."

Helmut's ready confirmation of what I had already gleaned from the experiment was disquieting. Despite the clarity of the results, I'd been half hoping he would come up with a logical counter-argument why FRIP might still be useful in the brain.

"So it looks like your friend's DNA and antibody were *Scheisse* all along," Helmut was musing. "We have to obtain a better FRIP antibody from Rouyle's lab to confirm expression before we can publish this story. And of course also testing other neuronal cell types will be of importance. If it turns out to be a universal phenomenon...then our uncle is Bob."

He moved off with a jaunty swing to his step just as the computer beeped its new-mail alert at me.

I wavered for a few seconds over the temptation of Janice's envelope before choosing to open the e-mail.

```
Dear Andy,

Gina never came into the main Geniaxis complex at all this
morning, so maybe she never checked her e-mail. I asked
around, and Steve said she was up in the mouse room at some
ungodly hour, like 07.30, doing injections, but she's gone
now. She's taken today off for a long weekend in Cornwall
with darling Richard.

Didn't she tell you...???

See ya at 7,

Maria
```

The words on the screen knocked the air from my lungs.

I didn't know what was worse, that she was away or that she was with Rouyle. It seemed crazy for her to have left her mice unattended, especially with Christine in Newcastle, but then I remembered it would take a few days for the herpes virus vaccine to infect and spread in the animals. Presumably, she'd taken advantage of the down-time to be with Rouyle. But that left me, alone with my terrible burden of information, to stew the entire weekend. And all this, after having convinced myself that everything was going to be okay. Gina was supposed to have seen my warning, sought me out, listened to my arguments and reported to Boyd straightaway. Then, irrevocably, the African Phase I clinical trial would be cancelled, and Rouyle summarily dismissed, both from the collaboration and from Gina's affections. After my restless night, the morning was *supposed* to have brought a satisfying resolution.

When my knuckles started to ache, I realized I was still clutching the interdepartmental envelope. I ripped it open and slid out the fax. The coversheet was in English sprinkled with a few inscrutable, probably Lithuanian phrases, and there was a sprightly yellow sticky note affixed to the upper left-hand corner.

Dear Andrew,

Here's your far-flung article at last. I hope it's more informative than it looks.

Kind regards,

Janice

I peeled away the coversheet and stared eagerly at the first page of the reprint.

So much for linguistic similarities: the language was absolute gibberish.

Early in and early out: definitely atypical behaviour, I thought as I gathered up my things to meet Maria for our date. I couldn't honestly say that I was looking forward to it. I had been irritable all day, finding it difficult to concentrate on my work, let alone on basic social interactions. Magritte studied me with concern several times throughout the afternoon, but each time I'd caught her, she'd turned away. Even Paul had picked up on my mood and, aside from his early morning quips, hadn't teased me again.

I'd kept my experiments to the minimum and had mostly sat at my desk, hovering by my Inbox while pretending to catch up on my reading. I knew that Gina was in Cornwall, but I couldn't help thinking there might be a chance she'd check her mail remotely. I did receive a light-hearted message from Christine, telling me that her interview had gone well but not to bother replying because she'd been invited hill-walking over the weekend with some people from the department.

Duly reminded, I e-mailed Cameron and arranged to meet him on Saturday evening for a drink.

But primarily, I'd pored over Rouyle's old article, trying to glean something from the figures. There were a few tantalizing pictures of what looked like old-fashioned biochemical fractionation, supporting my theory that PAX was probably a biological extract containing some sort of activity. However, the majority were graphs of electrical traces, the type of data you'd gather if you were wiring up electrodes to individual neurons and measuring their signals—in other words, strictly specialist material. Even if the figure legends had been in English, I probably wouldn't have been able to understand the results until I had read their actual written descriptions in the body of the text, where it was traditional for the author to digest the raw data and provide an attempt at logical interpretation. Accordingly, I wasted an amazing amount of time searching the Web for an online Latvian-to-English translation programme sophisticated enough to handle scientific prose—and came up with nothing.

As I put on my coat, Paul looked up slyly from his gel apparatus. "Off early, then? Hot date?"

"In a manner of speaking, yes."

Paul mentally regrouped, putting down his pipettor. "Who with?"

"Maria." I grabbed my rucksack from underneath my desk, preparing myself for the onslaught.

"I approve," he said quietly.

"Thanks, Dad. I won't stay out too late."

"Although, it's a pity it didn't work out with..." He stopped. "I mean, have a good time."

"Yeah, okay, Paul, whatever." I definitely preferred his smart-arse side. "See you Monday."

"Don't blow it!" he yelled after me. That was more like it.

I took the stairs down and made my way towards Geniaxis. Maria wasn't waiting outside yet, but I was a couple of minutes early. I leaned against the wall across from the door to wait. It seemed as if whenever I stopped doing something concrete, my mind would slide into the churning mess of the whole Gina/Rouyle/FRIP debacle. It was only the *clank* of the door release that jarred me back to the reality of the corridor.

I looked up, expecting to see Maria. Instead, two extremely tall black men in expensive suits were making their way out, jabbering in a musical tongue. They ignored me completely. One seemed angry, while the other was bobbing his head in a deferential, agitated manner as they flowed past down the corridor. I remembered that critical Phase I arrangements were being finalized here in the next week; perhaps these men were representatives from the African nation in question. If so, they didn't seem to share Boyd's confidence.

Maria appeared in the lobby, her face brightening as she waved at me behind the glass doors. After the way she had neatly manoeuvred me into this date, I had been feeling wary; the invitation had seemed mostly about scoring points against Gina. But her smile was genuine as she let herself out, and I felt myself relax. I did like Maria, after all, and it would be a relief not to be alone with my thoughts for one evening.

She greeted me with a kiss on the cheek, her lips almost hot against my unshaven skin. Even her perfume seemed more like warmth than scent.

"You're cold, Andy, and you look shattered. Tough day in the lab?"

There was something about the look in her eye—as if she truly cared—that made me feel reckless. I didn't know what was going to happen, and furthermore, I didn't *want* to.

"Not really...just a lot on my mind." I kept my tone incidental.

Maria threw me a curious glance as we waited for the lift.

"There's a great Tandoori place near my flat in Brixton," she finally said.

"It had better be good, if you're going to drag me south of the river."

"You North London men are so squeamish." She slipped her arm through mine as the door swished open.

Maria signalled to the waiter for two more bottles of Cobra. I didn't protest, even though I'd only had poppadoms and chutney so far on an empty stomach, and the world was already starting to appear more colourful and vibrant. I found myself momentarily bemused by the lights twinkling off the cutlery and the empty pint glasses. If this was part of her plan, it was working nicely.

"Thanks, Maria." I felt that familiar, alcoholic tendency to start baring my soul.

"For what?"

"Asking me to dinner, taking my mind off things."

I expected her to respond sweetly, but my comment set off a spark of anger instead. "Maybe I should apologize for the way I did it, but honestly."

"What?"

Her hand clenched into a fist on the table. "It winds me up the way Gina plays with you like a cat batting around a mouse. No offence meant, Andy, but she's leading you on something chronic. She knows exactly how you feel about her—so how could she not warn you that Rouyle was coming to visit? *We've* all known about it for ages. Instead, she just lets you make a fool of yourself."

"It's not fair to blame Gina that I've been acting like an idiot."

"Andy." Her gaze was as fixed as a wrestling hold. "You're an intelligent man. I know you think you're in love with her, but if she were giving you absolutely no encouragement, you'd've moved on by now. Look me in the eye and tell me I'm wrong."

I studied her dark eyes, with their candid challenge, for a few long seconds before having to shake my head.

"And so very convenient for her to keep you in that state," she said, "as you seem to be her slave in the lab as well!"

"That's not fair either," I said. "I'm helping her because I want to, because I think it's important. Because we're friends."

Maria just stared at me sceptically.

"And I don't think she's purposefully leading me on," I added. "I think she's genuinely mixed up."

"I know you *think* that, Andy. Only it doesn't seem so obvious from the outside perspective."

You're not exactly unbiased yourself, I thought, watching her adjust the arrangement of cutlery, the candlelight reflecting off the jet black of her bowed head.

"How much did you overhear?" I asked calmly.

She jerked up, face guarded.

"Come on, Maria," I said. "It's all got to come out here, I can see that."

She dipped her head in a small motion of acquiescence. "Enough, Andy. I heard enough. I'm not stupid, you know—I had my suspicions even before I walked in on you two."

I let out my breath in surprise, and she leaned back in her chair, gave me a calculating smile. "She and Christine have been inseparable in the Mouse House, always whispering and then going silent every time someone comes near. I don't know the entire story with you three, but it definitely involves mice. So as Gina's made it no secret at staff meetings how displeased she is about the premature, third-world exploitational Phase I, from tissue culture to innocent patient with no animal trial in between, I can pretty much guess the rest."

Silence hung over the table. Eventually, I began to nod.

"I knew it!" she said. "But I thought it was too outrageously daft to possibly be true."

"I'm afraid not," I said.

"Any results yet?"

I shook my head. "She only injected the combination vaccine into our test animals this morning."

"So nothing's going to happen until Monday at the earliest," she said thoughtfully. "The acute viraemia takes a few days to resolve before the viruses start infecting the nervous system."

"That's what I assumed...why else would she have gone off to Cornwall?" I shut my mouth as a whole flood of new images infected my own mind. "You're not going to turn us in, are you?"

She looked me over for a few moments.

"Maybe you're helping Gina for the wrong reasons, but the cause is certainly good," she said at last. "I have to admit I'm impressed by Gina's initiative, mad though it is. She's got a passion for this project that goes far beyond corporate loyalty—you wouldn't catch me doing something so idiotic for a mere job."

This comment had hit me like a ten tonne dose of reality. What if Gina and Christine got caught? Maria had seen through their activities effortlessly—so might anyone else.

Maria continued, "No one at Geniaxis—except for Boyd and the shareholders—is happy about this latest development with Pfeiffer-de-Vries. Most of the lower ranks have grown to distrust Rouyle. He was popular at first, but he's become insufferably arrogant lately, and rumours have been circulating that his track record is hardly exemplary."

To say the least.

"So are you going to tell Boyd about the mice or not?" I said.

She sighed noisily. "Jesus, Andy, do you think I'd be low enough to grass on a fellow employee? More to the point, d'you think I'd risk getting *you* in trouble?"

I reached over, covered her hand with mine. "Sorry—I'm just spooked."

"You're forgiven, I suppose." Her fingers insinuated themselves among my own, belying the sharpness of her tone.

I was sitting on the floor against the sofa, hardly able to maintain my vertical status. My memories of the walk from the curry house to Maria's flat were patchy at best, and were becoming more distant with every sip.

Maria held up the bottle of the cheap but respectable brand of Irish whiskey we were in the process of demolishing, and I nearly knocked over a lamp in my expansive acquiescence. She tried to refill my glass, giggling as the stream went slightly off target and pooled onto the coffee table. When the bottle stopped producing fluid, she smacked its bottom optimistically, and I dissolved into uncontrollable laughter at the sight.

Maria pushed my glass closer and joined me on the floor, palm sliding up my chest. Our humour gradually trickled out.

"You still want her, don't you?" she said, managing not to slur her words despite the vast quantities she had already drunk. I thought about her robust Irish genes, wondering if Cameron might be interested in them as a replacement for his doomed yeast hangover project.

"Don't you, Andy?" There was tacit danger in her question, but I just nodded, finding it impossible to dissemble in my current condition.

She stretched her head upwards, started to nuzzle my neck with her mouth. I felt the top fastening of my shirt mysteriously spring apart.

"Are you trying to seduce me?" I said.

She relapsed into giggles against my neck, and then I was putting my arms around her, falling onto my back and pulling her down on top of me, burying my face in the softness of her hair, kissing her forehead, her ear, her lips. Some part of me was aware of her eager response. But there was another thing distracting me, something important that I was supposed to remember, worry about, deal with. Eventually, the two opposing forces cancelled one another out, and I stopped thinking altogether.

22   *The Last Inconsistency*

*W*hy was it you could always tell straightaway when you'd woken up in a woman's bed? Of course there was the scent: alien washing powder at the foreground with traces of something floral and undeniably feminine just underneath. But there was something in the very texture of the sheets that exuded safety and comfort. Not that I was in the habit, but waking up in another man's bed probably wouldn't convey anything other than the fact that you were in a bed, quite possibly one in a dubious state of hygiene.

Hang on. *Why* was I in a woman's bed, exactly? My eyes popped open and scanned the unfamiliar ceiling. Sunlight formed a diffracted pattern on the opposite wall, hinting at net curtains—photons diving through with Heisenbergian uncertainty. There was a framed poster of some familiar piece of art—Hopper, I thought—in an otherwise blank, lemon-yellow expanse. Sleepily, I rolled my head over, decanting a sudden headache into the right side of my brain.

I nearly cried out in surprise when I saw Maria. She was asleep, her dark hair spread out on the pillow in spirals like a fresco angel. The duvet was pushed halfway down her torso, the interim territory protected—barely—by a scant piece of satin.

I took stock of my own state of dress...boxers, check...and that was all. Otherwise, I appeared to be unscathed. It looked quite incriminating so far, but I had to admit I didn't have the slightest idea how I had ended up there.

I resumed my inspection of Maria, moving past her overt sex appeal to something beyond: an innocence not evident when she was awake. I experienced an unexpected twinge of affection. But at the same time, I was sharply conscious of exactly where my feelings still lay fixed. Maria had been right: why had I allowed myself to accept

Gina's non-verbal come-on when all the outward signs pointed towards futility? I just didn't want to go against my instincts, even though there were some excellent reasons, like finding myself in bed with an attractive, clever woman who happened to be crazy about me. I'd be a liar if I said I didn't want her, at some level, but going along with it seemed like a bad idea. Though perhaps it was already too late.

With the conviction of an addict, I decided that caffeine would make everything clearer. Slipping quietly out of bed, I located the bathroom, then the kitchen. The floor plan was starting to look familiar as yesterday's events reasserted themselves: the dinner (at least four pints there, easily, two before the meal had even been served), back to the flat, maybe a half a bottle of whiskey between the two of us. No wonder I had amnesia. And then I was sure there'd been some sort of kiss...but after that, it was just white noise.

I found the kitchen, blue tiles shining in the sunlight, and fumbled together two steaming mugs. On the way back, I noticed my missing clothes in a pile on the floor on Maria's side of bed. When I burrowed back into the welcoming warmth, Maria mumbled something sleepily. Her lashes parted, revealing wariness beneath. I had the distinct impression that she hadn't forgotten a thing.

"Coffee?" I said, reduced to mundanity.

A smile curved her lips, erasing all traces of apprehension. "In a minute—I'm not actually awake yet." She rubbed her eyes with an open palm. "What time is it, anyway?"

"Just gone ten." I settled back against the headboard, blowing on the scalding coffee with needy impatience.

"I half-woke up a couple of minutes ago, thought you'd done a runner."

"Don't be ridiculous." I set the mug aside and put an arm around her as she snuggled close. She ran a hand over the hair on my chest, then started to skim it downwards, to my belly, then —

I caught her hand, neatly arresting its southward motion. "Care to fill me in on last night's events?"

She paused, then said, "You have no idea how tempting it is to lie."

"What did happen, then?"

She squirmed her hand from my grip and slid it—chastely, this time—around my waist before giving me a sly smile. "We were right in the middle of an epic kiss when you passed out."

"God, how embarrassing." I shook my head.

"You partially regained consciousness long enough for me to wrestle you in here."

"How can I face you after such a blatant failure of manliness?" It was humiliating to have been out-drunk by a woman, and such a small one at that.

"I wouldn't worry about the manliness department," Maria said significantly.

"How do you mean?"

"I did undress you, remember."

"I see." I caught her eye, and we both started laughing.

She repositioned herself against me, the movement of her hair a rare pleasure against my skin. For the first time in days, I was relaxed, untroubled. It was a surprising relief to be held and touched by a woman, even if we hadn't done anything about it. Reinforcing my random thoughts, Maria started stroking my chest again, and a wave of sleepiness came over me.

"You don't know what you're missing," she said. "And I'm not just talking about sex."

"There's where you're wrong." I was unable to prevent my eyes from closing.

"You're not still holding back because you don't believe that Gina and Rouyle are seriously involved?"

I studied the pattern that the sunny room was making on the inside of my eyelids, shifting flames of black and crimson. "No, that delusion officially went off-line the night of Julie's party."

"And I went home with someone else...grand."

"It wouldn't have made a difference. I've never been very good at changing my focus at a moment's notice."

"Like Gina has done." She obviously couldn't resist a dig.

"She had her reasons." I opened my eyes, peering down, but all I could see was the top of her head nestled on my chest, and I allowed my eyelids to droop shut again. "Anyway, I think that's probably normal behaviour, and I'm the odd one out."

"The frustrating thing is that your elusiveness only makes you more attractive." Her voice was receding as another wave of sleep tried to pull me down. "I wish I knew how to *make* you like me."

"You know I like you, Maria. I'm just...hung up." I could feel her heartbeats mixed among my own. "That's why I don't want to trifle with you."

"Even if I fancied being trifled with?" Her tone was light.

"You don't actually mean that, do you? I've been at the receiving end enough to know that it would just make things worse."

She didn't reply, and my mental dialogue started to get tangled up in dream images until I reached the stage where I kept losing the linear progression of my own thoughts.

Maria spoke one last time, her voice sounding very far away. In fact, I would not be sure later that I hadn't dreamt it.

"I wish I could be her."

And then I was gone.

I leaned my head against the window as the Tube train rattled northward. I'd slept a couple more hours in the end, and the sensation of being well-rested was almost euphoric. My faint high made the sky-blue environment of the Victoria line seem ethereal and strange.

When I'd woken again, Maria's side of the bed had been empty. I'd found her bustling around the kitchen in a dressing gown, hair trailing down her back in damp coils. She was cheerful and businesslike, but her eyes looked unusually bright, as if she'd been crying. But it was clear from her manner that our moment of intimacy was over, and I sensed that she wanted to keep things inconsequential, so I had pretended not to notice. Only in retrospect did I realize how insensitive, and possibly self-serving, this interpretation had been.

The neighbourhood around Brixton station had been seething with people out enjoying the weather, and I had moved among them, still enjoying a residual sense of lightness and experiencing a generous goodwill towards my fellow humans, surging around me with their own thoughts, feelings, sorrows and aspirations.

When I changed trains at Green Park, a curious transformation began. The closer I got to the Centre, the more my contentment eroded, unease moving in systematically to take its place. Of course none of my problems had vanished while I had been with Maria; if anything, they'd gathered momentum. I was so disturbed that I got off one stop early, forcing myself to negotiate the crowds of tourists milling about Covent Garden. But I no longer received any comfort from the press of humanity around me and ended up feeling even more isolated.

I keyed my way into the Centre and went straight up to the lab, relieved to find it deserted. A quick e-mail check revealed no surprise messages from Cornwall, which reinforced that I'd have to brood over my disturbing news until Gina got back. But what if she was too busy to see me on Monday? I couldn't very well force her to talk to me, especially as our last meeting had ended so awkwardly. And with the Phase I negotiations and the animal trial to deal with inside business hours, and Rouyle to spend time with outside, it might prove difficult indeed to find the opportunity to make my point. *I'll probably be unavailable*, she'd told me. And she would be furious if I risked sending such sensitive information to her company e-mail account. Besides, I couldn't guarantee that Rouyle wouldn't see her e-mail, even unintentionally.

I rolled my chair over to the battered old CD player and started rummaging through the pile of discs, looking for something soothing to clarify my thoughts. There was an excess of Helmut's obscure stuff diluting the otherwise good quality of the lab's collection, and also a few data discs mixed in where they shouldn't be. I was just about to toss aside one of these—a box labelled "Jon's Confocal Scans"—when I was gripped by a brilliant idea.

"You forgot to sign in, O'Hara," Magritte said mildly behind me.

I gave a yelp and jumped in my chair, the disc flying from my hand and skidding across the floor.

"Christ, you could've warned me!" Pulse thudding, I leaned over to retrieve the plastic box.

"Thought no one was here." She shrugged, draping her coat over her stool and placing a bouquet of flowers carefully on her bench.

"Since when have you started remembering to sign in?"

"Since today," she replied unflappably. "Why so upset, O'Hara? What's got into you lately?"

"Nothing." I swivelled back to the computer, reached for the mouse.

I promptly found myself being rotated back to face her. Hand still clutching the back of my chair, she pinned me with an inescapable stare.

"Don't give me this *nothing*, O'Hara," she said, making each word distinct. "You have not been self, past two, three weeks. Something funny definitely going on." She let go of the chair, started to tick off items on her fingers. "First off, are collaborating in secret with Helmut. Not crime, but suspicious. Not like either of you not to keep me informed."

I opened my mouth to protest, but her glare stopped me immediately.

"Moreover, are highly distracted, and workload has dropped. Don't care about that, but again, not *like* you." Another finger folded down. "Found out you performed ELISA test recently, which makes no sense for current projects. Why do ELISA when you usually just run gel?"

I had never seen her so angry.

"I always give my people freedom to explore, to make own way in science," she went on. "But in turn expect common courtesy: to be informed what goes on under own nose in own laboratory! Have I not always been fair? Not demanded too much? Not try to control, hold you back?" With each question, her voice became incrementally louder.

I nodded. Extraordinarily, I felt the prick of tears behind my eyes, and she put a hand on my shoulder, her focus sharpening even further.

"Andrew, you are the best post-doc I ever had good fortune to train, and I train plenty in my day. Care about you. Know I don't show it...not my way. But without trust, I feel like failure as mentor."

That did it. Something caught in my throat, and then I was unable to keep the tears from spilling over at an alarming rate. Shocked, Magritte hesitated only a moment before pulling up a nearby chair and holding me as the inexplicable grief powered through me as if I were an irrelevant instrument. I was too distressed to be embarrassed, although I remember feeling grateful that she kept silent and just left me to it.

My guilt at letting Magritte down was only the beginning of the flood, which soon fanned out into a host of other anxieties. In the forefront of my mind was the fact that Gina was in love with someone else, but this was nothing compared to my growing fears about her safety. Not only was she vulnerable to Rouyle's bogus gene therapy collaboration, but she would probably get herself into trouble when she found out my news—she could be so stubborn, without any regard for common sense. The animal trial was still a major worry, of course, and what would happen if it were discovered. And then there was Maria: I was almost certain I was in the process of hurting her, despite all my attempts to keep it under control. Christine would probably move to Newcastle, after which we'd try to keep up the closeness of our friendship, all the time knowing it was largely futile. And then, there was the painful scene I'd had with my mother a few weeks before, which we hadn't mentioned again, but which had nevertheless cooled our subsequent communications.

And of course, all these threads were intensified by the source of our falling-out: the subliminal, unspeakable loss that had filtered through my entire adulthood.

There was something solid about Magritte's presence, and after some time, I found myself out of tears. Humiliating or not, I was relieved and drained after my unexpected catharsis. I backed away from her awkwardly, and she straightened up.

"Now," she said, her green eyes betraying much more emotion than I had ever before detected in them. "You tell me, yes?"

She grabbed a box of Kimwipes off the bench and I blew my nose, mopped up my face. I took my time at it, thinking furiously. Mentioning the animal trial was impossible: Christine was right, Magritte would report us even if it were the worthiest cause in the world. Likewise, I didn't dare bring up the mystery protein, because with such evidence of foul play, she'd be down in Boyd's office in an instant. Considering that Gina was still alone in the countryside with Rouyle, I couldn't take the risk of any harm coming to her. No, just as with Maria and Christine, and even Raim, I was going to have to choose only one piece of the convoluted story to reveal.

"I'm so sorry about everything." I paused to clear the muck from my throat. "I have the highest respect for you, and it was wrong to hide things. And please, don't blame Helmut—I take full responsibility for making him keep it secret."

She nodded approvingly. "Go on."

"It all started with Gina."

"Gina...that beautiful woman with clever herpes vaccine, yes?" The fact that a woman was involved, and perhaps this woman in particular, seemed to be confirming her suspicions.

"We were...well, things were progressing with us, but then she started talking to Richard Rouyle after her Cambridge seminar," I said. "And more than talking, to be honest."

Magritte muttered something in her native tongue. "Would've thought...but then, love is blind *et cetera*. Please, continue."

"This is all strictly confidential, right?" I waited for her impatient nod, then explained about the combination vaccine strategy.

Magritte looked as if she were trying not to smile. "Ah, yes— Rouyle's seminar question. So they decided to collaborate?"

"Yes, but Gina was concerned by how fast things were escalating, was worried that there hadn't been enough *in vitro* testing to justify the idea. But she's not a cell signalling specialist."

"And you are," Magritte said, still amused. "But not virologist, clearly."

"No, that was Gina's jurisdiction. What are you getting at, Magritte?"

"In a minute." She waved me on. "Finish story first. I'm completely ears."

So I mentioned Helmut's discrepant SLIP experiment, and revealed how we had decided to test whether FRIP was also unable to muster an antiviral attack in neuronal cells.

"*Now* I understand. Good idea as always, Andrew: debunk Rouyle to help get girl, simultaneously help colleague get publication." Magritte's ill-informed consent made me feel ashamed. "So Helmut eventually got blood from stone—FRIP DNA from Pfeiffer-deVries. I remember signing their MTA. And your test showed...?"

I opened up my notebook. "We didn't have a good FRIP antibody," I said, glossing over that bit, "But you can see here that —"

"Yes, yes, yes, it's clear, O'Hara," she said, already having taken in, digested and interpreted the maze of black splotches with ease. "Your theory correct: FRIP useless as co-factor in Gina's vaccine. But beside point—we already knew that for more fundamental reason."

"We did?" I gaped at her.

"FRIP is similar to better understood antiviral pathways like interferon," she said. "Only stimulated by invasion of *double*-stranded RNA viruses, not those made of single-stranded RNA, or DNA. Gina clearly said in seminar, Vera Fever Virus genome is composed of *single*-stranded RNA."

Of course. That was what had been bothering me since the beginning. It was a fact I'd acquired from some long-ago undergraduate immunology course and subsequently forgotten. Magritte was right: it didn't matter if the antiviral TRAP protein wasn't turned on by FRIP in neuronal cells, because FRIP wasn't ever going to get co-activated by Vera Fever infection. The whole point was well and truly moot.

"Christ," I breathed. "And Rouyle would have known this, wouldn't he? It couldn't have been a careless mistake." As soon as the words were out of my mouth, I regretted them.

"Maybe not thinking with brains on this one," she said with a smirk. "Chance to collaborate with a woman like that..."

I forced myself to smile along with her.

"That's better," she said, nodding at my expression. Her eyes were restored to their normal opaque equanimity.

"Magritte...is this going to ruin things between us? My deception, I mean?"

She regarded me in surprise. Silence fell heavily between us then, even the sunlight weighing in with a fluid presence, and I became aware of the sounds of the lab, welling up from the background to fill my ears with irrelevancy.

"I tell you a little something," she finally said. She settled a bent arm against the bench, seeming to take on some of the gravity of the atmosphere. "At this stage of life, am used to living with secrets— my own, and those around me. Before I escaped my country, had to live with colleagues, friends, family unable to divulge truth. People would be there one day, gone next. We called it *jumping over*."

Her hand sketched a bridge through the air, and my eyes followed, transfixed by the unprecedented disclosure.

"Happy when they disappeared, sad simultaneous—could never be sure they'd made it safely. Maybe arrested, maybe dead." Her face absolutely neutral, she stretched a hand to the bouquet of flowers and fingered a rose, smoothing its petals like an old memory. "I kept my secrets too, and when it was my turn, couldn't even say good-bye to own parents. Never saw them again."

I opened my mouth, but she warned me off with a quick shake of the head. "So I grew up learning never to question, never to judge people by what they do or do not do, say or do not say. Can only know people by more important things, things you learn to read with heart, not ear or eye. Do you understand?"

I nodded, feeling the renewal of emotions massing just behind flimsy membranes. But this time, I managed to suppress them.

"Nevertheless." A smile hovered mere millimetres from actually landing on her mouth. "Things feel better when out in open, yes?"

She inspected me so closely that I was forced to look away. In that uncomfortable moment, I felt she was analyzing my thoughts and remaining cache of untold truths as expertly as she might decipher a pattern of black bands scattered across a piece of film. Then she patted me on the arm, and the moment passed.

"If you explain everything to Gina, she should understand," Magritte said. "Would make very nice couple—you both need someone sharp, someone to keep you on toes."

"Thanks for the advice," I said. "I just wish it were that easy."

"Put some *effort* into it, Andrew, like you do with research." Her smile finally touched down. "Think of it as an experiment of the heart."

I had to wait several hours for Magritte to leave before I could implement the first phase of my recent idea. The minute she was out the door, with a stern command not to stay too late, I prised off the FRIP film from my notebook and retrieved the matching rectangle, containing the black signal of the mystery protein, from my file drawer. Assembling the pieces carefully on the scanner, I zapped the reconstructed experiment into the computer. Using a standard graphics programme, I dressed up the images as if I were preparing a figure for an article or a scientific poster, adding explanatory labels and arrows, putting a question mark next to the mystery protein. I wanted to add a footnote about the requirement of FRIP kinase for viral genetic material comprised of double-stranded RNA, but thought it was too risky. I was trying to make the figure cryptic enough so that Rouyle's suspicions would not be aroused if he happened to get a casual glance, but not so cryptic that Gina missed the point altogether.

When I was finished with the labels, I typed in bold face at the bottom:

MAJOR CONCLUSIONS:

1. Protein of interest non-functional for desired activity in neuronal cells.
2. DNA and antibody provided do not encode or recognize, respectively, protein of interest.

I burned the file onto a fresh data CD and opened my desk drawer to stash it away. Dad was giving me that look.

"See?" I said. "I told you he was up to something. But I've got him now."

The shops were closed, but I'd have plenty of time to complete my plan before Gina arrived home on Sunday evening.

I put on an upbeat album and went back to my experiments with renewed energy. Stupidly, I was convinced that the straightforward nature of my solution would set everything to rights. Of course, I was completely unaware that my actions would end up making the situation much, much worse.

23   *A Few Pints Later*

I sat at a corner table in the Henry, a fixed point—blind, deaf and dumb—in the usual Saturday bustle. I was seriously regretting that Magritte had witnessed my emotional outburst earlier in the lab. I couldn't remember the last time I had wept; I supposed it must have been the day of the funeral, years ago. But those tears had been more angry than sad, the anger that had propelled me to crush my most treasured photograph into a wad and pelt it into the bin (only to be fished out sheepishly and smoothed, minutes later, too ashamed ever to ask Mum for a replacement). I'd forgotten how it felt, the sense of losing complete emotional control: overwhelming, as if I'd caught a stranger inhabiting my own body.

"Here sits a forlorn sight: a man with a half-pint glass in need of a refill." It was Cameron, smiling down at me. "Care for an upgrade?"

I nodded, making an effort to unstring my tension while he was busy at the bar.

"I've been slaving in the lab all day," he told me, unloading glasses onto the table. "My student is just too keen—please tell me we weren't so idealistic at that age."

"You've probably just repressed it."

"Do you know what happened today?" He rolled his eyes. "He had a go at me because his latest experimental result was ambiguous and—get this—*science is supposed to be black and white*. That's the only reason he wanted to be a scientist in the first place: to get some clarity and control over his life!"

"The poor guy." I couldn't help laughing. "Did you break it to him gently?"

"It's kinder in the long run to tell them the ugly truth." He made a dramatic gesture in the air. "The only certainty about science is that science is never certain, I told him. Results baffle, theories arise and get debunked, facts give way to fashion, and the kudos usually goes to the people who haven't done the work or come up with the brilliant idea in the first place."

"And how did that concept go down?"

He frowned. "I was hoping he'd slink away in a bout of existential angst. But it backfired: he insisted on setting up twice as many experiments, which I had to oversee."

"How much trouble could he get up to on his own?"

"Unfortunately for me, he isn't ready to work unsupervised." Cameron sampled the froth in his glass happily.

"Maybe we should set him up with our student. She's hardly ever in at weekends." I dissected a packet of salted peanuts in one swift motion.

"Kathy's far too nice...and normal. I wouldn't dream of inflicting this lad on her—he's a complete geek." He gave me a look. "Talking of geeks having a life, how did you get on with Maria last night?"

I stopped chewing on my mouthful momentarily.

"You're looking unshaven and disreputable," he said, eyes wisely amused, "so I'm guessing you weren't tucked up safely into your own bed by nine."

"How did you find out?" At least he hadn't noticed I was still wearing yesterday's clothes, but then again, he wasn't a woman, was he? It all fitted with my hypothesis.

"Andy, my lad, we work at the *Centre*! No amount of gossip, no matter how trivial, is above instantaneous transmission and, eventually, total coverage!" He paused. "Of course, a full disclosure now would be treated with the utmost discretion."

"Why do I somehow doubt your sincerity? And anyway, you're not going to like it."

"Don't tell me the odds weren't in your favour—you don't need a PhD to see she's mad about you."

"We had a nice evening," I said. "Got a bit drunk. Next thing I knew, it was morning, her place. In short, nothing happened."

"Major strategic error, O'Hara, with regard to the alcohol intake." He shook his head at me over his pint. "Wasn't there at least a chance to rectify the situation in the morning? Or was the moment gone, as the saying goes?"

"I'm not expecting you to understand, because I don't fully myself. I *like* Maria..."

"*But*. But what?" Cameron seemed agitated. "She's devastating. She adores you."

"The truth is that I like someone else."

He sat back, stared at me. "Who is it, then? Be honest with me."

I was confused by his level tone. "Gina Kraymer, of course."

"Gina?" An odd mixture of expressions flitted across his face. "I thought you two were over ages ago, last summer."

Clearly Christine had been more discreet than I'd given her credit for. "Well, yes and no, but...am I missing something? Who did you think?"

Cameron wouldn't meet my eye, knuckles clamped around his pint.

"Christine's been acting so strange lately, I thought she might be having an affair." He was speaking so softly that I had to lean forward to hear him. "And when I thought about who the offending party might be, there weren't any other logical options. I know she used to be interested in you, before she met me. You spend a lot of time together, and recently, I've had the feeling that your conversations have been a bit...well, secretive."

I was so shocked that I couldn't speak.

"And then this business with Maria seemed like the ultimate proof." He was starting to sound sheepish. "There had to be a truly compelling reason why you wouldn't want her. And so, I just started...but you're not, are you?"

"You have my solemn word, Cameron," I said. "And she can't possibly be having an affair—between the lab and the two of us, where else could she be?"

Cameron thought about this, finally nodded. "I'm sorry, Andy—I feel like an idiot. Thanks for not being angry. It's just...she *has* been acting funny." He took a defensive gulp of beer.

Frankly, I felt more offended on Christine's behalf than my own. "Let me ease your mind about our secretive behaviour. There's a valid reason, but it's part of a confidential collaboration with Gina's company."

He waited, then looked disappointed when I didn't elaborate.

"And about acting funny," I went on, "Christine recently used the same expression to refer to you. She's reacting because *you're* reacting to the whole Newcastle thing."

He slammed his glass down on the table. "I wouldn't be so worried if she would ever talk about it! But every time I bring it up, she changes the subject. You know how stubborn she can be."

"To put it mildly, mate."

"But she's talked to *you*, hasn't she?" He sounded resentful. "What's going on?"

I chose my words with care. "I gather she's nervous because you told her you'd prefer a job in the London area. Maybe she feels her options are being restricted. You know she's got strong feminist tendencies, and the idea that she might have to tailor her career around that of a man..."

"That's ridiculous!" he burst out. "I have mentioned London, but that was aeons ago, back when we first met."

"So you *haven't* told her specifically that you wouldn't follow her somewhere else?"

"Of course I haven't—she won't give me the opportunity! If she'd only *listen* for two seconds..." He shook his head, eyes still fiery. "I'd follow her to Outer Mongolia if she wanted me to. What good would a swanky position at UCL or Cambridge be if I couldn't be with her?"

We both drank in manly silence for a few moments, then Cameron ventured, "Thanks for enlightening me. I was completely out of line earlier, but the whole prospect has been scrambling my mind. What I really need to do is sit her down and dazzle her with my eloquence."

"Might need restraints and a muzzle."

He grinned. "Not a bad idea. But I'm not sure I can wait until tomorrow night—I'll call her when we're through here."

I perked up. "I thought she was incommunicado, hillwalking?"

"No, she called this afternoon, said the weather deteriorated and they cut the trip short. She's spending the rest of the weekend inspecting the insides of all the pubs within a two-mile radius of the lab—purely for research purposes, of course."

"I couldn't even get a connection."

"That's because she's finally replaced her dodgy mobile—I'll jot the new number down for you."

I rummaged around in my rucksack until I'd found a pen and notepad. When I slapped the pad down on the table, the fax of Rouyle's first article slid out and was arrested prematurely by Cameron's pint of Guinness.

"What's this?" he asked, picking it up. "I didn't know you were bilingual."

I shrugged. "It's meant to have a piece of data that might be remotely related to something I'm working on, so Janice tracked it down for me. But I couldn't figure it out from the figures."

He studied the front page curiously. "What language is this, anyway?"

"Latvian. I've been trying to find a way to translate it."

"No problem there—you know Ainikka, don't you?"

I straightened up out of my slouch. "Yeah, but she's Finnish, isn't she?"

"Only half. Her mother's Latvian, and Ainikka can speak it fairly well. Well enough to do freelance translating. And she's always looking for chances to earn money, because her frequent trips home mount up. If you wouldn't mind paying..."

"Definitely not!"

Cameron pulled out his phone and squinted at its tiny screen. "She's usually in the lab on Sundays...why don't you pop in tomorrow and see if she's up for it?" He pressed a few buttons, then started to copy down Christine's number.

"Thanks for the tip-off."

"It's the least I could do after you cleared things up for me." He paused, eyes taking on that telltale faraway haze. "Why is it that even the most straightforward situations tend to go awry where women are concerned? Might we be able to invoke the principles of chaos theory..."

He trailed off when he noticed the expression on my face. "Listen, Andy, I know it's none of my business, and you've probably been receiving unwanted advice and possibly outright molestation from my well-meaning girlfriend for months, but what in hell is going on with you and Gina? If you're not together now—and you never properly were before, were you?—then why is she still an issue?" He paused, added, "Feel free to tell me to shut up."

"No, it's all right." I realized that an independent male perspective had been conspicuously absent during the entire affair; Paul's barbed commentary hardly counted. "I've liked Gina since I first met her, and while I sometimes seem to be making progress—enough to keep my hopes up—nothing ever seems to *happen*."

"Well I suppose there's nothing wrong with being patient if you think she's close to coming round."

I shifted in my seat. "That's just it—she's not close at all. In fact, she's seeing Richard Rouyle."

He nearly spat out his beer. "That ancient relic from Pfeiffer-deVries? Of soporific seminar fame? Although he's handsome enough, I suppose. *And* a celeb."

"Actually, the general consensus is that he's arrogant, condescending, and maybe a bit dodgy."

"Isn't Gina meant to be amazingly astute?"

I shrugged and repeated what Magritte had observed earlier on in the afternoon, about love being blind.

Cameron looked disgusted. "If you want my honest opinion, I think that's a fatalistic cop-out."

"In what way?"

"I personally believe it's pathological to overlook obvious negative qualities in another person," he said. "I'm not saying Gina's a bad person *per se*, but do you really want someone with such poor discrimination? First Miles, and now this guy. Have you ever stopped to consider how her judgement might be a reflection of her personality?"

I just looked at him, not sure I wanted his opinion after all.

"Andy...I like you." He sighed. "I know we haven't been terribly close after this past conflict of interest over Christine, but I hate to see you making yourself miserable. Maybe you shouldn't excuse Gina without thinking hard about what it might mean. Isn't it possible you're idealizing something that doesn't really exist?" He stared into the distance for a second, then added carefully, "I guess what I mean is... if you allow yourself to make excuses for *her* excuses, you're guilty of the same weakness. It's contagious, like a virus."

I developed a pressing interest in my pint glass. Pub chatter lapped against my ears as I battled against my first instinct: to dismiss what Cameron was saying as rubbish.

"I'm in too deep now," I finally confessed. "I've never wanted anything as much as I want this...to have her. It's *worse* than a virus." *Don't you see that this desire overrides everything else in the end—common sense, fairness, self-respect?*

"I understand only too well," he said, grimacing. "Still, it might not hurt to think about it."

But the words had been firmly implanted in my brain. I felt the xenograft of foreign and possibly malignant ideas start to divide and colonize.

✦ ✦ ✦

Sunday morning found me alone in the lab, trying to lose myself in mindless tissue culture and deafening music, but diversion proved elusive. After speaking to Cameron the previous night, I'd been determined to tell Christine the whole story about Rouyle's past, along with the alarming results of the latest *in vitro* test. But when Christine hadn't picked up her phone or responded to any of my messages, my anxiety only increased, until it was all I could do to remember what my hands were supposed to be doing.

Around lunchtime, I slipped off to Oxford Street and, after successfully completing the next part of my plan, I was elated to see that Ainikka's name had appeared on the register in my absence. I jogged up to her lab two steps at a time and found her hunched over a dissecting microscope with her back to the door. She swivelled around at my greeting.

"Hi, Andrew. What can I do for you?" Her lake-blue eyes were distracted. "Quickly though, because the carbon dioxide will wear off at any moment."

She indicated the plate of fruit flies under the microscope, its denizens splayed out like drunks at closing time.

"Cameron said you might be willing to translate for me...for the going rate, of course."

"Absolutely." Straight airbrushed teeth like a magazine smile: I had her attention now.

I unzipped my rucksack and dug around until I'd pulled out the article, now beer-stained as well as dog-eared and rumpled.

She skimmed the abstract, made a face. "This looks really boring."

"What's it about?" Anticipation welled up and ejected the words from my mouth.

"I don't have time to get into it now, but I'll work on it tonight. Can we meet tomorrow, late morning?" She took another glance at the abstract, still clearly baffled why a biochemist might find something useful in a forgotten Baltic psychiatry paper.

Just then, a twitch of movement tickled my peripheral vision: her flies were coming around, staggering across the plate. "Er..." I pointed.

"*Perkele!* If you would excuse me." She tossed the article aside and peered down the scope's oculars. Picking up a few instruments, she began transferring individual insects to a fresh vial, swearing again as one of them escaped. I ducked as the fly whizzed past my left ear. I had wanted to press her to reveal the gist of the abstract at least, but further conversation was clearly impossible.

I sat down at my desk without taking off my coat and removed the new CD from its carrier bag. Even the largest shop on Oxford Street had offered nothing to compare with Helmut's premiere bootleg collection of suicidal German albums, and the specific disc I'd wanted was unavailable. But then I'd decided Gina's taste was too good to distinguish one obscure Kraftwerk album collection from another and had chosen at random.

I opened up my drawer and took out the data disc I'd burned the day before. Removing the Kraftwerk disc from its nest, I pressed the data disc into the box and forced the music CD down on top of it. I wrapped the case in the glaring pink paper I'd bought, fished out my last purchase, a birthday card, and scribbled a note inside:

Dear Gina,

Happy birthday! At least I'm fairly sure you told me it was today. I remember how much you enjoyed this CD when Helmut was playing it in the lab. It's so special and personally meaningful, I highly recommend taking the time to enjoy it in solitude!

Take care, and I hope to talk to you soon.

A.

Secret signals, but would she be undistracted enough to notice them?

A winter trick: the afternoon light had already faded when I emerged from Finsbury Park station. The smoked glass sky hung low and dirty, and a drizzle had started up while I was underground, the sort of fine spray that would impact noiselessly with an umbrella yet could still swarm underneath and soak you in minutes. Not that I was sufficiently organized to have an umbrella.

The bus bays were empty, so I turned up my collar, crossed Seven Sisters Road and started trudging eastward through leaf-clogged puddles, past fried chicken outlets, Asian restaurants and corner shops, everything reflecting the scruffiness I'd come to associate with the more disreputable parts of Zone Two.

After about five minutes a bus lumbered past me. I ran for it and climbed to the empty upper deck, settling into the front seat. The bus careered northward in rocking hypnosis. I watched the shops scroll by in an endless stream, blurred by the rain dribbling across the windows, droplets crawling downward, merging with other droplets until they gathered momentum and whizzed off the bottom into darkness.

It seemed like a long time since I'd gone this way with Gina before, that momentous Friday night. I remembered that we'd laughed every time the movement of the bus threw one of us into the other. True, she'd been rather preoccupied with her troubles, but I'd still felt a heady sense of freedom knowing I was going to spend the evening exactly where I wanted to be. Where I belonged, even—but I had been deluded then, full of unvoiced expectations and undashed hopes.

I pulled the cord at Stoke Newington Church Street and muscled my way off the bus. There was salsa music coming from the Spanish bar on the corner where I paused to orient myself. I made my way cautiously up the main street, which was strangely devoid of people, taking a turn when it seemed correct, and then another. When I was fairly certain I was in her street, I started scanning individual houses on the terraced row. Probably because the horrific events on her front step had been seared in my memory, I recognized the flat easily in the end.

I mounted the steps and stood in front of her door. The flat was dark, but I rang the bell just in case. Waited. Time did its funny shifting trick, and I was blasted with melancholy, as emphatically as if someone had turned on a tap. I could feel the sun on my face, see the way Gina had smiled up at me the morning after the attack, the image flickering against the rainy night in disjointed superimposition.

As I stood there, I remember feeling poised in a strange web of time and contingency, aware of the past as a signalling pathway of choices made, decisions executed, fine lines criss-crossing between all the possible outcomes in my life. But it wasn't just the major things that mattered, like failing to alert Gina to Rouyle's suspicious behaviour in time. Even trivial choices could have drastic consequences. Arbitrary examples clamoured for consideration, trying to flesh out this unsettling theory. If I had gone down to Geniaxis the evening I saw Gina weeping at her bench, if it had been me instead of Maria who'd eventually comforted her, how different might things have been now? Maybe she wouldn't have spent so much time talking to Rouyle in Cambridge and being persuaded into the ill-fated collaboration because she'd have been laughing and drinking in the bar with me instead. Perhaps it would have been me steering her about the dance floor, holding her at night, taking her off to Cornwall for a weekend break.

Enough. It was too late, and now I just had to get on with things. The flat remained silent, patently abandoned.

Looking around furtively, I posted the gift and card through the letterbox.

24   *Proof of Principle*

I awoke on Monday morning with a sense of tightly-wound expectation. As soon as I opened my eyes my thoughts took up precisely where they'd left off when I'd finally fallen asleep: Gina was due back, and *something* was bound to happen.

As I'd lain in bed the previous night, I'd envisaged many scenarios: Gina being immediately sensible and going to Boyd with my evidence; Gina being in denial and needing to be persuaded; Gina believing me, but deciding to take up the matter privately with Rouyle. There were many other permutations, but I'd just have to wait and see. And meanwhile, I had to squeeze in time to tell Christine the whole story as well as talk with Ainikka about the *Arch Lat Psychiatry* translation.

I have to admit that in all the excitement, I'd completely forgotten about the mice.

When I stepped into the lab, its cheerful normality made a surreal contrast to the close-circuited anxiety of my journey in. I forced myself to respond to the chorus of greetings, with a special smile and nod in Magritte's direction. I'd managed to get seven hours' sleep, had shaved and had taken care to dress respectably. She subjected me to careful inspection and seemed satisfied.

"Andy, my lad," Paul said in a stage whisper, descending on me as I was starting up the computer. "How'd it go Friday night?"

I shrugged, produced a self-conscious smile. "You were right...I am definitely in with a chance."

If he found out the truth, I would never hear the end of it.

"Playing it cool, then?" He nodded wisely. "Sounds sensible, mate."

"Paul," Marcy called over, using the polite tone she reserved exclusively for asking favours. "Can I steal some of your Lac-zed DNA for my transfection? And can you show me where it is...*now*?"

Paul rolled his eyes as he moved away, and I clicked into my e-mail, eager to see how Gina had reacted to the CD.

My Inbox was crammed full of junk—and only junk.

I was so astonished that I ran down the list of senders a second time in case I'd missed her name. Could it be that she hadn't had a chance to look at the CD last night? Maybe Rouyle had been sticking close. She couldn't possibly have failed to notice the conspicuous gift lying on top of her other mail. Or had she missed all the hints and not realized that something was hidden under the music CD, in which case she probably thought I was extremely odd as well as pathetic? Even if all else had failed, there was still the imperative e-mail I'd sent her on Thursday. Why hadn't she got in touch?

A hand landed on my shoulder, dispelling my fretful funk, and I ducked unsuccessfully as Christine planted a purposefully sloppy kiss on my cheek.

"*Oi!* What was that for?" I wiped my face with my sleeve, relief coursing through me in an unexpected rush at the sight of her.

She pulled up a chair, emanating smugness. "For whatever you said to Cam on Saturday night. We had a long conversation about things on the phone afterwards, and then yesterday we stayed up half the night talking."

"And?"

"Everything's...well, perfect, Andy. And I'm not letting you wriggle out of responsibility for your part in it."

I forced myself to set aside my troubles for the moment. "I'm glad. And the job?"

"They still have to interview a few more candidates, but they've hinted that's just a formality."

"Sounds as if you're going to take it if they offer, then."

She nodded, eyes going dreamy.

"Listen," I said. "That's great, but I've got something really important to speak to you about, in private." I lowered my voice still further. "It's to do with those *in vitro* tests I ran, and a few other things."

She looked at me curiously. "Okay, but first I should go upstairs and check on the baby," she said. "See how... it...got on over the weekend. Have you seen *her* around yet?"

"No, but if you see her first, could you tell her I've got something urgent to tell her?"

"I'll bet you do," Christine said, still studying my face solemnly.

I passed the time doing some calculations for the mass of transfections I wanted to perform in the afternoon, entering strings of numbers without much thought. I was just toying with the idea of sending another, not-so-subtle e-mail to Gina or going downstairs in person when my mobile rang.

"Andy, there's something massively wrong up here." Christine's voice contained an element I had never heard in it before: *fear*. "Meet me at the Smoker's Wall in five minutes. And have you found out where the hell Gina is yet?"

"No, I haven't," I said calmly, for the benefit of my audience. "Coffee sounds great—see you down there."

I hung up as coldness began to diffuse throughout my body.

When I entered the crowded lift, Christine was already inside, on her way down from the animal facility. She just looked at me, emotions barely under control during the descent, and we made our way out to the Wall in continued silence, the leaden sky sagging down on us.

I hunched up, wishing I'd brought my coat as the cold pierced my thin cotton T-shirt. Christine seemed oblivious to the temperature as she attempted to light a cigarette with shaking hands, but the wind was too strong. I cupped my hands around hers until the tobacco caught fire.

"*Jesus*," she breathed, a stream of exhaled smoke snatched away by the wind.

"It's the mice, isn't it?"

She nodded darkly. "They're in trouble, but Gina moved them into the virus isolation room on Friday morning, so I can't get a good look at them—my keypass isn't coded for it."

"How do you know there's something wrong, then?"

"I can see our cages through the observation window, and the ID tags are legible." The wind pushed a skein of brown across her face, and she turned her head to allow the hair to whip up and away. "Our mice are just lying there—all the rest of the animals in the room are scurrying around, waiting for feeding time."

"Are they dead?" My earlier fear coalesced into an indigestible stone.

"I have no idea—I can't tell from the window. But that's the least of our worries: if anyone notices, Theresa will be informed and then we're finished."

Rain splattered against my face, reminding me that this was actually happening.

Christine took another shaky drag. "Theresa throws a fit if a mouse even sneezes out of line—she's terrified of a repeat of that coronavirus epidemic we had a few years back. Inquiries will be made, and Gina won't be able to come up with a good reason for the pathology, and certainly won't be able to match the ID tags to any approved project license."

"But surely Gina's taken precautions in case the mice reacted badly—it was one of the logical possibilities."

"Yes, but Gina's not *here!*" she snapped. "I called down there and nobody's seen her. I can't *believe* she's left me alone in this mess with no way into that room! Are you sure she was due back last night?"

I paused, realizing I wasn't so sure anymore. "Maria mentioned a weekend break, that she'd be back on Monday. But not what time."

It hit me then that if Gina were still en route, she might not stop home first. If so, she wouldn't know anything about the CD or my e-mail, although the mystery protein was surely trumped by this alarming new development.

"Later would be too bloody late!" Christine's voice rose in pitch, and she stood up. "Theresa makes rounds right before lunch. And someone else might stumble across them earlier—like that horrid Steve person. *He's* got access."

I put out a hand to prevent her flight, finally starting to think clearly. "Wait, I've got an idea: we can go to Maria for help. She's probably authorized for virus work."

"We can't risk telling anyone else." Chris glared down at me, struggling to free herself from my grip.

"She already knows."

"You *what!*" Christine exploded. "How could you have been so bloody stupid, Andy, to —"

"I didn't tell her!" I stood up too, grabbed her by the shoulders. "Just calm down and *listen.*" I explained what had happened, then said, "Now, does Maria have access or not?"

Christine just stared at me. I gave her a shake, and she blinked, pulled herself together. "Yes, she does...in fact, she's got about six infected cages in the isolation room right now. Gina mentioned we'd have to be careful working around her."

"Excellent," I said. "Come on, we don't have much time. Do you want me to find her?"

Chris got up too, flicking her cigarette onto the pavement in a shower of sparks. "No, she usually makes an appearance upstairs directly after morning coffee. I'd better head her off before she reports those mice as ill."

I reckoned that Maria was clever enough to work it out and that we could rely on her to be discreet, but Christine was already sprinting across the street. There'd been no chance to tell her about Rouyle, either, or the mystery protein.

It was clearly going to have to wait.

I sat across from Ainikka in one of the private study rooms in the library. She rummaged through a pile of papers until she found Rouyle's article, now covered with illegible marginalia as well as beer stains.

"I managed it in just under two hours," she said. "I don't know if it's the author or the person who translated it into Latvian, but it was fairly tortuous."

I kept my suspicions to myself. "How should we do this, then?"

"Why don't you read a complete transcript of the abstract, and then we can go through each of the results one by one?"

She took a piece of A4 from a file folder and slid it across to me.

Dominant passivity factors and pliancy criteria in rhesus macaques exposed to the PAX fraction.

Rouyle, R, Viknar, PM, and Maaros, E.

The neurobiochemical mechanisms underlying basic emotions and behaviours in higher primates are still poorly understood. In this study, we attempted to determine the factors involved in one fundamental characteristic: passivity or submission in the face of a dominant authority, even when such behaviour is clearly detrimental to survival. We noticed one male rhesus macaque in our colony that repeatedly demonstrated highly exaggerated submission behaviour, and that this feature was passed on to all offspring, even those never exposed to their sire, suggesting heredity over learned behaviour. We fractionated the brain of one male offspring and purified an active fraction, called PAX (for passivity activating extract), which, when injected intracerebrally into normal adult animals, transiently caused the same exaggerated submission. Moreover, these animals were highly obedient and suggestible using a variety of behavioural tests, even in the presence of painful stimuli. This obedience in disregard for well-being in the presence of PAX suggests that the extract contains a novel, unique neurotransmitter or other biological agent that controls submission or passivity in a dominant fashion.

I stared at the sheet of paper, trying to keep a normal expression on my face. Inside, my stomach was still in free-fall.

"This isn't the type of study I was led to believe was in the article," I finally said, so steeped in auto-pilot deception at this point that the next lie emerged almost effortlessly. "A colleague told me there might be something about a certain signal transduction pathway in the nervous system that I could use to scoop my competitors."

"Well, there might be something useful later on," she said doubtfully. "Shall we continue?"

She took me through each of the figures and the accompanying interpretations. Except for the biochemistry experiment describing the original fractionation, most of the data consisted of electrical measurements of the test animals, which had been wired up to electrodes while being put through their often painful paces—a disturbingly gruesome affair.

"Their methodology seems unethical to me," she remarked. "But animal regulations were more lax back then, I suppose."

Not necessarily, I thought, remembering what Raim had told me about the rejection of Rouyle's primate research application.

"I want to read you something from the final part of the Discussion section," she said. "I know it isn't relevant to your research, but you've got to hear this!" She held up a finger. "*Further studies with this fraction may lead to promising new methods for controlling troublesome human elements, such as criminals or psychiatric patients. Moreover, mass administration of the PAX fraction could be highly effective for instilling harmony and stability into highly volatile regions of the world, ultimately resulting in increased productivity and economic and social improvements.*"

She paused. "So far, so good...well, it's a bit wild, but still within the standard exaggerated Discussion style people use to convince people that the work is worth funding. Agreed?"

I nodded, speechless.

Ainikka tapped a scarlet fingernail on the next block of text. "But then the author goes on: *Our research supports the notion that all*

275

human behaviours are controlled by simple molecules; if passivity can be transferred experimentally, then so might aggression, love, hate, fear and the like. This hypothesis could be tested by isolating as many of these substances as possible and introducing them into humans under controlled circumstances." She met my eye. "It's one of the strangest proposals I've ever read in a paper—my boyfriend couldn't believe it either."

I swallowed down a lump of nausea. "Yes, well...I'm afraid this has all been for nothing."

"Sorry you've wasted your money."

Duly reminded, I reached for my wallet.

"You can keep my notes on the article in case you have any more ideas." She flipped platinum hair out of her eyes and stood up. "Are you coming?"

I gathered up all the papers. "I think I'll go over it one last time to make sure I haven't missed anything."

As soon as she shut the door, I read the abstract again. Everything was coming together, and the picture was shaping up to be very ugly indeed.

✦ ✦ ✦

From: glkraymer@geniaxis.com
To: a.ohara@rcc.cmb.ac.uk
Subject: understood

Andy,

I've got literally two minutes to write this e-mail. I only just got into work, after stopping home to change clothes — there was a serious accident on the M4 and we were severely delayed. Thank you so much for the CD...you were right, those songs were very disturbing, best savored on one's own. I wasn't sure at the time, but having thought about it, I suspect that R. might benefit from a discussion about the meanings behind the lyrics. As soon as I get a private moment today, I'll talk to him about it. It might be possible to clear up any misunderstandings about your interpretations.

There's a phone message from Christine, wanting me upstairs, but it's impossible now because I'm in a last-minute conference all day with R., the boss, and some people from out of town. Could you convey my apologies?

The message had arrived while I'd been upstairs with Ainikka. Right now, Gina was probably sitting around a conference table, listening to plans being made about a virus that she now knew contained something completely other than what she'd intended.

What was going through her mind? Perhaps she was being cautious because she didn't know exactly who was in on the secret. On the other hand, her e-mail implied she thought there might be a perfectly reasonable explanation for the mystery protein. Maybe she feared she'd taken the wrong tubes from Germany by mistake. She now knew that FRIP's antiviral activity didn't work in the brain, but naturally she'd want to confront Rouyle about it privately so he could save face if it were a stupid error. She'd spared his dignity before, at his seminar, when he was a complete stranger; surely now, as a lover, he would receive even more careful treatment. It was this very discretion, on top of her naïvety, that was going to land her in serious trouble.

Shit, shit, shit. I felt completely helpless. Thanks to my CD, she was going to confront Rouyle without hearing about his exploits in Estonia, the PAX fraction or the sick mice. I certainly didn't share her optimism about how he would react. In the best case, he'd just laugh at her worries and attempt to explain away all the evidence. She was probably susceptible enough to his charms to believe him, as she had already demonstrated a marked immunity to other duplicities. But in the worst case, he'd see her as a serious obstacle in his plan. Why hadn't I gone to her after I'd spoken to Raim? Why had I dropped off that CD instead of waiting until we could speak in person? I had completely miscalculated, and now it had all backfired explosively. I couldn't very well go downstairs and barge in on her meeting. Instead, I was forced to wait until the evening, an incomprehensible amount of time.

The text message alert on my mobile phone beeped me out of my preoccupation:

I fretted through the next twenty minutes, then stood up and announced that I was going out for lunch.

Magritte beamed at me, obviously encouraged by such signs of normal, non-workaholic behaviour. Maybe she thought I'd sorted things out with Gina.

"We won't wait up!" Paul said with a ludicrous wink, probably favouring the Maria hypothesis.

The wind was still gusting, stirring up leaves and bits of litter into tiny localized vortices that dispersed almost as soon as they formed. Clouds scuttled across the sky in a shifty backdrop. For a brief moment, I felt a surge of vertigo, paused, then carried on.

Christine was already seated when I arrived.

"Tell me," I said, anonymous café chatter roaring in my ears. I bit into my sandwich more because it was in front of me than from hunger.

She nodded at me across the table. "It's sorted. Gina never turned up or responded to my phone message, so Maria and I had to make an executive decision." She sounded defensive.

"She couldn't get away—she was really sorry."

"She'd better have been." The pleasantness of her tone didn't entirely mask the chill underneath.

"Anyway, what executive decision?"

She dug into her BLT, obviously not suffering from a similar lack of appetite. "We sacrificed them," she mumbled around her mouthful.

"You didn't!"

"There was no choice, Andy." She glowered at me. "We had to get rid of the mice and then swap in new cages before Theresa showed up. We were bloody lucky there were extra litters still available."

"But those mice represented important evidence for Gina's attempts to get this Phase I cancelled!"

Her face was set. "They also represented the end of my promising career as a group leader in Newcastle—or anywhere else, for that matter—if we were discovered. And I'm not stupid—I *know* she needs the evidence. We did a very thorough observation on a few of the subjects, took videos, blood samples, even saved one corpse in the freezer in case anyone needs to prove later what virus went in."

She paused to swallow, took another bite. "By the way, there was no difference in the response of the normal SCIDs versus the

SCID/pbls—the presence of a human immune system obviously did bugger-all one way or the other." She looked at me carefully. "But you already knew that, didn't you? You said you had urgent news about the *in vitro* trial, so it wasn't likely to have been good."

"It's not surprising," I confirmed. "I'll fill you in in a second. Just...how were the mice acting? Did you perform a necropsy to see what was wrong?"

She took a swig of Coke, a funny expression on her face. "There was nothing *physically* wrong with them, inside or out. They were just in some sort of stupor—dull eyes, not even reacting to being handled. I've worked with mice for years and these weren't acting any way I recognized. It must be a freak cross-reaction between FRIP and Gina's Verase gene, right?"

"Chris," I said. "There's been some information I've been keeping back."

She put down her Coke slowly. "Why do I suddenly have a very bad feeling?"

"I just thought things were too premature or unlikely to be worth mentioning before, that —"

"Out with it, O'Hara." Now her stare was positively steely.

It was then that I saw things from her perspective for the first time. How could I possibly justify having kept her uninformed for so long? She'd risked her career mainly because of our friendship, and I'd led her along like everyone else.

I began to explain, haltingly at first, gathering momentum as I went on. I didn't have to worry about any outbursts, because soon she was completely hooked on the story. I started at the beginning, with Dan's recollection and then Raim's anecdote about the Estonian affair. When I mentioned Rouyle sleeping with the animal caretaker to further his primate trials, Chris stared at me with widening eyes.

Next, I passed her Ainikka's translation of Rouyle's abstract and showed her the ominous-sounding sentence about mass administration of the PAX fraction. Christine frowned as she read but refrained from any commentary.

"But after he switched fields at Pfeiffer-deVries and started working on FRIP, he obviously didn't forget about PAX," I theorized. "He must have identified the PAX gene on the sly, because there's nothing published on it."

"You're way ahead of me here," she said, irritated. "Tell me what happened next—in *order*."

So I told her about my experiments with Helmut proving that FRIP was useless as an antiviral messenger in the brain, and Magritte's reminder that Vera Fever Virus wouldn't have been able to stimulate FRIP anyway.

"But none of this mattered in the end except to suggest that Rouyle was a fraud," I said. "Because when Gina went to Germany to create the combination virus, I think he gave her the PAX gene instead of the FRIP." I explained how Gina had stolen reagents from Rouyle's lab, and about the experiment which had led me to conclude that Gina had been tricked into inserting a small gene of unknown origin into her herpes vaccine.

"I don't have definitive proof, but I'll bet you any money you like that it's PAX."

"It might explain the mice's reaction," Christine said thoughtfully. "I mean, what does a submissive mouse look like? Or maybe this primate neurotransmitter is a lot less subtle in a rodent brain."

We both lapsed into silence, fiddling with the remains of our crusts, and eventually she raised her head, examined me with a neutral expression. "So I take it you've not told Gina any of this either?"

I squirmed in my seat. "It was a tricky situation, with them sleeping together. I didn't tell her when I was first suspicious because I had no proof. By the time I got the result about the mystery protein, she was already in Cornwall, and I only got the article translated this morning." My guilt wasn't even remotely relieved by Christine's slow nod. "Anyway, I left a message about the mystery protein at her flat over the weekend."

"How on earth is she going to deal with it?"

"It sounds as if she's going to confront Rouyle in private."

"And she doesn't have enough information to realize what a bad idea that is," she said grimly. "If you're right that Rouyle's been hung up on PAX his entire career, maybe he's come up with this scheme to test it in humans when the normal scientific channels failed."

"That's exactly what I was thinking."

"After waiting so long, he's probably not going to tolerate any unforeseen obstructions."

"Are you saying Gina's in danger?"

She paused. "Well, it's a possibility. We've got to get her away from Rouyle—maybe she can stay at your place tonight. And then tomorrow we can go to Geniaxis and show them all the evidence."

"Not the mouse trial, though!"

"Of course not. Your information should be convincing enough."

I remembered something. "Are you sure that Boyd isn't...?"

She blinked. "I guess I'm not. Well, first we make sure Gina's safe, and then we can decide what to do."

"She arranged to meet me tonight."

"So you just spirit her away. Romantic, isn't it?"

Beneath her careful humour, I could tell that she was still hurt that I hadn't trusted her with the full story. But this concern was nothing next to my fear. The taste of dread kept coming back no matter how hard I tried to swallow it.

The afternoon passed in an unknowing blur. Somehow, I managed to speak intelligibly to my colleagues and put on a convincing impression of normality. I bantered with Marcy, who was irate that my stacks of plates were taking up too much space in the incubators. I fended off Paul, who kept trying to extract more details about my date with Maria. I managed to reassure Magritte, who'd approached me in a private moment to make sure that I wasn't trying to do too much because of her comments on Saturday. And I performed an absolute marathon transfection session in the tissue culture suite, introducing DNA after DNA into the hundred or so plates I'd seeded the day before. I did all this in a daze, relying on years of practice to coast through the intervening hours until I could finally see Gina again.

It was just past ten and I was alone in the lab, tensed at my desk in almost unbearable anticipation. Gina's window remained dark, but there was another square, lit behind blinds a few rooms over that I supposed was the Geniaxis conference room. I stood up, paced the lab without purpose, and when I returned, Gina's lab had flooded bluish-white, and the conference room was darkened. After a few moments, Gina herself came into view, followed closely by another person. When he turned in profile, I saw that it was Rouyle.

Gina spoke, sketching frenetic gestures in the air. At first, Rouyle looked to be trying to calm her down, both palms held outward in exaggerated reasonableness. But when she persisted, he began to react with an equal measure of agitated body language. As their argument intensified, she stabbed the air with a finger to make some point, and then he loomed over her, responding in kind and gripping her by both shoulders.

I stood up involuntarily, poised to run, but found myself transfixed. Gina's mouth worked in what looked like passionate anger as she struggled to free herself. She wrenched away, her hair fanning outward in response, but he made a successful swipe for her arm and began pulling her towards the door. She tried to escape his grip, but he muscled her from view with apparent ease.

The light was snuffed out, restoring the matrix of windows to dark uniformity.

I snapped out of my paralysis and pelted down the corridor, past shadowy empty labs on my left and right. I threw myself into the stairwell and hurtled down the steps, stumbling one step above the first landing in the sickly-green glow of the emergency exit sign. I grabbed at the railing, but it was too late: I was already going down, sprawling heavily onto the floor.

My body slid to a complete stop, all the air kicked from my lungs. After a few shocked seconds, a hot pain bloomed in my right knee. I levered myself up and limped as fast as I could down the rest of the stairs, but my knee refused to take any weight. Just as I was pushing through the fire doors, one set of lifts opposite the Geniaxis main entrance swished closed. The company was clearly darkened and lifeless.

I wavered in agonizing indecision by the stairwell. Rouyle must have overpowered her and forced her into the lift. According to the illuminated display above the doors, it was already sinking past the third floor. I didn't think I could negotiate that many flights quickly enough even without an injury, so I hobbled over to the lifts and hit the button.

While I was waiting for the second lift, I crossed the corridor and leaned on the Geniaxis after-hours bell for a few seconds, just to be sure, listening to its fruitless summons through the thick glass. When I turned around, the display showed that the current occupants of the other lift had arrived in the Centre lobby. The porter went off-duty at eight, and the area around the building was deserted at night, so in all likelihood, there would be no one to detain them. An important visitor like Rouyle would probably have a hire car parked in one of the VIP spaces in the car park.

The second lift arrived at last, and I dived in. When I erupted out again, the lobby was empty, and outside, the automatic gate of the Centre's car park was just closing with the crashing finality of iron on cement. Ahead, there wasn't another living creature in any direction, not on the pavements, not on the street, not in the quadrangle park. Just the distant tail lights of one lone car, turning the corner at dangerous speed. When I blinked the sweat from my eyes, it was already gone.

25   *Serious Resignation*

I stood in the Piccadilly Line carriage, clinging to a pole as if it could haul me from my nightmare. I felt disjointed by the morning rush hour: thousands of people who had no idea that the universe had lurched out of its enclosure and was loping wildly across the fields.

Many of the events directly following Gina and Rouyle's hasty exit from the Centre the previous night were lodged in my mind with unavoidable clarity, but others had somehow been struck from the record. As this hardly ever happens to me, I found the blanks almost more disturbing than the actual memories.

After the car had disappeared, I'd stood next to the car park exit gate, in shock, for a good few minutes. This is a part I still don't remember, aside from the irrational conviction that I must have been mistaken about the identity of the people in the lift and later, the car. I thought that Rouyle might still come charging out of the building with Gina in his grasp, that I could somehow take him on.

When a few more minutes had elapsed with no sign of the pair, I pulled out my phone, forgetting in my state that Gina's numbers weren't listed. What I should have done was ring the police straightaway, or Magritte, or at least search the building. Instead, I made the stupid decision to take a cab to Gina's flat in Stoke Newington. Of course she wasn't there, but I hadn't known where else to look. Then, as I'd been too flustered to remember to ask the cab to wait, and no other mode of transport was evident, I was forced to make my way back to Manor House on foot, which had taken quite some time with my injured knee.

I'd been thinking even less clearly when I finally ducked into my local police station, but what I had witnessed was not a crime, according to the officer on duty, and the rest was sheer speculation.

I was too mentally dishevelled to press the issue, so I just apologized for having troubled her and extricated myself as soon as possible.

The rest of the walk home was a haze of jumbled impressions. The next thing I remember was being slumped on the sofa, listening to Christine's voice on the telephone.

"He was probably just a bit rough in his anger. It's not necessarily as bad as you think."

"Chris—he's about to pull off a serious crime, and she's just caught him!"

"Let's see whether she turns up tomorrow before assuming the worst." But her voice sounded uncertain, and I was far from pacified.

I had sat on the sofa all night, oscillating between fear and denial. At one point I looked up and realized the sun had risen, so I took a shower like an automaton, put on fresh clothes and made my way awkwardly to the Underground, my knee still aching. It was a fine day, but the deep-blue November sky seemed as if it belonged on another planet.

I stepped into the Centre lobby, scanning the usual morning flurry with anxious focus. I wondered what I would do if I saw Rouyle, if I should—or could—restrain myself from challenging him outright. I was waiting for the lift when I spotted Maria with other Geniaxis people, coming from the canteen exit. When she saw me, her eyes widened. She murmured a few quick words to her companions, cut away from them and approached.

"Have you seen Gina yet this morning?" I burst out, without even bothering to say hello. "Or Rouyle?"

Her eyes grew larger. "You haven't heard about Gina yet, have you?"

My stomach plunged. "I haven't heard anything, I've only just got in."

She looked over her shoulder, agitated. "The whole company's in chaos today—no one's going to notice if my coffee break drags on."

I took her arm and steered her over to a quiet corner by the payphones.

"What's happened?" I prepared myself for the worst.

"She's only gone and resigned, that's all!" Her eyes were sharp with anger. "By letter, no less, delivered by special courier this morning, and effective immediately—not even having the courtesy to explain herself to Thomas in person!"

"Resigned?" I slumped against the wall.

"She's just buggered off back to America and isn't coming back—you have no idea what a mess the Gene Therapy Division's in right now!"

"What did the letter say?" I asked, keeping my tone level.

"It was all very self-righteous, apparently. She couldn't carry on with the Phase I in good conscience when the principle hadn't been tested in animals. " Maria lowered her voice. "But it doesn't make sense: she didn't have a chance to find out about the sick mice. Why quit right in the middle of the trial when those mice could've provided the means for stopping the Phase I altogether?"

When I didn't respond, mind racing, she went on, "I'm sure she'd get in trouble for breaking the rules, but she'd be forgiven in the end. Geniaxis would be history if this trial ends up harming any patients, but Boyd's made it very clear today that the Phase I will continue on schedule, Gina or no Gina."

"This is..." I trailed off, overwhelmed by shock.

"It's a major quandary for me, too," she said. "I can't look the other way now I know the damned virus is toxic. I didn't want to be involved, but now I am, and I don't know what to do."

It wasn't that I hadn't been listening to her lengthy speech, but I was stalled somewhere at the beginning, a certainty crystallizing around one of her earlier statements.

"It was a hoax," I murmured, so softly that Maria leaned forward, shook her head.

"It was a hoax," I said, louder. "The resignation letter, I mean. She didn't write it."

Maria was dumbfounded. "What on earth are you on about?"

I was almost too unstrung to stand still. "I was working late in the lab last night and I saw them—Gina and Rouyle—have a scuffle through the window. I didn't get down there in time. She never made it home. And we had an appointment at ten that night, and she never rang to cancel!"

"What are you saying, Andy?" Her face reflected a fusion of disbelief and grim humour. "That she was abducted?"

I nodded my head smartly. "And Rouyle probably fabricated that letter to cover up the fact that she's gone missing. You're absolutely right that it's not like her to have bunked off just when the mice were ready."

Maria crossed her arms. "It's a daft idea, Andy—and what would his motive be? She couldn't have confronted him about the mice, obviously."

"True...but she *did* confront him, about other things." I brought her up to date on the mystery protein and Gina's cryptic e-mail.

"Jesus," Maria said. "He wouldn't actually..."

"I'm not so sure." I gave her the highlights of Rouyle's shady history. "So which is more likely, that she's actually resigned, precisely when it makes the least sense, or that Rouyle's detained her? She has the knowledge to get him into serious trouble, and from what I saw of their argument, she wasn't going to be fobbed off easily."

"What are you...we...going to do?" For the first time, I could see I'd half-convinced her. "Go to the police?"

"Already tried it, last night. Because Gina and Rouyle are a couple and I only witnessed a bit of pushing and shoving, they didn't want to know."

"But now that's she's turned up missing, surely —"

"But that's just it, we have no proof! It looks as if she's left a note. I don't imagine the police will be any more concerned than they were last night."

"I'm not sure I agree." Maria looked at her watch. "But I don't have time to argue about it now, because we've got an emergency staff meeting in five minutes."

"Listen, have you seen Rouyle around this morning or not?"

"No, but we've been gossiping in the canteen for ages. I might not have —"

"When's your staff meeting over?" It made me heartily uneasy not to know Rouyle's precise whereabouts. "Because I think I'm going to speak to Boyd myself."

I was more convinced than ever that Rouyle's exploits were a solo job, just like in Estonia. Anyway, I didn't have the luxury to be cautious.

"Are you sure that's wise?"

"What else can I do?" I slammed a fist into my palm. "I know her vaccine's been sabotaged, and I've got the data to back it up. I don't have to say anything about the mice. True, Gina shouldn't have been telling me corporate secrets, but revealing this to Boyd won't get her into any more trouble than she's in already. And it's not as if I've broken any rules by listening to Gina's indiscretions."

She tried to interrupt, but I overrode her. "I can't just sit around when Gina might be in real danger! Nobody's going to look for her if they think she just resigned and left town—we've *got* to grab people's attention. The police will be more likely to listen to Boyd than to me. And if I do this properly, we can get the Phase I aborted without divulging the mouse trial."

Maria started to nod, although she didn't seem completely convinced.

I pushed open the glass door and stepped into the lobby of Geniaxis. It was the first time I'd been there in daytime, and it had a completely different atmosphere splashed in sunlight from the courtyard window and busy with employees coming in and out over the lunchtime break. But beneath the bustle, I could sense that these people were tense, distracted—that the entire place hummed with an undercurrent of uncertainty.

I approached the woman sitting at reception and said, "I've got something extremely urgent I need to discuss with Dr Boyd."

"I don't even have to check his diary," she said with a strained smile. "I'm certain he's all booked up for today. Perhaps an appointment later on in the week?"

I put my palms flat on her desk and spoke softly. "If you tell him that I know something helpful about Gina Kraymer, do you think he could squeeze me in between appointments?"

She took her bifocals off and inspected me with frank interest before asking my name.

I sat down on the sofa to wait. The severe old man in the white coat frowned down at me in lofty disapproval from his gilt frame, and passing Geniaxis employees stared. Self-consciously, I picked up one of the corporate brochures from the coffee table, its cover displaying the colourful Geniaxis logo and beneath it, the sweeping and rather arguable claim, *No disease is beyond the reach of the modern miracle of Gene Therapy.*

Maria had said that Geniaxis couldn't survive any clinical trial fatalities. In recent years there'd been a rash of negative media coverage about a few mishaps with gene therapy—fatalities, even some cancers. But these thoughts steadied me: Boyd had struck me as a rational man. Surely he would take me seriously if his company's reputation were in jeopardy.

"Dr O'Hara?" The receptionist was standing before me. "If you'd just follow me? Dr Boyd is having lunch in his office, but he can see you now."

Boyd was sitting at his desk, hands and mouth busy with an elaborate sandwich. He indicated the seat opposite him with one elbow, and while I was making myself comfortable, he managed to swallow long enough to mumble, "Dr O'Hara...Andrew, isn't it? Please, sit down, apologies for eating in front of you, but..." He shrugged, eyes burning with curiosity as he took me in.

"Thanks for agreeing to meet at such short notice."

"How could I not, after Ellen told me your reason?" He leaned forward, pinning me with a candid stare. "You know where she is, don't you?"

I opened my mouth to respond, but Boyd pressed on. "You could pass on a message from me, then, that her point has been made and that we would agree to forget all about this mad escapade if she'd only come back to work. Frankly, we still need her knowledge."

"I don't know where she is." I hesitated as his face compressed in disappointment, then went on before I lost courage. "But I'm certain that her resignation letter was faked, and furthermore, that Dr Rouyle has tampered with your combination herpes vaccine."

Boyd looked incredulous. "What in heaven's name are you blathering about? And how do you know about the virus? It's strictly confidential!"

"If you'd just hear me out, I can explain everything."

"This ought to be interesting," he said, voice tight with controlled anger. "Don't tell me Gina's been leaking company secrets on top of everything else? If so, I am excessively, excessively disappointed."

"Gina came to me for help because I'm a signal transduction specialist," I said. "It was her great concern about the haste of the collaboration that drove her to it. And I did sign a confidentiality agreement." I neglected to mention that I hadn't kept my promise in the end.

He looked me over, clearly unimpressed.

"I'm extremely busy today, so let's cut to the interesting part: Richard Rouyle's alleged *criminal activities*." His mocking tone made it clear I'd have to work quickly.

"I have three lines of evidence suggesting that Rouyle never intended to put FRIP into your herpes vaccine," I said. "First, our laboratory has proof that FRIP is unable to stimulate the antiviral TRAP pathway in the nervous system. Second —"

"Wait, let's address these points one at a time," he said, a knowing look developing on his face.

"Fine." I pulled out a folded piece of paper from my back pocket and smoothed it out on the desk: a printout of the definitive FRIP experiment. I pointed out the black bands proving that FRIP was competent for growth signalling but not for antiviral activation in neuronal cells.

Boyd shrugged. "So how about an experiment in human primary neurons, the cell type the herpes vaccine actually targets?"

I cleared my throat. "Well, I haven't done those experiments, but it seems to me that —"

"Seems?" His voice was low and perilous. "You call yourself a *signal transduction specialist*, yet you are drawing premature conclusions about an experiment done in an artificial rat cell line, when you should appreciate that signal transduction pathways are notoriously cell-type variable, not to mention species-specific!"

I opened my mouth, but nothing came out.

"You might as well know," Boyd continued inexorably, "that Richard has already called me this morning. He told me all about what happened with Gina last night before she disappeared. Apparently she unloaded a list of perceived problems with the FRIP kinase strategy, and concluded that she wanted nothing more to do with him or Geniaxis. And now I know where she was getting her information!"

The words hit my brain in discrete packets that took a few seconds to form comprehensible sentences.

"Richard was worried about her mental health," he went on. "Despite the vicious personal attack, he was still gentleman enough to excuse her behaviour on those grounds—far better than she deserves, I'm afraid."

I was now thoroughly disorientated. Why would Rouyle tell Boyd about the problems with FRIP? It made no sense. But then I realized that Rouyle must have feared that Gina had told other people, and the best defence was a pre-emptive strike. Thanks to me, he knew every piece of scientific evidence incriminating him.

Boyd produced an arctic smile at my speechlessness. "At any rate,

Richard assures me that his own lab has tested FRIP in the relevant human primary neurons quite thoroughly. Next point, please?"

There was still the matter of the mystery protein, which Rouyle couldn't have been able to explain away so easily. Unable to keep from stammering, I pointed out the appropriate places on the printout, but to my chagrin, Boyd just looked amused.

"Richard was *very* concerned when Gina brought up this point," he said, "but it made one thing clearer to him: it seems that two tubes mysteriously disappeared from the freezer when Gina left Pfeiffer-deVries, causing much consternation. These tubes were nothing to do with FRIP, but with another gene that his lab works on."

"Gina is intelligent enough to remember which tubes she used!"

"Richard said there are hundreds of tubes in that freezer, all labelled similarly. Anyone could make a mistake. And the fact that she stole reagents, even the wrong ones, is shocking. Now, I'm most eager to hear your third point."

I swallowed hard. "FRIP is like interferon—it only responds to attack by double-stranded RNA viruses." My voice didn't sound confident at all.

Boyd snorted. "Better stick to the signal transduction, Andrew. Even I know that interferon can mediate indirect protective effects against all sorts of viruses, including those comprised of single-stranded RNA. It's true that FRIP hasn't been as well-studied for secondary effects, but Richard confirmed that his lab has performed all the appropriate tests with FRIP and Vera Fever."

"And did he also *confirm* that he was getting rough with Gina in the lab? I saw it from my window!"

Boyd nodded. "Yes, he told me she was hysterical—he had to restrain her for her own good."

I had run out of options. "Rouyle got chucked out of the Brain Research Institute in Tartu for performing illicit primate trials. He's got a history of dubious behaviour!"

"Do you have proof for this fabulous accusation?" He was interested in spite of himself: obviously a point that Rouyle had neglected to mention.

I was just opening my mouth when I remembered my promise to Raim. He was terrified that scandal could still harm his institute, so he would probably refuse to back me up. Numbly, I shook my head.

"This discussion is over," Boyd declared. Then he paused, sighing. "Except for one final word. I know you're probably quite upset about Gina's defection. It was obvious from your manner the other evening how you feel about her."

I swallowed convulsively.

"Furthermore, she's clearly manipulated you into believing her warped side of the story." His voice remained mild, only the eyes taking on an edge. "None of us realized she was so unbalanced. Given the data you just showed me, and what you saw last night, it's no surprise you reached the conclusions you did."

I was so desperate to blurt out something about the mouse trial that I had to clench my jaw. But if I betrayed Christine, I would never, ever be able to forgive myself.

"I guess I have been a bit distraught since I heard about her resignation," I said. "I don't know what came over me."

"Say no more about it." The amiability, like my contrition, was forced, and he stood up pointedly. "And in the unlikely case that Gina does get into contact with you?"

"I'll pass on your message." I realized I was trembling, and was relieved that he made no move to shake my hand.

I pushed through the press in the Henry that evening, late for an emergency meeting with Christine and Maria. I located them immediately but was thrown off balance by the presence of a third person: Cameron.

Christine looked up guiltily at my approach.

"He knows, Andy," she said simply. When I just looked at her, she added, "I had to tell him. It's become too much to keep to myself, and we need all the brains we can muster."

"I don't mind," I said. "Sorry about all the subterfuge, Cam, but you probably understand now why we had to..."

"Absolutely." He was unaccustomedly serious. "It's a terrible business."

"We took the liberty of buying you something a bit stronger." Christine slid a small glass towards me as I slotted myself next to Maria.

I took a generous sip, the neat whisky burning down my throat. "Is everyone *au fait* with recent developments?"

"Everyone except you," Maria said, exchanging glances with the others.

"Rouyle's gone!" Christine said.

"What?" I stared at her.

"I didn't see him around today," Maria explained, "and then a rumour started circulating that he had to fly back to Frankfurt last night—some 'pressing emergency' in his lab. And he's not returning until Thursday!"

"We were just speculating that what really happened was that he was taking Gina back with him," Cameron said.

"In the midst of all these critical Phase I negotiations, it's hard to imagine what else could've been so important," Maria said.

"Christ." I studied everyone else's grim faces. "Have any of the gossips noticed the coincidence between the two disappearances?"

"Of course," Maria said, "but not in the way you're thinking. *I've* heard that Boyd's worried that this 'emergency' is bogus too. Except he thinks Rouyle's been recalled because Pfeiffer-deVries is planning to bail out of the collaboration now that its key person, Gina, has gone."

"How did your meeting with Boyd go, anyway?" Christine asked me.

I rubbed my eyes; my sleepless night was catching up with me. "It was a complete cock-up, basically." I proceeded to relate the painful details.

"This proves Rouyle's got something to hide," Christine said. "You don't think he's going to...do away with her, do you?"

Everybody flinched, and I must have looked particularly bad because Christine slid a hand across the table and touched my forearm apologetically.

"I don't think so," I said, after taking a few breaths. "Gina still has important knowledge about the herpes virus project. Boyd admitted he'd take her back even after all he claims she's done—and his anxiety about Rouyle's disappearance reinforces this. Surely Rouyle knows even less about her vaccine."

Maria nodded. "Of course we all keep notebooks, but you know how it is: you can't write down every last detail, and Gina was definitely the herpes specialist. Other labs are starting to use herpes viruses for neuronal DNA transfer, but she was way ahead of everyone else. She designed this entire system herself...it was her baby."

"I think we're all in agreement that Gina is indispensable for Rouyle to achieve his goals," Cameron said.

"But *what* goals?" Christine asked in frustration. "Yes, he wants to test PAX, but why? He's known for promoting the clinical applications of research, but I just don't buy that PAX could be medically relevant when there are so many sedatives on the market already. Who'd risk gene therapy when you could just as easily administer Valium?"

"I reckon his goals are practical, all right, but not medically so," Cameron said, eyes narrowing. "*Politically.* I bet he's developing a bioweapon—a way to control enemies without the outside world realizing what's happening."

"Daft," Maria scoffed. "Really, Cameron."

"Let's stay focused here," I said, a bit louder than I'd intended.

"Right," Christine said. "So Rouyle can easily keep the Phase I trial afloat by passing off Gina's coerced advice as his own insights."

"Gina would never tell him anything," I protested.

Christine looked at me sourly. "Don't be naïve. Rouyle probably wouldn't stoop to torture, but there are drugs that can definitely loosen the tongue, and one thing Pfeiffer-deVries isn't short of is drugs."

"Sheer intimidation can also be quite effective," Cameron added quietly.

I conceded the point. "But she's going to be redundant eventually, and furthermore there's the Phase I, which has the potential to harm innocent people. The real problem is that we can't convince anyone without revealing the existence of the animal trial. Which is out of the question, because Christine would take the entire blame now that Gina's gone."

I felt Maria's hand find mine under the table, seeking reassurance.

"There's only one thing for it," she said. "I've got to pretend it was me helping Gina, not Christine, and go to Boyd with the evidence."

"You can't go down alone when you weren't even involved initially!" Christine said. "It's absolutely out of the question!"

"Just let me finish, please." Maria sounded confident, but I could detect her nervousness through our physical contact. I gave her hand an encouraging squeeze. "I've managed to locate Gina's descriptions of the trial protocol. She kept very detailed notes, though they were completely cryptic unless you knew the ID tags of the animals, which Christine was able to supply. And don't forget, we've got video footage of the mice's strange behaviour, blood samples and one frozen mouse, all stashed away safely if anyone requires further proof. I'm convinced I won't get in trouble if Boyd believes the data."

"That's a big if," I warned. "I got massacred in his office today, and I thought my evidence was solid."

"But Rouyle had already contaminated your case," Maria pointed out.

"True, but even if you get to Boyd first, he'll just go to Rouyle and come back with another logical explanation," I said.

"Yeah, like they sent her the wrong virus batch from Germany," Cameron said. "He could just say his technician mixed up the preps or something."

"Exactly. Boyd's already sceptical, thanks to me," I said. "I don't doubt you've got enough evidence that the mice were sick, but we've got to prove that it was *his* combination vaccine that actually went into those mice."

"Andy's right," Christine said. "We can't go to Boyd until we've PCR'd up the viral sequences from the dead mouse."

Maria nodded. "I see your point. Fortunately, it's fairly easy. If the gene does encode PAX, like Andy reckons, and PAX only runs at about five kilodaltons on a gel, then the protein is quite small, only about, what..." she paused, doing the maths, "forty-five amino acids long, which is..."

"A hundred and thirty-odd nucleotides for the insertion," Cameron said. "Assuming the DNA isn't padded with irrelevant flanking sequences."

"Even assuming some extra, that's still within easy sequencing distance," I said. "So we can probably get the entire stretch using forward and reverse primers based on the surrounding herpes virus sequence."

"And those already exist," Maria said. "Gina's got loads of primers in her freezer, all very well organized and cross-referenced in her notebook."

"Okay," I said, stretching out the last syllable as I considered all the possibilities. "This sounds great. But how are we going to prove that the mystery gene is PAX? The sequence isn't published, and I already checked all the genomics databases—Rouyle hasn't deposited the sequence anywhere."

"Is that really necessary?" Christine asked. "Won't it be enough to show that it's not FRIP?"

"Sure, it'll be better than nothing. But I'm worried that he can always claim an error, that Gina put the wrong gene in without him knowing. But if we show it's PAX, we can link it back to his Latvian article, and from there, to the Estonian monkey scandal."

"But you said whassiname, Raim, wanted to keep it secret," Christine said.

"Yes," I said. "But if he knew the lives of human patients were at stake, he'd probably make a statement—he's a decent man. Then we'd have demonstrated a pattern of bad behaviour. And I reckon Rouyle cloned PAX illicitly on Pfeiffer-deVries time and expenses. We could get him on that as well."

Everyone was nodding. "I'll go ahead and start the PCRs anyway," Maria said. "Then if anyone can think of a clever way to figure out the sequence of PAX, short of sneaking over to Pfeiffer-deVries and committing corporate espionage..."

I stared at Maria, unable to speak. She had just given me a brilliant idea. Crazy, but brilliant.

26   *Interview Etiquette*

I leaned my forehead against the aeroplane window. The landscape below was transforming from patchy fields and clusters of red-roofed houses into a grey sea of buildings. A focus of pressure lodged in my temples as the plane angled on its final approach. My body was taut with expectation, but I was energized by an unusual sense of optimism. It was probably because I was actually acting, rather than sitting around waiting for things to happen. When had I believed in something—someone—so much that I had been willing to take real risks? I felt awake for the first time in years, free to respond to stimuli without a barrier of equivocation and cowardice in between.

In the end, it had been easy to arrange everything last-second—an ease that brought with it its own momentum. After our pub meeting the evening before, I'd gone back to the lab and sent off two hasty e-mails.

```
From: a.ohara@rcc.cmb.ac.uk
To: breckenridge@metzger.de
Subject: visit

Dear Sandra,I know this is massively short notice, but I
happen to be giving a talk in Frankfurt (at Pfeiffer-de-
Vries) this week, so I'll be in town. I was wondering if
you fancied getting together for a scientific discussion
at Metzger? I could even give an impromptu seminar if you
could find a free room. It was such a shame not to have
had a chance to discuss things properly — including my
most recent unpublished findings — in Cambridge.Let me
know ASAP, and I hope to see you soon.

Andy O'Hara
```

✦ ✦ ✦

From: a.ohara@rcc.cmb.ac.uk
To: r.rouyle@pfeiffer_devries.de
Subject: post-doc position

Dear Dr Rouyle,

I am a post-doc in my third year in the laboratory of
Magritte Valorius at the RCC in London. You are probably
familiar with our work on cell growth kinases in the development of cancers. I have been thinking about my next
career move, and am convinced that I would like to switch
to the industrial setting. Moreover, I have always been
extremely impressed with your work. It just so happens
that I will be in Frankfurt on Wednesday/Thursday giving
a talk at Metzger. I realize this is extremely short notice, but would you have time to fit in a brief interview?
I have attached an updated CV. If you are interested and
have a position available, please e-mail me immediately
and I can arrange to stop by your office during my visit.

Kind regards,

Dr Andrew O'Hara

p.s. I would appreciate if you refrained from asking Dr
Valorius for a letter of reference unless we both agree to
proceed further. Thank you for your understanding of this
delicate matter.

About an hour later, Sandra had replied:

Andy!

Totally floored to get your e-mail this evening! Sniffing
around for an industry job? I must say I'm surprised — I
always thought you were hard core. Anyway, this week is
perfect because Stan is out of town — no offense, but you
know how much he hates your boss. Also, we have a signal-
ing discussion group that meets every Wednesday at 4 — in
other words, tomorrow! The student who was going to present says she's happy to give up her spot. So bring your
hottest data — I'm salivating with curiosity.

see ya,

Sandra

I'd arrived at work the next morning with a rucksack packed in the
hope that Rouyle had responded favourably, but I was jittery with tension. It had only occurred to me after I'd sent the e-mail that my
application to Rouyle's lab, coinciding almost exactly with Gina's disappearance, might come across as suspicious. I had no idea how much
Gina had said to Rouyle on Monday night. She must have mentioned

my incriminating results, but had she revealed their source? Rouyle probably knew that Gina didn't have the reagents to have performed the FRIP experiments herself. But he would know that Magritte Valorius's lab was housed in the same building, and to make matters more precarious, Helmut had recently requested some FRIP DNA from Rouyle's own technician.

No, I could only hope that the combination of Gina's usual discretion and Rouyle's preoccupation with the unplanned kidnapping would have distracted him from making connections. There wasn't anything I could do about it now, anyway.

Rouyle's reply was already waiting in my Inbox, sent just a few minutes before. I held my breath as I clicked it open:

Dear Dr O'Hara,

I was pleasantly surprised to receive your e-mail. Certainly I would be pleased to meet with you to discuss a possible post-doctoral position — in fact I am quite eager to fill a recent vacancy. Your lab has a formidable track record, and furthermore I happened to notice your poster at Cambridge and was impressed.

(*The smarmy, lying bastard!* I fumed internally.)

There are no free seminar slots available on such short notice, but I would be happy to speak to you informally and then show you around our facilities.

This afternoon would be the better choice for me, but if that doesn't suit I can fit you in first thing on Thursday morning. Contact me with the details of your arrival, and I will be ready for you.

With best wishes,

Richard Rouyle

- - -

Richard F. Rouyle, PhD
Head, Department of Immunity Signalling
Gene Therapy Section
Pfeiffer-deVries A.G.
Frankfurt, Germany

I knew Rouyle was a master dissembler, but the innocuous reply reassured me nonetheless.

After that, it was just a matter of booking a last-minute plane ticket and notifying Magritte that I'd been invited to give a talk by the Fortuna lab in the afternoon. Magritte, though surprised, was amenable; she was always pushing us to get as much seminar experience as possible.

"Just watch that Sandra," she'd warned. "Don't let her take you out for drinks. Are too lightweight to handle."

"Please, Magritte," I'd replied with dignity. "I can look after myself."

She'd just sniffed.

Later, about half an hour before I had to dash for the airport, Maria had stopped by to brief me about the PCRs.

"It's going a treat: I got decent amplification with the first primer pair I tried." Maria's eyes were full of excitement.

"Well done. What did you use as a template?"

"I just dissected out a bit of brain and homogenized it. The size of the DNA fragment I pulled out was consistent with it being PAX, based on the mystery protein's molecular mass: roughly 160 base pairs, not including the viral flanking sequences."

"There's no way the insert is FRIP, then," I said. "It's far too small." Then something occurred to me. "I'm surprised Gina didn't notice the size discrepancy in Germany when she was cloning the DNA into her vector."

She shrugged. "It's not standard cut-and-paste plasmid cloning—she has to use recombination because the herpes genome is so large. Besides, I doubt she did the dirty work herself; she had several technicians at her disposal."

"What's next, then?"

"I'm purifying the fragment right now, so I should have it down to Xavier for sequencing before lunchtime."

I deflated. "Sequencing's going to be a real bottle-neck. I sent Xavier some work last week and I still haven't got my traces! I gather there's a hefty queue at the moment."

Maria's dimple materialized. "Not a problem, Andy. Geniaxis has a special agreement with the Centre's sequencing facility. We pay more than you lot, but in return our samples have priority."

"You're having me on! That is so unfair!"

She laughed. "Well, it works in your favour this time—we'll probably know by tomorrow afternoon at the latest." She lowered her voice, even though the lab was empty. "Christine tells me you've devised some deranged plan to go to Frankfurt and sniff around Rouyle's lab."

"That's right." I felt rather sheepish at the unequivocal disapproval transmitted by the angle of her raised eyebrow. "I've got to do *something*. Besides, maybe I can get my hands on that PAX DNA sequence while I'm at it."

"I don't like it one bit, Andy. It seems so unnecessary. The last thing we want is for you to get in more trouble."

By the *we*, it was clear she meant *I*. I couldn't help feeling touched.

"I promise I'll be careful," I said. "But I want to see if I can get some clue about what he's done with her."

Maria's dark eyes appraised my own. "If it were me instead of Gina, would you go to all the trouble of flying over?"

"What a question!" I replied. "Of course I would: post-docs have to stick together."

❖ ❖ ❖

Was I really here, drinking in a smoky bar in the middle of Frankfurt? Actually being in Germany had increased the disjointed sensation that all of this might very well be happening to someone else, and I hadn't even got anywhere near Rouyle yet. I felt guilty, too, that I was socializing while Gina might be in real trouble. But there was nothing I could do about it until the following morning, and meanwhile, I hoped to learn more about Rouyle from his Frankfurt colleagues.

When I'd called Rouyle and told him the details of my Metzger seminar, he'd decided that Thursday morning was more convenient. So I'd managed to secure a hotel and, despite Magritte's warnings, hadn't been able to get out of the customary post-seminar session. However, by the time my talk was finished, I was happy to join them, as they'd turned out to be unexpectedly forthcoming.

Sandra's voice roused me from my preoccupation.

"A big *prost* to Andy for having the balls to bare his unpublished soul," she declared, clashing her cloudy glass of *Hefeweizen* against my own before attacking all the others.

"So, Andy," she went on. "Spill the beans about your Pfeiffer-deVries interviews tomorrow. Which labs are you visiting?"

Everyone else's banter subsided, and I sat up, seeing my opportunity.

"Well, there are some good people there," I said. "The Schmidt lab has done some interesting stuff with MAP kinases, and Kruller had that *Nature* paper a few months about that novel lipid-activated protein...what's it called..."

"TAK-1," supplied one of the senior post-docs, a long-haired blond man who fulfilled every Californian stereotype I'd ever absorbed from television.

"That's it," I said. "And then there's Rouyle's lab, working on FRIP kinase."

"Puh-lease!" Sandra hooted, taking another swig of her beer. A few of the others chuckled at her response. "The man's an asshole—you can't seriously be considering his lab!"

"*I* think he's cute," one woman said defensively, only to be pelted with a barrage of nuts and pretzels by some of the others. Sandra just shook her head disapprovingly.

"What's wrong with him?" I kept my expression neutral. "I don't know him personally."

One of the PhD students leaned forward. "He's got a majorly bad rep, Andy. His street cred is sub-normal. There's, like, serious word out about him."

"In what regard?" I asked, after I'd waded through his linguistic quagmire.

Sandra shrugged. "Nothing concrete. Just...rumours. Post-docs quitting—or getting axed—for no apparent reason."

The blond guy nodded. "*I* heard he's in trouble—his last post-doc packed up her things last month and he's been having like major problems replacing her."

"He'd snap a hotshot like you right up, Andy," another said. "But you *so* don't want to go there."

"They say he goes postal if you disagree with any of his pet theories," Sandra said. "There's talk of hidden agendas, odd behaviour, frequent affairs with his students."

"And he's a big-time hypocrite too," the blond guy added. "He doesn't care about patients at all."

"Besides," Sandra said, "If you're after an industry job with all the advantages of academia, you can't do better than Metzger. We like it *much* better than UCSF." She paused, added, "Well, aside from the crummy weather, of course."

"Want us to look into getting you head-hunted?" the blond guy asked.

The others were nodding with enthusiasm, making me feel unexpectedly despicable.

❧ ❧ ❧

"It's a pleasure to meet you at last." Rouyle grasped my hand over his desk, a vast sea of gloss.

"Likewise," I said, calling up all the suave confidence I could muster. Despite my best intentions, the evening before had been longer and more alcoholic than had been prudent. The details started to get hazy after we'd started on the *Jägermeister*, and now, I was almost vibrating from the massive dose of compensatory caffeine I'd administered to myself at breakfast.

"First off," Rouyle said. "I must confess that I'm booked on a flight to London in under three hours, so this will have to be quite efficient. Now, I'm curious: what brought you to e-mail me?"

I pretended to consider his question, but in fact, I was experiencing a reoccurrence of paranoia.

"Well, your impressive work on FRIP over the years clearly has parallels with my own line of research," I said. "But the time has come for me to branch out into something a bit more clinical, more relevant to actual patients. My cell division stuff is interesting, but it's *abstract*. And that's a sentiment I could honestly apply to all of academia."

Rouyle bobbed his head, playing absently with his azure-blue silk tie and looking a bit disgruntled at my admission. "Go on."

"I'm confident I could apply my expertise very effectively to FRIP research. But to be honest, I'm more captivated by your earlier work."

Rouyle looked at me inquiringly. "You mean, the more virological aspects of the FRIP pathway?"

I shook my head. "No, I mean the *earliest* work." I took a breath, forced myself to say it. "What you were working on in Estonia: the PAX fraction."

There was a moment of charged silence, a blip in time while my stomach roared silently downward and Rouyle blinked several times, seemingly in slow motion.

"How do you know about that?" he finally said, in a passable facsimile of his normal relaxed tone.

"Well, it *is* in PubMed," I remarked. "I had your paper translated.

And I was impressed, both by the research as well as the potential applications for treating human disorders. I know I don't have any neurological background, but it would be interesting to explore the signal transduction pathways associated with PAX. Of course," and here I tried to sound disappointed, "you've probably stopped working on it altogether, as nothing more's been published."

Rouyle hesitated. "That's not completely true."

"Really?" Blood began to thrum behind my ears.

"I've maintained...an interest in that particular field." His gaze skittered over me.

"But you haven't published anything more on it, have you?"

"If you're truly committed to a career change, you'll have to come to grips with how industry actually works." He shrugged, rolling a gold pen between his fingers. "We don't want other companies subverting potentially fruitful lines of research. This PAX gene has huge potential, as you've cleverly realized, and we plan to keep it out of the public domain until it suits us."

"This PAX *gene*? I mean, you've actually been able to clone it?"

Rouyle paused again. "Well, I was speaking hypothetically. It wouldn't be easy to pull out the protein, I can assure you, as the activity is a vanishingly small fraction of the entire extract, but using a brute-force approach with dozens of monkey brains, one might obtain enough material for mass spec sequence analysis."

Hypothetically. He must be lying; there was no way I could be wrong about him having isolated the PAX gene, was there?

"Brilliant!" I said. "So then we could over-express or knock down the gene in neuronal cells and see what sorts of pathways are affected."

"Indeed...that would be enormously helpful." As he leaned forward, eyes intensifying, I could see the possibilities racing across his face. It was as if I had become a thousand times more interesting than I'd been only minutes before. Despite my hatred, I could feel his aura drawing me in, a compelling sense of excitement and purpose.

"There are still so many things we don't know about PAX," he murmured, more to himself than to me.

"Of course, the most interesting approach"—I was probing even further into dangerous territory—"would be to transfer PAX into humans."

"Now why would we want to do that?" The words came out in a drawl, and as he continued to look me over, I noticed that beads of sweat had appeared on his brow despite the carefully regulated chill of the room.

My mind went blank for a moment in a sudden panic.

"Answer the question, Dr O'Hara." A smile, carefully sculpted.

"Well," I said. "If this primate neurotransmitter really could control human behaviour, it would be a significant breakthrough."

"Indeed." He seemed to savour my response, drumming his fingers against polished wood. "But how could one deliver the gene to the right tissue?"

All at once, I understood what was happening: I was being tested. Relief seeped out of my pores. "I suppose...one could use a neurological virus?"

"Very good." His eyes were glowing with concentrated feeling, connecting with my own in a way that made me want to shiver. "In fact, Pfeiffer-deVries has been considering a new herpes-based virus vector in collaboration with a small British company."

I coughed, shifted in my chair. "Really, which company is that?"

"It's highly confidential, of course." The radiance about him dampened as he glanced at the front page of my CV.

"Well, it's all very fascinating," I leapt in, trying to divert him. "So are you close to obtaining the sequence of PAX?" Maybe I could manipulate his single-minded ardour and induce him to pull out a copy of the sequence.

"In some respects." He cleared his throat, eyes now devoid of undue luminosity or feeling. "Of course, if you came to work for me, I'd be free to give you more details."

"Of course," I echoed mildly. "Something to look forward to, then. And how soon do you —"

The telephone trilled, and he picked up the receiver and spoke in German. From his end of the conversation, I deduced that he was arranging a taxi to Frankfurt-Main airport, then indulging in a rant about a mix-up with his hotel reservation in London.

"If you'll excuse me," he said. "I have to sort out something with my excessively dim secretary. Why don't you have a look at this lab prospectus while you're waiting?"

"With pleasure," I replied, slapping my palm down on the stapled sheaf of papers as it whizzed across the desk.

As soon as the door swung shut, I stood up and tossed the useless prospectus aside. Heart starting to beat faster, I leaned over his desk, scanning the surface for anything that looked like a printout of a DNA or protein sequence. In retrospect, it's clear I was being absurdly optimistic. There were multiple stacks of papers, which I riffled through, but I came across nothing resembling a string of one-letter code. Yet this wasn't too surprising on further reflection. Despite Rouyle's intimation that his lab was studying PAX, I was convinced that Pfeiffer-deVries was not aware of this, in which case Rouyle wouldn't leave such sensitive information lying around.

I have always prided myself on my steady hands. After all, I was a man who, fuelled only by vending machine snacks, could go for two nights without sleep and still operate a pipettor skilfully enough to string together chains of DNA into bold new configurations. Yet as I looked over my shoulder at the closed door, went around to the other side of the desk and crouched there opening one drawer after another, my hands were shaking uncontrollably, fumbling and dropping things like the greenest undergraduate who ever decimated a lab's supply of glassware. And at the same time, it was as if the scientist in me were standing by, watching critically and making pointed remarks along the lines of *what in hell do you think you're doing?*

What does it look like? I retorted, searching the drawers as best I could in this sorry state, but all I found was typical office detritus. I noticed a briefcase underneath the desk, but when I bent down and tried to open it, the lock firmly resisted my efforts.

Straightening up, my knee throbbing from the effort, I scanned the room again. A suitcase rested against the far wall, and above it, a travel garment bag dangled from the lip of a bookshelf. These items, along with what I'd picked up from his telephone conversation, suggested that he planned to go straight to the airport after our interview. I was not unaware of the opportunity this presented, if Gina were being left behind in Germany. After all, it was too risky to transport her back and forth: I reckoned he had her detained somewhere, and what safer place than his own home?

His own home. With a flash of inspiration, I strode over to the suitcase, flipped up the leather tag and branded Rouyle's home address into my memory.

I turned, gaze finally alighting on the Burberry coat hanging on a hook at the back of the door. Sidling up to the coat, I frisked the pockets until I felt a mass of hard objects within. I slid my hand inside, connected with jagged metal, and—brain curiously empty of thought—transferred the bunch of keys into my own trouser pocket.

I forced myself to sit back down and flip unseeingly through the prospectus, with tiny needles of adrenaline simmering at the base of every hair and a cold sweat condensing on my skin. Thinking of something, I went back to the first page where the titles of Rouyle's projects were listed.

The word PAX did not appear anywhere.

The door opened, leaking corridor chatter into the office, and Rouyle poked his head in, brow creased. "Sorry about that. Time's getting on...shall I give you a tour of the labs now?"

When I jumped to my feet, the awkward bundle of keys jingled in response, as conspicuous to my own ears as a strident accusation.

27   *Key Question*

*T*aking a glance at the map spread out on the passenger seat, I took a turn and eased the hire car into the afternoon traffic. The city was enveloped in a light dusting of rain. I had about two miles to go on this main road until I had to watch for my turn-off. An endless line of red tail lights strung out ahead, alternatively sharply focused or bleeding fuzzily through the beads of moisture on the glass, morphing back and forth in the relentless sweep of rubber blades.

I'm still taken aback when I remember my activities that day. I have always been a law-abiding person, polite to my elders, respectful of authority, taking care to ring my mum most Sundays. Of course I broke the occasional rule, but never one of much consequence. Yet in recent weeks I'd slipped into a secret life, effortlessly misleading employer, acquaintances and friends alike.

The dissembling I'd been forced to do while negotiating the convoluted waters around Rouyle's plot—meeting Raim, doing experiments on the sly, keeping my friends in ignorance until the last possible second—had been minor compared to the Frankfurt trip. Nevertheless, I had kept on one side of reasonableness until the moment I'd stolen Rouyle's keys. Now, as I made my way towards his house, I recalled Christine's border between futility and facilitation: she'd said you had to step over before you could even know which side you were on. Maybe this was me, finally crossing.

I spotted the signpost for Rouyle's street up ahead. At the sight, I became acutely aware that I was driving on the wrong side of the road in a strange car, in a foreign city, about to do something exceedingly stupid. But that was the aspect of courage I hadn't fully comprehended before. Courage didn't mean you weren't scared; it meant you went on despite the fear.

Resolutely, I turned into the wooded lane. The fading daylight deepened further under the canopy of maples, branches glistening with fiery colours. Driving slowly, I scanned the numbers until I located the correct address, a two-storey house of handsomely painted wood and graceful bay windows. Unlike most of the other dwellings in the street, there were no signs of habitation within.

I continued to the end of the road and parked by an alley running behind Rouyle's house. After inspecting the map, my plan had been to access the house through the rear to avoid exposure, but when I got out and took a closer look, I saw this was going to be impossible. The back garden was walled off by a high wooden fence, reinforced by vertical metal struts and topped with artistic but effective-looking spikes. There was a gate, but the mechanism for opening it was only accessible from the inside.

At this point, I almost lost my resolve. Keys or no keys, it was one thing to slip in unobtrusively and quite another to commit to a full frontal assault of the house. I stood there dwarfed by the massive barrier and felt the full weight of what I had to do. And what came to mind then was Gina. Not my last memory of her, frantic and overpowered across the courtyard, but my first: dancing in the lab as if there were no place she'd rather be.

I shoved my hands in my pockets and circled back to the street. The rain had dwindled, but falling leaves spiralled around me like perturbed bats. An old woman walking her Alsatian stared at me from two shrewd points in the surrounding folds of wrinkles. The dog growled as it passed, and for the next dozen steps I was convinced that her eyes were eating their way into my back. Neighbours weren't the only thing on my mind, though; there were alarms, trained hounds and housekeepers to think about too.

When I reached Rouyle's house, I went up the flagstone pavement, mounted the front steps and pulled out the keys as if I had every business being there. I'd done my homework earlier, separating the three most promising candidates from the rest. Part of my mind was occupied with physical manipulations, and the other was racing ahead, perfecting a story for why I was there in case anyone decided to challenge me. I made sure the appropriate German vocabulary was at the ready: *cousin from abroad, house-sitting, last-minute arrangement...*

In my peripheral vision, I was almost certain that the old woman had paused in the distance to watch.

I scanned the area above the door for anything that looked like a house alarm, but the brickwork seemed unadorned with any security arrangements. My hands were clearly becoming comfortable with this new concept of wild shaking as I faced the lock. Succeeding with the second key on my shortlist, I let myself in and leaned against the closed door—no warning buzz, no flashing lights. I felt terror and relief all at once, like standing on the edge of a cliff, imagining that I was about to jump and knowing simultaneously that I would not.

The house was shrouded in gloom, every detail reflecting expense and a decidedly masculine taste that had been allowed to escalate a touch too far. I registered a blur of glass and mahogany, chrome and onyx, black leather upholstery and strange minimalist sculptures. As I took the first step into the unknown, my foot slipped against something unexpected on the polished marble floor. Leaning down, I picked up the note, written in German, which I translated as follows:

Franz,

The latest files are on the computer — please deal with them in the normal way. And ring me with an update when you are finished here.

- R.

I became drenched in perspiration. I didn't know which was worse, that Rouyle was expecting a visitor, or that him expecting one meant it wasn't too likely that Gina would be locked up here. At any rate, I'd better hurry. Putting the note back, I started downstairs, going through the kitchen, dining room, lounge, study. Up the grand staircase then, and a hurried inspection of the upper rooms: bath, another study and two bedrooms, all of them tidily made up, no Gina.

I had been wrong, I was suddenly certain. I moved towards the end of the corridor, pulling open the doors to a linen closet, a utility room, an airing cupboard, each empty lead solidifying my disappointment. I had been convinced she was being held here, but now that I considered the matter, it was clear she could be absolutely anywhere. It was even possible that she was still in London, detained in her own flat. I hadn't seen any signs of occupation there on Sunday, but Rouyle would have been discreet.

The bleakest possibility of all was one I wouldn't let myself dwell on: that Gina really had resigned and gone back to America, abandoning her vaccine, her company—and me.

Reaching the end of the hallway, I came across an unexpected alcove towards the rear of the house, terminating in one last door. I turned the handle fatalistically, but unlike the others, it was locked.

Chemical tension fizzled in my bloodstream.

"Gina?" The house swallowed up my voice as I bruised knuckles against wood. No response.

I fished out the clutch of keys and eventually found one that slid in and turned. As I moved forward into blackness, stale air assaulted my nostrils. I couldn't find a switch, so I opened the door completely, allowing a rectangle of weak light to fall across the room. This was clearly the master bedroom, and someone was lying motionless in the bed.

I crossed the room, drawing in my breath when I translated what I was seeing: Gina, lying beneath the covers, arms flung up by her head like someone being mugged at gunpoint. When I sat on the bed, her body rolled unresisting into the dip in the mattress, and when I touched one of her forearms, I found that her skin was cold.

At that terrible moment, I felt as if I had jumped from that cliff after all, with a roaring in my ears and nothingness on all sides. Dropping into the future, too fast to prevent the sensations from flashing by: the dark mouth of an open grave. That empty feeling when you first wake up and remember all over again what you've lost. Resigned to a lifetime with someone else, my too-little-too-late heroics forever taunting me with their ultimate ineffectualness.

All of this took only a second, and then my eye was caught by the motion of Gina's chest rising and falling, and I slammed to a stop mid-plummet, dizzy with relief. I switched on the bedside lamp. When the dazzle subsided, I soaked in the sight of her. She was shockingly pale, with shadowed eyelids and the purple blotches of bruising marring the insides of her arms. On closer inspection, I made out a series of tiny red spots within the discoloration, smeared with dried blood: the needle marks of injection.

And just like that, I was falling again, thinking about the combination vaccine, about Rouyle's desperation to test PAX in humans and his need to get scientific information out of Gina. Amongst her many qualities, submissiveness was not high on the list.

Pressing my fingertips against her throat, I grasped a pulse, faint but regular, but when I shook her, she didn't react. I went to the *en suite* bathroom, dampened a cloth with cold water and applied it to her face, shook her some more. But then, just as I was resigning myself to carrying her downstairs and back to the car with my dodgy knee, she made a sound. After a few seconds, her eyelashes fluttered, and she was looking right at me.

"What are...*you* doing here?" Her eyes slid from mine towards a space over my shoulder. "Where's Richard?"

"He's gone," I said, not quite believing that she was actually speaking to me. "You're safe now."

She struggled to sit up, but her elbows gave out and she collapsed back onto the pillow.

"What do you mean, safe?" Her voice was rough and bewildered, and then she seemed to zone out for a moment.

"Gina, you're confused." I put my hand on her face, roused her again. A strange feeling was growing inside, the feeling that something wasn't making sense. "You're being held captive in Richard's house. In Frankfurt."

"No...no I'm not." She looked incredulous.

"He abducted you from the lab!"

She blinked at me. "What are you talking about?"

"You were fighting—he attacked you, and —"

"No, he didn't. It was just an argument, Andy. It was..." Her eyes widened. "Oh, God—I've made the most awful mistake, Andy. With the combination vaccine. I've come to fix it."

"Mistake?" I said slowly. "What mistake?"

She seemed to be struggling to dredge up her most recent memories. "I was too ashamed to tell Thomas, so Richard agreed to help...arranged the trip...promised to make up some excuse for Thomas, take me to Pfeiffer-deVries, help me correct the error..."

"Wait a minute," I demanded. "You came here voluntarily?"

"Of course I did. What other..." Her gaze wavered across my face, anxious with confusion.

I stared back in wonderment. How could I, with all my scientific training, have so drastically misinterpreted what I'd seen? Acted on so many unfounded assumptions? But then—the craziest part of all— to have been so intuitively correct in the ultimate essentials?

"It all happened so fast," she murmured. "Off to Heathrow...forgot to call you to cancel..." Her eyes closed and I shook her again, initiating another dribble of words. "I told him about your evidence. The wrong size...the TRAP data."

"You didn't mention my name, did you?"

She shook her head feebly. "I made up a colleague at Berkeley. I was so upset with him, but then he explained how I must've made a mistake when I constructed the virus...put the wrong gene in by accident...we'd had sequencing problems, so it's true we hadn't confirmed it absolutely...I must've screwed up...he said...so stupid."

"You didn't make any mistakes, Gina." I was so angry with Rouyle that I wanted to hit something.

"Oh, but I did." She looked at me miserably, eyes dull and drifting. "Because then he called his technician, had him check the notebooks more carefully. The insert was the wrong size, apparently. I must've messed up...deleted part of it, or picked up the wrong tube...it was all so fast, so many shortcuts...but Thomas would've been furious if he knew—I could get fired, and then what would happen to my village?"

"Gina, listen to me. There's something I have to —"

"But I'd constructed the new virus in duplicate, as a backup," she said. "It would still be in the freezer in his lab...wouldn't take more than a day to see if the other version was okay, nobody would have to know."

"Gina! I —"

"And he also wanted to show me the experiments proving FRIP worked in the brain, in the right sort of neurons." Her distress was mounting. "He thought I should see it with my own eyes...so reasonable, after he'd calmed down...such a good sport about my accusations, which I didn't expect, after..." She trailed off, a person relating a nightmare who's slowly realizing the story is nonsense. "But why do I feel so ill? And why are *you* here?"

I took her hand in mine.

"Rouyle's duped you into inserting the wrong gene; there isn't time to explain." I thought about the note in the entrance hall and my words started to speed up. "Your discussion Monday night, the phone call with his technician, the so-called sequencing problems—it was an act. You didn't do anything wrong—he's tricked you into coming here."

"No." Her head moved weakly back and forth on the pillow. "No, that can't be right."

"Gina," I said. "What day is it?"

She thought a moment, obediently. "It's Tuesday morning...we came in on the last flight, went straight to bed."

"It's *Thursday* evening. Your door was locked from the outside, and I think you've been sedated." I made her look at the marks on her arms.

She regarded the wounds solemnly, as if they didn't belong to her. Then a fuse in her brain seemed to blow and she was abruptly terrified, choking out a few words about needing air.

I wrestled open the curtains and tried to push up the sash, but it was locked. I found a key that fitted the mechanism and hauled up the window, flooding the room with coolness. It had started to rain again since I'd come inside, and I could hear it hissing against the trees. The angle of the window allowed a view only of the wooded back garden, smudged in twilight. Even if she had managed to wake up or stand, she couldn't have easily attracted the attention of neighbours.

"Andy," she called out, "I think I'm going to be sick."

I hastened back and helped her to a sitting position, grabbed a nearby bin. She retched violently over it, but there didn't appear to anything in her stomach. Had he been starving her as well? Then her head sagged against my shoulder, and I held her close, stroked her hair. She opened her eyes and the panic in them gradually subsided, like the rippled surface of a lake going still.

"I'm not quite...this is really happening, isn't it?" she said.

"I'm afraid so."

"It's starting to come back now." Her gaze flickered. "I think I woke up a few times...I felt the shots...I remember *him*..."

She drew in her breath, and my arm tightened around her involuntarily. I looked at the bruises and jab wounds and wondered what else Rouyle might have done to her while she couldn't defend herself. I felt the urge to kill, simple and swift: a latent urge that must have been encoded in my genes millennia ago.

"Can you walk?" I asked, filtering the murderous edge from my voice.

"I'm not sure." She took a breath, a trembling hand passed experimentally over her eyes, her face. "I feel so weird."

"Where are your clothes?" I stood up, paced around the room, flung open the wardrobe. Now that the relief of finding Gina had dissipated, the animal urge to flee was mounting.

"My suitcase was by the bed last...I mean, Monday night." She looked around the room, at a loss.

"There's no time to find it. Wait—here are your shoes at least."

I helped her on with those, grabbed one of Rouyle's fleeces from the wardrobe and yanked that down over her nightdress.

"Come on." I stood up and hauled her to her feet. "You can lean on me."

She clung to me as I helped her down the stairs, my injured knee spasming in sharp complaint. Eventually we were standing in the corridor by the kitchen on the ground floor, both of us short of breath.

"I need to go through Rouyle's files before we leave," I told her. "There's no time to explain."

"Are you absolutely sure he's not coming back?"

"Positive." I thought again about the note and decided she was in no condition to hear about it.

I guided her to the study and she wilted into a chair, scarcely conscious. I surveyed the room, which I'd only glanced at the first time around. Desk, computer, filing cabinet, bookshelf: I knew what I had to do. While the computer was booting up, I turned to the filing cabinet. Sliding open the top drawer, I started pawing through the tightly packed hanging files of bureaucratic paperwork from Pfeiffer-deVries. Reaching the end, I slammed the drawer closed and started on the next, feeling like I was in one of those never-ending, slow-motion anxiety dreams that often trap me just before my alarm goes off.

After a few minutes my fingers stumbled on a tab labelled in neat script, "PAX". For a second or two, I thought I was still dreaming. I pulled out the thick file, flipped through it. As the papers fluttered by, I caught snatches of words: *injection, herpes delivery, purified extract, acquired suggestibility, side-effects, chemical consciousness*, interspersed with colourful intermezzos of graphs and charts. Among the letters, scientific reports and other items were printouts of DNA and protein code, the results of various database searches—I had no way of knowing for certain if any of it represented the PAX gene, but it was promising. Stapled to one of the sheets of code was an envelope containing a CD.

I turned to Gina with satisfaction. "Right, I think we've —"

There was the unmistakable sound of a key turning in the front door.

Gina stiffened in the chair, eyes enormous.

After an eternity that probably wasn't more than a second, I crept to the closed door, leaned down and peered through the keyhole. A fair-haired man about my age was standing in the foyer, shaking the rain from his umbrella and clutching a briefcase. He bent down and retrieved the note about the files on the computer. The computer that was sitting not two feet away from me.

I straightened up and Gina's eyes flung me a drastic question. I gestured for her to keep silent, racing through my fabricated story, wondering how to bolster it to explain my intrusion into Rouyle's study with the added plot complication of a desperately ill woman. It was never going to fly; I knew that with numb certainty. When I looked back through the keyhole, the man was hanging up his leather coat with fastidious care. Then he started moving towards me. I watched, paralyzed with the inevitability, as he came a few steps closer—then angled to his right, slipping past my limited view.

The main staircase creaked.

"We've got to get out of here." I was practically mouthing the words.

Gina had already burst to her feet: a testimony to the inspiration of adrenaline.

"We can slip out the back," I said.

Switching off the computer and lamp, I helped her into the corridor and we slunk to the kitchen, the ceiling protesting as footsteps paused directly above us, carried on. Where was he going? The creaking started to move again, towards the end of the corridor.

Towards the master bedroom. Awareness dawned.

"Come on." I tightened my arm around Gina's waist and reached for the back door.

"Oh, God—I've just thought of something."

"What?" Our conversation was as soft as breathing.

"My passport, Andy. We've got to find it or I won't be able to leave the country."

"Shit." I ran my fingers absently through my hair. "Where did you see it last?"

"I dumped all my loose stuff on the antique writing desk—the one in the living room."

"I didn't notice anything there earlier." I was unable to prevent panic from seeping into my voice. "Maybe he's tidied it away."

Above us, I heard a door opening, and then an explosive curse.

I grabbed the handle and opened the back door.

"Go outside." I put my hand on her shoulder. "Wait behind the door. If I don't show up in ten minutes, go to a neighbour and call the police. This information might help your credibility." I passed her the file, and she took it reluctantly.

"But Andy, I can't leave you —"

"Just go!" I hissed, shutting the door on her frightened face.

By this time the man was bounding down the stairs, cutting off my access to the main corridor. I slipped towards the kitchen's side entrance, struggling to listen between the riotous heartbeats in my ears.

"Are you here, girl?" the man called out in slipshod English, sounding half angry, half frightened. Floorboards responded audibly as he moved towards the kitchen.

I went through the side door, passed through the dining room and into the murky light of the lounge. The old roll-top desk skulked in shadows against the far wall, its polished surface as bare as I'd remembered. I eased open the centre drawer and saw it straightaway: battered blue leather, eagle insignia and the words *United States of America* stamped in fake metallic leaf along the bottom.

I snatched the passport along with the unmarked envelope stuffed between its pages, shut the drawer carefully and crept past the study towards the main corridor. It sounded as if the man were retracing my steps through the dining room, so I circled back to the kitchen. I thought I heard the muted chirps of buttons pressed on a mobile phone as I went through the back door.

Gina was still leaning against the wall, shivering in the dark and clutching the PAX file to her chest.

"Mission accomplished." I took the file from her and waved the passport before tucking it into my coat pocket. "Let's move it!"

"You're amazing," she said as I took her hand and helped her down the steps. As we left the protective overhang of the roof, a spotlight blazed on, hurling our shadows to the far end of the lawn in grotesque proportions. Seconds later, a dog started to bark maniacally on the other side of a fence.

My legs began running beneath me, the pain in my knee forgotten as the biochemistry took over. I half shoved, half carried Gina to the gate, expecting at any moment to hear an angry challenge from the kitchen door, or irate neighbours, or a pack of rabid hounds. I fumbled with the gate's sliding bolt, and then we were out, dashing down the alley towards the safety of the car. Gina lost consciousness when she slammed into the passenger seat, but there wasn't time to deal with this. The tyres sprayed gravel before catching the road, and then we were zooming off.

I'm trying to remember if I managed to breathe before we made it to the motorway. Of course I must have done, but when I think about those ten or so minutes now, all I can recall is the grip of my hands on the wheel, the tension of my leg depressing the accelerator and the sensation of perpetual breathlessness, like a swift intake of shock that I somehow never managed to exhale.

Later, as I settled into the rhythm of driving, three shifting lanes of traffic braiding before and behind me, the enormity of what had happened began to sink in. That's when I became aware of my lungs again, the flow of air and the restoration of reality. I had done what I had set out to do, but it was all too much to absorb. The most important thing was that Gina was breathing too, a simple fact that I could no longer take for granted. Whenever I risked a glance, she was still there, visibly respiring, head rolled to one side, eyes closed and face pale but peaceful.

There was something familiar about seeing her in the seat next to me, about having her under my protection. If I allowed the motorway light to smudge the moment and time and place to become flexible elements, we could almost be returning from a holiday trip, pleasantly exhausted from sea and sun. My father used to drive us to Brighton one summer weekend a year—strictly rationed quality time—and we'd return as late as possible on the Sunday. I'd be drowsy in the back seat with Liz, still feeling the rocking motion of the waves imprinted in my muscles, the flush of sun on my skin, and Dad would be at the wheel, keeping us safe.

I could sense something in my body now as well. But it wasn't the cradle of surf; it was the trough of stillness between one wave of fear and the next. Because it wasn't over yet—not even remotely.

After I parked at the hotel, Gina revived with only a touch and seemed fairly animated, which fooled me into believing that her condition was improving. We spent a few minutes in the car trying to smooth down her hair and cover her inappropriate clothing with my coat, but the looks people gave us in the lobby made it that clear that something had to be done.

So after I'd brought her up to date on the situation, got the bath running and ordered some dinner from room service, I ventured out to take care of a few things. When I returned, Gina was curled up on the bed in a towel, much more listless than before. I noted uneasily that she'd hardly touched her meal, despite her frantic hunger earlier, and her smile at my entrance was small and lost. With her hair wet like that, she looked as if she'd recently washed up on shore.

"I've booked your ticket." I closed the door and placed a bag down beside her on the bed. "And I bought you a toothbrush and some clothes. They're a bit corporate *über-frau*, but there wasn't much of a selection."

Gina peered into the bag, suddenly distressed.

I sat down on the bed, taking one of her hands in mine. "The dress isn't that unfashionable, is it?"

Her smile had hardly formed before it slipped away, and I saw the shimmer of tears.

"What is it, Gina?'" I moved my other hand along her forearm, avoiding the bruising, which seemed even more appalling under the harsh fluorescent lights. Her gaze saturated me, pupils bloomed unnaturally wide, and I was just opening my mouth to say something else when she looked away.

"I'm a bit overwhelmed," she said. "You're being so kind, and I was so terrible to you." She was still inspecting the ceiling, not me, and when she paused to swallow, her face was etched with discomfort.

"Gina?" I felt a lurch of worry, but she silenced my concern with a scant movement from fingers resting against her chest.

"I owe you an apology, Andy." She rolled her head to one side to meet my eye, and this time she didn't waver. "This whole thing with Richard: I don't know how I got into it. I guess I was caught up in some misconception in the beginning, and then later —" Her voice slammed to a halt. "I have no idea how I missed the warning signs. How I allowed myself to get lured into this dangerous situation."

"Nobody's blaming you." I slid my hand up to her bare shoulder, rubbed the damp fine hairs at the back of her neck. A burst of gooseflesh radiated outward underneath my fingers as she shivered unconsciously, completely transfixed by her inner turmoil, and went on as if I hadn't spoken.

"I really was terrible to you, wasn't I?" She waited, distraught, for confirmation, and a tear slipped down her cheek.

"Forget about it, Gina. People do what they do—like who they like—for their own reasons."

She quieted then, turned her head to look at me more closely with grey eyes full of that familiar seriousness. I reached over to wipe away the tear, and her eyes closed in response to my touch.

"I've got to return the car now," I said. "You'll be okay?"

She nodded reluctantly, but her eyes were already closing again, and in a few minutes, her breathing betrayed the regular patterns of sleep. There was an extra blanket folded at the foot of the bed. I tucked it carefully around her, inventing a few dozen excuses to keep sitting there, just watching her drift.

Clots of snow melted against the windows, and the road shifted in frictionless patches underneath the wheels of the bus. I sat near the back, chewing over my anxieties, naming them like novel species and then classifying them into groups. I was worried about Gina being on her own, of course, wondering if I should have taken her to the police, or even to hospital. But she'd insisted she was fine, just a bit weak, and my instincts were driving me to return to London. I needed Maria's help to convince Boyd, otherwise it might prove difficult to persuade anyone with such a far-fetched story, especially on Rouyle's home turf.

Meanwhile, I was thoroughly spooked about the man in Rouyle's house. There was no doubt he'd contacted Rouyle. Even if he hadn't spotted us dashing across the lawn from the kitchen window, he surely knew that she couldn't have escaped without assistance. Rouyle would then realize how his keys had gone missing, and would hasten to Boyd with yet another tale, this time about my supposed—or was it actual?—criminal activities, which Boyd might find corresponded well with my mad behaviour in his office on Monday. I hadn't made any efforts to be discreet, and my fingerprints were all over the house. For all I knew, the police could have been contacted already, and be waiting for our return. In that case, the only things that stood between us and disaster were Maria's PCR results and the information I'd stolen from Rouyle's study—neither of which was guaranteed to be useful.

I shifted in my seat and felt a jab in my side. Slipping my hand into the inner pocket of my coat, I pulled out the offending item: Gina's passport, and the thick envelope in between that I'd forgotten about. I opened up the booklet, momentarily arrested by the confident smile on that younger Gina's face, her shorter breezy hair and fearless eyes. Then I slipped fingers into the envelope and removed what was inside: a single ticket in Gina's name, on a flight departing to Nairobi in a few days' time.

When I got back to the hotel, Gina was awake and wearing the dress I'd bought her. The PAX file was open and its contents were strewn all over the covers.

"You shouldn't be upsetting yourself with all that right now," I said. "We've got to leave for the airport in a few minutes."

She had an expression on her face that scared me.

"Andy," she said, the softness of her voice not diminishing its urgency. "I've found something unbelievable in here. You'd better have a look."

28   *Blast*

Sometimes when there are too many things to worry about, you find the easiest way to cope is to focus on the simplest. Right now, for me, that was Gina. Her condition had deteriorated soon after the taxi had dropped us at my flat, and now she was submerged in feverish dreams on the sofa. When her eyelids twitched open occasionally, revealing slivers of grey iris beneath, it was clear that she wasn't fully conscious.

I was still torn about keeping her here. She clearly belonged in hospital, but if I had to explain exactly why she was in her present state, I would be forced to reveal the story prematurely and jeopardize our position. While my fears about being detained at the airport had proved false, I was convinced that the police would arrive at any moment to take Rouyle's domestic intruder into custody.

As if on cue, the doorbell rang.

I peered through the peephole before opening the door.

"It's about time!"

"Nice to see you, too," Maria said, pushing past me into the room. Behind her, a cab squealed off into the drizzly night. Then she turned back to me, body still charged with anxious irritation, only her eyes relenting. "It *is*, you know." She kissed me on the cheek. "Welcome home."

Before I could comment, she went over to inspect Gina.

"How long has she been like this?" She put a hand on Gina's forehead.

"About an hour." I paused. "Do you happen to know the symptoms of acute herpes simplex virus infection?"

She glanced up in alarm. "Please tell me you're joking."

"She's been injected multiple times. It could just be drugs, of course, but..."

Maria pushed up one of Gina's sleeves and inspected Rouyle's handiwork. "Natural herpes just causes sores in the mouth, and sometimes the eyes, but Gina's souped up the original virus beyond all recognition." She frowned. "A person might react against such a modified virus injected directly into the bloodstream; it could induce a fever. I simply don't know."

"She was perfectly fine before, just tired," I said, a bit defensively.

"Well, we don't know anything about the infection process or side effects in humans; that's the whole point of a Phase I trial. Fortunately for you, me and everyone on that aeroplane, the virus isn't contagious—Gina put in safeguards."

"Christ, I hadn't even thought of that!"

"Anyway, if she did get jabbed, it's not just the viral infection *per se*," she said. "There's the mystery protein to consider. It could be having an effect, like on those mice."

"Is there an antidote?" What if there wasn't? Gina had explained in her seminar how she'd designed her viruses to stay perpetually active as they secreted their alien genetic messages into the brain. It was a horrific irony to think of her trapped in a viral prison, mind being slowly poisoned by her own creation.

Maria reached over, started unzipping her laptop case. "Let's not jump to conclusions, Andy. In all likelihood she's just reacting poorly to drugs."

"But —"

"The sooner we see if the sequences match, the sooner we can ring an ambulance. Andy, what's your wireless password?"

While Maria busied herself setting up on the coffee table, I rummaged around in the PAX file until I found the disc. I didn't want to contemplate my next move if the DNA sequences didn't match.

Maria cast me a curious look. "Is that the file you mentioned when you rang me?"

"Yeah—sorry there wasn't time to —"

The doorbell cut off my words.

"Christine and Cameron, I presume?" she said.

"Let's hope so."

Christine came in, gave me a quick hug. "I was incredibly worried when you didn't get off that earlier flight," she murmured in my ear as her arms went around my neck. "The airline refused to give me any information."

Cameron was close behind. "Good to see you're intact, Andy." He gripped my shoulder, the pressure at odds with his light tone.

Maria looked up from her computer, face illuminated in a bluish-white glow. "Perfect timing—we're just about to compare the sequences."

"How's Gina?" Christine threw her damp coat at me and strode over to the sofa. "She looks awful."

I filled her in about the injections, and on Gina's fluctuating health since I'd found her.

"Jabbed, you say, but with *what?*" Christine wasn't fooled by my carefully factual report.

I sighed. "We don't know."

"You didn't explain why you didn't take her straight to hospital." Christine stood with arms crossed, frowning as Gina murmured something in her delirium. She reached down, brushed a strand of Gina's hair away from her eyes. "It looks to me as if she could be in real danger."

"I haven't had a chance to tell any of this properly," I said. "Let's just compare the sequences. After that we can call an ambulance, and there'll be plenty of time to update everyone. Five more minutes isn't going to —"

"You're over-ruled, O'Hara." Christine flipped open her mobile and poked it with three decisive motions.

"Well, I'm ready to go here, Andy," Maria pronounced, as Christine murmured into the phone. "Pass me that disc, will you?"

Everyone else crowded around the screen. Maria popped open the CD tray and pressed in the disc. I was assuming it contained a computer file of the code on the attached printout; otherwise it would take us ages to type in the sequence by hand.

"Let's have a look, shall we?" Maria navigated into the CD drive. There were three documents listed on the disc:

```
humanPAX_nt
mousePAX_nt
simianPAX_nt
```

"*Yes!*" Cameron and I exclaimed simultaneously.

"Looks as if Rouyle's been busy," Maria said.

Christine snapped her phone shut and joined us on the carpet.

"We go with the human version, agreed?" Maria looked around, and we all nodded. She clicked on the first file, revealing a screen full of G's, C's, A's and T's, abbreviations for the four different nucleotide bases that together spelt out, in millions of different combinations, the twenty-thousand-odd genes encoded in human DNA.

"That's much longer than it should be," Christine said. "Didn't you pull out a short sequence of about a hundred and fifty bases?"

Maria copied the entire sequence. "This file might include upstream and downstream regulatory sequences, or bits of the cloning vector."

"She's right," Cameron said. "You can already see it doesn't begin with a start codon."

Maria connected to Blast, a suite of programmes designed to interface with the genetic databases. She clicked on a button and a new window opened, featuring two white query boxes.

"I'll paste in Rouyle's PAX sequence here." Maria performed a swift keystroke, and the first white box filled up with rows of nucleotide letters. Then she shuffled though folders and directories, finally alighting on a particular icon. "And here,"—she zoomed over to the second query box—"I'll stick in the results from the sequencing department. Xavier managed to generate about four hundred bases into it, high-quality readout, so I'm assuming we'll run into some herpes DNA sequences on either end that won't match." Another few manipulations, and the lower box became filled with the second mass of letters. She moved the cursor to the final button and pressed it with a flourish.

A few seconds passed as the programme digested the strings of code, but it seemed like hours. An expectant silence amplified the sounds in the house: the whirring of the computer's fan, the buzzing refrigerator in the kitchen, a metallic twang from one of the radiators, expanding on the microscopic scale. Gina made a distressed noise before falling quiet again. Looking over, I saw that one arm was now flung over the side of the sofa. Reaching behind me, I took her hand momentarily in mine; it was hot, and remained unresponsive to my squeeze. *Just a few more minutes*, I promised her silently, just as I became aware of the faraway wail of a siren.

"Here it comes," Christine said. I thought she was referring to the ambulance, but when I turned back, I saw the screen sprout an elaborate new window.

"There!" Maria stabbed a finger at the graphical representation of the alignment results: two horizontal, slim rectangles one on top of the other. At either end, the rectangles were black, indicating no significant similarities in sequence. But in the centre, the majority of each rectangle was coloured sky-blue, denoting a match. There were a few cheers and a scattering of applause as Maria scrolled down, past the statistics and into the area where Blast lined up the matched sequences, letter by letter. In the central blue region, Blast had found a perfect fit along a stretch of one hundred and forty three nucleotide bases: the DNA from the infected mouse brain sample and the DNA sequence of the human PAX gene were clearly identical.

"*Quod erat demonstrandum,*" Cameron murmured irreverently.

The paramedics had just departed from my flat along with Christine and Cameron, who were riding along in the ambulance. I had wanted to be the one to go, but I'd been instructed to stay behind with Maria. Thomas Boyd and the police were en route, and we'd be needed to give a statement. Meanwhile, I was using the quiet spell to organize my thoughts and bring Maria up to date on the rescue and what Gina and I had pieced together on the flight back to England from the various reports, letters and personal writings enclosed in the PAX file.

"Rouyle had *already* performed a Phase I trial on PAX?" Maria settled back on the sofa, sipping at her mug of tea with wide eyes. It was probably the first time I'd seen her drop her sceptical stance and just absorb information with childlike credulity.

"Not actually a proper trial," I said. "And of course not with the combination vaccine. But last month, Rouyle injected two of his technicians with a single dose of the PAX extract purified from macaque brains, the same stuff he used for his Latvian article."

"Why on earth would anyone agree to that?"

I shrugged. "Maybe some of Rouyle's people are as fanatical as he is. Or else he intimidated them into it."

"So his whole lab was in on the secret?"

I shook my head. "FRIP was just his day job, to keep Pfeiffer-deVries happy. The temporary staff—students and post-docs—did the FRIP work and had no idea anything else was going on. But it seems as if the permanent technicians were heavily involved in PAX-based experiments."

"Why would he chance injecting his own people if the African Phase I was practically assured?"

"I think he thought the long-term risks were minimal," I said. "He already knew from animal studies that the natural extract, once injected, was extremely unstable. Whatever it did to his technicians wasn't going to last more than a day or so. But the impending Phase I actually forced his hand."

"How?"

"The trial would be cancelled immediately if any patients became seriously ill, and Rouyle had been growing nervous about possible side-effects in humans."

"Understandably," Maria said. "If something went wrong, his reputation could be damaged."

"No, because everyone thought FRIP was the second gene, and FRIP's already gone through Phase I alone with minimal side effects," I reminded her. "Any toxicity could justifiably be blamed on Gina's herpes virus, which has never been tested in humans."

"And then Geniaxis would've gone down for sure!"

"That was of no real personal concern to Rouyle. But he did want to avoid that possibility, as he'd probably never come across another opportunity so ideal."

"But you said his Latvian paper showed no side-effects in treated macaques."

"Yes," I said. "But he'd recently done a few PAX injections in mice and was shocked to stumble into the same problem that we did."

"Massive toxicity?"

I nodded. "His test monkeys had been fine, but the sick mice alerted him that not all animals would respond to PAX in the same manner when it was delivered in unnatural amounts."

"But humans and macaques are extremely similar."

"Yes, but they can still respond differently to drugs and infections." In fact, Magritte had told me once that she could foresee the day when testing drugs on animals would be abandoned, not for ethical reasons, but from mounting evidence that even genetically related animals were still too different to make good predictors.

"If he did see anything weird in the reaction of his jabbed technicians," I continued, "he was prepared to invent an excuse to pull Pfeiffer-deVries out of the trial, bide his time and cultivate some new opportunity to test PAX in the future."

"But everything went fine?"

I showed her the key paragraph in the relevant report.

Six hours post-injection/summary: subjects obtained mental competency test scores comparable to pre-injection indices. No overt symptoms of mental impairment or other detrimental effects. In contrast, passivity index test numbers increased 30-fold over baseline (see Appendix 4).

Maria passed back the papers, disquieted, and asked how Rouyle was going to get away with performing those same neurological tests in Africa.

"It was one of the negotiation points," I said. "He wanted to fly down there with his PAX team and be in charge of the patient analysis."

"The local medics wanted to do that," Maria said, frowning. "I did get the impression those foreign representatives trusted Geniaxis more than Pfeiffer-deVries. But a colleague told me that Pfeiffer-deVries have been using that region for years to perform cheap, rather cavalier drug trials on the local populace." She ran a finger under one tired eye, then the other. "And that was all he wanted, then? PAX passing its secret Phase I as a proof of principle?"

I hesitated. "Well, ironically, Rouyle seemed convinced that Gina's portion of the vaccine would be effective against Vera Fever. Inevitably, there would be a Phase II, then a Phase III, and he planned to take PAX along for the ride as a stowaway."

"Still, eventually the testing would be over—then what? Any evidence in the file to support Cameron's mad theory about a PAX-based bioweapon?" She couldn't help smiling.

"No—in fact, it turns out that Rouyle loathes applied research," I said. "All that public bluster was just to enhance his power and reputation at Pfeiffer-deVries, which in turn gave him more money and resources to work on PAX. Also, it gained him access to potentially exploitable human trials."

"So what was he up to?"

"I don't know," I said. After a pause, I added, "My main theory is that he's pathologically fixated on the fundamental biology of PAX and other behavioural modulators."

"Pathologically fixed...you mean, he's insane?" Maria looked intrigued.

I considered that description. "Not exactly. Just incredibly... focused. I think he decided long ago that studies using monkey brains would be an ideal way to unlock the mysteries of human behaviour, and PAX was his first attempt."

"Well, that seems reasonable, aside from the obvious ethical questions of using higher primates."

"Yes, I agree. But where he differs with his colleagues is in the importance of subsequently testing these findings on humans. Human experimentation involving very risky procedures is never approved for mere basic research; there has to be a disease involved, usually a life-threatening one. He disagreed, thought it was right to use volunteers and prisoners for fundamental research."

"Now that's truly radical," she remarked.

"But of course he was never able to convince anyone who counted. He couldn't even secure the use of monkeys, let alone humans. After the incident in Estonia, it seems he just withdrew into his own world, where testing PAX in humans took precedence over everything else." I patted the file. "I found notes alluding to a book he's writing, a life's work on biochemical consciousness. I think he believed that the pure intellectual value of the work justified everything." I paused. "I have to admit he did an amazing job of pushing PAX almost all the way to the clinic on his own."

Maria half-smiled. "All obsessions are relative—and some people don't know when to stop." She met my eye, and I felt my face grow warm. "So how did Gina fit into his plans?"

"He needed her knowledge to pull off the trial, but how he would get that cooperation isn't clear."

"It's utterly daft—he never would've got away with it."

"I don't know," I said. "Everything was in place: the financing, the patients, even the scientific theory. We know Gina's viruses should have delivered PAX to the appropriate neurons in the brain. And Rouyle had gathered solid data over the years suggesting that PAX truly was a *bona fide* submission-controlling protein."

"Still, the combination virus has never been tested in humans..." Maria's voice dwindled off.

I finally voiced the question that had been weighing me down all day. "If Rouyle did infect Gina, and Boyd can't figure out how to cure her, do you think she could learn to resist? She's an extremely strong-willed person, after all." I could see quite a few laws of nature bending around someone like Gina.

Maria put her mug on the coffee table and wrapped her arms around herself, appearing suddenly vulnerable. "It's not necessarily as straightforward as mind over matter when it comes to brain biochemistry, is it? More the reverse. Just look at schizophrenics...it's not as if they want to be paranoid and hear voices. But they're completely at the mercy of the neurotransmitter imbalance."

I didn't respond, and after a moment I felt her hand slip over mine, between us on the sofa. We just stayed like that until the doorbell rang.

The cab swerved around the corner, the momentum making Maria's body heavy against my own. I nudged open the window, letting in a blast of rain-laced wind. We were flying down Green Lanes on the way to University College Hospital. The city was full of impending dawn, the wet streets glowing in response.

"I thought we'd never get out of there," Maria said, yawning and making herself more comfortable against me. Over the past hours, her solidity and earthy commentary had kept me grounded in this whole dreamlike scenario.

I just nodded, looking out the window. The sky was streaked with orange over the row of shops and a crescent moon hung like an impossible ornament. Even though Christine had rung recently to tell us that Gina was in a critical but assuredly stable condition, I felt a strange dread at the prospect of seeing her. As more time had elapsed and the daze of my heroics faded, so had the shininess of the prize. What had replaced it was a growing sense of uneasiness, tangled green weeds smothering the flowers beneath until I couldn't see anything clearly.

I had become hung up on one particular point: how could Gina ever have loved a man who was corrupt enough to do what he'd done to her? Of course I knew she'd been deceived and that Rouyle could be very charming and persuasive. But the scientist in me couldn't let it go unquestioned, even though it was clear that fundamentally, I still wanted her. That I might want her no matter what she'd done—the most disturbing prospect of all. And then, the inevitable rebound: feeling ashamed that I was even questioning her integrity when she was so ill, and fear that it was all irrelevant anyway, that my hasty decisions had delayed medical attention until it was too late.

"Did you and Gina ever get a chance to talk about what's going on between you?" Maria asked, perhaps continuing a thread of her own private thoughts.

"No, we had bigger things to worry about. But she did apologize."

"Did she now? For what, exactly?"

I thought back. "For liking Rouyle, I suppose, for not seeing through him. And for being so ambivalent, even though I'd stood by her."

I could tell that she was looking at me, but I kept my gaze directed out the window, half-mesmerized as Angel Tube station streamed past.

"So what are you going to do?" she finally asked.

"I have to decide," I said. "But I've been on auto-pilot for so long, obsessed with how to win her, that now I'm a bit lost. It was never an active choice."

"It's human nature. We may no longer live in trees, but we still don't do many things consciously."

"That's what I always believed, that I should go on blind instinct. But I was having a conversation with Cameron recently..."

"What did *he* say?"

I shrugged, rubbing palms over the rough stubble on my face. "He said I was idolizing a Gina that didn't really exist."

Maria laughed, jarring the otherworldly dawn atmosphere. The driver met my eye in the rear-view mirror before returning his serene gaze to the road ahead.

"With all due respect," she said, "it doesn't take a scientist."

"That's why I've been re-evaluating. Even if she's...okay, and she decides she wants me after all..."

"What are you saying, Andy?" She sat up, all traces of humour vanished.

Over the past days, Cameron's advice had been multiplying inside me like an infection, and now I was alarmed to hear it coming out of my own mouth.

"She's shown questionable judgement," I said, "and on top of that she's repeatedly rejected me. Maybe she's not the right woman for me."

Maria's expression fluctuated like the surface of a pond on a gusty day.

"I thought you'd be pleased," I said at last.

"Are you sure you want to know what I think?"

"I'm certain I can guess."

"Can you?" She produced a cryptic smile. "I think there's a lot to be said for forgiveness."

"But you're the one who kept urging me to drop her!"

She sighed.

"There've been extenuating circumstances, to say the least. She's apologized, shown evidence that she's learned from her errors of judgement." She paused. "It's obvious her past is riddled with them."

An oncoming car dimmed its headlamps too late, and I was momentarily dazzled to blindness. "Does this mean you've...changed your mind about me?"

"Of course not." Voice rich with scorn at my denseness. "This isn't easy for me, you know."

"Yet now you're recommending I stick with Gina." I heard the incredulity in my own voice. "I can't keep up with you, Maria. Where's the catch?"

"Do you want to know the tragic truth?" She smiled again, her skin seeming to glow in the milky light. "I don't think I'd still want you if you were the type of person who couldn't forgive her."

As I sat by Gina's bedside, the feel and smell of the place brought back effortless memories of visiting my father. It was all so familiar: the sadness, the fear, the pessimism, the sense of being completely out of control.

Then as now, fluids dripped, lights flickered, the instruments of science played mute witness. I had long since lost my coordinates in time: everyone else had drifted off either minutes ago, or hours.

Time was playing tricks with Gina as well. Her face, wiped clean by sleep, appeared both younger and older, or perhaps ageless, if age—before the indiscreet betrayal of wrinkles—is something transmitted largely through behaviour, movement, speech, expression. Without the animation of consciousness, she looked like another person altogether—or perhaps, like any person. And without these cues, or my former blind convictions, I suddenly didn't know where I stood. Even though I'd been gazing at her and dreaming about her for months, it was as if here, in the impersonality of the hospital bed, I was seeing her for the first time.

She was still beautiful, of course, a beauty intensified by the indigo afterglow of the digital equipment shadowing the topography of her face, her throat, her slender arms. The past evidence of her pros and cons became starkly tabulated before my scientific mind for due consideration. It was all a matter of perspective now whether she was fatally tainted by her mistakes, or rather enriched, made more complex and human by them. Two opposing theories, posed by two independent observers, each with my best interests at heart. And somehow, I had to choose. In my current detached state, the time couldn't be more appropriate.

Ever since I had met Gina, I had given her the benefit of the doubt, assumed that she had good reasons for the choices she'd made. I had blamed everything else—unfortunate timing, her past difficult circumstances, even my own behaviour—but hadn't once questioned her own understanding, let alone factored that in, allowed it to influence my desire. If Gina had been one of my experiments, I had committed the classic novice's error of overlooking incriminating data in my final interpretation, allowing sentiment to sway me towards a favoured hypothesis. But if she was a flawed creature, and I was a flawed observer, then where did that leave us?

Taking her hand in mine, I waited for a sign. Not from above, but from within.

29 *In the Dark*

*E*ven the strangest episodes eventually swerve back to the mundane. And as I came off a week-long high of epic proportions, reality was not only beckoning: it had landed on me with a heavy thud.

It was early on Saturday evening, the first time I'd stepped into the Centre since coming back from Frankfurt two nights previously. In the spirit of this return to routine existence, I couldn't resist going straight to the Board. Sure enough, an irreverent homage had appeared in my absence: a rash of new postings, almost every inch scrawled over with amusing commentary in various colours of ink.

Scientist implicated in GM virus scandal

A respected British scientist at the pharmaceutical firm Pfeiffer-deVries in Frankfurt, Richard Rouyle, was arrested early this morning on charges of kidnapping, fraud and assault in a case that may have a profound impact on the approval and monitoring of gene therapy trials in the future.

Police say Rouyle abducted his scientific collaborator, Gina Kraymer, last Monday when she found out about his illicit activities: tampering with a genetically modified virus about to undergo clinical trials.

Kraymer, an American virus specialist employed by the London biotech firm Geniaxis, is in a critical condition in hospital after being enticed by Rouyle to Frankfurt and held captive there.

Kramer was rescued on Thursday by British scientist Andrew O'Hara, a colleague who discovered the plot and broke into Rouyle's Frankfurt home in order to free her.

It was at this point that the margin scribblers had been most prolific:

Way to show us how it's done!
Always suspected he was a closet nutter.
A mild-mannered lab drone by day, but at night, he puts down his pipet-tor, dons spandex underpants and transforms into...Superdoc!
Could it possibly be the world's most elaborate scoring strategy ever??

And so forth.

A hospital spokesman said today that the cause of Kraymer's collapse was still under investigation.

Lawyers representing Rouyle have so far maintained their client's innocence.

A Pfeiffer-deVries spokesperson said today that they were unaware of any illegal activities surrounding the collaboration with Geniaxis, stressing its 21-year reputation for integrity in international drug development.

Elizabeth Lord of the anti-GM organization NatureFirst called for caution in approval of future gene therapy trials. "This just goes to show that scientists cannot be trusted. If this scheme had been carried out, human beings would have been, in effect, genetically modified against their will by an untested agent."

The director of the Royal Cancer Centre, scientist Sir Harold Dinstag, whose organization is a major shareholder of Geniaxis, disagreed. "Gene therapy is a respectable alternative to standard drug treatments, and one bad apple shouldn't be held against the entire barrel."

Picture of A Mad-Man: Portion III
-Science NewsBytes, The Mirror Online
    translation by OneWorld.com

Following up of yesterday's reports, we bring you further detection around Rouyle scandal (clicking here for two earlier reports). The German scientific community is still in shock after learning of Rouyle's dark effort to unload Pandora's container on the Third World.

We are succeeded in tracking down Dr Helmut Meier, German lab-fellow of Dr Andrew O'Hara, the collegiate which achieved the rescuing of Rouyle's whistle blowing collaborator. Meier helped perform key experiments that pointed O'Hara to the path.

"I am saddened learning of Rouyle's deeds," said Meier in an exclusive interview at RCC in London.

"It was extremely difficult, but with Andrew's help, I manage to solve the mystery," adds Meier modestly. "FRIP kinase is not functioning in the brain, and such irrefutable data is meaning that Rouyle was up to no good."

Post-Doctoral Haiku No. 32
by: Dr Anonymous

Damsel in distress
A post-doc to the rescue:
Free world safe again.

I felt unexpectedly touched.

Leaving the common room, I walked down the darkened corridor and into the lab. After taking comfort from the familiar scene, I switched on the lights, stripping off my coat as I made my way over to my desk. Out of habit, I peered across the courtyard towards the bank of windows, but all was quiet at Geniaxis as well. In fact, not a single lit window could be seen along the entire side of the building.

After the anarchy of the past few days, the tranquility was a relief. I'd scarcely had a chance to think, let alone see any friends or come to work. There'd been extensive meetings with the police, debriefings by the Geniaxis legal and PR staff, and a number of interviews with the television and press, both British and German. Much to my mother's delight, several reports had even been headlined on the BBC news. And there'd been an emotional encounter with Gina's parents, just flown in from Chicago and so worried and exhausted that they'd stammered over their gratitude.

Naturally I'd visited Gina in hospital as much as I could, but she'd been so overrun by visitors—friends, family, colleagues, baffled consultants and more police—that I'd decided to back off until things settled down. There'd be plenty of time to talk later. At any rate, I still wasn't sure that she even wanted me, that there was still anything to discuss. But on my end, I had reached a decision. During my long vigil that first morning at her bedside, forgiveness had come effortlessly—who wasn't guilty of similar misjudgements? Still, I had eventually decided for a number of reasons that I'd be better off without her.

I noticed a warning reflection in the lit glass of my own window. Clearly, the peace was destined to be short-lived.

"Nice of you to join us at last," Magritte said from behind me.

I turned around, having been dreading this moment for days.

"Boss," I acknowledged, faltering halfway into a smile.

She was standing in the doorway, hands on hips, dressed for the Siberian wastelands in her ratty old fur hat and coat. She was surely now aware that, even in the midst of our frank discussion, I had only revealed a fraction of the truth. From the enigmatic expression on her face, I was unable to tell whether she was angry, but I feared the renewal of her disappointment in me more than any rant.

"Thank goodness you're all right!" She shot over and enveloped me in a furry hug. "Was worried sick when I found out what you did! But so proud, simultaneous!"

Pulling away, she gripped me at arms' length and subjected me to a thorough scrutiny as I tried to regroup.

"Nice work, O'Hara," she finally said. "How did you like hero thing?" Her eyes were intense and inquisitive. "How did it *feel?*"

I thought about it. A few of the journalists had posed similar questions, and I'd offered the stock phrases people always say in these sorts of situations: *I just got on with things. I acted without thinking. I did what I had to do.* But now I understood why people used them: they were placeholders for ideas that could never be properly expressed, at least not in words, or in one glib sentence, or immediately, before enough time had gone by to make sense of it all.

"It was scary," I said. "And liberating. And I had lots of doubts—I still do. And sometimes it still doesn't feel as if it really happened."

She nodded. "Know what you mean—felt like that after my defection. All this sneaking, running, hiding—like movie, yes? Embarrassing on one hand, deadly real on other."

"That's it exactly."

"Advice to you, Andrew." She let go of my arms at last and took a step back. "Don't stop thinking, synthesizing, trying to figure out how it feels. *Use* it, yes?"

"I'll try, Magritte." I paused, then said, "Listen, I really need to apologize for lying to you again, about that whole Metzger seminar thing."

"Nonsense: you already know how I feel about all that. Besides, had clue even before Tuesday. But was sworn to secrecy of own, couldn't discuss."

"What are you talking about?"

She actually blushed. "Heard part of story from Ra...from Dr Aidula." My eyes widened, and she hastened on, "He didn't want Rouyle story getting out, also not that he'd been indiscreet to me with your private affairs."

"You...and Raim?" I couldn't help myself: a huge grin was breaking out on my face like a rampant epidemic.

Magritte's colouring deepened. "He e-mailed invitation to his seminar at Institute of Child Health. Know next to nothing about vision, brains et cetera, but like to support Eastern European scientists, had free afternoon, thought why not? Went out for drinks after...then more drinks..."

"Finally met your match in the vodka-drinking department, I take it? Of course you were at a severe weight disadvantage."

She nodded, not bothering to hide her happiness any longer. While enjoying this immensely, I was also a bit taken aback. It was the first time Magritte had ever revealed anything about her love life. Maybe Raim had thawed her out...the old goat.

"It's a long way to Estonia," I ventured, suddenly anxious.

"Irrelevant. That seminar was for job. He got it, starts December."

"That's great!" I shook my head in disbelief.

"Anyway, he's visiting this weekend, must go to meet now—just stopped by, off-chance you were here. Always seem to end up here Saturday night." She frowned at me. "Assumed you'd be with *her*."

"She's still in hospital as far as I know."

"As far as you know?" She gave me a look of sharp surprise. "You mean you aren't...?"

I shook my head.

"Surely after romantic rescue, old boyfriend awaiting trial?"

"You would think..." I looked away, not having the heart to explain my decision.

"Listen, O'Hara. Made good start in Germany, but not quite finished. Have to follow through, yes?" She gave me that trademark penetrating inspection. "Some scepticism is healthy, but don't let doubts stand in way of common sense."

After she'd evaporated, I just stood there, laid bare and wondering how she could possibly have seen through me.

A few minutes later, a second visitor arrived.

"I kept missing your calls," Maria said, laughing self-consciously as I lifted her off the floor in a hug.

"Haven't you heard? Our voicemails are having a torrid affair." I set her back on her feet. "How's Geniaxis handling the furore?"

"Well, Thomas is in a bit of a state." She paused with the careful timing of a practised gossip. "On top of everything else, he found out yesterday that *Steve* was the mole who leaked all that information to the animal rights activists."

She gave me the highlights: disgruntled PhD student, too incompetent to finish his degree but blaming the system in general for his failure. For revenge, he'd agreed to pose as a technician and dig up material to fuel FUR-IE's media campaign.

"But the best bit," she crowed, "is how completely FUR-IE misjudged the situation. That Leicester dog scandal they abandoned us for was a media flop, based on a faulty tip-off, and they ended up looking ridiculous. Whereas if they'd only stuck with us a bit longer, think of the publicity wave they could've ridden!"

"As if Boyd wouldn't already have enough to deal with."

"By the way, he's still berating himself about having dismissed you so severely."

"I don't blame him in the least," I said mildly, leaning against the bench. "Rouyle was a fast talker."

"Well, no one's listening to him now," she said.

"You've heard about the new charges, haven't you?"

Maria nodded solemnly. A close inspection of Rouyle's financial affairs had revealed a long history of embezzlement from PfeifferdeVries, much of these funds having been diverted to his illicit PAX research and development team.

"By the way," she said, "I presume you and Gina have spoken by now?"

"We haven't had the chance, I'm afraid."

"Have you made any decisions about her?"

"Not yet." I forgave myself the deception. But the last thing I needed right now was further input, tilting the fragile balance with more opinions. Instead, I just said, quite honestly, "It's very complicated. You do understand?"

"Actually, Andy..." She looked positively awkward.

"What?"

"Maybe now's not the best..."

"Go on," I prompted.

"Well, I've been mulling over what we were talking about before, about idealizing people."

"Yes, and you had a good laugh at my expense."

"At the time," she said. "But later, I realized I might be guilty of the same thing myself."

"Are you saying what I think you're saying?"

"I think I am." She looked up at me, gaze unwavering. "Quite honestly, I've spent the last few days asking myself hard questions about my feelings for you."

"Such as?" The irony here would be amusing if it didn't sting quite so much.

"Such as, do I want to be someone's second choice?" She shrugged. "And even if I settled for that, are you really up to the task of dealing with someone like me?"

"I have been making some progress lately." I couldn't help smiling at the look on her face.

"And I've noticed. But it's just not enough. Maybe in a few years' time?" She smiled too, and I received the distinct impression that she would rebound with her usual streetwise equanimity; indeed, that she was already well on her way. "Meanwhile, I think you just *might* have what it takes to be an excellent friend."

She truly was something, with her teasing dark eyes. Somewhere underneath my relief, I felt an illogical sense of let-down.

"Any time I need emergency PCR and sequencing done, I know where to go."

"Xavier and I are like *this*." Maria laughed, crossing her fingers, then stood up on tiptoe to give me a lingering kiss on the cheek. "Best of luck with your decision. Just don't do anything hasty."

I watched her stride from the lab, not looking back.

I stared with utter lack of comprehension at the results of a routine PubMed inquiry, a listing of the hundreds of articles in my field that had accumulated just in the past week. I hadn't really wanted to know; if anything, I'd hoped that losing myself in something familiar would shake the disjointed feeling that had welled up in Maria's absence: a sense of purposelessness, of incompleteness that had been plaguing me since returning from Germany.

"I can't believe you're in the lab after everything you've just been through!" Christine swept in, brash manner not hiding the fact that she was excessively pleased to see me. She pulled up a chair and gave me a hug. "Coping okay with the paparazzi?"

I shrugged, rather glumly. "Gina's getting most of the attention."

"Don't take it personally, O'Hara. Given the choice between a gorgeous super-scientist babe, abducted by a mad professor bent on dominating the world with an evil virus, and a sad loser like you, sitting in front of a computer in a laboratory on Saturday night, who would you choose to interview?"

"Cheers, Chris, for putting my heroics into perspective."

She cuffed me on the arm. "Don't be stupid, Andy—you know I'm proud to death of what you did, and honoured that someone like you is my friend." The line was delivered straight, but with Christine you could never be sure. "To be honest, I'd been quite worried about your assertiveness problem, and although you may've overcompensated just the *tiniest bit* in this affair, the whole thing was a glorious confirmation of my whole theory."

"And that being?"

"That there was someone halfway useful trapped in that apathetic body."

"Thanks a lot!"

As usual, my sarcasm just slid off her. "So how's Gina? I popped by yesterday but couldn't get anywhere near her."

"The main thing is she's tested negative for the PAX virus," I said. "And as of yesterday evening, the doctors were fairly sure there hadn't been any long-term damage from the drugs and dehydration. They just wanted to observe her for a bit longer."

"That's a relief." She eyed me curiously. "Why aren't you at the hospital right now? Doesn't look as if you've anything better to do."

"You saw how it was—I was just underfoot. And..." I lowered my voice. "I honestly don't know if she wants me around."

She sat back in amazement. "Let me get this straight. You go all the way to Germany, meet Rouyle face to face, steal his keys, break into his house, rescue the girl whilst simultaneously stealing the evidence to put Rouyle away, reinstate said girl in her job—with a massive promotion, according to Maria—and save the Third World from viral oppression, and you *honestly don't know* if she wants you around?"

I squirmed uncomfortably in my seat. "People don't like people for what they do, Chris. They like them for who they are."

"Which is exactly why you have nothing to worry about."

When I didn't say anything, she looked at me more carefully, and then she began to frown. "Wait a minute. What aren't you telling me?"

"Just leave it, Chris, please."

She stared. "You can't seriously be having doubts."

I sighed, knowing escape was impossible now. "I can't square her behaviour—getting involved with Rouyle in the first place, I mean."

"Are you mad, Andy?" Her voice was drenched with incredulity. "She's just been a bit stupid—it could happen to anyone. *Including* a certain person I know rather well."

I felt my neck go tense.

"I'm just not sure I can trust her," I said. "I'm not sure there's enough evidence."

She crossed her arms. "For Christ's sake, Andy—this is your future happiness we're talking about here, not some stupid experiment! She's a decent woman."

"How can you be sure?"

"Female intuition," she said.

"Oh, great."

"Or if you want evidence..." She shrugged. "We spent a lot of time together in the Mouse House. I got to know her. She cared more about her vaccine, and helping those patients, than about anything else—including her reputation and career. That's a mark of true integrity, Andy."

The room hummed with its usual sounds.

"You're probably right," I said eventually. "But what if I'm never really certain about her? Won't it always bother me?"

"Two things, O'Hara." Her irritation, as it so often did, had slipped into sympathy. "First, we can never be one hundred percent sure of anyone, or anything—that's where faith comes in. It's the same in science as in life."

She watched me think about her words.

"And second," she said, "maybe she did do something wrong, but that doesn't mean she wasn't still an innocent victim. Have you two talked it over thoroughly?" When I shook my head, she said, "I think you need to listen to what she's got to say before you do anything asinine."

"Okay. You're probably right."

She patted my knee. "Good. Now, to change the subject completely, I want to tell you something before rumours start flying around."

"Let me guess: it's about the job in Newcastle."

She nodded. "I did get the job, and I have accepted it, but —"

"That's brilliant!" But when I tried to embrace her, she held me off.

"Easy, there. I'm not finished." She paused, suddenly shy. "Cameron's coming with me—and we're getting married."

My mouth fell open. This time she did let me hug her, an all-encompassing hug that squeezed the breath out of her.

Christine started mumbling into my shoulder. "...not general knowledge yet, so if you could keep it to yourself for the moment..."

I backed away. "As if Cameron won't have told half the Centre by now."

She tried to clout me, but I snared her wrist. Our eyes met then, both of us going serious at the same moment.

"Are you sure this is what you really want?" I spoke softly, choosing my words with care. "You were a bit unsure about things not long ago."

"I know." She looked at me earnestly. "It's been a difficult prospect for both of us, the move...and the commitment too. But together, we finally decided where our priorities lay. And do you know what helped settle my mind, at least?"

She gave me a strange smile, and when I shook my head, she said, "Seeing the way you looked at Gina in that hospital bed."

My equilibrium shifted, and I felt a funny ache in my throat.

"I suddenly recognized the expression," she said. "It's how Cam looks at me. And I realized then that I don't ever want him to stop."

I let out my breath. "If that's really true, then I approve whole-heartedly. I just want you to be happy."

"Oh I am, Andy," she confessed, ardently. "Very much so. But it would be that much more complete if I knew you could find something just as good, after everything that happened—or didn't happen—between us."

"Don't worry about me, Chris. I always float to the top."

I released her, continuing to be assaulted by a muddle of emotions. Sadness seemed to be at the fore, at the vagaries of the scientific career, poised to whisk closed the curtains and change the set, the actors, yet again.

She stood up, eyes still shining. "Cam's waiting in the Henry. You want to join us?"

"I'm more in the mood to be alone right now."

She nodded, and I was relieved to see that she understood.

The lab now seemed about a thousand times emptier. Christine was right: what in hell *was* I doing here? I should just go down to the pub and get slaughtered. Instead, I opened my laboratory notebook to the last entry, Monday afternoon. The few random sentences reminded me of my abandoned experiment, the billions of transfected cells languishing and ruined in the incubator, the theorem still waiting its proof. In fact, the last few weeks had been useless. It was time to get back to my experiments after so many distractions. I felt the familiar tug of science—my original obsession—enticing me downward into calm clarity.

I rummaged around my drawer for a pen, then paused, snared by the photograph. I had noted, over the years, that I seemed to have a barometric response to the static image of my father's smile. Sometimes the grin made me feel optimistic that things would work out eventually.

And other times, like tonight, it simply hurt.

I slammed the drawer shut, and as I turned back to my notebook, I began to pick up a familiar prickly sensation. I was pretty sure I knew what it was. Sure enough, when I peered over my shoulder, I saw Gina leaning against the door frame. Somehow, I wasn't surprised: all the other women in my life had been by, so why not her?

"I saw your light," she said.

"You're out of hospital," I noted intelligently.

She nodded, straightening up and sauntering over. The sleeves of her black blouse covered up the bruising on her arms, and though her skin still seemed a bit translucent, in all other respects she looked fine. More than fine.

"I was discharged this afternoon." She had an irregular shape to her lips that wasn't quite neutral, but wasn't exactly a smile either.

"Shouldn't you be taking it easy?"

"I know. But I've been so bored with all this lying around."

I wanted to kiss her in greeting, but felt paralyzed by her manner. After all our intimacy during the rescue, and my subsequent agonizing over what to do, I didn't know how to act.

"So, can I help you with something?" I finally broke the lengthening silence, indicating the metal cassette held unobtrusively at her side. "Have you run out of film?"

"No, our developer's broken. Can I use yours?"

I looked at her narrowly. "What sort of result could possibly be so pressing that you'd have to get up from your deathbed?"

"I put a virus assay down on film before I went to Cornwall." Her eyes remained inscrutable. "I'm curious to find out what happened."

"Well, you know where the darkroom is."

"Aren't you coming?"

I stood up, mystified, and she retreated so smartly that I had to hurry to keep up. When we reached the darkroom, Gina spun the barrel door around and stepped inside. As soon as the dominant stimulus of vision ceased, all my other senses woke up. I could detect her warmth, only inches away from me, the soft sound of her breathing, and above all, her scent: a confusion of perfumes and subtle traces, no doubt her microscopic chemicals, invading my skin and docking relentlessly with my own defenceless receptors.

I manhandled the barrel around and followed her into absolute blackness. Gina switched on the safelight and strode over to the workbench as if she frequented the place every day. Her form was just barely visible in the scarlet gloom as she tossed the cassette onto the bench, turned towards me. Kept coming, then, and before I knew what was happening she had slipped her arms around my neck and pressed herself against me. Her kiss came out of the darkness, softly at first and then gathering momentum.

I was shocked—in fact, my whole body appeared to be electrified. Rather irrelevantly, I only had time to think *God, that's one major uncertainty cleared up* before she had drawn her face away.

"That was for rescuing me." Her voice contained an intimate teasing quality I had only ever imagined in my dreams.

Steady on, the winking eye of the developing machine cautioned me over her shoulder.

"Well, if you didn't keep getting mixed up with animal rights terrorists and mad scientists, I wouldn't have to —"

She cut me off with another kiss. And I could only react again, my fingers intertwining through the thick currents of her hair with the grip of a drowning man, drinking her in and sinking down until I was ready to forget everything. Then panic dragged me to the surface by the scruff of the neck and slapped the water from my lungs, and I found myself backing away, breathing heavily, pushing her back to extricate myself.

"What's wrong?" She sounded disorientated, like a roused dreamer.

"There's something I've forgotten." I slipped past her and fumbled for the door.

"Andy, where are you going?"

"I'll be right back." I stepped into the cylindrical chamber. "Don't move an inch."

The rotation of the barrel severed her confused response. Escaping into the corridor, I burst into the departmental office next door and flung myself into the secretary's chair. My heart was still thudding, but the tidiness of the office, with its uncomplicated world of in-trays and paper clips, soon brought the calmness I needed to think.

When I'd decided Gina wasn't right for me, my resolution had felt unshakeably wise. Of course it's so obvious now how thoroughly I'd been deceiving myself, but run aground there in the office, gasping for air, I was overwhelmed by the way she'd come back to life and ambushed me.

Go with it, seemed to be the inner consensus. Yet the essence of my main grievance remained unchanged. I had never once been in control of the situation, and worse, I had allowed Gina to lead me on, buffeted helplessly in the wake of her fluctuating whims.

But recent events had forged a kernel of steel inside, gradually reinforcing itself with layers of resolve. For the first time in years I was letting myself see clearly, think clearly, and act accordingly. After breaking free on my trip to Frankfurt, I was unwilling to relapse into the passive role I'd adopted since I'd allowed work to take over my life, or to dwell in the grey uninspired world of missed opportunities that had resulted.

But the escape route had to come from me. I didn't want Gina to make the decision, even if it happened to be the right one, and I didn't want my fate orchestrated by a third party, either. And above all, I didn't want to get swept away by blind passion.

I bolted to my feet, energized. It was time to do things my way for a change—and the first thing I needed was more data.

✦ ✦ ✦

After I stepped back into the darkroom, it took a few seconds to locate Gina, sitting on the workbench in subdued silhouette. I felt along the wall and hit the switch.

She turned her head against the assault of light, a belated hand thrown over her eyes. Wordlessly, she placed the other palm flat down, tensed to slip off the bench.

"No!" I blurted out. Then, more calmly, "Just stay right where you are. I can't think when you're anywhere near me."

"What are you trying to think about?" Carefully, as if one ill-chosen word might make me vanish again.

"Chemistry."

"In what sense?" She had removed the hand from her eyes and was blinking at me.

"Yours."

"Ours," she corrected, almost pedantically. "Chemistry is a two-way phenomenon."

"Ours, then."

"I've hated it," she said, with sudden fierce candour. "I've hated that I couldn't stay rational around you."

"*You* couldn't?"

"My reactions were out of control," she said. "It all started when I asked you for that drink, despite having a boyfriend, and deteriorated from there. It wasn't like me—so I was tricked into running the other way. It got us off on entirely the wrong foot."

"And now?"

"I've decided it would be idiotic to let fear of my own feelings sabotage what I really want."

"What do you want, exactly?"

She threw me a look, half impatient, half imploring.

"I want *you*, Andy. I've wanted you since the very beginning, even though I've been too stupid to..." I watched her face work with powerful emotions. "I've made the most terrible mistakes at every turn."

I took stock for a moment, then said, "What bothers me the most is that I don't have the slightest idea what it is you like about me. I don't have any *evidence*."

She didn't hesitate even a second.

"I like the way you think, Andy. I like the way you look, the way you speak. Even the smell of your skin drives me mad." Her words felt physical, like hands grabbing at my clothing. "And you're the only man I've ever met who seems to see who I really am."

I couldn't suppress a laugh. "How can you say that? I've completely idolized you."

"Maybe, but you *see* me, too. Just like I see you." Her gaze remained immovable. "You know I'm right."

"That's for me to decide, not you."

"Yes, but you said yourself that we make a great team."

I didn't answer. Eventually she deflated, and when she spoke up again, her voice was bleak. "I've spent all these months denying the obvious fact that I love you, and now it's too late, isn't it? You don't want me anymore."

"It's not that simple. I do want you." Her admission of love crashed through me, shedding implications in slow motion like discarded rocket stages flung out into space; ruthlessly, I refused to let it show.

"You do?" She reddened, floated a hand to her cheek. "But then why...what's the problem?"

I gripped the developing machine to prevent myself from touching her. "Here's the thing, Gina: I have to make a real, objective decision or I'm never going to be in control of my life."

"And the chemistry's getting in the way?"

"Exactly," I said. "It's not an intellectual decision."

"But why shouldn't feelings or instincts be just as trustworthy as the intellect?"

As she stared me down in flushed disarray, I saw then that she was prepared to fight with everything she had, with her wits as well as her passion. Somehow this affected me deeply.

"Because they're the opposite," I said, playing along for the moment.

Gina's face was gravely serious, but her eyes had lit up with their old scientific enthusiasm. "What about PAX, to take a recent example?"

"What about it?"

"Being passive is an emotion of sorts. A state that feels a bit out of control, a bit random—right?" She cocked her head at me, and I nodded, guilty as charged. "But it looks like it's all regulated by precise chemical reactions. When introduced artificially, PAX can actually subvert human will."

"That's hardly a natural process." Only scientists could be having a conversation this weird at such a crucial juncture.

"True. But even under normal circumstances, you can't possibly think that we actually control our own wills." She smiled at me, an action that set off the usual physiological responses. I thought about biochemical substances shooting purposefully across synaptic gaps, obeying rules invisible to the brain's owner and exerting absolute dominance. I thought about gut instincts, pheromones and sexual fixations.

"Thinking *is* chemistry," Gina continued, calmly persuasive. "The mind is an organic, messy system...and we should listen to it. In all of its manifestations."

She flowed off the bench, and this time I didn't prevent her approach. It was almost scary how perfectly she fitted into my arms. It would be so easy, too, to take her hand, take her home and never look back, to never even bother thinking at all.

"Please give me a chance, Andy."

She pressed her head against my chest, where she was at risk of being deafened by the pounding of my heart. And when she looked back up, all her glib assurance was gone. This made it almost impossible to put my complicated reluctance into words, but then I saw it wasn't necessary: she had already decoded the answer on my face.

Her eyes faltered before dropping like birds shot out of the sky.

I put an apologetic hand on her cheek—the molecules of the room seemed to be raining down around us too. "I need to think—a lot. Not just about you, but about everything. I need to go slowly." I cleared my throat of accumulating emotion. "I need time."

She finally looked up at me again, not attempting to mask her intense disappointment like she once would have. I wondered how I could ever have thought her eyes to be unreadable, unknowable.

"How long?"

"I'm not sure...maybe a few weeks. I'll give you a call."

"I'll be waiting, Andy. I'll wait as long as it takes."

She released her breath, and I held her close a few seconds longer, trying to convince myself that I wasn't the world's biggest idiot.

"Let's get out of here," she finally murmured. "I'm supposed to be in bed."

I stepped back. "There isn't anything in that film cassette, is there?"

Gina turned around and opened the empty metal device with a flourish.

"So this was your master plan?" I said. "Lure me in, give me a few kisses and everything's fine?"

"That was the general idea. From there, I was going to improvise."

"Great minds think alike," I said. "Remember the night we first met? I didn't actually need that Taq."

Her eyes widened in appalled surprise, and I had to labour to keep a straight face.

"Do you know how *expensive* that stuff is?" she finally demanded.

"Don't worry—Helmut put it to good use."

We both burst out laughing. Eventually Gina had to grab onto me in her weakened state, and we were still chuckling faintly when the rotating chamber expelled us out into the real world.

30 New Development

Two weeks later, I crossed the bridge and made my way towards the prearranged meeting point.

It was one of those freakish early winter days when, with no apparent warning or reason, the air thaws and a spring-like softness permeates the world. The South Bank was thronged with tourists enjoying the reprieve, most of them in short sleeves and sunglasses. They seemed much more willing to embrace the weather in easy-going holiday stride than the natives, who scurried along, still stubbornly sporting overcoats, unbuttoned as a sole concession. The mild air brushed against my face and through my recently cut hair. The tide was up and the river sparkled, making my eyes ache. Naturally, as a native in denial, I wasn't wearing sunglasses.

It had been a good break. I'd informed Magritte that I needed some time off—a plan she'd heartily endorsed. I'd spent the first couple of days catching up on my sleep, sleep so deep that I didn't remember my dreams, so thorough that I would wake up stiff and heavy-limbed, still locked in the same position I'd adopted before drifting off. In short, I slept like a champion sleeper, making up for months of deprivation.

On Wednesday, I'd travelled down to my mother's and stayed a few days, most of the time spent relating the convoluted story of Gina, Rouyle and the PAX virus. I'd originally planned on keeping it simple, but my mother's lively questions drew out hundreds of nuances, stretching my memory to the limit, and it took several enjoyable sessions until she was satisfied. On the last night, I surprised both of us by asking to see the old photo albums. We spent the evening staying up too late, getting tipsy and swapping stories about Dad, and though the process made me sad, it was gratifying to find that there was still a lot to laugh about too.

When my mother turned a heavy page to reveal my treasured photograph of the Cambridge lab, I was momentarily confused. But of course she would have a print of it as well—and of course it would be smooth and perfect, unmarred by the creases of thoughtless anger at the unfairness of the universe.

"Do you still have your copy?" she asked, noticing my expression.

"More or less." I explained about its unfortunate condition with a deep sense of shame. "I've always felt terrible about throwing it in the bin."

"Oh, love." My mother gave me a sympathetic smile. "It was perfectly natural to be angry. After all, he went away—and he was never around much in the first place."

A silence stretched out, punctuated only by the popping of sparks in the hearth.

"You used to fight about his long hours, didn't you?" I finally asked.

"Yes." Her blue eyes were placid, untouched by rancour over the rim of her brandy glass. "It wasn't that I didn't understand his passion, or respect it. But there was more at stake than just his work."

"Your relationship, you mean." I still had difficulties conceptualizing my mother as a real person, with the potential to have ordinary men problems—and that the man, the problem, could have been Dad.

"Actually, no. I knew full well what I was in for when I married him. But you and Liz were too young to understand the compulsion that kept him eternally away."

"I'm not sure I agree." I swirled my own glass, watching the flames through the burnished liquid. "Of course I didn't understand the details, but as far back as I can remember, its importance seemed clear."

But even as I spoke, I recalled dozens of instances of neglect: missed birthdays, unanswered pleas for advice, the way it felt when he retired to his study and positioned the solid oak barrier firmly between himself and the rest of the family.

"Perhaps you're right, dear." she said. "Perhaps he transmitted everything to you in a gene—the interest...the *passion*. Just as Liz ended up being influenced by the artistic regions of my DNA." The skin around her eyes crinkled even more in amusement, then smoothed away as she considered me carefully. "I'd been rather worried over the years that you might have inherited more than just your scientific bent from Charles."

Molten fire in my glass, clockwise, anticlockwise. I forced myself to look at her, not at my drink. Speaking and listening: these were simple acts I was never again going to underestimate.

"I managed to distract your father from the lab long enough to win him over," she said. "But I'd started to lose hope that anyone would ever break through to you."

I didn't dare say anything, shifting away from the heat burning at the surface of my clothing, my hands, my face. Something hit me then, a realization so obvious that it must have been standing quietly, just on the other side of the door, for years. The very attribute of my father that had angered me the most was precisely the trait we'd had in common all along.

"The strange thing about love," Mum continued, "is how, even at its most desperate, inappropriate or unrequited, it can shape you in ways nothing else can. Even after you'd despaired of ever risking it again." She was poking at the glowing embers with the tongs, and the sudden burst of flames lit up her fond smile—a smile not directed at me.

I missed Gina then, like a swift assault to the gut, a tingle to the skin and a hand squeezed around my heart all at once. I thought about the way she had brought me out of my two-dimensional life. Of course you could argue that Christine, with her constant nagging and indoctrination, had shaped the complex reactions of my transformation.

But Gina, and the way I felt about her, had been the catalyst.

The next week, I'd shunned company and not done much of anything—visiting a museum or two, sipping cups of tea in cafés, watching people flow past outside. I'd gone running along the steep pathways in the grounds of Alexandra Palace, breath steaming and the city spread out below me. I'd finally finished a book about the history of science that Christine had given me ages ago. And, as promised, I'd spent a great deal of time just thinking, weighing everything in my mind and trying to put into context the events that had happened to me. I didn't come to any earth-shattering conclusions, but I did feel different, somehow. Not being in the lab was a novelty, and letting go of my experiments and focusing on the wider world was like the release of a muscular tension I must have been carrying around in my body for a decade.

It was a sensation I thought I could get used to.

Midway through this almost illusory period of non-work, I received an envelope in the post from my mother. It contained no words, no cheerful remarks or scientific cuttings. Instead, I pulled out an unblemished copy of my favourite photograph, freshly printed from the old negative. Without the crease marks, the expression on that three-year-old boy's face was restored to happiness at the weight of his father's hand.

I promptly went out, bought a frame and hung up the photo in my kitchen where I would be sure to see it every morning.

I skirted the tables displaying second-hand books for sale outside the British Film Institute café, the calm of my time off twisting into a coil of expectation. I located Gina immediately, sitting on one of the outside benches. She was blending in well with the tourists in a sleeveless blue dress, and her bowed head was shot with coppery-brass in the sun. She half-looked up from her paperback, not seeming to see anything, but smiling at something she'd read. Then, prompted by an unknown cue, she raised her head further and met my eye unerringly.

I made my way over and sat down next to her.

"You look great," I said. And she did, with her face coloured by renewed health. I leaned in to kiss her on the cheek, and her skin was sun-warmed and smelt sweet—not seductively deadly, just human, with a trace of soap and her familiar perfume.

"I was just about to say the same thing myself." She took me in as she tucked the book into her handbag. "You seem different."

"That would be the sleep," I told her. "And the proper meals. And the fact that I've stayed away from the lab for two entire weeks."

"And have you been thinking?" When I slipped an arm around her, I could feel her suspense. And something else: the stirrings of our mutual attraction, stubbornly undeterred by the leave of absence and any number of hours engaged in intellectual abstractions.

"There was a lot to take in," I said. "I've given up coming to terms with some of it. All that stuff about obsession and chemistry—it's too much part of the same linked system to think about rationally. One probably shouldn't even try."

"But?"

She was scared, I realized, and it gave me a pang.

"I've decided we can't go any further until you explain why you stayed so long with Richard, even though you claim to have loved me. Until I understand that, I can't understand you."

There was a slight pause, and then she shook her head.

"I can't."

"Why not?"

She slipped out of my embrace and stood up, shifting her weight as if she were thinking about bolting. Her hair was lit up against the falling sun, her expression lost in shadow.

"I know it's hard to talk about," I said, "but I just need a general idea of —"

"You don't understand," she said. "I *can't*. If you knew the truth, you'd never forgive me."

I stood up as well. "Gina, if you can't be honest with me now, what hope is there for any sort of a future between us?"

She studied me with her serious grey eyes, seeming to waver over the options.

"Okay," she finally said. *You asked for it*, was the unspoken continuation, and I could sense the surrender in her posture as she turned towards the riverside and walked to the embankment wall. I followed, edgy with apprehension. Of all the ways our conversation could have played out, this was not a scenario I had prepared for.

She stopped next to one of the lamps and leaned against its podium, the evil-looking black dolphins curling over her bare shoulders.

"When I spoke with Richard in Cambridge," she said, "I was struck by his interest in Vera Fever." Now that she had given in, a calmness seemed to settle over her. "Not in the details of my research *per se*, but the predicament of the afflicted people. I finally thought I'd met a scientist who truly cared about developing world diseases."

"You were as deluded as the rest of Europe on that point," I said charitably.

She nodded. "But I want to be clear that it wasn't a romantic attraction. To be honest, I was still very much focused on you then, despite your marked inattentiveness at the symposium."

"But you went back to his room, didn't you?"

She shrugged. "I was drunk. And after I saw you kissing Maria, I was angry too. Richard's persistence did the rest."

"But that didn't mean anything!" I said. "I can't believe I let that happen."

"Don't berate yourself, Andy. It didn't change anything, trust me."

"But that's when I lost you."

"Hardly," she retorted, with a strange smile. She was silent for a few moments. "I woke up the next morning with a headache and serious misgivings. I managed to hide my uneasiness, but made it clear that the evening had been a one-off. And he seemed to take it well, promising to contact me about the collaboration."

"But you must've known fairly soon that Maria and I never got together," I said. "So when you found out I still liked you that night in the Timelapse room, why didn't you just go with it?"

"I was caught off guard," she admitted. "And I didn't know how enthusiastic you really were. It wasn't always easy to tell, Andy."

"I realize that. I've been...practising, in the meantime." I reached over and took her hand.

"I noticed, in Frankfurt." Unexpectedly, she smiled, and our eyes met, both of us going silent. There was something about that moment I will never forget—the way she looked against the dark blue sky with her hair blowing across her face, the raw feeling that we were teetering on the edge of something, but neither of us knowing whether it was the beginning or the end.

Then she seemed to remember where she was, and intertwined her fingers more tightly among my own.

"Something you've probably worked out," she said, "is that I've had bad experiences with men in the past."

I nodded, watching the flux of thoughts across her face.

"I kept choosing the wrong attributes," she said, "mistaking glibness for kindness, bluster for confidence, jadedness for experience. You name it, I've misinterpreted it." She paused. "And something about me seems to bring out cruelty in the wrong sort of man."

"I'm so sorry, Gina."

"Anyway." She let go of my hand, as if she didn't have the right. "The point is that I was still feeling burned by my most recent mistakes, so I decided not to leap into anything. I needed time to see if desire had blinded me to any surprises you might be hiding."

Gina resumed walking upriver, and I fell into step alongside. The London Eye loomed into existence from behind the Royal Festival

Hall, giving the illusion that the giant wheel was slowly rolling towards us down the South Bank. When I took a peek at Gina's profile, I saw both resolution and resignation.

"But in the end, I didn't have that luxury," she said, "Thomas called me into his office to tell me that Pfeiffer-deVries had offered to extend our collaboration to modify my vaccine, pledging to finance an eventual Phase I clinical trial. He was frank about how Geniaxis's very existence hung on this cash infusion. When he told me I had been chosen to go to Frankfurt, I tried to get one of my technicians sent in my place. But Richard had specially requested my presence—it was non-negotiable."

"You didn't *want* to go." I dwindled to a stop as various bits of the past struggled to settle into this new context.

"That's a bit of an understatement," she said, pausing too. After an uncertain look at me, she leaned out over the embankment wall to contemplate the churning of the tides.

"When I got to Germany," she said, "Richard didn't waste any time trying to repeat our previous alliance. He worked on me relentlessly." A pause, her eyes still directed at the water. "Here's where it starts to get bad, Andy. He was very charismatic, and had power over me, and eventually, I couldn't seem to help myself."

I felt knee-jerk jealousy like a blind synapse flashing in the dark. There it was all over again, no matter how I tried to reason it away: how on earth could she have gone off with him? What did it mean? How could this piece of data ever integrate into the theory I was trying to construct around her? Around us?

"What happened next?" I kept my voice even.

"I started to have doubts almost as soon as we'd begun," she said. "I missed you terribly. I couldn't stop thinking about that night you helped me with the mice. And then Richard—there were incidents— inconsistencies, losses of temper, cold-blooded opinions dropped in conversation. He started getting rough...in bed, I mean." She avoided my eye. "But the cancellation of the animal trial was the limit."

She had begun to shiver, but when I took off my coat and passed it to her, she slipped into it without seeming to notice. "We had our big fight the night before I flew back to London. When it was clear my refusals were absolute, Richard decided on a new strategy: blackmail."

"What are you talking about?" I stared at her, a scaffolding of forgotten clues trying to slip into place.

"If I didn't agree to keep sleeping with him," she clarified, "he made it clear he could convince Pfeiffer-deVries that my entire herpes vaccine strategy was flawed. Apparently Thomas had been indiscreet about our finances, so Richard knew the precise consequences."

"But your vaccine is brilliant! You could have found other collaborators, other capital." I was starting to feel undeniably uncomfortable.

"Not after Richard finished disseminating his professional opinion of my work, and of Geniaxis, to the rest of the pharmaceutical industry."

I felt my mouth open in shock.

"That's when I realized he didn't care about Vera Fever at all." She could no longer keep the distress out of her voice. "Of course I had no idea about PAX, but I assumed he was bullying me to have control over the collaboration. And I had to go along with his demands, because Geniaxis would never recover from such slander."

"No," I said slowly. "I suppose not."

"Still," she went on, as inevitable as a landslide collapsing into the sea. "As much as I cared about Geniaxis, that wasn't the deciding factor. If we sank, so would my vaccine, and all those villagers would keep dying." A note of bitterness crept into her voice. "No other companies, or the academic community, have given Vera Fever a second glance, and I couldn't live with letting those people down. And Richard was acutely aware of that fact. That weakness."

A moment of silence: wind, water, and the ancient stones of the city, patently unperturbed.

"Gina." I began, then had to stop, start again. "I understand your dilemma, but letting him...that's almost like..."

"You see now why I couldn't tell anyone, not even my family," she said. "They would never have understood. *You* wouldn't have."

I shifted uneasily. "But surely you could've done something, called his bluff earlier before things got out of hand. Complained to Boyd—cried sexual harassment, whatever."

"I know that now." She was clutching the coat closed over her chest. "But he had this *force*—it was like I couldn't think straight. I've been trying and trying, but I still can't work out what I thought I was doing at the time."

Then she was putting both elbows on the stonework, covering her face with shaking hands. "And the even sicker twist was that he didn't even seem to enjoy my company. He just wanted to...*subjugate* me. And not only because it turned him on. It's clear now that he needed absolute psychological control in case I found out about PAX."

"But instead, you threatened to turn him in," I said. "That's why he tried to turn the blame on you—and then got you out of the way."

She dropped her hands, let them flop helplessly over the side. "I'm sure he never intended to use force—*physical* manipulation wasn't his style. The entire plan was improvised...clumsy. Did he think he could keep me locked up forever?"

Gina had finally started to cry, cradling her head in her arms. As I stood there watching her shoulders shake, I realized that she had run out of ammunition at last, that her fighting had come to an end. In a moment, she was going to offer me her hand in farewell and disappear forever.

It's strange how the balance can just tilt. I experienced a wrench of emotion at the prospect, and just like that, my selfish concerns, wounded pride and petty jealousies became insignificant. I'd been cross-examining her like a scientist trying to dismantle a competing hypothesis, reading her actions and words instead of her underlying intent. It was time to retire all the blunt instruments and start listening with my heart.

"Come here," I said. "You don't have to tell me anything else. I forgive you."

She tried to pull away, and when I wouldn't let her, she tried to turn her face to one side, but I prevented that too.

"How can you?" she said, still refusing to look at me.

"Because I love you." The words came effortlessly. "Because you've forced me out of my solitary world and restored something I didn't even know I'd lost. Because nobody's perfect, least of all me."

Gina finally raised her eyes. I wanted to soak in the way she was looking at me, commit it to long-term memory, but was foiled when she buried her face in my neck. The curve of her smile impressed itself on my skin, my pulse thudding against her mouth, and everything about her—her own skin, her hands on my back, her chemicals, even her cells—seemed to be in the disorderly process of trying to push in amongst my own. There must have been dozens of people swarming around us, but I don't remember any of them now. Maybe memory is only truly reliable when you're not distracted by life.

"I think the best plan is just to start again." I'd finally drawn my mouth away from hers, but only the scant millimetre required for cogent speech.

"That's what I want, too," she said. "There's still a lot you don't know about me."

"There's a lot you don't know about me either."

"So tell me something I don't know." She seemed to be giving off heat and light: her habitual blaze of scientific curiosity. "What was it you lost, that I helped you find?"

"You don't miss a thing, do you?"

She laughed, and I tightened my arms around her, tried to pinpoint the beginning of the story, the proper way to unfold it: the crystallization point. The first concrete thing that came into my mind was the late-night lit square of Gina's lab window.

So where does a story end? This one certainly hasn't—in a way it's only begun. I can tell you that I took Gina home that afternoon, and that there were more tears, and hours of talking, and plenty of chemistry. Much later, I lay with her in my arms, watching her sleep in a pool of moonlight and too full of emotional energy to let the evening end. I didn't know then, and I still don't, whether we'll last forever, but I do know that I'm going to try harder at this than at anything I've ever tried before. Gina's not the only fighter around here. We have to try, just for the chance. Because in the end, nothing else matters—not science, not success, not any of the modern obsessions that blind us to essentials.

Epilogue

Gina Kraymer and Andy O'Hara swap places
- by J. Smythe, *Centre Monthly Newsletter* reporter

Feelings were mixed last Friday when Geniaxis and the Cell & Molecular Biology Department held a joint gala party in the main lounge to bid farewell to two valued post-doctoral employees.

Gina Kraymer, Head of Virology at Geniaxis, was instrumental in placing two of the company's gene therapy strategies into Phase I clinical trials. However, she is leaving shortly to start her own group at Oxford, focusing on fundamental molecular mechanisms of the Vera Fever Virus.

Her return to the academic fold has caused a flurry of interest in the scientific press, including a recent profile in *Nature*. Of course Gina is no stranger to media attention after last year's unfortunate PAX affair, but it was this very notoriety that heightened public awareness of the African disease, leading to a surge in donations worldwide and the formation of the Oxford lectureship.

Thomas Boyd, Geniaxis's Scientific Director, was visibly affected. "We are all still devastated, but I understand and respect her need to push Vera Fever into the limelight."

Andy O'Hara, a post-doctoral fellow in Magritte Valorius's lab, has made ground-breaking discoveries in growth signalling during his four years at the Centre. After taking a few months of well-earned holiday with Gina, he will cross the line to industry, having been head-hunted by a small company in Reading (Melanex Ltd.) seeking to discover innovative cures for malignant melanoma.

"Andy has learned how to take it easy this past year," said Magritte. "With new relaxed attitude, will do great things in translational research."

After finally managing to prise the guests of honour apart, I asked each how they felt about moving on.

"I'm sad to be leaving Geniaxis," said Gina, "but I sincerely hope we will stay in close contact and work in collaboration wherever possible."

"Basic research is important, but I'm ready to get more concrete about fighting cancer," said Andy. "Melanex's slogan is that theories really can become cures. It sounds promising, but I won't believe it until I've seen all the evidence."

361

Acknowledgments

Writing a work of fiction that contains a lot of scientific detail is a careful balancing act: an author must make the science simple enough for everyone to understand without impairing the integrity of that information. Equally, the science must not eclipse or disrupt the story. In revising this novel, I relied on a legion of volunteer readers to help assess and tweak the inevitable imbalances: non-scientists who flagged up (sometimes brutally) every paragraph that left them puzzled, uncomfortable, or derailed, and scientists who warned me when I'd dumbed down a concept right out of existence. There are too many to name here, but the following people were especially helpful: David Weinkove, Clare Isacke, Armand Marie Leroi, Adam Lauring, Jon Hallé, Alison Lloyd, Matthew Day, Tom Hopkinson, Sally Lowell, Francesca Pagnacco, Sally Leevers, Vicky Long, Jonathan Halstead, Eve Laur, Helen Cole, Sherry Pickett, Rachel Brennan, Elaine Thomas, Michele Garfinkel, John Weinkove, and Sheila Leevers.

I would like to thank Caroline Davidson for her valuable lessons on the art of fiction. Thanks are also due to Kris Franks for designing the cover; Lewis Wolpert, Sara Abdulla, and Martin Raff for their encouragement; and Carl Djerassi for his friendship, advice, and support. I am indebted to Denise Weiss, Kathleen Bubbeo, and Mala Mazzullo at Cold Spring Harbor Laboratory Press for their hard work on the production side. Finally, I would like to express my deep gratitude to John Inglis at the Press for his faith in the project and to all the regulars of LabLit.com for their unstinting belief in the idea that science and scientists really do have a place in mainstream literary fiction.